RISE OF THE VANQUISHED

TALES OF THE MISPLACED

BOOK SIX

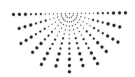

ADAM K. WATTS

CHARACTERS

Agaeran Zabala: (AH-geh-rahn zu-BAH-lah) *Félbahlag* count.

Ager Sagasti: (AH-gayr suh-GAH-stee) *Félbahlag* baron. Member of the Félbahrin senate.

A'iwanea, Mama: (AH-ee-wah-NAY-uh) *Noélani* referred to as the Great Mother, primary mother goddess of the *Kajoran* people.

Akajokira, Auntie: (uh-KAH-jo-KEE-ruh) *Noélani* daughter to Mama A'iwanea and Papa Mohanga. This is the goddess of protection for the *Kajoran* people.

Akani, Auntie: (uh-KAH-nee) *Noélani* daughter to Mama A'iwanea and Papa Mohanga. This is the goddess of the harvest for the *Kajoran* people.

Akshira: (ahk-SHEE-rah) *Rorujhen* spouse to Farukan and mother of Barashan.

Alénia: (uh-LAY-nee-ah) A human woman living in the Shifara area. She is an expert with the long sword and seeks out any who are proficient to challenge them.

Alex Stone: *Daruidai* agent.

Anazhari: (AH-nah-ZJAH-ree) *Rorujhen* mare who agrees to become Mira's mount.

Ancaera: (ahn-KAY-rah) *Ashae* widow to Vaelir, whom she had married out of convenience to maintain control of her family estate of Shianri.

Anjenig: (AHN-jeh-nig) *Wyl-Dunn* man that Mira befriends.

Aputi: (uh-POO-tee) King of the *Kajoran* people.

Aradi: (uh-RAH-dee) Daughter to Duanna and mother to Nimué. The second *Baensiari*. Aradi brought the secret of witchcraft to Earth at the behest of her mother, who was also known as Diana.

Arama Elizondo: (AH-ruh-muh eh-lee-ZOHN-do) *Félbalag* queen of in Félbahrin.

Arané-Li: (uh-RAH-nay-LEE) *Ulané Jhinura* Chamberlain in Su Lariano.

CHARACTERS

Arduanna: (ahr-doo-AH-nuh) See Duanna.

Astéa Wairua: (uh-STAY-uh wun-NO-uh) See Bright.

Astrina: (uh-STREE-nah oo-LAH-nay po-LO-so) Astrina Ulané Poloso. *Ulané Jhinura* queen of Su Lariano.

Ayrik: (AI-rik)*Dannu Fé* king on Danu.

Bastien: (BAS-chehn) *Tékoran* (manticore) that Nora adopts.

Bavrana: (bah-VRAH-nah) An *Urgaban* merchant and the Merchant Guildmaster in Pokorah-Vo. Part owner with Mira of the Raven's Nest Restaurant in Su Lariano.

Bénca: (BAYN-kuh) *Bahréth* second wife to Médard.

Berowen: (BAIR-o-wehn) *Ande Dannu* king in Solaian on Danu. Also known as Oberon.

Bijoux: (BEE-jhoo) *Jahgreet* cub. Rispan's companion.

Bright: *Shian Shariel* (originally a *Kree*) that Nora saved and who has become her companion. Bright has evolved into a new and sentient creature. Also known as Astéa Wairua.

Carmen Cansino: (KAHR-mehn kan-SEE-no) This is a false identity used by Mira as a way of paying homage to Rita Hayworth, one of her favorite actresses.

Chenosh: (CHEH-nosh) *Qélosan* who is referred to by the *Bahréth* as The Envoy and granted status in their religion as an angel.

Cirilia: (sih-REE-lee-uh) *Jhiné Boré* (Dryad) who lives on Earth in the heart of the small wooded area near the Ramirez home.

Corlen Veranu: (KOHR-lehn vehr-AH-noo) *Kajoran* that meets Nora on the island of Carabora.

Dagda: (DAHG-duh) *Uthadé.* Traditionally known as the father-god of the *Tuatha de Danann.*

Dajhanok: (DAH-zhah-NOHK) *Jyyeh* god of chance for the *Bahréth* religion. Trickster god.

Danel Gartza: (DAH-nehl GAHRT-zuh) *Félbahlag* baron. Member of the Félbahrin senate.

Deirdre Leland-Rinn: Nora's biological mother.

Duanna: (doo-AH-nuh) Also known as the Great Mother of the *Uthadé* and is the namesake for Danu. She had many names, including Arduanna, Arduinna, Dunna, Dana, Danu, and Diana. She was the first *baensiari.* Mother to Aradi and many other gods of the *Uthadé.*

Dwayne Hawthorne: *Human* father of Emma and Shelby. Husband to Parker Hawthorne.

Dyani: (dee-AH-nee) *Ranolan* woman of the *Sokwané* clan who helps Nora and her party get back to Carabora.

Dzurala: (dzu-RAH-lah) *Ulané Jhinura* General of the Investigations and Intelligence Branch (IIB) in Su Lariano.

Edrigun: (AY-dreh-goon) *Kagan* (king) of the *Wyl-Dunn* on Danu.

Elishat: (EH-leh-SHAHT) *Rashi* woman on the ship *Lantees* at the bottom of the Lantesian Sea.

Emma Hawthorne: Shelby's younger sister from Earth. Daughter to Dwayne and Parker.

Eremon Igonez: (AY-reh-mohn EE-go-nehz) *Félbahlag* general. Member of the Félbahrin senate. Advisor to King Inigon Elizondo the Third. Eremon the Victorious.

Ezhti: (EHZH-tee) *Jhyeh* mother-goddess of the *Bahréth* religion.

Farukan: (FAH-roo-kahn) The *Rorujhen* formerly enslaved by the White Riders on Daoine. He serves Mira as mount and partner. Spouse of Akshira and father of Barashan.

Felgor: (FELL-gor) *See Mouse.*

Fernan Gabiran: (fehr-NAHN GAH-bee-rahn) *Félbahlag* duke, merchant, and member of the Félbahrin Senate.

Gathrael: (GAH-thray-ehl) *Qélosan.* The strongest of the *Qélosan* and the one who first established contact with Olsahg of the *Bahréth.*

Genevané: (gen-neh-VAH-nay) *Darakanos* befriended by Rispan.

Goibhniu: (GOYV-noo) Master *Uthadé* smith. Creator of Mira's daggers.

Grace Ndané: (n-DAH-nay) A witch and half-owner of Herbs, Antiques and Curiosities (HAC.) Mentor to her partner, Katya.

Gralbast: (GRAHL-bast) An *Urgaban* merchant. Formerly the Merchant's Guildmaster. Mira's business partner in Pokorah-Vo.

Gurutz Baroja: (goo-ROOTZ bah-RO-hah) *Félbahlag* count and member of the Félbahrin senate.

Gylan: (GUY-lahn) *Ulané Jhinura* armorer and leatherworker. Husband to Félora and father to Tesia.

CHARACTERS

Hoa: (HO-uh) *Pilané Jhin* who helps Mira to heal after she was severely wounded and helped her to learn pixie magic.

Inigon Elizondo: (IN-ih-gohn ay-lee-ZOHN-do) *Félbahlag* prince in Félbahrin. Nephew to the king and heir apparent.

Igonez: *See Eremon Igonez.*

Iratzé: (ee-RAHT-say) *Kaganum* (queen) of the *Wyl-Dunn* of Danu.

Istas: (EE-stahs) *Ranolan* chief of the *Sokwané* clan. Father to Dyani.

Itara, Brother: (ee-TAH-ruh) *Noélani* referred to as the *awa'ia* of the sun by the *Kajoran* people.

Iwalani, Auntie: (ee-wuh-LAH-nee) *Noélani* daughter to Mama A'iwanea and Papa Mohanga. This is the goddess of communication and learning for the *Kajoran* people.

Jack: *Jakarael Abalaan. Daijheen* who encounters Nora shortly after she first arrived on Danu and became her companion.

Jakarael Abalaan: (JAH-kah-ray-EHL AH-buh-lahn) *See Jack.*

Jakeda: (jah-KAY-dah) *Urgaban* head chef at the Raven's Nest restaurant.

Jill Ramirez: Mira's foster-mother on Earth.

Jorge Cervantes: Mira's biological Father.

Kaiaru, Uncle: (kai-AH-roo) *Noélani* son of Mama A'iwanea and Papa Mohanga. He is the god of the sea to the *Kajoran* people.

Kaléa, Aunti: (kuh-LAY-auh) *Noélani* daughter of Mama A'iwanea and Papa Mohanga. She is the goddess of the dance.

Karis Ulané Panalira: (KAH-ris oo-LAH-nay pah-nah-LEE-rah) Younger cousin of Neelu. Missing for many years. *See Rispan.*

Kartahn Zeg: (KAHR-tahn ZEHG) *Bahréth* religious leader, mage, and necromancer. He has a more human appearance, but this is a glamour used to disguise his true nature.

Katamakutu, Uncle: (KAH-tah-muh-KOO-too) *Noélani* son of Mama A'iwanea and Papa Mohanga. He is the god of chance to the *Kajoran* people.

Katya Zahradi: (KAT-yah zuh-RAH-dee) A witch and half-owner of Herbs, Antiques and Curiosities (HAC.) Apprentice to her partner, Grace.

Kékoatalki: (kay-KO-uh-TAHL-kee) *Borosoor* resident of the abandoned city of FIndias in Danu.

Kemen Agéra: (KEH-mehn uh-GAY-ruh) *Félbahlag* baron. Member of the Félbahrin senate.

Képa: (KAY-puh) *Wyl-Dunn* healer.

Kholinaer: (ko-lihn-AIR) The *Ashae* king in Shifara Castle.

Korana, Sister: (ko-RAH-nuh) *Noélani* referred to as the *awa'ia* of the moon by the *Kajoran* people.

Korashéna Ulané Sharavi: (KO-rah-SHAY-nuh oo-LAH-nay shah-RAH-vee,) *See Shéna.*

Laila: (LYE-luh) *Impané* mage. Mother of Yormak.

Lélé Corana: (LAY-LAY koh-RAH-nuh) *Kajoran* ship captain.

Lo-An: (LO-AHN) *Pilané Jhin* who helps Mira to heal after she was severely wounded and helped her to learn pixie magic.

Luana Alaso: (loo-AH-nuh uh-LAH-so) *Kajoran* princess. Heir to the *Kajoran* throne.

Luciana "Luci" Leon: (LOO-see-AH-nuh lay-OWN) Social worker assigned to Mira and Nora for their foster care. She is also Mira's aunt, and formerly with the *Daruidai.*

Lugh: (LOOHG) *Uthadé* who was half *Fu-Mo Ri* and a king at one time. Son of Duanna.

Luisanto Eskivel: (loo-ee-SAN-to AY-skee-vehl) *Félbahlag* baronet appointed as alcalde of Carabora.

Maeve: *Dannu Fé* queen on Danu.

Makati, Auntie: (muh-KAH-tee) *Noélani* daughter to Mama A'i-wanea and Papa Mohanga. This is the goddess of the wind for the *Kajoran* people.

Martin Laurent: Nora's biological father.

Marua, Uncle: (muh-ROO-uh) *Noélani* son to Mama A'iwanea and Papa Mohanga. This is the god of healing for the *Kajoran* people.

Médard: (MAY-dahrd) *Bahréth* mage that Mira encounters in Tyr nya Lu.

Mehrzad: (mair-ZAHD) *Rorujhen* stallion who agrees to become Luci's mount.

Merlain: (mehr-LAYN) Also known as Merlin. A biological ancestor of Nora's.

Milani: (mee-LAH-nee) *Awanjii* sent as Mama's Mercy.

Mira: (MEE-ruh) Mirabela Cervantes Ramirez. Nora's foster-sister.

Moépatu, Auntie: (MO-ay-PAH-too) *Noélani* daughter to Mama A'iwanea and Papa Mohanga. This is the goddess of death for the *Kajoran* people.

Mohanga, Papa: (mo-HAHNG-guh) *Noélani* referred to as the Sky Father, primary father god of the *Kajoran* people.

Monollo: (mo-NO-lo) *Awanjii sent as Mohanga's Revenge.*

Mooren: (MOO-rehn) *Ulané Jhinura* assigned to accompany Mira and advise and protect her on her missions to Pokorah-Vo and Shifara. Holds the rank of Lance with the Su Lariano Palace Guard, which is equivalent to corporal.

Motiho, Uncle: (mo-TEE-ho) *Noélani* son to Mama A'iwanea and Papa Mohanga. This is the god of music for the *Kajoran* people.

Mouse: Also known as Felgor. Close *Ulané Jhinura* friend to Mira and Rispan since her early days in Su Lariano. Becomes manager for the Raven's Nest Restaurant.

Neelu: (NEE-loo oo-LAH-nay POO-lah-kah-SAH-do) Neelu Ulané Pulakasado. *Ulané Jhinura* daughter to Queen Astrina. Mira's first friend in Daoine.

Nériala Elizondo: (nay-ree-AH-lah ay-lee-ZOHN-do) *Félbahlag* princess in Félbahrin.

Nimué: (NEE-moo-ay) Daughter of Aradi and Oisin Rinn. A biological ancestor of Nora's. The third *baensiari*.

Nora: Leanora Leland. Mira's foster-sister on Earth.

Nuada: (NOO-uh-duh) Also, Nuada of the Silver Hand. Known as the first king of the *Uthadé* (*Tuatha de Danann.*)

Ogma: (O-muh) Master *Uthadé* smith. Creator of Mira's pendent.

Oisin Rinn: (oh-SHEEN RIHN) Nora's ancestor. Husband to Aradi and father of Nimué.

Olsahg: (OL-sahg) *Bahréth* prophet who introduced the Transcendent (*Qélosan*) into the religion.

Orton: (OR-tuhn) *Uthadé* harbormaster of Tyr nya Lu.

Palben Ayala, Father: (PAHL-ben ai-AH-luhn) *Félbahlag* Grand

Inquisitor of the Jhunélin Order within the Most Holy Church of Ah-Shan.

Palila Aloso: (puh-LEE-luh uh-LAH-so) *Kajoran* queen. Mother of Luana.

Parker Hawthorne: *Human* mother of Emma and Shelby. Wife to Dwayne Hawthorne.

Poldi: (POL-dee) One of three *Bahréth* who, urged by Mira, decided not to attack the camp of healers and injured *Wyl-Dunn*, breaking away from Kartahn Zeg.

Radomér: (RAH-do-mair) One of three *Bahréth* who, urged by Mira, decided not to attack the camp of healers and injured *Wyl-Dunn*, breaking away from Kartahn Zeg.

Ree: (REE) *See Reelu Ulané Pulakaloso.*

Reelu Ulané Pulakaloso: (REE-loo oo-LAH-nay poo-lah-kah-LO-so) *Ulané Jhinura.* Older sister to Neelu. Rispan's mother.

Rispan: (RIS-pehn) Close friend to Mira and Mouse since her early days in Su Lariano. Is assigned to join her first mission to Pokorah-Vo.

Rizina: (rih-ZEE-nuh) *Ulané Jhinura* bodyguard assigned to protect Mira when holding the rank of Bar, equivalent to private, with the Su Lariano Palace Guard.

Seighdlacht: (SAYGD-lahkt) Unidentified dark figure in Nora's dreams.

Sena: (SEH-nuh) One of three *Bahréth* who, urged by Mira, decided not to attack the camp of healers and injured *Wyl-Dunn*, breaking away from Kartahn Zeg.

Shahz Dega: (SHAHZ DAY-guh) *Félbahlag* first mate to Lélé Corana.

Shan: (SHAHN) God of the *Félbahlag*.

Shelby Hawthorne: Went to high school with Mira and Nora. Older sister to Emma. Learns how to use magic after seeing Nora do magic accidentally.

Shéna: (SHAY-nuh.) Korashéna Ulané Sharavi. Last surviving member of the royal family of the *Ulané Jhinura* city of Su Astonil. Enslaved in Pokorah-Vo all her life until she was freed by Rispan.

Shian Shariel: (SHEE-uhn SHAH-ree-ehl) *See Bright.*

CHARACTERS

Shigara: (shee-GAH-rah) *Ulané Jhinura* Chief Healer for Queen Astrina in Su Lariano.

Sophia "Sofi" Leon Cervantes: (so-FEE-uh lay-OHN sehr-VAHN-tess) Mira's biological mother.

Ta'uira, Auntie: (TAH-oo-EE-ruhn) *Noélani* daughter to Mama A'iwanea and Papa Mohanga. This is the goddess of the storm for the *Kajoran* people.

Tavarnin: (tuh-VAR-nihn) *Wyl-Dunn* father to Zoriaa and Arrosa.

Té Niya: (TΛY NEE-uh) *Ande Dannu* queen in Solaian in Danu. Also known as Titania.

Tesia: (TEE-zee-uh) *Ulané Jhinura* master mage in Su Lariano. Friend to Neelu and daughter of Felora and Gylan. Trains Mira in magic and accompanies her on her mission to Shifara.

Tony Ramirez: Mira's foster-father on Earth.

Uftzi Elkano: (OOFT-zee ayl-KAH-no) *Félbahlag* count. Member of the Félbahrin senate.

Unais Elizondo III: (oo-NAY-us ay-lee-ZOHN-do) King of the *Félbahlag* in Félbahrin.

Usoa: (oo-SO-uh) *Wyl-Dunn* woman assigned to assist Mira. Later becomes a traveling companion and apprentice to Zoriaa.

Valdis Rotger: (VAHL-dihs ROHT-gehr) *Félbahlag* baron and appointed governor of Kajo.

Veeluthun: (vee-LOO-thoon oo-LAH-nay gah-BO-lay) Veeluthun Ulané Gabolé. Younger brother to Neelu in Su Lariano.

Veron: (VAY-run) *Ulané Jhinura* weapon's master in Su Lariano. Assisted in training Mira in martial arts.

Véshdani: (vaysh-DAH-nee) Androgynous god of the ancient *Félabhlag* religion of Fél Naran.

Ysiola: (EE-see-OH-lah) *Ashae* queen in Shifara Castle.

Zoriaa: (ZO-ree-uh) *Wyl-Dunn* keeper of the old ways, similar to a priestess. Eldest daughter of Tavarnin and sister to Arrosa.

Maps

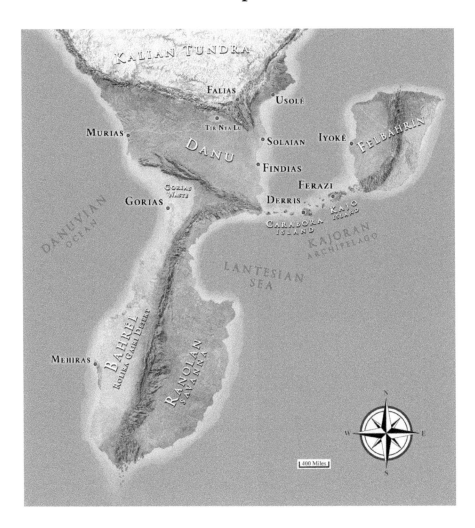

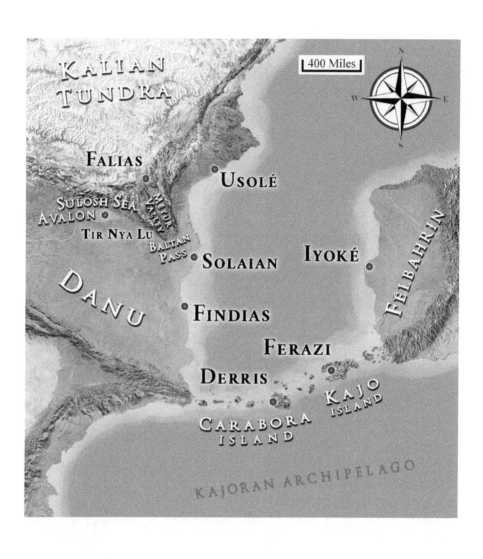

AUTHOR'S NOTE

Throughout my stories, you may note the use of names (or words) either taken directly from various ethnic groups or are some variation thereof. This is my way of tipping my hat in appreciation to those groups. I in no way attempt to portray the culture of these groups as I could not even pretend to do them justice, though there may be some cultural aspect that inspires me in the development of my fantasy cultures. Likewise, the fantasy races for whom these names are used is just random assignment, often it is simply based on a particular sound I was going for at that moment. If you read a name that appears to be from your people or culture, know that it is done respectfully. If you are reading a name that is unfamiliar to you, I encourage you to see if you can figure out its origins and look into those cultures for yourself. Perhaps inspiration will strike you as well.

CHAPTER ONE

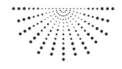

MIRA

The huge *Wyl-Dunn* camp I'd visited before was gone; there was nothing left but destruction. And the dead. My first instinct was to look for familiar faces among the fallen, not that I had known many of them. There were too many bodies to be able to easily tell who was here, but there weren't anywhere near enough to account for the entire camp. Somewhere, there were a lot of survivors. I also saw a number of bahrantu, those giant scorpions, or sometimes just pieces of them. I saw a gajhanti corpse not far off; one enormous tusk pointed at the sky.

"This isn't all of them," I said. "They must have gone somewhere."

"And they'd just leave their dead like this?" Luci asked.

"They may not have had a lot of options at the time," I pointed out. "Do you think you can track any survivors? The ones who were on foot, anyway?" She wouldn't be able to track those who flew off on *gurpahn*-back. The griffins.

"I have no idea," she frowned. "With armies coming in and out, trampling tracks far and wide…" She shrugged.

"I know where they went," a voice said.

I spun to face the speaker. It was a *Wyl-Dunn* woman. Her hair was ragged and filthy. There was a bloody gash on her head, and she seemed to be favoring one leg as she stood leaning on a staff that she gripped with both hands. She was familiar.

"Usoa?" I asked.

She gave a nod. "I don't see the child. Was your mission not successful?"

"We found her," I said. "She's safe. What happened here?"

"Kartahn Zeg," she said simply.

"He attacked you?"

"He sent a message to parley," she explained. "His army was somehow… cloaked. We couldn't see them until they attacked. We were overrun almost immediately. Most of the kaganesh escaped to the air. The fallen here bought them time to retreat. The *Bahréth* were far too vast in numbers to stand and fight them. Our kagana have taken our people

2

to Solaian to support the *Ande Dannu* against Zeg's army."

"What about Jack?" I asked her. "Did they take him with them? And the sword?"

She shook her head and winced at the motion. "Jack and many of our wounded were taken with Képa, our healer, north into the hills. I saw them as they were leaving; Zoriaa and some others were with them."

Usoa seemed to swoon for a moment and caught her balance. I dismounted quickly and rushed to her side.

"Why didn't you go with Képa?" I asked as I helped her from her feet. "You need a healer, too!"

"I was buried under a fallen tent," she said. "When I came to, they were already leaving. Besides, my duty was here."

"Why? What's here?"

"I knew you would come back," she answered. "Kaganum Iratzé assigned your care to me. You would need answers when you returned."

"But you clearly need medical attention," I scowled. "You can't very well give me answers if you die."

"Then it is fortunate I did not die," she said, smiling.

Luci was already getting out what first aid supplies we had and we washed and bandaged Usoa's head wound.

"I'm sorry," I told her. "I never managed to learn healing magic."

She gave another wan smile. "Few have the calling. It would have made my parents happy, but it was not my path."

"Is something wrong with your leg?"

"A bahrantu sting," she answered. "I managed to find some of the antidote, but I don't know if it was enough."

"We should probably get you to Képa as soon as possible. You need a real healer."

"I would not object."

"You can ride with me," I told her. "I'm sure Anazhari can carry us both easily."

"You even had to wonder if I could manage a couple snippets like you two?"

It was nice to hear Anazhari joking, but I got the idea she was doing it for Usoa's benefit. Anazhari knelt and I climbed into the saddle, putting Usoa in front of me sitting sideways to keep from putting too much pressure on her injured leg.

I had long since stopped judging age by height. The *Wyl-Dunn* were *Loiala Fé* by another name and their average height was about four and a half feet. As Usoa directed us where to go, I realized she was much younger than I'd originally assumed. She'd always been so serious and formal.

"How old are you?" I asked her.

She stiffened slightly before answering. "I am

sixteen as of last month when I was taken into the kaganum's service," she said sternly. "I am fully adult."

"I was only curious," I assured her. "I'm younger than I look. Not much older than you now. I'm eighteen."

She gaped at me. "Why do you look so old?"

It was the first thing she'd said to me that didn't sound formal. Maybe the fact that we were so close in age let her feel like she could be more herself.

"There was a spell," I explained. "It sped up time. When I dismantled it, it aged my body."

"Well," she said after a moment, "I suppose you don't look *that* old."

"Gee. Thanks."

"At least no one questions your ability because of your age," she said.

I had to laugh at that. "People will always question your ability. If it's not because of your age they'll find some other reason."

"Xantif is also eighteen," she said. "He's not too much older than I am."

"Xantif?"

"He was the one who saw to your *Rorujhen* when you first arrived at the kaganesh," she looked at me. "You must remember him. You even talked to him."

"Right." I vaguely recalled the conversation.

We were a good hour out from the ruined camp when Luci pulled up.

"We have a problem," she said. "The footprints of the *Wyl-Dunn* here are trampled by some others. We're not the only ones tracking them."

"*Bahréth?*" I asked her.

"Looks like it."

"Can you tell how many?"

She shrugged. "It's not a huge group. Less than a half dozen, anyway. The tracks are pretty fresh."

"That's plenty to be a problem for healers and injured people," I frowned. "Let's pick up the pace. Hopefully, they haven't caught up to them yet."

"You do realize we'll probably be outnumbered, right?"

I nodded. "Too bad I don't have a bow. I trained with one. I'm no expert, but I can definitely hit something as big as a *Bahréth.*"

"I'll stick to my Hellcats." Luci patted one of her pistols.

Right, I thought. *Those will definitely come in handy.*

"You trained with a bow?" Usoa asked. "You trained to be a hunter?"

"Not a hunter," I shook my head. "It was part of my martial arts training from the *Ulané Jhinura.*"

"Martial arts?"

"Yeah. You know… Military. Fighting. I learned how to use a lot of different weapons. Everyone had to have at least basic competence in pretty much everything."

"My parents didn't let me train for fighting," Usoa's eyes were downcast. "Now that I am an adult, I can choose for myself." Then she looked at me hopefully, "Maybe you could teach me!"

"Um," she had caught me by surprise. I'd never thought about teaching. "I guess I can show you some of the forms. But I'm not an instructor. And you need to heal first, anyway."

We were nearing the top of a small rise and Luci held her hand up for silence.

I let Anazhari slowly advance until I could just see over the top of the rise. About fifty yards from us, four *Bahréth* were arrayed in a semi-circle facing a rocky overhang near the base of a steep slope. The four *Bahréth* were just common soldiers, shakahr, rather than the elite Anointed.

Old soot stains on the rock told me that the overhang had seen repeated use as a shelter. A shallow stream flowed on a diagonal across the area in front of the slope and I could see several people in the recessed area. I could tell that the ones standing were the size of *Wyl-Dunn*.

I eased Usoa to the ground as she slid down Anazhari's side.

Most *Bahréth* soldiers carried an oversized falchion-type sword and a war hammer. They could wield the sword in one hand and the hammer in the other. The head of a *Bahréth* war hammer was roughly two or three times the size of what you'd expect on a normal construction hammer, but instead of a claw on the back for pulling nails, it had a six-inch long spike. It would be a bit heavy for me, being normal, human-sized. The handle was about four feet long and the whole thing could pack an incredible punch in the hands of the huge *Bahréth*.

The only thing I'd seen that could go one-on-one against a *Bahréth*, muscle for muscle, was an *Ogaré*, and they lived on Daoine. The *Ogaré* were taller, but the *Bahréth* had tails that were spiked like a stegosaurus.

I'd gotten lucky with Médard when I'd knocked him out. I'd caught him by surprise. Plus, he'd been a mage and not a warrior. The staff he'd carried had a decorative headpiece and was more a symbol of his position; it was not intended to be used for fighting like mine was.

As the *Bahréth* drew their weapons, I was reminded of that day so long ago, my first day on Daoine, when several *Urgaban* had me cornered. That's when I met Neelu. She'd saved me. I remembered how she'd handled it. I glanced at Luci and saw that she held one of her pistols in her hands.

I slid to the ground myself after Usoa. Then I connected to the *Ralahin* and used it to project my voice.

"What kind of shakahr attacks healers and injured people?"

The four *Bahréth* paused and looked around. Because of how I'd projected my voice, they couldn't tell where the sound was coming from. Only my eyes and the top of my head were above the level of the hill, so they couldn't see me.

"Leave now or the shame of cowardice will stain you for the rest of your miserable lives," I told them. "Short as that may be."

"Easy to speak of cowardice from the shadows," one of them growled.

The first time I'd done this it had almost killed me, but I'd long since mastered the flit. I leaned into the *Ralahin,* and in an instant, I had traveled the distance and stood with my knife against his belly.

"Is this better?" I asked him.

At first he was stunned that I seemed to appear out of nowhere, but then he looked down at me and felt less threatened.

"Little thing, aren't you?" he smirked.

I pushed lightly with the knife to get his attention.

"This blade is big enough to gut you right here," I told him. "Do you want to try me?"

"You made your point, little one."

"My *name* is Mira," I told him. "What's yours?"

"I am called Radomér."

One of the other shakahr raised his war hammer and stepped toward me.

"Ah!" I pressed harder with my knife.

"Hold!" Radomér ordered the others. "I can sense you would not hesitate to plunge the blade to the hilt," he said to me. "Why not just kill me and have done? With your speed, you could probably cut us all down."

"I almost did just that," I said. "But the truth is we have no reason to be enemies. I am no enemy to the *Bahréth*, and neither are the *Wyl-Dunn*."

"Kartahn Zeg would disagree with you," he pointed out.

"Maybe so," I agreed. "But there is no honor in killing the wounded or their healers."

"Honor or not," Radomér frowned, "we have our orders. Kill any *Wyl-Dunn* we find."

"Rashka the Destroyer would scorn such orders," I told him.

"You know of our *Jhyeh*?" He was surprised. *Jhyeh* was what they called their gods.

"I have read the *Tolkéda*," I answered. "I admire its beauty. Except for the heresy of Olsahg."

"Heresy?" He looked uncomfortably at his fellows. "You speak dangerous words."

"I speak truth. Olsahg and his Transcendent are contrary to everything the *Jhyeh* stand for. To follow them is to betray the *Jhyeh*."

"You believe in our *Jhyeh*?"

"I don't know whether the *Jhyeh* exist, but I believe in their words," I said. "Olsahg is the only prophet who did not claim to speak with the *Jhyeh*. These supposed Transcendent are the *Qelosan*; a race from another world that feeds on the emotions and life energy of others the way a leech feeds on blood. Olsahg's words were false, whether he knew it or not."

"Heretic!" One of the shakahr snarled and launched himself in my direction.

There was a loud report and a hole appeared in his forehead before he dropped lifelessly to the ground.

"Nobody move!" I commanded. "Do not throw your lives away for nothing!"

"Stand down!" Radomér ordered. "Sheathe your weapons. If they wanted to kill us, we'd all be dead." He raised his palms and stepped back away from my knife. "We cannot have peace over a knife point."

I nodded and sheathed my own blade.

"The last thing I expected was to discuss the *Tolkéda* with a foreigner in the wilderness," he said with a smile.

One of the other shakahr made a sound and looked pointedly away. "Why not?" She mumbled. "You speak of it with anyone else who'll listen."

"Radomér," I arched an eyebrow at him. "Did you miss your calling to be a monk?"

He laughed. "I'm just a simple *Bahréth*. I'm not a holy one."

"As were most of the prophets of the *Tolkéda* before they became prophets."

"Perhaps so," he shrugged. "And what did you learn from reading the words of our prophets?"

"Besides Olsahg, you mean?" I thought about that. I was glad I had taken the time to read their scriptures. I still had pieces of Médard's memories, but my own memories were more sure. "We know from the First Book of Lantos that the *Jhyeh* aren't interested in being worshiped. And that it is Ezhti's hope that the *Bahréth* take responsibility for themselves."

"Yet the Book of Olsahg says we should take responsibility for more," he answered. "For the world even. And to bring others into the fold of the *Jhyeh*."

"And that's what this war is about?" I asked him. "What of the Second Book of Lantos?"

"What of it?"

"You shouldn't ask for more than one is willing to give," I reminded him. "Forcing others to accept your beliefs is a violation of those same beliefs."

"That is my feeling as well," he sighed. "But Kartahn Zeg is in power now, and he has very different ideas."

"Those ideas will cost the lives of many good *Bahréth*," I told him. "And the lives of a lot of others, too. It's a needless waste. Radomér, you don't need the words of the *Jhyeh* to tell you about waste. The *Bahréth* live in the desert. Your lives are anything but frivolous. But you don't just live in the desert; you *thrive* in it, and not by being wasteful."

"How do you know so much of our people?" he asked me.

"That's a long story for another time," I said. "And I know the *Bahréth* well enough to know you aren't really our enemies. Not if you don't make it that way."

"I cannot speak for Kartahn Zeg or his armies. And I cannot speak for tomorrow," he said. "But I will say that none of us here today are enemies." He signaled to the other shakahr. "We will assist as we can with your wounded."

"What about your orders?"

"There is no honor in attacking healers and wounded," he smirked.

"These shakahr will honor that?" I asked. "Even after…" I nodded to the body of the *Bahréth* Luci had shot.

"They will," Radomér assured me. "That one was new to our unit and not well liked. He had a bad attitude."

The *Wyl-Dunn* in the little camp under the overhang, the ones who were conscious anyway, had been watching our conversation with worry. We weren't close enough for them to hear what we were saying and when the shakahr started walking toward them, they began to panic. I could see Zoriaa and Képa standing protectively in front of the others.

"It's alright!" I called out. "They're going to help!"

"Mira?" Zoriaa stepped forward. "What's going on?"

"Let them know what they can do to help," I told her. "I'll be right with you."

I went to the top of the hill and Radomér followed curiously. When we got to Luci and the others, she still had her pistol in her hand.

"Are you sure we can trust them?" she asked.

"I believe Radomér," I answered. "Radomér, this is Luci, Anazhari, and Mehrzad. And this is Usoa."

Usoa was lying on the ground and only semiconscious.

"I'm worried about that head injury," I said. "Let's get her to Képa."

I started toward Usoa, but Radomér moved quickly to her side and gently picked her up in his massive arms.

"I can walk," Usoa said.

"No need," Radomér told her. "I have you."

CHAPTER TWO

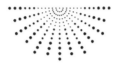

MIRA

"Thanks for the assist back there," I said to Luci as we started down the hill to the others. "That was a pretty good shot at that distance."

"I was aiming for his chest.," she scowled.

I bit back a laugh, but she noticed and her scowl deepened.

I studied the wounded while Képa directed Radomér and the other shakahr. There were about two dozen of them in various conditions. At least a half-dozen were unconscious, Jack among them. I'd hoped that by now he would have come out of whatever was going on with him.

"Most of the wounded were evacuated to So-laian with the rest of my people," Zoriaa said. "But we couldn't get everyone. These were the last few and it was a struggle to bring them this far to get them away from the fighting."

"This is as far as they can go for a while," Képa looked up from working on Usoa. "Several people would die if we tried to move them again."

"How soon will they be able to travel?" I asked her.

She considered that for a moment. "At least a week. Probably longer. We have no wagons to carry them and we have no *gurpahn* to fly. It's a long way to Solaian on foot. If we had more resources here, or more healers..." She shook her head. "We're not going anywhere soon. And some of these may not survive either way."

I didn't like the delay, but what were the alternatives? I couldn't open a portal to Solaian since I didn't have anything to use as an anchor.

"What if we could take them someplace else?" I offered. "Someplace with resources and more healers?"

"Solaian is the closest place," she answered.

"It might be the closest," I agreed, "but not the easiest to reach."

She looked at me, waiting for me to go on.

"I'd have to check," I said. "But I can open a portal to Su Lariano on Daoine."

"Su Lariano?" Her brows furrowed. "*Ulané Jhinura?*"

"Yes," I told her. "I have some connections there."

"I doubt the sprites would be of much help," she said dismissively.

"They have some of the best healers," I told her.

"Really." Her tone and expression told me she doubted it.

"You think you're better off here?"

"No," she sighed. "If you make this portal, will they accept us?"

"All I can do is ask," I said. "But I think it is likely."

"I suppose even the sprites will have better accommodations than this," she commented.

"Alright, I'll see what I can do. But one thing…" I met her eyes. "I don't know where this derogatory attitude about the *Ulané Jhinura* comes from, but it stops now. I've known good and bad people among every race I've encountered. The *Ulané Jhinura* of Su Lariano include some of the best and noblest people I have ever met. They saved me and took me in when I was a stranger on their world. They fed me and trained me in military arts and magic. They marched in support of the *Ashae* in Shifara against a rebel faction and helped to preserve the throne. They've made advances in uses for magic that even the *Ashae* didn't have. If it weren't for the *Ulané Jhinura*, I wouldn't be here right now. And you'd be dead."

Her expression had become pinched when I started, but gradually turned to surprise and then embarrassment.

"Of course," she agreed. "You are right. There's no basis for that bias. Just because they are smaller doesn't make them less. And if they agree to take us in, I will have nothing but gratitude."

I breathed a sigh of relief. I hadn't been sure how Képa was going to respond, but there was no way I was going to let her take that attitude to Su Lariano, even if that meant leaving her here. Maybe I was being unreasonable, but I didn't care. I'd seen racial bias and discrimination before, both on Earth and on Daoine, and it only led to problems rather than solutions. Maybe I was quibbling over something small, but I wasn't going to put up with it. It was too easy for things like that to just become normal and people didn't realize what they were doing.

Fortunately, Képa had been able to see that she wasn't being fair, but I had to wonder how much more of that I was going to see. Anything different was reason enough to make members of one group leery of another. Some of these things were obvious, like the color of someone's skin. Other things weren't so obvious, like size or age.

"Where's Xantif?" Usoa was looking around. "Is he here?"

"There is no Xantif here," Képa told her.

"Did he go to Solaian with the others?" she asked. "I'm sure he was very brave during the attack. He'll probably be promoted!"

"Usoa," Zoriaa spoke. "I saw Xantif during the fighting. He was very brave indeed. But... he did not go to Solaian."

"Why not? Was he sent on some special mission?"

"I am sorry," Zoriaa told her. "He was killed in the attack."

"No!" Usoa shook her head. "You are wrong! Or you are lying! Xantif is just fine, he's—" Her voice broke. "It's a mistake! It *has* to be!"

"I'm sorry," Zoriaa said again.

"He can't be dead! He can't be! He's beautiful and smart and brave and sweet!" Usoa looked around in desperation, hoping for what, I don't know. Then her eyes landed on Radomér, and she launched herself at him.

"How could you!" Her breath was coming in ragged sobs as she beat her fists on his chest. "How could you? I hate you! I'll kill you!"

Radomér stood unflinching, at a loss for what to say. I had to turn my eyes away at first. I understood her pain too well and it brought back memories of my own pain. But Usoa's pain overrode my own and I stepped to her.

"Usoa, it's not Radomér's fault." I gently pulled her from him.

19

"How do you know?" She demanded, her grief fully turning to anger. "Maybe he's the one who did it!"

"I don't know who did it," I admitted. "But still, it isn't his fault. I understand how you feel—"

"No, you don't!" She pulled away. "How could *you* know?"

"Because I *do*."

She looked at me searchingly for a moment. Then her anger evaporated, and I caught her as she collapsed into sobs. I wrapped my arms around her to give her what comfort I could. She pressed her face into my shoulder and I could feel my own hot tears running to join with hers.

Once Usoa had calmed down, she admitted to being hungry, but then she only picked at her food. I remembered how I'd dealt with my own grief and was thankful she was in a different situation.

I worked up a tentative plan with the others and made a portal to my suite in Su Lariano. As soon as I was there, I went in search of Neelu. I found her sparring with Veron, the queen's weapons master. Her eyes brightened when she saw me.

"You got your body back!" She smiled.

"Yes." I gave her a hug. "This is much better! Hello, Veron. Good to see you."

"And you as well." He grinned. "Are you here for some sparring? Has a life of leisure gotten you rusty?"

"Ah, no," I answered. "To both of those questions."

"Is this a social call?" Neelu asked with one raised eyebrow.

"I wish it was," I frowned. "I think I told you about Kartahn Zeg?"

"Even if you haven't," she rolled her eyes, "I've heard about him and everyone else you met on Danu countless times from Emma."

"Right." I agreed. "How's she doing?"

"Good. Tesia has been teaching her to use magic."

"I'll get her home as soon as I can," I told her. "And once I'm on Earth, I have to find out what happened to Jill and Tony." At her questioning look, I went on. "That's why I had to leave Emma here. I was in that *Bahréth* body, so I took her to my house, but it was burned to the ground."

"What happened?"

"I have no idea," I frowned. "But first thing's first. I have about two dozen *Wyl-Dunn* refugees. Mostly wounded. Some are seriously wounded. I wanted to know if I could bring them here."

"Of course!" She was all business. "Let's go to the infirmary and set up a space so you can portal directly there."

We said goodbye to Veron and headed straight away to the healer's wing and found Shigara, the chief healer. She agreed to the plan immediately and began giving orders to her staff.

I looked around and realized I couldn't bring the *Rorujhen* here. I turned to Neelu.

"We should go to the pasture where the *Rorujhen* graze so I can set up an anchor there for a portal."

We made our way quickly and I connected a thread for the anchor. By the time we got back, Shigara had cleared a space in one end of a large room and empty beds waiting on the other end. Orderlies and healers were standing by.

"If you will permit it," I said to Shigara, "I will attach a thread of magic to you to use as an anchor for this end of the portal."

"You may," she answered.

I reached for the *Ralahin* and pulled a thread which I tied around Shigara. I added the other end to the collection I had going around my wrist. Then I found the thread tied to Anazhari. I formed a portal and stepped through. To my surprise, Neelu came through on my heels. I kept the portal open behind us.

"I thought you were going to wait?" I asked her.

"I decided to take a look at Danu instead." She shrugged with a grin.

"Well," I smirked, "if that's the way you want to play it..." I turned and spoke loudly to the faces that were all looking in our direction. "Everyone, I present to you Neelu Ulané Pulakasado, Princess of Su Lariano!"

There were a lot of surprised expressions and several people who were standing started to kneel.

"No!" Neelu objected. "Stop! No kneeling! Or bowing, either!" Some had awkwardly tried to change from a kneel to a bow. "Just carry on with whatever you were doing. And call me Neelu." She gave me a scathing look and I just smiled.

Then Neelu saw the *Bahréth,* and I put my hand on her arm as she reached for her blade.

"I forgot to mention," I told her. "We do have some *Bahréth* with us. They're helping."

Her brow furrowed for a moment before she relaxed.

"You weren't appointed to the Diplomatic Corps by accident," she said with a smile.

"Képa," I called out. "Shigara has a space ready for you. She's the chief healer at Su Lariano."

I turned to Anazhari and Mehrzad.

"I'll make a portal to the pastures outside Su Lariano for you two first," I told them.

"We have been discussing this," Anazhari told me. *"You will need to return to this world, yes?"*

"Nora is still here somewhere," I said. "So, yes."

"And these injured will need to be returned to their people once they have been treated?"

"I hadn't thought that far ahead," I admitted. "But that's true as well."

23

"*Your ability to create portals has a weakness,*" she said. "*This anchor that you require for the destination. You or someone you are connected to has to go there first, correct?*"

"Right." I agreed. "If I know a place well enough, I can anchor the other end there. Otherwise, I need a thread to follow. A magical thread, like the one I attached to you."

"*Mehrzad and I will continue to track the* Wyl-Dunn *from their camp and discover where they have gone,*" she said. "*That way, when you are ready to return, you should be able to go directly to them.*"

"Good thinking," I agreed. "That will definitely save some time."

"*However,*" Mehrzad put in, "*we would appreciate it if you could take the saddles with you. You can bring them when you return.*"

"Right. Of course. I should have thought of that, too."

Once the saddles had been stripped from the two *Rorujhen,* they didn't waste any time hanging around; they were off through the trees and gone.

Képa was already prepared, so I located the thread to Shigara and opened a portal back to the infirmary. The patients that could walk went first. Then the shakahr began carrying the others through and returning through the first portal, which I'd kept open for the purpose. In no time at all, everyone had been moved to Su Lariano, bringing the two saddles and any supplies as well.

Radomér had talked about it with the other two shakahr and they had decided it would be better to come along for now rather than risk retribution for doing what they'd felt was right. Neelu, Luci, and I were the last ones through and I closed both portals.

Arané-Li was there with Shigara to help work out where non-injured people would stay. I turned to Neelu.

"If you've got this under control, I'd like to go back to Earth and find out what happened with Jill and Tony."

"What about Emma?" she asked. "Do you want to bring her with you?"

"Not yet," I shook my head. "Let me find out what's going on first. If it's safe, I can come back and get her."

"No problem. Shigara and Arané-Li have things under control here," she said. "And I'll keep the little birdie under my wing until you get back."

"Thanks." I turned to Luci. "Maybe we should go to the back room of Grace's shop. We can probably use that as a base of operations while we figure things out."

I dug through my pack and found my cell phone; it had worked its way to the bottom. It was also very dead.

"This is going to need a charge," I frowned. "Yours is probably the same. I'll have to use the shop phone."

I formed an image in my mind of the back room of HAC – Herbs, Antiques & Curiosities – the store that Grace and Katya ran. Just Grace now. I formed a portal as soon as I had an anchor in place and Luci and I stepped through.

It was after hours, so the shop was closed for the day. The room was lit up only from the dim light of the exit sign by the rear door. I stepped into the office and flipped the light switch. The first thing I did was plug my phone into the charger that Grace kept on the desk. Then I dug through the bottom drawer and pulled out a spare charger for Luci. I tucked my pack into the corner of the office out of the way.

I used the land-line phone on the desk and tried Tony's cell phone, but it went straight to voicemail. I got the same thing with Jill's number.

"It just means their phones are off," Luci said when I told her the results.

"*Both* of them?" I asked.

"We shouldn't assume the worst, that's all I'm saying."

"The house burned down," I pointed out. "So much for the protection of the *Daruidai*."

"I can make some calls," she said. "See what they know about it."

"Alright. While you're doing that, I'll take a look around what's left of the house. Plus, I'll look in on Emma's house. I'd like to get her home and out of this mess as soon as possible."

"What will you tell her parents? You're going to need to have a story to tell them about where she's been. Something that Emma will have to back up when she's asked about it. You can't very well tell them she's been on another world where there's magic."

"I don't know," I admitted. "But I'm not going to talk to them now. I'm just going to take a look around. We'll have time to figure something out. And who knows? The truth might actually work with her parents. It worked with Jill and Tony."

"Not everyone has such amazing parents."

"No, you're right," I said. "Emma's parents might not be able to handle it. Emma's a good kid, though. Her parents always struck me as a bit controlling, but somehow Emma would still manage to sneak out."

"Didn't you say something about her having a sister?"

"Shelby…" I frowned, remembering my last encounter with her. "That's another subject entirely. To be honest, I don't think anyone in Emma's immediate family is very good for her, but they *are* her family."

"Are you thinking of leaving her on Daoine?"

"No," I shook my head. "Her family might not be great, but I wouldn't want to do that to them. We'll get Emma home as soon as we can."

I didn't want to portal directly to my burnt-out bedroom, so I decided to go to Nora's tree in the woods. It wasn't too far of a walk and I could swing by Emma's house on the way to mine.

As I stepped through the portal and into the clearing, I remembered the last time I had been here. It had been evening then, as well. There'd been a *Jhiné Boré*, a wood nymph or dryad, who'd been living in the ancient tree for who knew how long. What had been her name?

"Cirilia?" I called out. "Are you here?"

If she was there, she wasn't answering. That was her prerogative, so I turned and started through the woods toward home.

I went by Emma's house. The lights were on and I could see someone moving around inside. The blinds weren't all the way down on the window to the front room, and from across the street, I could see Emma's father sitting and watching TV. I remembered his name was Dwayne. Dwayne Hawthorne. After a few minutes, Emma's mother, Parker, came in from the kitchen and I could tell they were talking and then she went back to the kitchen.

There was no sign of Shelby, but that didn't mean anything. Maybe she wasn't home. Maybe she was in her room. Either way, things at their house appeared normal. I didn't see any red flags that would indicate Emma couldn't come home right away.

I continued up the sidewalk and around the corner to my street. To what had been my street, anyway. The house wasn't totally gone. It looked like the fire had started in the front room and that part of the house was the worst. The roof in front had collapsed. Rafters showed through like the ribs of a half-decomposed body.

I felt sick. Everything I owned had been in that house. Everything except for the odds and ends I'd brought with me in my pack. All my books. My movies. My clothes. The dress I'd worn for my quinceañera. School yearbooks. Pictures. Everything. All gone.

Oh, maybe there'd be something in the closet or dresser that hadn't burned, but there'd still be smoke damage. Not to mention water damage from the firemen putting out the fire. Maybe there was a way to fix the smoke damage using magic. I glanced around, but the street seemed deserted.

The front of the house was too big of a mess, so I went around to the back. The sliding glass door had been blown out. The pieces made a scratching sound on the concrete patio as I walked over them. I looked around the ruined kitchen, thinking of all the meals Jill had made there. From here I could see how the fire had gutted the front room. Tony's favorite chair was nothing more than a misshapen lump.

I started toward the hall when I heard the scratching of someone walking on the broken glass on the patio. I turned my head to look, but the sound stopped. I couldn't see the patio from where I was standing, but I knew someone was there. As softly as I could, I made my way down the hall into my bedroom. I barely registered that the fire hadn't been so intense here and I went to the window.

I looked out cautiously, but there was no light in the back and I couldn't see into the shadows. The glass was gone, so I quietly climbed through the frame and lowered myself to the ground outside. As I turned from the wall, I felt a hand grabbing my shoulder.

"Ha! Got you, witch!"

Then I felt a sharp pain in my side, and I staggered from the blow.

"I knew that was you, nosing around outside my house." It was Dwayne, Emma's father. "Shelby told me what you did to Emma!"

"What are you talking about?" I gasped through the pain.

"I know all about you." His grin was cruel. He brought his hand up, taunting me with a long kitchen knife. There was blood on a good eight inches of the blade. "Suffer not a witch to live!"

He came at me then, lunging forward with the knife. I slapped it to the side and tripped him as he went past. I had to get away; I was in no shape for a fight. I forced myself to move and I heard him getting to his feet.

I formed a portal to my suite in Su Lariano. If I could get there, they'd get me a healer right away.

"You won't get away," he snarled.

I couldn't spare a glance and moved into the portal. As I started to step through I felt the blade strike again, this time an overhand blow to my shoulder. I fell forward and lost my focus. The portal shifted as I passed through. I found myself on the ground in a forest and he had fallen with me.

I rolled over and pushed him away with my feet. I forced myself up and stumbled away from him. I made it three steps before I tripped on a root and fell headlong to the ground. There was a commotion all around me and I saw that I had fallen into a *Pilané Jhin* garden. I could see a swarm of *Pilané Jhin*, pixies, forming in the air above me.

"I'm sorry!" I tried to get the words out. I knew how deadly they could be to trespassers. "I didn't mean to!"

"Now you die, witch!" Dwayne stood above me in the garden, his feet straddling me.

He sank to his knees on top of me, holding the kitchen knife in a two-handed reverse grip. I was too weak to push him off. As he raised the knife, the *Pilané Jhin* struck. There were thousands of them. Three-inches of winged fury times thousands. Knife forgotten, he started flailing his arms, trying to knock them away. There were too many of them. I could already see blood from hundreds of cuts, shredding his skin. He leaped up and started running, but instead of running into the forest he ran deeper into the garden. His incoherent screams turned to whimpers and then fell silent after only a few minutes.

I heard a sound like the buzzing of wings approaching and the swarm was back above me. I tried to say I was sorry again, but I couldn't get the words out. I knew I was losing consciousness. With what was coming, unconsciousness would probably be a blessing.

CHAPTER THREE

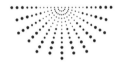

NORA

It took us a full day to navigate the narrow channel that went north from Carabora. The entire Kajoran Archipelago was thick with underwater mountain ranges and coral reefs that prevented access from ships with deep keels like what the *Félbahlag* used. The *Kajoran* had created a single narrow passage through the reefs to each of the two main islands, Carabora and the larger island of Kajo. Other passages existed, but they were highly guarded secrets among *Kajoran* ship captains and navigators, committed to memory and never written on any charts.

Once we were free of the reefs, the warship *Gechina* headed northeast under full sail to Iyoké, the *Félbahlag* capital. Captain Corana had stayed behind. She had recruited a new crew and taken possession of the *Resolute*, the *Kajoran* ship that Monollo and Spike had cleared of living occupants. While I wasn't happy about the loss of life, I was glad Corana had her own ship again. Shahz had decided to come along with us to Iyoké, the *Félbahlag* capital, and I was grateful for that. It would be good to have at least one *Félbahlag* around I knew I could trust. Dyani had come with him rather than return to the Ranolan Savanna.

The effects of Mohanga's Revenge started out similar to mild hay-fever, but quickly escalated. There was a pale green film that was evident in bodily fluids such as mucus and even sweat. The spores that had once been Monollo began to eat away at the skin and internal organs, but I knew that while this process was very slow for the first few days, it would speed up exponentially after that. At a certain stage, it would reach a tipping point and there would be no coming back from it if they hadn't left the islands in time.

The *Félbahlag* evacuation of Carabora had been difficult to keep orderly. A panicked mass exodus would just have resulted in a confusion of ships vying for position in the narrow channel. The Baronet Luisanto Eskivel had maintained tight control without ruffling too many feathers. Of course, it helped that he outranked any of the dignitaries and such who had been on the island.

At night, I had started avoiding the dreamspaces. I felt bad about shutting Katamakutu out. That was like having a whole separate life and my life by day gave me enough to think about. Since my nightmares had stopped, all my nightly dreams were just normal ones. It was strange to have my nights be so normal for the first time I could remember.

Eskivel had been very courteous on the voyage, though he wasn't happy about Spike coming along. After the first two days of the voyage, his symptoms, and those of his crew, had faded. The *Gechina* had been the last ship to leave, but once we were under full sail, we were quickly overtaking the other ships en route to Iyoké.

"All these ships are evacuating from the Kajoran islands?" I asked Eskivel.

"Yes." He replied. "They are having to abandon their homes. We annexed the Kajoran Archipelago two decades ago. Some *Félbahlag* lived there even before that."

"Annexed?" I raised an eyebrow at him. "Don't you mean forcibly occupied? Excuse me if I don't seem sympathetic."

Eskivel was saved from having to respond. Another ship was sailing towards us from the east and he ordered the captain to alter course. Once the two ships were side by side, lines were tossed back and forth to keep them together. An officer came aboard from the other ship and gave a brisk salute to Eskivel. They spoke for several minutes before the officer saluted again and returned to the other ship. Lines were cast off, and the other ship moved away.

Eskivel looked troubled and unsure of his next move.

"What's going on?" I asked him.

"It's not good," he admitted. "Baron Rotger has evacuated Kajo, but he had his ship firing cannon at the city. He's only leaving long enough for his symptoms to go away, then he intends to come back and attack again from sea."

"What?" I was shocked. "We have to stop him!"

"I have no jurisdiction over the baron," he shook his head. "He is my superior."

"I don't care! You *know* this is wrong. We have to do *something!* He's just killing innocent civilians!"

Eskivel sighed and shook his head. "We can go, but I do not know that we can change anything."

"We have to try. The worst thing we can do," I told him, "is to do nothing."

"Captain!" Eskivel called as he walked toward him. "Change course! We sail for Ferazi on Kajo. Get us there as fast as you can."

"Yo-ah," Corlen said to me. "Why dat *lako* say change course? Why we not go to Princess Luana?"

Corlen was dedicated to his princess, and nothing was more important to him than finding her and freeing her from the *Félbahlag*.

"We will," I told him. "But that jerk baron is shooting his cannon at the city."

"So? How you gwan stop 'im?" he asked me. I could see his anger at the news. "You gwan use magic stop cannon?"

"No. I don't know," I frowned. "The baronet is going to see if he can do something."

"Baronet tell baron?" he scoffed.

"Do you have a better idea?" I demanded.

His only answer was a narrowing of his eyes.

"I'm sorry," I relented. "That wasn't fair. None of us know what we can do, yet. But we have to do something."

"Aye, dat." He gave a single nod before walking away.

"*Can you do what he asked?*" Bright's voice sounded in my mind. "*Could you use magic to stop the cannon?*"

"I have no idea how I could do that," I answered. "I don't know if that's possible."

"*Not knowing how hasn't stopped you before.*"

"Maybe, but this is different," I told her. "A cannon is like a really big gun—"

"*Gun?*"

"Um… Never mind, that's not important. The thing is that it uses an explosion in a confined space and that's what shoots the cannonball out of the end."

"*What causes this explosion?*"

37

"Gunpowder, I guess," I shrugged.

"But how does this gunpowder cause an explosion?"

"They touch it with fire, or maybe a spark, and it explodes."

"Fire is something I know about," she said. *"From what you say, this gunpowder must burn very quickly. Different things burn at different speeds. Pine burns more quickly than oak."*

"Right." I agreed. "And gunpowder explodes because it burns so fast."

"If you had a way to make gunpowder burn more slowly, there would be no explosion? The cannon would not... fire?"

"I suppose."

"Then you have your answer."

"What do you mean I have my answer?" I asked. "Make the gunpowder burn more slowly?"

"Yes."

"But I don't know how to do that!"

Her only response was a sort of mental shrug.

It was a dumb idea. Even if I could figure out how to make gunpowder burn slowly, I wouldn't have access to it to put a spell on it or whatever. Plus, they'd have plenty more gunpowder to use. Was I supposed to figure out a way for *all* gunpowder to burn slowly? That wasn't possible.

Maybe I could make one of those dreamspace bubbles where gunpowder burned slowly, but this was the real world, not a dream. But what had Kata said? Something about reality just being another dreamspace?

How did that help me?

He said every dreamspace had its rules. That meant that anytime magic was used anywhere, somehow it was within the rules of wherever it was being used. Then I thought of the transformation of Monollo and Milani. I didn't have a clue how that could possibly fit into the rules. I shook my head. That wasn't my problem to solve. My problem had to do with fire.

I'd created fire out of thin air. I'd made flames to see by. I'd lit candles. I'd even lit an entire ship on fire. An entire ship! That was it! It didn't matter where the gunpowder was as long as my spell affected the whole ship. Anything *within* the ship. Then it couldn't fire its cannon.

But that still left me with the basic problem of how to make things burn too slowly to explode. I knew how to make things burn. Could I do the opposite? Actually, I knew I *could* do the opposite; I could put out a flame. Could I create some kind of field that would prevent fire inside of it? Maybe that was overkill though. I didn't need to prevent all fire; I just needed to prevent a fast fire. I needed a spell that would put a cap on how fast things could burn.

I'd just go with whatever was going to be easiest. Maybe this was something I could do after all.

The first thing would be to figure out the spell to control fire within a given area, then I'd have to figure out how to attach it to that area. It couldn't just be a one-off that would let them fire the cannon the next time they tried. I'd need to disable all the cannon on a ship and keep them disabled.

I went below to the small cabin I'd been assigned to share with Dyani. She was there and looked up when I came in.

"I recognize that look," she said. "What are you up to?"

"Baron Rotger is using his cannon to attack the main city on Kajo," I told her. Her face hardened with anger. "I'm going to see if I can figure out how to stop the cannon from firing."

She nodded. "Don't let *me* stop you."

I looked around and found a candle. First, I lit it using magic. That much I could do, no problem. Then I used magic to extinguish the flame; not to blow it out, but to stop the combustion. Then I worked at alternating it, on and off, to light it and put it out. I got to where I could do that quickly without any trouble.

Dyani watched silently as I went. I knew I'd done some of these drills before, but going through them again helped me to get my head around what was next. Could I make it burn more slowly? I wasn't even sure how I could tell if it was working. I lit the candle and focused on the flame, feeling how it was consuming the wax. This seemed more like a science experiment than magic. There was a chemical process going on; molecular. I just needed to slow the reactions.

The thing was, I *didn't* really understand the process that was occurring. It was like my sight zoomed in and I watched the burning. Then I willed magic into it. The flame suddenly shot up and half the candle had burned away before I could stop what I was doing.

"This isn't working!" I mumbled.

"Keep trying," Bright said. *"You're getting there."*

I shook off my hands and focused again. As I willed the magic this time, I was thinking of the particles being like someone trying to walk through water; they could get through, but it was slow. As I did this, the candle dimmed. I'd done it! I'd slowed the fire!

But was it enough? I'd have to see about fine-tuning later. The next thing was to see if I could do the same thing with a field instead of working directly with the flame. I wouldn't be able to see every cannon.

Leaving the candle burning on a wooden stool, I held out my hands and concentrated on making a ball of magic between them that would cause the same walking-through-water effect on a flame within the ball. Once I had it, I carefully moved the ball over to the candle and lowered it so that the flame would be inside the ball.

The flame dimmed!

Okay, now the next step. I noticed absently that Dyani wasn't in the room anymore and I'd no idea when she'd left.

I set the candle on a side table and focused again at creating the same ball of magic as I'd just done. Then I anchored the ball on top of the stool. Once I was sure it was in place, I took the lit candle from the side table and set it on the stool inside the area of the magic. It dimmed!

"It worked!"

"*I told you you could do it.*" Bright sounded smug. How could she get those emotional undertones in her mental communication?

I ran up on deck and found Dyani talking with Shahz and Corlen. They all looked at me as I approached. I must have spent a lot more time working on the spell than I realized because it was fully dark outside.

"Did you figure it out?" Shahz asked.

"Yes!" I told him. "Well… mostly. Come see!"

They followed me to the cabin, and I set the candle up on the side table and lit it.

"Alright," I said. "I've already attached a magical field to the top of the stool. Watch this."

I took the lit candle and moved it to the stool. As

soon as the flame was inside the field the candle flame dimmed considerably.

"See?" I asked. "The spell slowed the flame."

They looked at each other, clearly not understanding the significance of what I was saying.

"Look," I explained. "The cannons shoot the cannonballs when the gunpowder explodes, right?"

They nodded, waiting.

"The explosion is just the gunpowder burning really fast. If I can slow down how fast the gunpowder burns, it won't explode. The cannon won't shoot!"

"That makes sense," Shahz said. "But a candle is not gunpowder."

"I know, I know. I still have to try this with actual gunpowder. Then I should be able to get the spell just right."

"But how will you get to the cannon to put the spell on them?" he asked.

"No," I shook my head. "Once I get this working with gunpowder, I can anchor the spell to an entire ship and none of the gunpowder on the ship would be able to explode. Of course, they'll still be able to have lanterns and fire for cooking and such."

"Nice of you," Shahz raised an eyebrow.

"Well," I shrugged. "You still might need to burn the ship up, right?"

He laughed at that. "It seems we need to get you

some gunpowder to experiment with," he said. "But you should probably do it up on deck instead of down here."

"And only little bit," Corlen said. "Big mistake wid little bit not so bad. Little mistake wid lotta bit not so good."

"I guess we should talk to Eskivel," I said. "See if he'll let me use some gunpowder."

"Good luck with that," Dyani smirked.

It took some convincing, but eventually Eskivel agreed to provide small amounts of gunpowder for my experiments starting the next morning, but only under his direct supervision and only on the top deck away from anything important. The idea that magic might be used to nullify cannon was both appealing and disturbing to him.

Adjusting the spell to hamper the rate of burn for the gunpowder was actually easier than I thought it would be. It didn't take much and all it would do was fizzle a little and burn. Eskivel nodded his approval at the result.

"But we still have to make sure," I told him. "I should put the spell on one of your cannon and we'll see if you can fire it."

He raised an eyebrow at me. "You may try this with *one* of our cannon. No more. I cannot have you disarming my ship. Try the aft chase-gun on the starboard side."

By this time, I was getting pretty adept at anchoring the spell where I wanted it. Once I figured out which of the cannon he was talking about, I put the dampener spell around it. Then Eskivel ordered the cannon crew to load the cannon with gunpowder and wadding. That would be sufficient for the test and we didn't need to load a cannonball.

When the cannon was ready, one of the crew touched off the short fuse. The fuse lit, but burned slowly, giving a lot of smoke but no sparks. I watched impatiently as the burn inched its way toward the gunpowder charge at a glacial pace. Then there was more smoke, but no explosion.

"It worked!" I practically jumped up and down. This was huge. I wondered whether this spell would work on regular guns back on Earth. If all schools were protected with a spell like this, school shootings would be a thing of the past.

"Try it again," Eskivel told the crew. "Try it several times and we will make sure the results do not vary."

The spell was locked in place on the cannon, so I didn't see how it would make any difference, but he was right. We should make sure. The crew tried six more times to get the cannon to fire. It was a long process. They had to clean out the barrel after every attempt, sponging it clear to make sure there weren't any lit embers before they packed in more gunpowder.

Finally, Eskivel was satisfied. Now we just

needed to get to where I could use the spell and hope Baron Rotger didn't do too much damage to the city or its population before we got there.

We spent three more days sailing before we finally had the port city of Ferazi in sight. For four hours before that, we'd seen smoke in the sky. I stood on the deck, feeling helpless and wishing the ship could go faster and was frustrated when we had to slow to navigate the narrow channel between reefs to get to the south side of the island.

We still had miles to go, but we could see a *Félbahlag* ship firing cannon toward the shore. There was nothing I could do from so far away. I needed to be a lot closer to work the spell. Sailing along the shore as we were, we were closer to the city than we were to the ship.

"That's the *MHS Victorious*," Eskivel said, looking through a telescope. "Rotger's ship."

"MHS?" I asked.

"Most Holy Ship," Shahz explained. "Their prevailing thought is that the *Félbahlag* navy is blessed by their god."

"What ship dat?" I heard Corlen ask from nearby.

He pointed to a second ship that was sailing toward the first one, coming from the west.

"Are there going to be two ships firing at the city?" I asked.

The second ship was under full sail and moving

along quickly with the wind coming from behind her. It had closed to three-hundred yards and showed no signs of slowing.

"That's the *Resolute*," Shahz was looking through another telescope. "That's Corana. She must be trying to stop Rotger."

I reached out my hand for the telescope and he handed it to me. I looked through, trying to see if I could find Captain Corana on the deck of the ship. The telescope was very powerful, and I wondered if maybe it was magically enhanced.

"Why isn't she firing?" I asked him. "That ship has cannon, too. Right?"

He shook his head. "Cannon don't do you any good if you don't have a crew trained to use them."

I turned the telescope to the shore. A number of the buildings were burning and many more had been demolished from the bombardment. I could see *Kajoran* people pulling others from the wreckage. One boy, who was maybe twelve years old, was struggling to carry an old woman into the jungle. I saw he was saying something to her and smiling.

I could also see unmoving bodies in the streets.

The only *Kajorans* I really knew were Corlen and Luana, and Captain Corana and her crew. They seemed like good people. No better or worse than any other I suppose. They certainly didn't deserve this. They were just trying to live their lives. What right did anyone have to come in and tell them how to do it?

We were less than a mile from the *Victorious* now, but still too far for me to work any magic on it. Corana's ship was still closing on the other one.

"She can't hope to survive ramming," Eskivel said as he joined us.

"It's a desperate move," Shahz agreed. "Her ship won't survive, but it might get the job done."

I could see people scrambling on the *Victorious* and a few cannon fired in the opposite direction of the shore and toward the *Resolute*. One of the spars was struck, but it was too late. There was no stopping the ship and it rammed into the side of the *Victorious*. I could see how much damage it had done to the *Victorious*, but the bow of the *Resolute* was smashed. The sound of the collision came to us seconds later.

Sailors were rushing across, and the deck of the *Victorious* swarmed with a melee of fighting. Other sailors on the *Resolute* were throwing lines with hooks into the spars and masts of the *Victorious* and hauling them tight.

Corana's ship was taking water through the damaged bow and was sinking fast. Within minutes, the deck of the *Resolute* was below water. The lines to the masts on the *Victorious* were causing it to heel over from the weight of the sinking ship.

Fires were being lit and soon smoke was billowing from several places on the *Victorious*. We were getting closer, but we were still too far away.

"If the fires reach any gunpowder," Eskivel said, "that ship will blow. Can you cast your spell?"

"I can try," I said. "But we're still so far away."

Actually, we had neared to roughly the distance we'd been when I'd burned that ship before, when we were first coming back from Ranolan with Dyani.

"I think I can—"

Before I could finish, the *Victorious* was rocked with an explosion, then another. A few seconds later, a larger explosion from lower decks blew upwards.

"That was the main store of gunpowder," Eskivel said. "Both ships are finished now. Captain!" he called out. "Have your men prepare launches! We'll need to search the water for survivors!"

CHAPTER FOUR

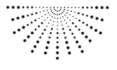

NORA

The ship had a few small boats amidships on the top deck. As soon as we were close enough, they were lowered with several crewmen on each. By then, the *Victorious* sat lower in the water and burned furiously.

This had started as a rescue mission to prevent the slaughter of *Kajoran* citizens and the destruction of their homes. Now it was a different sort of rescue mission. There were a lot of bodies in the water, but many of them were dead. If we'd gotten there sooner, maybe my plan would have worked without so much loss of life. The boats were pulling survivors from the water and shuttling them aboard the *Gechina* as fast as they could.

By the time the sun was nearing the horizon, we had put into the pier and the *Kajoran* survivors of the *Resolute* were taken ashore. The survivors of the *Victorious* had to be kept aboard the *Gechina* to keep them safe from Mohanga's Revenge. No other *Félbahlag* ships remained near Kajo, so we would have a crowded trip to Iyoké.

All of the rescued sailors from the *Victorious* showed signs of the spore. Setting out to sea for it to fade and immediately returning hadn't worked as well as Rotger had thought, and onset was much faster the second time.

Rotger had survived the battle, but he was barely conscious and incoherent. The left side of his face and left shoulder had been badly burned and he'd lost that eye. The burned flesh of his face was mottled with the green of the spore.

There was no sign of Captain Corana.

Eskivel and his crew were already showing signs of the spore returning, so Eskivel decided we wouldn't wait until morning to depart. We used the last rays of the sun to put as much distance between the ship and the islands.

"Do you think Corana made it?" I asked Shahz.

"There's no way to know for sure," he answered. "But I fear it is unlikely."

"The *Kajoran* captain is certainly to be commended for bravery," Eskivel said. "It's too bad things couldn't have been resolved more peacefully."

"You can thank Baron Rotger for that!" Shahz scowled.

"I cannot speak to the Baron's actions," Eskivel frowned. "But I do not agree with them."

"Bout time you baggies got run out." Corlen gave a merciless grin. "Dese islands not for you. You come all dese years. Tell us learn from you. Tell us how talk. How dress. Tell us what believe an' what not believe. Now you learn you not so smart, eh?"

"We were simply trying to enrich the lives of the *Kajoran* people," Eskivel told him. "To bring you civilization."

"Civilization?" I snapped. "You think just because you like to organize your lives a certain way that makes you more civilized? It *doesn't*! You know what makes you civilized? How you treat people. If what I've heard is true, if what Rotger was doing is *any* way to judge, then your people are the barbaric ones! You call that civilized?"

Eskivel's lips narrowed into a hard line.

I'd heard the argument about spreading civilization before. It was just an excuse to steal the resources of another people and enslave or slaughter them. Manifest destiny? More like might makes right, as though whoever was the bigger bully was morally, ethically, and in all ways superior. What a load of bunk.

Eskivel had seemed a lot more reasonable than

Rotger, but he was still part of the same machinery. I noticed Dyani helping to care for the injured *Félbahlag*.

"Why are you helping them after what they did?" I asked her.

"They are people," she said. "Same as any other. They bleed. They suffer. Their pain can be lessened and their lives improved."

"They deserve to be punished." I scowled. "Not have their lives improved."

"Perhaps," she shrugged. "Who am I to judge?"

"All anyone *can* do is judge," I told her. "People use judgment every day. That's how we make decisions."

"That's not the same as judging others."

"It's not so different," I argued. "I'm not talking about slapping labels on people. But we look at what people *do* and we can *see* if it's right or if it's wrong. Are they helping the world or hurting it? Are they making others pay the price for their own selfishness?"

"If helping is good," she pointed out. "Then I should help them."

"They don't deserve it."

"Even if that judgement were true," she answered, "it changes nothing about how I should conduct *my* life."

That made me stop and think.

"I think I've heard this one before," I said with some chagrin. "Two wrongs don't make a right."

"Indeed." She agreed.

Maybe I was insisting on the idea of punishment so strongly because I felt guilty about the hurt I had caused before when I'd burned the *Félbahlag* ship days before. I'd had to do it, but I didn't *like* having to do it.

"Fine," I sighed. "What can I do to help?"

I'd never done this kind of thing before. The work was exhausting. The lucky ones were unconscious. It's not like we had morphine for the pain. The more seriously injured were moved below to the infirmary, but there just wasn't room for all of them. I followed the instructions of Dyani and the doctors – whatever they called them here – to do what I could. Mostly washing and helping to bandage wounds.

Lanterns were hung, and even Bright helped to provide light. The hours wore on and I realized the sky was turning pale. I no longer looked at the injured as undeserving. I knew that these men had been firing on the *Kajoran* citizens and remembered the damage I had seen there. And yes, that had been wrong. But the truth was, no one deserved to go through this. Several of them didn't survive the night.

Finally, Dyani pulled me away and sent me to bed. I was asleep before my head hit the pillow, but

I could hear the moans of the injured *Félbahlag* from my cabin and I was up a few hours later and back at it. There was too much pain and suffering for me to feel comfortable resting. It didn't matter who they were or what they'd done. This was the result of war, and there was nothing good about it. I'd never seen it before. Not for real. TV and movies just don't count. And this was only a small glimpse of what war was like. I hoped that I would never have to see war again for as long as I lived.

I've heard that some people find it rewarding to work with sick or injured people. I did not.

It's not that I didn't want to help, but it was just too much ugliness for me to have any good feelings about it. We lost a few more over the next several days, but most of them stabilized. The wounds would heal, though not all the bodies were whole.

Meanwhile, I needed to start thinking about the next steps of our mission. What exactly was my goal here?

I needed to find Luana and get her the Heart-piece back. I also needed to tell the *Félbahlag* king about Mohanga's Revenge and how it wasn't safe for his people on the *Kajoran* islands anymore. He probably wasn't going to be very happy about that.

What else?

I needed to get back to Danu and find a way to take Emma back to Earth. I still didn't know how to get home, but at least Danu was reachable.

55

I approached Eskivel on deck. Communication between us had been a bit icy after my comments about the *Félbahlag* not being as civilized as they claimed, but he'd still been polite.

"Do any of your people travel to Danu at all?" I asked him.

"Not officially," he answered. "I imagine there might be some traders who go there. Why?"

"Well, I'm really just the messenger here," I told him. "Once I've delivered the message to your king, I have my own business to get back to. For that, I need to go to Danu."

He was silent for a moment as he mulled that over.

"You may see yourself as merely a messenger," he finally said, "but King Elizondo may see things differently."

"I don't know why he would. I don't represent the *Kajorans*. I really don't have anything to do with them."

"And yet you are the one who understands this new plague against the *Félbahlag*?" he asked.

"That's only because I went to A'iwanea—"

"The *Kajoran* mother goddess," he said.

"Yeah, but that wasn't my idea. Luana sent me there."

"Princess Luana entrusted a mission to you to go and speak with her goddess, which apparently you did, and then you return with news of a new plague—"

"It's not a plague," I objected. "And I didn't have a lot of choice."

"You return with news of some curse against the *Félbahlag*, which immediately is proven to be true, and you expect Elizondo to believe you are simply a messenger?"

I pressed my lips together.

"Alright," I said. "When you put it that way, he may think there's more to it."

"Isn't there?"

"Not as far as I'm concerned, there isn't."

Eskivel wore an amused expression but didn't reply.

"Fine," I sighed. "What would you recommend, then? What's the best way to… extricate myself after delivering my message?"

"It is difficult to know for sure," he answered. "But I would recommend being as impartial as you can."

"Impartial?"

"You have been quite free with your opinions," he pointed out. "If you do that with the king, he will very likely take offense."

"My opinions? You mean like about how the *Félbahlag* have been oppressing the *Kajoran* people?"

He raised a silent eyebrow at me.

"Come on," I said. "You *know* what's been happening is wrong."

"Even—" He stopped as he glanced around to see who might be listening before continuing with a lowered voice. "Even if I agreed with you, and I'm not saying I do, I couldn't say so openly without serious repercussions. Surely, you must realize that."

"Why can't you just say what you think?"

"I can do more good if I can continue breathing," he growled at me.

I could feel my face flush. I hadn't even thought about that. I knew that as governor, Rotger was his boss, his superior, but I really hadn't thought about what it would mean in practical terms. It was all very good to assume a position of moral superiority and talk about what *I* would do in someone else's situation while remaining blissfully ignorant of the reality of that situation.

I'd had repercussions in my own life for speaking up, for not going along with the flow, but that had been pretty mild compared with what he could face. It seemed like ages ago when I'd been called to the vice-principal's office. There was no comparison to what Eskivel would face, and I had no right to assume I knew best about what he should do.

It was more than a week later before we finally reached Iyoké. I didn't know what to expect, but the massive walls that ran around the city and along the cliffs overlooking the ocean were truly daunting. The ship entered the port through an enormous gateway into a channel that was also enclosed in the huge walls. At the far end of the channel was a huge wharf structure shaped like a circle with an opening to allow entrance and exit from the circle's interior. At the center of the circular wharf was a solid area with a single bridge on the far side to the wharf on the shore. The walled city lay beyond.

In the distance, I could see a colossal ziggurat with a stepped pyramid on its peak.

"Welcome to Iyoké." Eskivel smiled. "Is it not magnificent?"

"I've never seen anything like it," I admitted.

I could tell they had put a lot of attention on defense when they had designed the city and the port. Iyoké wasn't anywhere as beautiful as the white towers of Tyr nya Luc on Avalon, but it was definitely impressive.

"It seems someone has been watching for us," Eskivel tipped his head toward a small group of people standing on the dock. "We aren't the first ship to arrive from Kajo and Carabora."

"Why do I get the idea this isn't necessarily a good thing?" I asked him.

"Politics," he shrugged. "It is a way of life."

"It doesn't have to be," I scowled. "I don't see why people don't just do what's best or what needs to be done and ignore whatever political games people might be up to."

"In Félbahrin," he arched an eyebrow at me, "these *political games,* as you call them, can be quite deadly. You don't survive by ignoring them. You survive by navigating them."

"If you say so." I resisted the urge to roll my eyes.

Eskivel gathered our party at the head of the gangway as the ship tied up to the dock.

"We must try to move quickly through the port and the city," he told us. "Stay together. If you wander off, I cannot be responsible for your safety."

As soon as the gangway was in position, he led us off. We had no sooner put our feet on the wharf when a man in a coarse brown robe, flanked by two soldiers, stepped forward.

"Baronet Eskivel," the man started. Then his eyes bulged when he saw Spike coming up behind me. He struggled to regain his composure. "The Grand Inquisitor Palben Ayala commands you attend him at once at his residence."

"Thank you, Father," Eskivel gave a polite bow. "Please inform His Holiness that I will present myself to him once I have reported to the king."

"It is the Grand Inquisitor's intent that you see him first," the man replied with a frown.

"And you may extend my apologies that I may not act freely until I have discharged my duty."

Eskivel didn't wait for an answer but moved past the man, leaving him floundering. I glanced back and saw the man talking with a boy, who then took off at a run.

We had traveled maybe three miles through the city, getting stares along the way – more than a few people hurried off when they saw Spike – when eight men carrying an ornate palanquin jogged up and stopped in the street ahead of us. Curtains were pulled aside and a tall narrow man with a pinched expression stepped out. He wore a robe similar in cut to what the priest had worn, but rather than being coarse, this man's robes were a very fine linen. I recalled Luana had told me this was something her people produced from a type of flax that only grew on their islands. She'd said the fibers were longer, thinner, and more elastic than with other linens and were as soft as silk.

The man also wore a heavy silver chain around his neck holding a large pendant that had a circular center with three rays extending outward from points. The center and the three rays appeared to be carved from a blue gemstone that seemed to glow from the slightest light.

"Greetings, Grand Inquisitor Ayala," Eskivel said, taking a knee as the man stalked toward us.

"Did you not receive my orders to come to me at once?" The man's deep voice had the quality of fingernails on a chalkboard. "I would hear of your failure in Carabora, though it should be of no surprise given your obvious inability to follow simple instructions."

"I did get the message, Grand Inquisitor," Eskivel replied evenly, getting to his feet. "And it *is* my intention to come to you at once after fulfilling my duty to report to the king."

"You put earthly duty ahead of Shan?" Ayala snapped. "You dare to put God in second place?"

"Of course not. The Great Father Shan is always above all else," Eskivel raised his palms and looked upward in a sign of devotion as he said this. "Shan has seen fit to see me entrusted with a duty to serve His Majesty, whom Shan has ordained should rule our people. I serve the will of Shan doubly by obeying my king according to those duties. Shan has also entrusted me with the safety of crew and soldiers who are in need of succor, and I must make arrangements for them or I betray my oath to both Shan and king."

"I care nothing for your oaths!"

"Naturally not," Eskivel agreed. "As is proper. My oaths to Shan are between myself and Shan and He will hold me accountable, just as your oaths are between you and Shan and not for me to question."

"Shan endured forty days and forty nights in the pits of hell to pay the price for our eternal redemption," Ayala snapped. "You should be grateful and obey him in all things to show you wish to be worthy of his sacrifice."

"This is always my desire," Eskivel said. "And while I will never be worthy of that sacrifice, I constantly turn my ear, imperfect as it is, to hear the will of Shan."

"I *am* the voice of Shan," Ayala grated. "When I summon you, you will come."

"It is my strongest desire to hear the words of Shan through your lips," Eskivel told him. "But alas, such decisions are not my own to make. I must obey my king, and he has not given me leave to deviate."

"You risk your soul with this mockery."

"I assure you, Grand Inquisitor, there is no mockery. And I would gladly sacrifice my life and my soul if that is the will of Shan. I am merely a humble servant going about his duty. And you will forgive me, but I must be about that duty now with all haste that I might follow your orders without delay." Eskivel executed a bow. "I will report to you as soon as the king gives me leave."

I felt Ayala's eyes digging into our backs as we continued up the street.

"Who was that guy, exactly?" I asked Eskivel.

"That was Father Palben Ayala," Eskivel told me. "He is the senior priest and Grand Inquisitor of the Jhunélin Order within the Most Holy Church of Ah-Shan."

"That's a mouthful."

Eskivel gave me a look from the side of his eyes.

"He is probably the most dangerous man in the city," he said.

"Oh?" I glanced at him. "Are you sure it was a good idea to disobey him like that?"

"It was not. But my first loyalty is to king, not clergy. The king must be the first to get my report."

"I'm more concerned with making sure he understands your people aren't welcome on the Kajoran Islands any more than I am about following you around so you can make your report," I said. "That and finding Luana."

"Staying with me is protecting you and your friends from being arrested or worse." Some frustration had crept into his voice. "You may think you can just walk in here and deliver a message and leave, but things are not so simple. Your naïveté is refreshing in some ways, but it is also dangerous. Our purposes may not be aligned, but I have given my word that you would be under my protection, and I will keep it, whether you appreciate it or not."

His outburst shut me up. He was right. The truth was that I was out of my depth and he was clearly skilled at navigating the dangers of this place. He deserved some credit.

"Thank you," was all I managed to say.

We continued on our way and finally came to

another huge, crenelated wall with a massive gate and gatehouse.

"This is the Iyoké Citadel, proper," Eskivel said as we went through the gate under the watchful eye of the guards. "The enclosure inside these walls contains the Ziggurat palace, which is both the home of the royal family and where all official state business is conducted. It also has various government buildings, lodgings for officials, and grounds for public meetings."

Buildings lined the inside of the citadel walls. The center opened into a large, open area in front of the Ziggurat itself. There was a moat around the building and a wide drawbridge to cross the moat. The Ziggurat had three front stairways, one extending forward from a broad landing at the center of the structure and two more going left and right against the wall from the landing. The landing was large enough to be used as a stage for ceremonies or such. The wide stairs continued up from the landing, and to either side was a door leading into the interior.

Eskivel led us up the main steps. Soldiers and guards along the way saluted him with a closed right fist over their hearts.

The building didn't have much in the way of windows, so torches were affixed in sconces to the walls. The place was designed with good ventilation though, and the flames fluttered from the flow of air. I'd never thought of that, but I supposed it would be needed to keep the air fresh with all of those fires going indoors.

We came to a stop in what appeared to be a waiting area outside a large set of ornate double-doors.

"Is that where we need to go?" I nodded toward the doors.

"Yes," Eskivel answered. "As soon as we are summoned. The king will be aware that we are here." His eyes flickered over my shoulder to the side of the room. "Please wait here, all of you."

Eskivel approached a hooded figure and they started talking. They spoke too quietly for me to hear what they were saying. The figure glanced our way and I got a brief glimpse of a woman's face. I was trying to get a better look and I scarcely noticed when the doors opened briefly and a figure stepped though.

"Baronet Eskivel," a voice sounded.

Eskivel turned and walked to the speaker. The hooded woman had disappeared.

CHAPTER FIVE

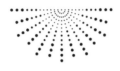

NORA

"General Igonez," Eskivel gave a salute.

"Who were you just speaking with?" Igonez asked him.

"Just a courtesan," Eskivel said dismissively. "Is the king ready to see me?"

"We have need of an official report," Igonez told him. "All we've had for the past two days are hysterical rumors. People talking about the *Kajoran* gods coming to life and cursing us, of all things. I hope you will be able to provide something more substantive than superstitious claptrap."

"I will report the situation to the best of my ability and understanding, General," Eskivel said. "And I have brought a delegation who can explain from the *Kajoran* point of view."

Igonez's eyes went to us, examining us in turn like we were insects in his private collection.

"That creature," he nodded toward Spike, "will not be allowed in the presence of the king. Why did you bring it?"

"It appears to be some sort of pet or mascot," Eskivel said. "It was of little enough importance to warrant an argument."

"Little enough importance?" The general's eyes narrowed at him. "A tékoran?"

"It hasn't been troublesome," Eskivel shrugged dismissively. "Of course, you are right about not taking a risk with the king, but I did want you to see for yourself and get a full picture of what we are dealing with. You should also be aware that the Grand Inquisitor attempted to intervene before I could report here."

General Igonez's eyes moved back to us for a moment before he finally turned to Eskivel with a nod.

"You have your report?" he asked.

Eskivel pulled a packet from under his coat and handed it to the general.

"I have detailed everything here," Eskivel said. "I have been as thorough as I could."

"Give me a summary," Igonez said. "What is the situation?"

"Some sort of affliction has come to the Kajoran Archipelago that does not seem to affect the natives," Eskivel told him. "To our people, it is deadly. However, only if we remain in the vicinity. A couple of days away from the islands and the affliction disappears. Or perhaps it goes dormant, of this I am unsure."

"And if you do not leave within that period?"

"It eats away at flesh and bone until nothing is left but powder."

"This is a disastrous turn of events!" Igonez threw a glare in our direction. "And who are these people? Only one appears to be *Kajoran*."

"The one with the red hair is apparently a messenger. The others of her group—"

"You know," I cut in. "It's rude to talk about people like they aren't there." I'd had about enough of that.

"We're here to talk to your king and to see Princess Luana," I told him. "After that, I'm done with this, and you can do whatever you want."

Igonez's eyes snapped to me as soon as I started talking. He turned back to Eskivel when I'd finished.

"You will need to get this one under control, Eskivel," he said. "Better to send the tékoran to the king than a disrespectful woman with a loose tongue. She will need a proper education if she expects to be seen in court."

I opened my mouth to object when I felt Shahz put his hand on my arm, cautioning me to silence.

"I will see to it at once," Eskivel told him.

"Meanwhile, I will review your written report with King Elizondo."

"Very good," Eskivel answered. "And what of the Grand Inquisitor? I was able to put him off, but he still expects me to attend him, and he will also be looking for information on the *Kajoran* developments."

Igonez mulled that over for a moment before responding.

"Leave it to me," he instructed. "I will send him a message saying you are indisposed and that he is welcome to come see me if he would like an update on the latest incident from the archipelago."

"He won't like that." Eskivel smiled grimly.

General Igonez gave an eloquent shrug.

"I hereby give you explicit orders that you are not to leave the citadel without permission," Igonez told him. "That is all the protection I can give you. Meanwhile, make *that* presentable." He nodded in my direction. "Take them to the Peacock House. They can stay there for now."

"By your command." Eskivel snapped his fist over his heart.

Eskivel turned on his heel and started down the hall, motioning for us to follow.

"Who—"

Eskivel interrupted me with a quick shake of his head. "Not here."

"Baronet Eskivel," a new voice called.

Eskivel looked around for the speaker and came to a surprised halt.

"Prince Inigon," Eskivel gave him a bow. "What can I do for you?"

The prince was looking us over. He was young; he'd probably be a sophomore in high school if they had such things here. When his eyes got to Spike, his expression was curiosity rather than fear.

"You've just come from Carabora?" the prince asked. "And these people came with you?"

"Correct, my prince," Eskivel affirmed.

"Is it true what they are saying? That the Kajoran gods are taking revenge? They've cursed us?"

Eskivel glanced around before answering, "There is truth to the tale, Your Highness."

"Did you see them?" Inigon asked. "These gods?"

"I did not."

Inigon nodded, seeming disappointed.

"Palben Ayala tells me that there are no other gods than Shan," Inigon said. "There is likely some natural explanation for whatever is happening."

"I met them," I said. "A'iwanea and Mohanga. And I met several other *Noélani*."

Inigon looked at me and tilted his head.

"And they are gods?" he asked. "Actual gods?"

"I guess that depends on what you mean by gods," I shrugged. "I've been trying to figure that out myself. I mean, they're pretty much immortal. They are incredibly powerful; they came up with this curse or whatever instantly. Mohanga's Revenge. I suppose they qualify as gods. I don't know what else to call them."

"That won't make Palben Ayala happy," he said with a grin.

I thought about the pinch-faced man we'd met on the street.

"I think he's probably too constipated to ever be happy about anything," I said.

"Ha!" The prince let out a short laugh before self-consciously putting his hand to his mouth. His eyes still twinkled with humor.

Eskivel was giving me a look, so I didn't say anything else.

"Prince Inigon, there you are!" A matronly woman bustled towards us. "You are late for your studies. Come along, Your Highness, your tutor is waiting in the library."

"I can learn more by seeing things for myself." He gave her a sullen look.

"I'm sure that can be very educational as well, Your Highness," she said, indicating with her hands that he precede her down the hall. "But your mother wishes you to also learn in a more formal setting."

Inigon rolled his eyes and headed down the hall, the woman following closely behind.

We followed Eskivel out and down the steps of the Ziggurat. Then he veered right and several minutes later led us into a building against the citadel wall that looked like a small villa.

"This is a guest house," he explained. "You will stay here for now. I will have all of your things brought from the ship."

I glanced around the spacious room. It was fairly Spartan in terms of decorations, but there were plenty of seats for everyone. I found a comfortable-looking one for myself before saying anything.

"Are you going to tell me who that other guy was, now?" I asked him as the others found seats. "I mean, I thought you said the king had to get your report? But you gave it to him instead."

"He is the next best thing, and he will ensure the king gets the report," Eskivel told me. "That was General Eremon Igonez. A very powerful man in Félbahrin. Possibly, as dangerous as the Grand Inquisitor."

"And he's your guy?"

"My guy?"

"He's your boss," I explained. "You… listen to him. You support him."

"He is my superior." His confusion hadn't lessened. "I must listen to him and support him. That is my duty."

"Yeah, yeah," I agreed. "But you seemed like you don't mind working for him. You know?"

Eskivel paused to take a breath before he spoke.

"Political intrigue is rife in Iyoké," he said. "Aside from the king, there are a number of men vying for power. It does not bode well that you have already met two of them: Grand Inquisitor Palben Ayala and General Eremon Igonez. Count Agaeran Zabala is another man of whom you should be wary. Duke Fernen Gabiran represents another faction—"

"I recognize that name," I interrupted. "Isn't he the one that Luana is supposed to marry?"

"He is. That was intended as a political move to bring him closer to the king without granting him too much power or prestige. But these things are not the issue at hand."

"Then what exactly *is* the issue at hand?" I asked him.

"There are certain conventions of behavior in our culture." Eskivel sighed. "I should have prepared you better, and for this I apologize. I assumed a certain common understanding that is clearly foreign to you. You come from a different culture, so I should have anticipated this."

I scowled at him. "Alright, tell me what I don't understand about the great *Félbahlag* and their conventions of behavior."

He shook his head. "You see? I had noted this

and thought it quaint. In this, I have done you a disservice."

"So now I'm quaint?" I raised my brows at him.

"In our culture," he went on, "women do not speak so freely as you seem to be accustomed to doing. Women are not seen as capable on intellectual topics, or of higher reasoning in general."

"It sounds like women are treated as second-class citizens who don't have a right to independent thought or opinions," I frowned.

"That observation would not be entirely inaccurate," he agreed. "It is the men who direct our society. Women function in a strictly supporting role."

"I think it's worse than that," I told him. "I've heard about your female genital mutilations. I think you call it female circumcision? It's gross."

"That is a common religious practice, yes," he said. "Particularly among the wealthy or the aristocracy."

"So much for being civilized," I snapped at him. "I don't see how you can believe that's anything but barbaric. *Any* religion forcing that on people is just wrong."

"I didn't say I agreed with it," he told me. "They say that women are impure until they have been... cleansed in this manner, and that this makes them more acceptable to God."

"Oh, really? It sounds more like the opposite to me."

"How so?" he asked.

"I take it your religion says that your God created all of you?" He nodded at this. "And, of course, your God is all-knowing, all-powerful, and basically perfect, right?"

"Naturally."

"So where do your religious leaders get off saying that your all-powerful, perfect God created women so *poorly* that *men* had to come in with a knife and alter them to make them acceptable? They must think that men are better than their God if they can do something their God *failed* to do." I let that sink in before I went on. "If your God is truly what you believe, then you are defiling his creations with this filthy practice. It's *not* about God or religion; it's about control, pure and simple."

"I don't disagree with you," he said, raising his palms. "But you should know that if you say these things in public, you will be imprisoned and burned as a heretic."

"That's not right!" I snapped at him.

"It is *reality!*" he snapped back. "The Most Holy Church of Ah-Shan is the official religion of the *Félbahlag*, and the Order of Jhunélin sees their primary duty as rooting out the heretics of the world and dealing with them. If you say these things in public, you will die painfully and there will be *nothing* I can do about it!"

"I can't believe that," I shook my head.

"He's telling you the truth," Shahz said. "That's the way it is here."

"But *you're Félbahlag. You're* not like that."

"I am an anachronism among my people." His eyes flicked to Eskivel. "I follow the old ways. The religion of Shan is only a couple centuries old. We had other beliefs before that. It is not safe for such as me in Félbahrin. You should listen to Baronet Eskivel, he is trying to protect you."

We turned at the sound of the front door opening and closing. A hooded figure stepped into the room and lowered her hood. Her black hair fell in tight, natural curls to frame her face. Her lips were colored a vibrant red and she looked at us with bright eyes. It was the same woman I had seen Eskivel talking to in the Ziggurat.

"You should not be here!" Eskivel said to her, his face etched in worry.

"Things are moving too quickly, Luisanto."

"All the more reason for caution," he admonished. "A misstep now—"

"A misstep now would be no less dire than at any other time," she cut him off. "We can only hope that fortune will favor the bold. Now. Introduce me to your guests."

"As you wish," he bowed his head. "This is Nora, an outworlder appointed as the messenger of this delegation. Our *Kajoran* friend is Corlen Veranu. This is Dyani of the Sokwané people of Ranolan. And this is Shahz Dega. My friends, this is Princess Nériala Elizondo, daughter of King Elias Elizondo the Third."

Nériala's eyes had gone to Spike, and she stepped toward him with a smile.

"And what is your name?" she asked him as she reached out to scratch behind his ears.

"That's Spike," I said.

"Perfect," she said with a grin.

"He forgot to mention me," Bright spoke into my mind.

"I noticed," I sent back. *"But maybe we should keep you a secret for now. It doesn't hurt to have a surprise up our sleeve."*

"I'm not in your sleeve," she said with a laugh.

Nériala must have noticed my amusement at Bright's joke because she gave me a curious look.

"I guess I know two princesses now," I said.

Realization quickly crossed her face.

"You must mean the *Kajoran* princess, Luana, yes?" she asked. "You are friends?"

"I don't know if I'd go that far," I frowned. "But I know her. We've talked."

"As have I," she said. "Though it is difficult to speak freely. What do you know of the current state of politics in Iyoké?"

"I was just getting into that, Princess," Eskivel said. "We have not gone into any great detail."

"I take it," she asked me, "you are here to notify

my father that our people have been ejected from the *Kajoran* islands and to declare *Kajoran* independence from Félbahrin?"

"That's probably a good summary," I admitted.

"Are you also going to negotiate agreements for continued trade?"

"Um… no. I wouldn't know anything about that," I shook my head. "I'm not an official representative of the *Kajoran* people."

"Oh? Who *did* send you?"

"No one really," I admitted. "I mean, I figured that you'd need to know the details and I guess I'm the expert on that. Plus, I have something I need to give Luana."

"And how is it that a non-*Kajoran* is an expert on these details?"

"It's kind of a long story," I answered. "It was supposed to be Luana. It was her mission. But she got taken and she sent me instead."

Nériala laughed. "With every answer you raise another question. Where did Luana send you?"

"To Lantesia, to see A'iwanea."

"Really?" She looked surprised for the first time. Then she nodded her head. "I take it the result of this trip is why our people had to flee the islands?"

"Pretty much," I agreed.

I wasn't sure what to make of her. I was getting a picture of what it would be like to be a woman in *Félbahlag* society and it was hard to imagine them producing someone with as quick a mind as Nériala.

"Did this A'iwanea actually exist?" She looked at me expectantly. "Or any of the other beings from the *Kajoran* religion?"

"You mean the *Noélani*? Yeah." I nodded. "They exist."

"That must have been a fascinating experience," she said.

"It's been… interesting," I acknowledged.

"No doubt! But we'll save that conversation for another time," she said with a smile. "More to our present situation; do these *Noélani* represent an on-going threat to us?"

"You mean are they going to take some action or attack you?" I shook my head. "I seriously doubt that. But with Mohanga's Revenge, they don't need to."

"Mohanga's Revenge," she said. "Tell me about it."

"The simplified version is that if any non-*Kajoran* go to the islands, they will die horribly in less than a week."

"And there is no cure?"

"The cure is to leave before it gets too advanced," I said. "There is a temporary… Well, not a cure, but it will keep you safe for several days. After that, you have to get another dose or you'd need to leave."

"What if you leave and come back?" she asked. "What would happen?"

"Baron Rotger tried that," Eskivel told her. "He left and then sailed back to bombard the city when the symptoms had faded, but they returned faster than before."

"Rotger is a fool!" she scowled. "It accomplishes nothing to attack like that." She shook her head. "But this Mohanga's Revenge is definitely going to cause us problems."

"It might cause *you* problems," I snapped. "But it's a big relief for the *Kajoran* people."

"I'm sure it is," she agreed. "And I am not unsympathetic to their issues, but—"

"Their *issues* are that they have been oppressed by *your* people." I wasn't going to let this go. Not after everything I'd seen.

"That may be so," she answered. "But *my* responsibility is to the *Félbahlag*. All other considerations are secondary."

"Well, *that's* pretty short-sighted."

My answer surprised her, and she narrowed her eyes at me. "Do tell."

"You achieve more through cooperation and collaboration than you do from conflict," I told her. Didn't they study history here? "Conflict just uses up resources, and *lives*, that could be put to better use. It's stupid. The only people who gain from conflict are the ones who sell weapons."

"Different peoples have different needs and goals," she said. "This can put them at cross-purposes which makes cooperation impossible."

"No," I shook my head. "It just means you have to put a little more thought into it. There's always a rational solution if both parties are willing to give and take. It's only when you want to take without giving that there's a problem."

"That is a highly simplistic view," she said. "As a general principle, I can see how it might provide better long and short-term results *if* an arrangement can be made. I thought you said you were not here to negotiate ongoing trade?"

"What? No, I'm not," I shook my head vigorously. "I don't know anything about that kind of stuff."

"Evidently," she smirked, "you know more than you think."

"If you want to talk about trade," I said grudgingly, "you'll probably want to talk to Luana. Speaking of, I'll make a bet that the wedding with this Duke whoever is off. There's no reason to force that now."

"Perhaps." Her face took on a more calculating expression. "But I would wager that the stakes have just become higher."

"You think you should still make her marry that Duke?" I couldn't believe what I was hearing.

"There is a clear advantage to moving forward

with that plan," she said. "But I fear things are moving too fast now and we must consider other marriages as well."

Eskivel gasped.

"If you are following my thought," Nériala chided him, "don't speak of it. To anyone." She raised her hood. "I have much to do."

"She isn't what I expected," I said to Eskivel after she left.

"She never is." He gave a wry smile.

"When can I see Luana?" I changed the subject. I didn't *really* want to see her, but I needed to get it over with.

"I don't know," he answered. "We haven't been here long enough to find out about her situation. She would only have arrived a couple of weeks ahead of us."

"The sooner I can talk to her the sooner I can be done here."

"And where do you intend to go?" he asked me.

"I want to go home," I said. "To Earth. But first I have to get Emma and check on Jack. They're with the *Wyl-Dunn*."

We were interrupted by a hurried knock on the door.

"Enter!" Commanded Eskivel.

A soldier entered.

"Baronet!" he said. "There has been a development!"

"Well, go on man! Tell me."

"The *Kajorans*," he answered. "They've sent a fleet of boats… those *wakoa* things they use."

"*Wakoa karua*," I supplied.

"Right." The man glanced at me. "About two dozen of them, and they are demanding the return of their princess."

"Demanding?" Eskivel replied. "That can't be going over well."

"I believe preparations are being made to use our cannon on the boats," the soldier finished.

"We have to stop them!" I jumped to my feet.

"There is nothing we can do," Eskivel told me.

"Yes, there is!" I said. "I can do what I was going to do to stop Rotger. We weren't in time to do anything there, but we can do something now!"

I was sickened by the thought of *Félbahlag* cannon killing more *Kajorans*. If there was something I could do to prevent the senseless slaughter, I would do it.

"It won't take them long to destroy those boats," Eskivel said. "I have been ordered to remain in the Citadel, I—"

"Take me there!" I told him. "Now!"

Eskivel gave some brisk orders. He scribbled off a letter addressed to General Eremon Igonez.

"Hopefully, the General will forgive my disobedience in this situation," he grimaced. "If not – I hope you are successful. The cost could be very steep."

A carriage was brought and we all piled in. The driver had us rushing past the Citadel wall and through the streets toward the harbor. All the while I was listening, afraid I would hear the sound of cannon fire.

As we reached the harbor, it happened. A single cannon fired. Then an entire fusillade.

The harbor came into view through the carriage window. I jumped out even before it fully came to a stop. Smoke was clearing above a bank of cannon and I could see that the harbor gates were closed. Inside the gates was a single *Kajoran wakoa karua*. Its mast was broken, and I could see other damage on the boat. The brightly colored sails were torn and tangled with lines and a fallen spar. The other *wakoa karua* must be outside the harbor gate.

"Reload!" an order sounded.

The soldiers manning the bank of cannon set to work. I couldn't let this happen.

I cleared my mind and concentrated on the line of cannon that faced the inner harbor. I formed the dampening spell, pouring power into it to make it big enough to cover the whole line of cannon. I felt the spell take shape and I anchored it in place. I looked the whole thing over, worried I'd somehow made a mistake. It looked right. Now we'd just have to wait and see.

The soldiers continued to clean and reload the cannon. Then they signaled their readiness.

"Fire!" came the order.

I saw fuses being touched-off and held my breath. After a moment, there was a brief sizzle and some smoke, but no explosions.

It had worked!

Confusion shone on the faces of the soldiers and the officers. More orders were issued, and the cannon were tipped forward to remove the balls, then they were washed out and reloaded. Again the order to fire and the same result. I couldn't help grinning.

Someone was standing on the *wakoa karua*, looking in my direction. It was Captain Corana! She had survived!

One of the officers was furiously shouting orders and soldiers were rushing to obey.

"Who's that?" I asked Eskivel.

"That's the general," he answered. "His position has become precarious. A failure today could precipitate his downfall. He may not be in position much longer to be upset with my disobedience."

The general was turning his attention to the outer wall that faced the sea. From where I stood, I could see the tops of the masts and a bit of the sails from the other *wakoa karua*. That's when I realized there were many more cannon and they were spread across a much larger area than I could hope to cover with my spell.

He's going to destroy the rest of the fleet!

I couldn't let him do it. I started to create another dampening spell, pushing the size to make it as large as I could. It wasn't enough; I didn't have enough power.

"Bright!" I sent to her. *"Help me! Please!"*

Immediately I felt the boost from her flow of power and the spell grew in size. It still wasn't nearly big enough to cover the cannon I knew about. Were there more somewhere else? If I disabled this line of cannon would they just switch to another one? I had to make the spell big enough that no matter where else in the city they had cannon, they wouldn't work.

I pushed more power, drawing more from Bright. Pulling from everywhere around me, desperate to make the spell bigger. Suddenly, a dormant connection flared to life and I felt a huge rush of power.

"Nora?" A familiar voice sounded in my mind. *"Is that you? Who is that with you?"*

"Mira?" I couldn't believe it. *"Oh, my god! I thought you were dead! We connected before and I saw your body... you weren't in it!"*

"It's a long story, but I'm alive," she assured me. *"And I've been looking for you. I just missed you in Tyr nya Lu. Where are you?"*

"You... What?" How could that be? *"I'm... in Iyoké. In Félbahrin."* I sensed someone else there. *"Who's that with you? Never mind, there's no time for that right now. Mira, can you use magic now? I can't explain now, but if you can help me, I need as much power as you can give me! Please!"*

The connection expanded exponentially, and a torrent of power came pouring through. I pushed all of it into the spell, making it bigger and bigger, expanding it further than I would have believed possible. It grew until in encompassed the entire city of Iyoké and for miles around. I anchored it at the Ziggurat. As I felt it fall into place, I let go of all the magic. With that, I felt my connection to Mira start to dissipate.

"Thank you!" I sent along the fading line.

"I'll come to you as soon as I can," I heard faintly. She was saying something else, but I couldn't hear it and I was falling to my knees, too tired to stand.

I knew the spell had worked, and the *Félbahlag* would find out for themselves soon enough. The *Kajoran* boats were safe. At least from the cannon. And Mira was alive! She was alive and she was coming to me!

CHAPTER SIX

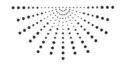

MIRA

*F*lashes. Pieces of concepts. Like overhearing parts of a conversation but not being able to understand what was being said.

As I struggled to push through the mental fog, to rouse myself, I realized I wasn't hearing spoken words, but thoughts.

What had happened? Where was I?

Then I remembered the fight with Dwayne Hawthorne. He'd stabbed me! Why had he done that?

I tried to move and the thoughts around me turned silent.

The *Pilané Jhin*! The pixies!

I knew they were very territorial and unfor-giving with trespassers. How was I alive? I'd been in no condition to defend myself. I still wasn't, that much was clear. Whatever they were going to do with me, there wasn't anything I could do about it. I felt the mental fog coming back, pulling me under.

"Mira!" The voice was strong in my mind, carrying an imperative. *"Do not sleep! You must stay awake!"*

I couldn't form words with my mouth; it required too much energy.

"I'm too tired," I thought back. *"I need to rest."*

"If you sleep you will die!" a new mental voice said. *"You have been badly wounded. We have done what we can, but it is not enough. You must stay awake to complete the healing."*

"Not a healer," I managed to form the thoughts. *"Can't heal."*

"You must become one with the rala *of the* Pilané Jhin." It was the first voice. *"It will transform you, but it will also preserve you."*

Rala. I knew that word. It was like *Ralahin.* It meant magic.

I tried to connect to the *Ralahin,* but I couldn't focus well enough.

"Can't," was all I managed.

"No." It was the second voice again. *"Not the* Ralahin *of the* Ulané Jhinura. *This is a different aspect."*

I floundered for thoughts, but I was too confused.

"The Ralahin *flows through everything, carrying it*

along like a river. The rala *seeps into you and becomes part of you. Like the* Ralahin, *it can illuminate, but the pieces of* rala *become embedded in your very nature. You must allow them in."*

"Don't know how."

"We will assist," the second voice spoke. *"But you must accept. You must open yourself. Do not resist; accept."*

I didn't understand what they were talking about and only barely managed to send back a feeling of agreement to them.

Something started to happen, and I realized there were more than the two of them who had spoken into my mind. I was surrounded by thousands. I could feel them. I could feel something from them. Individually, it would have been negligible, like a drop of water. But from all of them it was like fighting the tide. It was inexorable and I floundered as though drowning. I pushed back, struggling to rise above.

"Do not fight it!" The first voice commanded. *"Accept it! Allow it to join with you!"*

I tried to relax, but it wasn't working. I couldn't do it.

"All our young must undergo this process to fully become Pilané Jhin," the voice spoke in my mind again. *"You can do this."*

Bit by bit, I let go of my natural resistance, my instinct to fight against what in some ways felt like a violation. Then there was a tipping point and my mind expanded.

The thousands of *Pilané Jhin* around me began to coalesce into individuals. And I knew them. I knew them because they accepted me and knew me. Tan. Nhi. Laman. Vinh. Dieu. Binh. Keemo. Lo-an. Minh. Duy. Yen. Truc. Quangtu. Sen. Xuan. Trai. Phouc. Mychau. Lam. So many more names. So many more people. And I knew them all.

Something else was happening. Something was changing within me, within my body. I was becoming... else. Not what I was. The magic was changing me somehow, transforming me, as if at a molecular level. I didn't understand it, but I wasn't afraid of it anymore. Then everything clicked into place, and I could feel the change settling in.

"*Very good,*" the first voice spoke again, and I knew it was Hoa.

"*Now you may rest,*" the second voice was Lo-an. "*It is done.*"

I still didn't know what *it* was, but I felt that it was a good thing. I let sleep take me.

Then I was awake.

Not fully awake, but the sort of awake you are when you've been sleeping really hard and you're still drowsy, but you know there's no way you're going to be able to fall back asleep.

I could feel the weight of a light blanket, or maybe a sheet over me, but it was also over my face and head and the air felt close. I pushed against it to pull it away. It had a strangely fibrous feel to it and it was stiffer than I expected, as though I was encased in something. I pushed harder and my hand broke through. Along with the fresh air came light.

I grasped the edges of the hole I'd made and pulled my hands apart to make it larger. My fingers shredded the material and it wasn't very long before I was free from whatever I'd been in.

I sat up and looked around. I was near the edge of a *Pilané Jhin* garden; home to a pixie community. *Why would I be here?* I thought back to the last thing I could remember.

I'd gone to Earth.

That's right.

To find Jill and Tony.

But I didn't know of any *Pilané Jhin* on Earth. What had happened after that? I felt a bit of *deja vu* as I again remembered the fight with Dwayne Hawthorne and trying to portal away to Daoine.

I absently brushed my hair away from my face, but something wasn't right with my hand. It wasn't shaped right. I held my hands up and was horrified at what I saw. *What happened to my hands?*

The skin of my right hand and arm had turned dark and leathery, the left side was so pale it was white. My fingers were too long and ended in claws. I sprang to my feet in panic, but immediately tripped and fell to the ground. Something was tangling my feet and I kicked to try to free them. It was my boots; they were only partly on and loose. The boots came free and what I saw was worse than my hands. My socks were torn and my feet had narrowed and stretched. Long talons had cut through the socks, the right was a dark blue-black and the left was white. Like my hands. But at least my hands still sort of looked like human hands. There was nothing remotely human about my feet.

What's happening to me?

"Peace," I heard Hoa's voice in my head.

Who is Hoa? How do I know her?

"Be calm," Hoa's thoughts came to me again. "The answers are within you. Give yourself a moment. Allow the knowledge to manifest."

I felt her thoughts influencing me. Not that they were overriding my will or manipulating me, but I could sense the certainty in them, the sincerity, and I could feel that she was somehow a friend.

I forced myself to calm down. I'd been in strange situations before and I'd come through it. I'd dealt with getting stuck in a reptilian *Bahréth* body, and a male one at that, and I was still okay; I was still me.

But I didn't feel like me. There was a strange sense that I didn't fit inside my body. This sensation was different from when I'd swapped bodies with Médard. Even though that hadn't been *my* body I hadn't felt like I didn't fit in it. I tried not to think of what I'd seen on my hands and feet and just tried to control my breathing.

"What's happening to me?" I asked. "How do I know who you are?"

"*Tell her.*" It was Lo-An.

"*The knowledge must come to her on its own,*" Hoa replied. "*This has always been our way.*"

"*She is not bound by our traditions,*" Lo-An told her.

"*She is one of us now and must learn.*"

"*She was not raised in our ways,*" Lo-An pointed out. "*Though she is now one of us, she is also apart from us, as she will always be. And she was not prepared. She needs help. Direction.*"

"*Very well,*" Hoa agreed with a mental sigh.

I was familiar enough with the type of mental communication they used to know that they were intentionally letting me hear their conversation. It didn't help. I had no idea what they were talking about. I could see the two of them, their small bodies hovering in the air above me. Lo-An's wings were a blur, like a dragonfly. Hoa's wings were different and they fluttered like a butterfly.

I felt Hoa shift her attention fully to me. I also felt a moment of discontinuity. I somehow thought of each of them more as *her*, being female, but at the same time I knew that wasn't completely correct. Then I remembered that the *Pilané Jhin* were alternately male and female and changed over a two-year period. But now I was aware of more.

The change they underwent was physical; male and female were aspects of biology and how a species reproduces. These weren't truly aspects of the spirit. Hoa's body might change between its male and female aspects, but the being that was Hoa was bigger than those concepts and encompassed them both. Was it the same for me? I know I had always felt very female. I felt attraction to boys. But was that *me* or just the influence of my physical container?

"The physical container does influence your drives," Hoa told me. *"But you are not wholly bound to that. The spirit is greater than the body."*

"But if the body… influences… why would some people… I mean," this wasn't a subject I spent much time thinking about, "isn't a body one way or the other?"

"Oh, no," Hoa answered. *"Even among humans, this is not the case. I sense the direction of your question and I can only tell you that there can be many reasons for variation, some physical and some not. Things are not always as simple as we would prefer. But I do not think this point of curiosity is your primary concern at the moment. You are distracting yourself from your main concern, yes?"*

"I suppose so," I agreed, trying not to look at my malformed hands. My thoughts became a jumble and I couldn't even form a coherent question.

"Alright," she said. *"First, I will tell you of the Pi-lané Jhin. Similarly to the Ulané Jhinura, we have a unique connection to rala. For the Ulané Jhinura, they call this Ralahin. It represents not only the connection, but the particular aspect of rala that they connect with. Pilané Jhin do not connect with the Ralahin aspect. What little I know of it indicates it has something to do with flows, and these may sometimes be seen as threads. Such things are ever moving in a constant state of flux. You may think of this action as motion."*

"That's not what you do?" I asked.

"The Pilané Jhin connect to the aspect of rala that deals with the is-ness of things. We call this Ralabo. Within Ralabo there is also a condition of flux. Something may be, without at the same time being static."

"Um, I think you lost me on that one."

"For example," she explained, *"my body may at some times be completely male. That would be its is-ness. At other times, it can be completely female. Between these lies a gradient scale. At any time, the body would be what it is, yet it can still change."*

"Okay," I nodded. "Like a snapshot of a certain point in time. But what does that have to do with me?"

"When you came to us, you were badly injured."

"I remember," my hand went protectively to my side where the knife had struck, but there was no indication of a wound. "It seems like you healed me, though. I should thank you."

"You were dying," she told me. *"Your wounds were too severe for us to be able to heal you."*

"But – What are you saying? Are you trying to tell me I'm dead?"

I felt amusement from her.

"No, you are not dead. But for your body to survive, you needed the transformation of the Ralabo.*"*

"And you lost me again."

"When our young are hatched, they appear very different from what you see in us," she said. *"When we reach a certain age, we undergo a change."*

"Like puberty?"

"Similar," she agreed. *"It is a time of change to adulthood. It joins us to the* Ralabo *and changes our bodies.* Ralabo *connects us as a people while enhancing our individuality. It enables the change between our female and male aspects. It gives us our wings. By joining with the* Ralabo, *you were able to transform rather than perish."*

"What do you mean *transform*?" I felt panic starting to creep back up on me. "What did it turn me into?"

"Don't worry," she assured me. *"You are still yourself, but you will experience… differences."*

"Is it going to make me change back and forth between male and female?"

"I do not believe so," she answered. *"That would*

not be according to your species. But I believe you will have more versatility in your form."

"Why can't you just tell me what's happening to me?"

"*Partly,*" Lo-An spoke up, "*it is because we do not know the extent of the changes. We do not know how the* Ralabo *will work with your individual nature as a being, nor how these permutations will manifest in your physical form.*"

"*Another aspect we did not anticipate,*" Hoa said, "*is that you already interact with* Ralahin. *Connecting with both* Ralahin *and* Ralabo *is unprecedented. We cannot fully predict the outcome.*"

I looked down at my hands and feet.

"So it turned me into some kind of monster?"

"*It changed you, yes,*" Hoa answered.

Now I was really afraid. I didn't want to hear anything else or know anything else. I just wanted it to all go away.

"*An important thing to realize is that you can connect or disconnect to the* Ralabo *at will,*" Lo-An said. "*You can control the level of connection. In this way, you should be able to control the physical manifestations that come with that connection.*"

"So, my hands... my feet... They aren't stuck this way?"

"*Once you learn to control your connection,*" Hoa told me, "*you should be able to control that as well.*"

Relief washed over me.

"Your hands and feet are not the only changes to your physical form," Lo-An said. *"Would you like to see the rest?"*

"What else?" I wanted to say no, but I couldn't.

"Look with my eyes," Lo-An told me. *"See for yourself."*

Look with her eyes? I wasn't sure what that meant. It must have something to do with our mental connection. I concentrated my thoughts more on her and I could feel her guiding me through the process. Then I had a moment of double-vision as I was looking through both her eyes and my own. I let my own vision fade so I could see what she saw.

I was looking down at a figure sitting on the ground. It was unlike anything I had seen before, except maybe in nightmares. *Is this me?* The skin all over was dark on the right side and pale white on the left, but didn't have the same leathery look I'd seen on my hands. The hair was jet-black on the right and white on the left, and it was completely straight now instead of wavy and came to a slight widow's peak above slanted brows. The face was titled up, looking toward me. This wasn't my face. Something about it was more angular. The eyes… they were a pale blue with vertical pupils. The partly opened lips were black, and I could see pointed teeth. I don't know if it was the eyes or the split coloring of the face that seemed more alien.

Could this really be me?

I touched my tongue to my teeth and felt the points. I felt the panic rising again.

Calm down! I told myself. *It's not permanent!*

My body shifted slightly and I noticed something else, two wings were partly folded along my back and sides. Wings. But they weren't like the wings that Hoa or Lo-An had. From what I could see, the right wing had jet-black feathers and the left one was brilliant white. I was still terrified, but also excited. I had to take a few breaths and my thoughts were jumbled. Was I some kind of harpy now?

"Why are the wings different from what you have?"

"That is part of the individual," Hoa answered. *"For* Pilané Jhin, *our wings take either of two general forms, depending on the winged creatures we have an affinity towards. But you are not* Pilané Jhin. *Perhaps you simply have a stronger connection to a different type of winged creature."*

That must be it. The raven. The *balangur*. By happenstance, I'd fallen into calling myself Raven when I'd masqueraded as a male merchant. The daggers I'd found among my mother's things had stylized ravens on the hilts; one black and one white. I'd even taken the word *balangur* as my official house name on Daoine.

"They're functional?" I asked. "I'll be able to fly?"

"*Of course,*" Lo-An said.

"And you're sure I'll be able to control this?" I asked. "Turn it off or on or whatever."

Hoa hesitated slightly before answering. "*We believe so.*".

"You're *not* sure?"

"*You are a unique case,*" Lo-An told me. "*But there is every indication that you can learn to control your physical manifestation.*"

"*That is true,*" Hoa put in. "*The length of time you've been in chrysalis would indicate your condition will be very stable. Had it been shorter, we would fear for a more volatile state.*"

"Chrysalis?" I asked.

My vision snapped back to my own and I looked up at them. Then I glanced around and realized that the material I'd shredded earlier, what I'd been wrapped inside of, had been some sort of cocoon.

"Exactly how long have I been here?"

"*You were in chrysalis for twenty-eight days,*" Hoa told me.

CHAPTER SEVEN

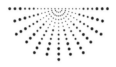

MIRA

"Twenty-eight days?" I was shocked. "I've been here for four weeks?"

What's been happening in that time? Luci must be going crazy wondering where I am. Emma would still be at Su Lariano. I still don't know about Jill and Tony.

"I have to get out of here," I said. "I need to find out what's going on, and I need to let people know I'm alright."

"*You will need to come to terms with your new self, first,*" Hoa told me. "*Adjust to your new form and abilities.*"

"I don't have time for all that," I told her. "There's too much to do."

"*By all means.*" I could hear Lo-An's sarcasm in my mind. "*Walk on those new feet of yours. Or perhaps you think you can use those enormous wings to fly and don't need to learn how first?"*

I scowled as that sunk in. I couldn't show up back on Earth looking like this. But I *did* know how to hide my appearance behind a glamour spell, I'd done that before. I would need to be able to walk, though. Lo-An was right.

Hoa and Lo-An thought that it would be easier to learn to control my changes if I focused on getting to know the new form first. That started with walking.

Walking ended up not being so much of a problem. However, the metamorphosis had worked, my changed limbs felt at least as strong as my original ones. I didn't have to develop new muscles. It was more like suddenly having to learn to walk on stilts, or grabbing things with your toes. It's not like I was new to having feet. After only a couple of hours, I was pretty stable on my new feet. Not quite as good as with the originals, but that would take time.

The hands weren't a problem either. They had narrowed slightly, the fingers were a little longer, and the razor-sharp nails were longer than what I was used to, but I could still grip or grab.

The problem was the wings.

I had no idea how to use wings. I knew there would be basic concepts like lift and drag, and I would need to move them to generate force to propel me through the air, but I had no idea how to do any of that.

I tried flapping my wings experimentally and it didn't result in me learning anything. How did baby birds learn to fly?

"Should I jump from a high place and learn to use the wings on the way down?" I asked them.

"*You are thinking of things too mechanically,*" Lo-An told me. "*The wings are a manifestation of* Ralabo. *Control is magical, not physical.*"

"Why wouldn't they be physically controlled?" I asked. "They're attached to me physically."

"*Are they?*"

"Of course! I can see them."

Lo-An's only response was a sort of mental shrug.

I turned my head, trying to see my wings better. I tried to extend them out to the sides, but all they did was give a slight twitch. *That's not very promising.*

I reached back with one hand and grabbed the top of my right wing, the black one, and held it out as far as I could. The feathers were jet-black and shiny. But when I looked at more of the wing I saw that the bottom edge was different. The feathers were quite large, but where I expected the biggest ones to be, they weren't really feathers. From about the middle of the wing along the bottom and all the way to the wingtip, each individual feather looked more like the membranes of a dragonfly wing and the black color gave way to deep blues and purples. I checked my left wing and it was the same.

"These are… beautiful," I said. "But they're still physical, right?"

"*They are magical,*" Lo-An corrected me. "*You must see with magical eyes.*"

I tried to connect with the *Ralahin*.

"*No,*" Hoa stopped me. "*You must use* Ralabo, *not* Ralahin."

"What's the difference?"

"Ralabo *does not flow,*" she said. "Ralabo *is.*"

That and a fortune cookie will get you a plate of fried rice, I thought to myself. Hoa must have picked up on the thought because I sensed confusion.

"Sorry," I said. I'd have to be more careful with my inner snark around telepaths. "That just sounds cryptic to me, and I have no idea what it means."

I heard a musical tinkling in my mind that I identified as laughter from Lo-An.

"*Use my eyes,*" she said. "*I will show you.*"

I focused my attention the way I had earlier. After a brief moment of double-vision, I settled into Lo-An's view. She shared more than just her view, though. I got a sense of the magic residing in her. It moved with her, but it wasn't a flow like *Ralahin*. Then she embraced Sight.

The world was lit with magic. I could see it everywhere, in everything; almost as if the universe was made of glitter. Or sequins. Rather than a stream or thread, it was particles. Or maybe not particles but points of reference that might or might not contain particles. They established dimension.

I remembered when I'd been looking at the connection between spirit and body when I was trying to figure out how to get my body back from Médard. What I was Seeing with the *Ralabo* was an aspect of that. Sort of. If I wanted to control the wings on this body, maybe I would need to establish anchor lines throughout the wings.

Something about the dimension points also reminded me of the anchors I used when creating portals. Portal magic didn't really use *Ralahin*. I'd been aware it was different, but hadn't really thought about it. When I'd first arrived on Daoine, Neelu had told me that there were many different kinds of magic, or many different ways to use or connect with magic.

"Do you See how I connect with the Ralabo?" Lo-An asked.

I studied her a moment before answering.

"I think so," I told her. "It's just a different way of looking. But it helps to know what you're looking for."

"Yes," she agreed. *"One cannot hear a robin in the forest without knowing what a robin sounds like. But once you know, you will always recognize it."*

I wasn't sure that analogy made sense to me, but it was good enough.

My connection to Lo-An was suddenly gone. How had she done that?

"Now you try," she said.

I recalled the feeling of how she had connected to the *Ralabo* and tried to duplicate it within myself. The connection came easily. Then I shifted my attention to Sight. Slowly, the world around me began to light up with dimension points. Seeing them directly, rather than through Lo-An's eyes, I got a better feel for them and their nature. Dimension points were *created* things. They weren't naturally occurring. Some of the points appeared to be as old as the planet, while others were much newer. I could get a general sense for who or what had created them.

There were more dimension points than there were stars in the universe. People – beings, souls, spirits or whatever you wanted to call them – were constantly creating these dimension points and had been doing this since the beginning of everything. They were everywhere. Some interacted with each other, some overlapped. I tried to deepen my Sight and saw that everything was constructed of these dimension points. They gave dimension to structure but weren't the structure.

Was this some aspect of physics? Were these dimension points somehow like atoms?

"What holds everything together?" I asked. It looked like these dimension points helped define structure, but it's like a connect-the-dots drawing. Until you connected them, you didn't have anything but a bunch of dots. "Something has to tie the dimension points together, right?"

"Intention," Hoa said. *"These dimension points, as you call them, are created with purpose and intention. However, they are most often created unknowingly."*

"Sometimes," Lo-An added, *"purpose and intention can waver. They can change or falter. They can become abandoned. They can also be repurposed."*

"Abandoned points are the most common," Hoa continued. *"They can be... not destroyed, but unmade, by their creator. But this rarely happens. And since most are created unknowingly in the first place, abandonment is the most common state."*

"That's all wonderful theory," I said. "But that doesn't tell me how to use them or help me understand why I turned into this... whatever it is I am now."

"By connecting to the magical properties of these dimension points," Hoa explained. *"You interacted with them in a way that results in an alteration of your physical properties and dimensions."*

"This is something that all Pilané Jhin *experience,"* Lo-An added. *"It is an aspect of the intention and purpose that comes with our connection to* Ralabo. *This*

change operates within a certain scope, but becomes individualized for each person."

"That's why you don't all have identical wings?" I asked.

"Correct," Hoa told me. *"That is one aspect which is strongly influenced by the individual."*

I looked at my wings again. They were actually pretty amazing.

"How do I use them?"

"First," Lo-An said. *"Look at your body. Do you see the* Ralabo *points in your structure?"*

"Uh…" I examined myself. "Yeah. I see what you mean."

"Good. Now the wings. Do you see it there as well?" she asked. *"And do you see how they are attached to your body?"*

"I don't know that I see *how* they are attached," I admitted. "But I see *where* they are attached."

"That is sufficient," she told me. *"What you must understand is that you are not your body. It is simply a vessel."*

That made sense. That whole business with Médard had been about trading *vessels.*

"I get that," I said.

"I can see that you are filling your body," she continued. *"At least, you are filling the portion that was your original body. You need to expand to include the new dimensions of your body."*

"How am I supposed to do *that?"*

"*It is simply your own consideration,*" Hoa said. "*What you call dimension points establish size and shape for the physical. The spirit that you* are *is not composed of the physical. A spirit does not have dimension. A spirit only has a scope of awareness, a scope of responsibility. That is what you must change.*"

"I have to change my scope of responsibility?"

"*Yes,*" Lo-An answered. "*If you want to use your wings, you must take ownership of the points which define their structure, and you must accept responsibility for them.*"

"I don't know how I'm supposed to take responsibility for them," I told her. "I didn't create them."

"*Didn't you?*" I heard her laughter again. "*Let's leave that question alone for now. Start by taking ownership of the points. Accept them as yours.*"

Accept them as mine.

I looked again at my wings, at their structure, at the points that defined the dimension of them. I saw how the points defined the shape of the structure, and how they connected it to the structure of my body and all the points that defined my body. Part of that was realizing that I was not my body; it was separate from me. I knew that already, and my switch with Médard proved it, but this was seeing it from a totally different perspective.

I am not my body.

But this body *is* mine. I own it. I control it. I am the one responsible for it.

But how far does that responsibility extend?

The deeper I looked at that question, the more my mind balked. Thoughts of molecules and atoms and electrons just didn't seem to fit into this new model of responsibility.

"Simplify your approach," Hoa instructed. *"A farmer tends his crop that it may grow, but he doesn't allow himself to be distracted by every leaf in the field, else he would never get his job done."*

"Right."

I took a deep breath. My body. My wings. *My* wings. Defined by all these dimension points I could see outlining every aspect. *My* dimension points. Exactly how they had arrived there didn't matter right now. What mattered was that they were mine.

As I focused my attention on the dimension points and the structure they defined, kind of like connecting the dots, I could feel myself expanding into the structure, accepting the structure as mine. I became more aware of sensations being relayed to me along the nerves. I could feel the rays of the sun warming my wings. I could feel the light breeze ruffling through my wingtips.

I spread my focus to my entire body. I realized that I had never really taken complete ownership of it before. I had simply assumed my ownership without actually asserting it. But this was *my* body, with all its faults and limitations. With all its imperfections.

With this acceptance, I became aware of a duality. Accepting the *Ralabo* of the *Pilané Jhin* had given me a second form for the body, but it didn't change the original form. I could also sense that this duality didn't have to be a binary on or off, but could manifest on a gradient. And every state along that gradient was mine.

I felt larger than I had ever been. I don't mean because my body was bigger with these huge wings. Me. The being that was myself, who owned this body, felt somehow larger. Even larger than the body that was my vessel.

"I can see you are settling in," Lo-An said. *"Very good."*

I stretched my arms and my wings and got to my feet. My new feet. They were very clearly talons. I stretched my toes to get a feel for them. I had a lot more control with these than I ever had with my original feet and toes. I held up my hands and studied them. They might not have the same level of dexterity as my original hands, but they looked stronger. The nails looked more like claws. I suppressed a laugh as I thought about how they'd look with pink nail polish.

"Do you think you could use your new hands and feet to climb that tree?" Lo-An asked.

I looked at the tree she was talking about. It was

immense. I walked over to it and looked up. The tree was thick with branches, but I should be able to thread my way through them. Tucking my wings as closely to my body as I could, I started up.

I had no trouble grasping branches with my clawed hands and talons. I could also grip the bark of the trunk. Something I'd never be able to do with my original hands and feet. In no time at all, I was near the top of the tree, high above the ground and looking down at the *Pilané Jhin* garden.

"*Excellent,*" Lo-An told me.

"*Now it is time for flying,*" Hoa said.

"Ummm, alright. How do I do that?"

"*Jump,*" Hoa instructed.

"No." I looked at the ground far below. "I mean how do I fly after I jump?"

"*That is for you to learn,*" she answered.

"I think I'm a little high to try it," I said.

"*Jump,*" she told me again.

"I'll fall."

"*Jump and open your wings. You will be fine.*"

"*Trust yourself,*" Lo-An added. "*Trust your wings.*"

"Can't you at least tell me *something* about how to fly?" I was *not* excited about the prospect of blindly jumping into the air so far above the ground.

"*Our wings are very different from yours,*" Hoa told me. "*We cannot instruct you in their use. But we have seen how birds with wings similar to yours learn to fly."*

"*You will be fine,*" Lo-An assured me. "*Go with your instincts.*"

I felt my stomach tighten as I looked at the ground again. It was a long way down. Why had I climbed so high?

"*Jump,*" Hoa told me again.

Putri firgolo, I thought to myself. Then I pushed myself away from the tree and into the air.

I was falling. Leaves and small branches slapped at me as I went down.

"*Open your wings!*" Lo-An told me.

My wings!

I snapped them open as fast as I could and felt them catch the air. My angle of descent shifted, and I slowed. I tried flapping a wing and I rolled uncontrollably and plunged toward the ground again. I extended both wings firmly, evenly, but the ground was still approaching quickly. I pulled my head back, arching my back. Almost immediately I leveled off. I was flying!

To be honest, it was more of a controlled fall, and now I was gliding along several feet above the ground and moving quickly across the garden.

How was I supposed to stop? The trees on the far side were coming up quickly. I tried the same arching maneuver I'd done before. I must have arched too much because I faltered and tumbled to the ground at the base of the trees.

"Woo-hoo!" I'd done it!

"*That was very well done for a first flight,*" Lo-An told me.

"*It was indeed,*" Hoa agreed. "*However, I think after this you should practice away from the garden.*"

I looked back and saw that my "landing" had plowed through several feet of the garden, destroying many of the plants.

"Oh! I'm so sorry!"

"*It was to be expected,*" Hoa dismissed my apology. "*You are still a fledgling. Fledglings can be forgiven much. But you are such a* big *fledgling.*"

"*It will take some time and much practice to master flight,*" Lo-An said. "*This is something you can explore on your own.*"

"*Somewhere other than our garden,*" Hoa put in.

"*Now,*" Lo-An went on, "*you must turn your attention to another lesson.*"

"*Yes,*" Hoa agreed. "*Shifting between your forms. Transformation.*"

CHAPTER EIGHT

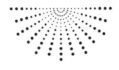

MIRA

Food among the pixies had been a problem at first. The *Pilané Jhin* were omnivorous; aside from harvesting from the vegetation, they also ate insects and rodents that posed a threat to their gardens. I couldn't bring myself to eat the insects, but I did manage to eat some roasted gophers. This wasn't something that I'd want to add to the menu at the Raven's Nest. Fortunately, they also brought me plenty of berries and mushrooms. The petals from a number of flowers were actually quite good, too.

It took me two days to figure out how to disconnect from the *Ralabo* in a way that let me transform back into myself. I needed that ability in order to do everything I had to do, and I couldn't wait any longer. I'd already been gone *way* too long. I told Lo-An and Hoa this.

"You still have much to learn about your new form," Lo-An told me. *"And you have only scratched the surface with* Ralabo."

"I've gotten better at flying, like you said I would. And I'll keep getting better."

"Not if you cannot freely transform to your Ralabo *form,"* Hoa pointed out.

"I know," I said. "And I'll work on that. I do appreciate everything you've done for me, both of you, but I can't stay. I'll have to figure out the rest on my own."

"You are not ready," Hoa said.

"I'm ready enough," I answered. "I'll have to be. But for now I have to go back to Earth."

"This world has a hold on you, too," Lo-An observed. *"A connection that is undeniable. You will return to Daoine, make no mistake. When you do, you should come back to us for more training. You are also one of us, now."*

"Thank you," I told them. "I was wondering though… When I first came here… I'd heard stories about what the *Pilané Jhin* do to trespassers, but you helped me. Even though I damaged your garden."

"You were pursued," Lo-An said. *"You had been attacked and were injured."*

"Your intent was clear," Hoa added. *"Even in your*

condition you attempted courtesy. Had you been disrespectful, the outcome would have been quite different."

I recalled flashes of what had happened to Dwayne and shuddered.

"You saved my life," I told them. "I'll always be grateful for that. And for teaching me."

"You need more lessons," Lo-An told me as she and Hoa flew away from me. *"Come back when you can."*

"Watch your step!" Hoa instructed. *"Your feet are too big!"*

I bit back a laugh at that. My mind was already going over what I would need to do. Where should I go? I formed a portal to the back room at Grace's shop and stepped through.

The only light was what was coming in through the window. The office was empty, so I went up front. The lights were out there as well, and the front door was locked. I checked the clock on the wall. At 10:30 in the morning, the store should be open. Where was Grace?

I went back into the office and retrieved my phone from the charger. I powered it up and called Grace while I put on some fresh clothes from my pack, but it went straight to voicemail.

"Grace, it's Mira. I was looking for you at the store, but it's closed. Call me."

I tried both Jill and Tony's phones and left similar messages. Luci at least had customized her voicemail message.

"Hi, you've reached Luci's phone." It seemed like she was trying hard to sound jaunty. "But you haven't reached *me*. I decided to take a vacation and get far away from the world. You can leave a message, but there's no reception where I'm going. *Bolejha'an!*"

That last word had been in the common tongue. It was a fairly common greeting for hello and goodbye. Was she trying to tell me she wasn't on Earth? If so, where had she gone? Danu? Daoine? How did she get there? Luci didn't know how to make a portal. I didn't know anyone besides myself who knew how to do it, though Tesia could probably manage.

No, there *was* someone else I knew who'd created at least *one* portal. I needed to talk to him anyway.

"Stone," he answered after a single ring. "Mira? Where are you?"

"Where's Jill and Tony?" I demanded. "You were supposed to be protecting them!"

"I did," he said.

"Some protection, the whole house burned down. What happened?"

"There was an attack," he told me. "But we got them evacuated. They're safe."

"What about Grace?" I asked him.

"What about her? Last I heard, she was with you."

"Never mind that," I told him. "Where are Jill and Tony?"

"After the attack, we took them to a safehouse in the country," he said. "But then Luciana Leon came and got them."

"They're with Luci?" I felt some relief at that. "Where did they go?"

"Ms. Leon wouldn't tell me where they were going." He didn't sound happy about that. "But I think they went to one of the other worlds."

"But Luci doesn't know how to create a portal."

"Create a portal?" he asked. "You don't just create a portal. You need to use an existing gateway, or you use an amulet keyed to open to a specific world."

I realized he'd never seen me make a portal, but if what I could do was so rare, I didn't feel like giving away my secret.

"That's what I meant," I covered. "That's what you used that time, right? But that couldn't have been keyed to my house."

"No," he admitted. "That was a special amulet that allowed me to focus on your location, and then to return me afterwards. But that went haywire when Nora broke it."

"Did Luci have one of those?"

"I suppose she might have," he said. "But if she

did, I don't know where it would take her. If you want to find your foster parents, you'll need to talk to her."

"Alright, thanks. I'll talk to you later."

"Wait!" He caught me before I could disconnect the call. "I need to know what's been happening! I haven't heard from you for at least six weeks."

"There's too much to go into right now," I said.

"I'm not a big believer in coincidences," he told me. "You've somehow been going back and forth between Earth and two other worlds, and then suddenly we get this stuff happening in Ireland. Is there a connection?"

"Ireland? What are you talking about?"

"All the sightings over the last few weeks," he said. "We tried to keep them under wraps, but that's almost impossible to do these days with everyone able to post pictures and videos to the internet." He paused. "You don't know what I'm talking about?"

"Not a clue."

"Damn. I was hoping you might have some answers."

"Sorry," I said.

"Did you find your sister?"

"Not yet," I told him. "It's… complicated."

"Keep me in the loop if you can," he said. "We've kind of got our hands full right now but if there's something I can do, let me know."

I thanked him and ended the call. But then I was curious, so I went to the computer on Grace's desk and did a search on "Ireland" and "sighting" for the past month. Several headlines popped up referring to the "Irish lizard hoax" in the area of Newgrange in the Republic of Ireland. I clicked for images and was rewarded with a high-resolution picture of a *Bahréth*.

It was an Anointed, one of the elite warriors. They were used as officers as well as scouts. And spies.

But what's an Anointed doing in Ireland?

"Jealousy!" The thought came from nowhere. *"Zeg wants everything once owned by the* Uthadé."

"Who is that?" I demanded.

Silence.

Was I going crazy? Hearing voices in my head?

But what if it was true? What if that *is* what Zeg is trying to do? The *Uthadé* had been in control of Danu, and Zeg was invading. He'd attacked Tyr nya Lu, which had been an important *Uthadé* city. The *Uthadé*, known on Earth as *Tuatha de Danann*, had also lived in Ireland for a time. Was Zeg planning on trying to take over Ireland? If so, I couldn't imagine him succeeding. Even with magic, there was no way he would be able to stand up to modern weapons and technology. He'd be completely unprepared for that.

Uthadé had also gone to Daoine centuries ago and became *Ashae.* Would Zeg go there, too?

"He must be stopped!"

"Who's there?"

Silence.

"Stop hiding," I growled, raising a ball of flame over my upturned palm. "Tell me who you are."

"Oh, don't be so dramatic." I heard a mental sigh.

"Wait," something was familiar about the voice, even in my head. "Yeravi?"

"Very good," she said. *"I always knew you were very intelligent."*

"But… you died."

"So much for intelligence."

"Just tell me what's going on." I frowned. "How can you be dead and still talk to me?"

"Now you're just being obstinate. Only my body died. You should know the difference by now."

"But… shouldn't you, I don't know… move on after your body dies?"

"Yes, that's always an option," she agreed. *"But I wanted to see what you would do next. In taking over guardianship of Daoine, you would do things differently than I, and—"*

"Guardianship of Daoine? What are you talking about?"

"Oh, that's right," she chuckled. *"I forgot that we had obscured your memory."*

"What?"

"*Relax,*" she told me. "*It's only temporary. It will come to you at the appropriate time.*"

"What did you do to me?" I demanded.

"*Not me,*" she said. "*We. All I can tell you now is that certain parts of your memory are temporarily hidden from you, and that you agreed to it.*"

"How do I not remember any of this?"

I heard her laughter. "*Not knowing is one of the easiest things for someone to do.*"

"And part of this is becoming some kind of guardian for Daoine?"

"*Everything will become clear at the proper point of your development, and I will say no more of it. Except that I decided to hang around and observe you for a while.*"

"Observe me." I thought about that. "And then you decided to talk to me?"

"*Well...*" I felt a mental shrug. "*It's dreadfully boring, not talking to anyone. Since I'm following you—*"

"Haunting me?"

"*Semantics. Either way, you were an obvious choice.*"

"And that's also something I supposedly agreed to?"

"*Well, no. Not precisely.*"

"You know," I said. "Now that I realize what's going on, I can block you out. I can make it so you can't reach me."

"*Yes, of course,*" she agreed. "*But I hope you won't do that. And I* can *be of assistance, you know.*"

"I'm not sure that I trust that you won't try to make me be more like you. To do things the way you would."

"*I can't tell you I won't have my own opinions,*" she admitted. "*But my way was clearly flawed. I failed. I won't argue my reasoning of the past. That is done. You showed me that my premise was short-sighted, and that inclusion provided more survival potential than exclusion. The irony of the fact that a human child was more far-sighted is not lost on me. After thousands of years of planning, it took nothing more than a snip of a girl to overturn it all. Yet, the victory was yours and I will not attempt to take that away or change it.*"

I thought about that. I knew that she was very knowledgeable, and she was offering me that. She had lived for thousands of years as one aspect of the triple goddess, the *Miréygna*.

"Can you help me with the *Ralabo?*" I asked her. "And changing between my physical forms?"

"*I did not use* Ralabo *specifically. But, with some effort, I was able to change forms. I cannot say for sure whether this experience will help. I will advise to the best of my ability.*"

"You've spoken to me a few times," I said. "But not while I was with the *Pilané Jhin.*"

"*I didn't want them to sense me,*" she admitted. "*I*

was afraid of a negative reaction. They have no love for me."

I could understand that. Yeravi and the other *Miréygna*, and their tools, the White Riders, had been behind the oppression of all the other races on Daoine, seeing them as inferior to the *Ashae*.

"Alright," I said finally. "I won't block you out. Not as long as you don't make problems for me."

"Understood," she said. *"And thank you. Now, what are you going to do about Zeg?"*

"That's not my first priority," I told her. "If Zeg is attacking Earth, he's in more trouble than he can imagine."

"You seem very confident about that."

"I am," I said. "Sure, he can cause trouble. But in the end, he'll lose. My priority is my family. My friends. Then I'll worry about the other stuff. I know that's selfish, but right now I don't care."

"I have been listening," she said. *"Do you trust this Luciana? Luci, you called her?"*

"I do," I affirmed. "She's been watching over me for years and I didn't know it. She's my aunt."

"For those of whom you are most concerned, who is in the greatest jeopardy?"

I thought about that. I had to assume that Jill and Tony were secure with Luci.

"Emma is safe in Daoine," I answered. "But I should check in on her. Maybe not right now, but soon. Nora... I don't know where she is, except that she's somewhere on the world of Danu. To track her down, I have to go back there. And I probably need to get help from Zoriaa. That works. Because she has Jack with her and I accepted responsibility for him, and evidently he's important to Nora somehow. I took them to Su Lariano, so they're safe, but I still need Zoriaa's help. Everything else is a big question mark. I will need to talk to Luci, and to Grace, but as far as I know, that can wait for now."

"I agree with your analysis," she said. *"Very logical."*

"If I can bring Emma back," I said. "Get her home. That takes her completely off my plate. I should do that straight away. Low-hanging fruit, as the saying goes."

I was already weaving a portal to my suite in Su Lariano. I grabbed my pack from the corner and stepped through.

My timing was good, because Tesia and Emma were seated at the table. Emma jumped up and ran to me, wrapping her arms tightly.

"Where have you been?" she asked. "I was afraid something bad happened to you!"

"I was attacked," I explained. "I was hurt and had to heal before I could travel."

That was close enough to the truth. It only occurred to me now that it might not be so easy to tell her that it had been her father who attacked me, and that he was dead.

She jumped back from me, a grin on her face. "I've been learning magic!" she said.

"Really?" I glanced between her and Tesia.

"I can light candles!" she exclaimed. "And I can move things! Well, small things, but I can do it! And I can make icicles!"

"That's great!" I told her.

"Did you really cut off all your hair and pretend to be a man?" she asked me.

"Um…" I glanced at Tesia. "Yeah."

"And did you really free all the telepathic horses?"

"That was more of a group effort," I said. "But I'm actually here to take you home to your mother. She's probably been very worried about you. You've been gone for a long time."

"I don't want to go home." She frowned. "I like it here."

"Maybe when all this trouble is over, I can bring you back for a visit."

"But I want to *stay* here!"

"Emma, you're only thirteen. You're a minor. You belong with your mother until you're older."

"I'll be fourteen soon!"

"That's still too young," I shook my head. "Your mother—"

"She doesn't want me!" She glared at me. "No-body does!"

"I'm sure that's not true," I told her. "She's probably worried sick about you and misses you."

"You don't know her!"

"You're right, I don't." I was surprised at her reactions. I knew there might be a problem at home from my previous interaction with her, but I didn't expect this. "But I do know you need to go home."

She rushed to Tesia and fell to her knees in front of her.

"Please let me stay! I promise I'll be good!"

"I'm sorry, Emma," Tesia told her. "But Mira is right. You should be with your parents."

Emma wiped the tears from her cheeks and got to her feet. Her expression had changed from pleading to anger.

"Thank you, Tesia," I said. "I'll be back as soon as I get her home."

"I understand." She smiled. "I'll see you shortly."

The closest place to Emma's house where I could easily anchor a portal was my house, but since that was burned down, I didn't want to go there. Instead, we stepped into the clearing in the woods by the ancient tree. Emma didn't say anything as she started walking through the trees. I closed the portal and hurried to keep up with her, but I didn't say anything about her attitude.

"It's probably best if you tell your mother you don't remember anything about where you were," I said. "If you start telling people about magic and different worlds, they'll probably think you're crazy and lock you up."

"I know," she grated.

I pulled up when we got to the corner of her street.

"Emma—" I started. But she ignored me and walked away.

I felt bad, but I was trying to do the right thing. I knew she was upset now, but I was sure she'd be alright once she settled in at home.

I tried Luci's cell, but it went to voicemail again. I'd have to come back and try again another time. I portaled back to the shop, just in case Grace had come back, but it was as empty as it had been earlier. I put my phone back on the charger and left it there, since I wasn't going to be able to use it in Daoine or Danu, anyway.

CHAPTER NINE

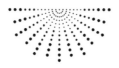

MIRA

*W*hen I arrived back at my suite in Su Lariano, Tesia had already left.

I made my way to the infirmary, since it was the last place I'd seen any of the refugees I'd brought from Danu.

Shigara and Képa were both there and the only remaining patient was Jack. He looked unchanged from the last time I saw him. I'd hoped Shigara would be able to bring him out of whatever was going on with him.

"You've been gone for some time," Shigara told me. "The last of our patients left more than a week ago."

"There you are." Neelu had come up behind me. "I'd heard that someone saw you in the halls. I thought you might be headed here."

"Hey!" I gave her a hug. "Yeah, I wanted to check in on the refugees from Danu, but they aren't here."

"No," she shook her head. "Most of them were moved to an empty barracks. Except the *Bahréth*. They were more comfortable above ground."

"How are they—" My words were cut short as I suddenly felt a connection blaze to life. Magic came alive in my Sight, and I struggled to identify what was happening.

"Mira?" I heard concern in Neelu's voice. "Are you alright?"

"I – Wait," I told her. I sent my awareness along the connection; there was someone on the other end. I was poised to strike along the line if this was some sort of attack, but when I sensed who was there, I was stunned.

"Nora? Is that you?" How could she be doing this? I knew she'd discovered magic, but I didn't know how this was possible. This was the second time she'd connected with me from far away. I also sensed that she wasn't by herself; that her mind was not alone. *"Who is that with you?"*

"Mira? Oh, my god! You're alive? I thought you were dead!"

"I'm alive," I said. *"And I've been looking for you. I just missed you in Tyr nya Lu. Where are you?"*

"You... What?" I could sense her confusion. *"I'm... in Iyoké. In Félbahrin. Who's that with you?"*

Who did she mean? Neelu? Yeravi?

"Mira, I can't explain. There's no time. Can you use magic now? If you can help me, I need as much power as you can give me! Please!"

I didn't waste time asking questions, I just started flowing power along the connection, feeding it to her. She drew it all in, the pull became a torrent. I could tell she was creating a complex spell on her side, but the details eluded me. I flowed more and more power to help feed it, pulling from all around me. I felt another connection to Nora flare to life, but I was too focused to be able to know anything else.

Then it was done, and the draw of power stopped. With that, the connection began to fade.

"Thank you!"

"I'll come to you as soon as I can!" Then the connection was gone, and I wasn't sure whether she'd heard my last message.

As my eyes focused, I realized that I was on my knees and Neelu was crouched down, worry etched into her face. Shigara and Képa had also come closer to see what was happening.

"Are you alright?" Neelu asked me. "For a moment, you looked… different."

Different? I glanced at my hands. Had I shifted forms without realizing?

"I'm fine," I told them. "It was Nora. She… needed magic for something."

"Your sister?" Neelu asked.

"I know where Nora is," I said. "Where is Iyoké?"

"I don't know," she answered.

"That's the capital of *Félbahrin*," Képa said. "Across the sea to the east of Danu."

"That is where Nora is?"

I turned my head to identify the source of the new voice. It was Jack. He was sitting up on the bed. He still had the sheathed sword clutched in his hands, but the glow was gone.

Shigara and Képa immediately rushed to his bed and tried to examine him, but he pushed them back and got to his feet. Jack flexed one hand, looking at it, and then around the room.

"I feel more myself," he said with a satisfied nod. "But I do not recognize this place or remember coming here." He looked at me. "I recognize you. You are Mira. Nora's sister."

"Right," I told him. "You've been... unconscious I guess, for over a month."

"That is extensive," he said. "I imagine that my injuries were such that I needed a more intensive period of healing. With the additional aid from the healing magic of the sheath, I have even healed from the theft of my powers. I can feel that they are returned."

"I went through something similar myself in the last month," I smirked.

He looked at me sharply. "Yes," he said after a moment. "I can see some fundamental changes in you. Interesting. But more importantly – am I to understand that Nora is on this Iyoké you mentioned?"

"Nora connected to me a minute ago," I told him. "She needed power for something."

"I felt that as well," he said. "And gave what aid I could."

I guessed that had been the other connection I'd sensed.

"Well," I went on. "She told me she's in Iyoké."

"If she is there," he said, "then there is where we must go. I assume that is your goal?"

"Yes. I just need to wrap up some things here," I said. "Then we can figure out how to get to Nora. Oh, sorry. Jack, this is Neelu. Or, I *should* say, Neelu Ulané Pulakasado, Princess of Su Lariano."

"I hate it when you do that," she scowled at me.

"This is Shigara," I went on, trying to hide my grin, "Chief healer of Su Lariano. And Képa—"

"Képa, I recall from the *Wyl-Dunn*," Jack said. Then he bowed with a flourish and grace that surprised me. "It is my honor and privilege to meet you all."

"You seem to have recovered from whatever magical condition encapsulated you," Shigara said with an arched brow. "In which case, I shall not keep you from continuing your conversation elsewhere."

Jack gave her a quizzical look. Before he could say anything, I grabbed him by the arm and started pulling him toward the door. Shigara had incredible skills as a healer, but she could also be a bit prickly at times. It was best to take her hint and clear out.

"Shigara, Képa," I said. "Thank you for taking care of Jack and the others. We'll get out of your hair. Have a wonderful day!"

Neelu chuckled as we went through the door.

"So," she said as we walked along. "You've been gone a lot longer than anticipated."

"I was attacked on Earth," I told her. "I barely survived."

"You look recovered," she observed.

"I... ended up falling into a *Pilané Jhin* garden—"

"And you lived?"

"Yes, they protected me. And they healed me."

"I think they did more than that," Jack commented.

"Evidently, the injuries were pretty severe," I explained. "In order to save me, I had to connect with their form of magic. Their type of *Rala*. They call it *Ralabo*."

"Interesting." Neelu looked at me from the side of her eyes. "Are you still able to connect to the *Ralahin*?"

"Yes. They're not mutually exclusive. But I'm still learning about the *Ralabo*."

"Isn't *Ralabo* how the *Pilané Jhin* develop wings?"

I wasn't quite ready to have that conversation, so I changed the subject.

"Where are we going?"

"I assumed you would want to check in on your refugees," she said. "We can go to the barracks and see the *Wyl-Dunn* or we can go outside and talk to the *Bahréth*."

I thought about that for a moment. I had some questions for Radomér.

"Let's check in on the *Bahréth* first," I suggested. "Then we can see the *Wyl-Dunn*."

Neelu took the next left turn followed by a right. We went up four flights of stairs and down another corridor. Then we were in the main cavern and went out through the main gates to the town outside the city.

We located Radomér and the other two *Bahréth* practicing just outside of town. I nodded to Radomér and he joined us under the shade of a tree.

"I wondered if you were coming back," he said.

"I got held up," I told him. "How are you and your unit holding up?"

He shrugged. "It's been difficult. We don't have anything to do. The *Ulané Jhinura* are friendly enough, but we're so much bigger than they are. It tends to make them uncomfortable. I think they'd be relieved if we left."

The other two *Bahréth* wandered over to join us.

"I don't think we've officially met," I said to them. "I'm Mira. Thank you for your help evacuating the injured."

"I'm Sena," one of them said. She was one of the rare female *Bahréth* who became soldiers. The second one I'd met. Becoming a soldier was one of the only ways for a female to attain a position even close to being equal to the males, but it wasn't an easy life.

"Poldi." The other one nodded.

"From what I've gathered," I said, "I take it you all aren't really happy about the war. How common is that?"

They exchanged glances before Radomér answered.

"It's hard to say," he admitted. "It isn't safe to speak against Kartahn Zeg or his war. Say something to the wrong person and the next thing you know, the Gastbaween are hauling you away."

The pieces I had left of Médard's memories told me that the Gastbaween were a sort of secret police for their religion, the *Jhye Hazhdi*. Once upon a time, they had simply been ethical advisors, but their role had changed considerably since the Book of Olsahg, and even more so since Kartahn Zeg came into power as The Prophet.

"Well, I was just on Earth," I told him. "One of the Anointed was sighted there. At least one. Do you know anything about Kartahn Zeg's plans?"

"Earth?" he asked me. "I don't recognize the name."

"Alright," I said. I felt disappointed though. I'd really hoped I could get some answers from him.

"This is another world?" he asked.

"Yes. The one I'm from."

"I've heard nothing of it," he said.

"That's fine," I told him. "It's just one more problem for me to solve. It can't be a coincidence that Zeg has launched his war and Anointed are wandering around in Ireland."

"That name sounds familiar," Sena spoke up. "The Land of Eire. It was once a stronghold for the *Uthadé*, right?"

Radomér nodded. "Zeg wants to show that the *Bahréth* are greater than the *Uthadé* by taking possession of anything they ever owned."

"Told you!" Yeravi's thought came to me.

"*Uthadé* came here to Daoine and became *Ashae*," Neelu said. "Is he planning to come here as well?"

The three exchanged glances again before Radomér nodded.

"From all the propaganda," he said, "Zeg intends to conquer the *Ashae* of Daoine, as well as all of Danu, Félbahrin, and the Land of Eire."

"Zeg is going to fail," Jack spoke up for the first time. "I'll make sure of that."

"Get in line, buddy," I said to him. "If Zeg's going to bring his war to Daoine AND to Earth, I'm definitely going to stand against him."

"After we get Nora." Jack looked at me.

"After we get Nora," I affirmed. I looked back at Radomér and the other two shakahr. "We could use your help here."

"We may not agree with Zeg's war," Radomér shook his head, "but we won't fight our own people."

"That's not what I meant. There are plenty of *Bahréth* that think like you do," I told him. "They lay low because it's not safe to speak up."

"You want us to commit sedition?" he asked. "To get other *Bahréth* to rebel against Zeg's authority?"

"What you have to decide," I told them, "is what you owe your loyalty to. Do you owe it to your people or do you owe it to Zeg?"

"He is The Prophet," Radomér said. "He represents our religion."

"Let's talk about that," I said. "Your *Tolkéda* tells how you are to live your lives in the world. And it worked. For thousands of years. Then, all of a sudden, Olsahg pops up and starts telling a very different story. That's the story Zeg is using to push this war."

"That's going a bit far," Radomér said. "The truth of Olsahg's words is evident by the presence of the Transcendent. They are immortal beings sent by the *Jhyeh* to guide us."

"They aren't immortal," I told him. "I killed one. Jack killed one, too, back at Tyr nya Lu. Right Jack?"

"I did." Jack gave a cold smile. "Chenosh. He called himself the Envoy."

"They aren't special or sent by your *Jhyeh*," I told them. "They just have a very powerful glamour spell to make you think they're these wonderful beings. It's a trick. And Zeg knows it."

Radomér let out a long breath, shaking his head.

"Why do things have to be so complicated?" he asked. "Let us talk about it. This is too big for me to decide for all of us."

"Of course," I said. "I was wondering… you're a better leader than one would expect from a shakahr. Why didn't you apply to become an Anointed?"

Sena smirked at my question and looked away.

Radomér frowned before answering her. "Let's just say that there are certain ideological vows one must take to become Anointed. It was known that I was not… pure enough to meet the requirements."

Sena barely held her laugh at his explanation

and his scowl only deepened. There was obviously a story there, but I wasn't going to push it.

"Alright," I told them. "Let me know what you want to do. And if you just want to go back to Danu and rejoin the army, I'll take you. But if you do decide to work against Zeg from within, here *or* there, you won't be alone. I can't tell you more than that until I know you're in."

Radomér looked at me speculatively. "Fair enough." He agreed.

We left the three shakahr and Neelu led Jack and I back through the gates into the main city.

"You killed a *Qélosan*?" Jack asked me as we walked. I nodded. "That is no small feat. Your species has no natural resistance to their glamour."

"It wasn't easy," I recalled. "I guess I just tried to hold onto the thought that it wasn't real. That it was a trick. I think it would have been easier if I'd had my daggers with me."

He raised his eyebrows in a question.

"They can cut through spells," I explained. "Of course, the release of energy when you do that can be unpredictable. If I'd tried to use them on that time spell..." I shook my head. "Anyway, they can be handy if someone is using a spell directly on me."

"Time spell?" he asked.

"There was a spell on this world that sped up time here," I told him.

"Interesting," he mused. "For what purpose?"

"The idea was to make it hard for people to come here from other worlds," I explained. "But it cut off travel in both directions."

"Yet, you somehow were able to come here despite the spell."

"That was an accident. Someone had created a portal using a pendant with a portal enchantment. Nora accidently shattered it with one of my knives as we all fell through the portal. I ended up here on Daoine and she landed on Danu."

"She had no such knife when I encountered her."

"I think she must have dropped it," I said. "And they're kind of linked to me, so I ended up with both of them. I met Neelu not long after that and she helped me to learn about this place."

"I sense you have many strong ties here," he observed.

I thought about that.

"I do," I agreed. "There are a lot of really amazing people here that I love. And I grew so much in my time here. It's a wonderful place. But… there are also some sad memories, too. So it's complicated."

"*I certainly underestimated the people of the other races,*" Yeravi spoke in my mind. "*As well as your ability to create allies.*"

"*Not now!*" I sent to her. Anger flashed through

me as I thought of the people who had died because of her. People I had loved. I struggled to keep my thoughts on the here and now; it would be too easy to plunge into the darkness of that pain and loss.

"I think much is complicated with you," Jack said. "From my experience with Nora, I think it is important that I tell you that I am highly receptive to thoughts."

I looked at him sharply.

"Nora admonished me about intentionally listening to another's thoughts without their permission," he went on. "And I adhere to her instruction on the matter. But those thoughts that are… of great volume… are impossible for me to ignore."

"Good to know," I said flatly. He was telling me he'd heard my brief interaction with Yeravi.

"Speaking of telepaths," Neelu said. "I'm curious about your time with the *Pilané Jhin*. I don't know that anyone has ever connected with both *Ralahin* and *Ralabo* before. And knowledge of *Ralabo* outside the *Pilané Jhin* community is practically non-existent. Just as *Ulané Jhinura* knowledge of *Ralahin* is not shared with others."

"I spent most of that time… unconscious," I told her.

"Yes," Jack said. "You indicated it was similar to my own condition. And I sense that we have another similarity. *Daijheen* have two physical forms and we can shift between them. This is one of the powers I had lost but has now been restored to me."

"Are you saying that Mira can change her form?" Neelu asked.

I came to a halt, trying to gather my thoughts. I wasn't ready to talk about this yet; I hadn't figured it out. But here it was.

"Okay. Yes," I admitted. "I was in some kind of cocoon and when I woke up… I was different. I spent the last few days trying to figure out how to get my regular body back."

"I think I saw it," Neelu said. "Your other form, I mean. Just for a moment earlier when you… with whatever you were doing with your sister."

I looked myself over with a feeling of panic. Was I wholly myself? Everything seemed normal and I let out a sigh of relief.

"What's wrong?" Neelu asked me.

"Nothing's wrong!" I snapped at her. "I just want to have my own body! I spent *weeks* stuck in that *Bahréth* body and just when I finally got my body back, it changed and I couldn't do anything about it."

I felt like the world was spinning around me and I had no control.

"Mira, look at me," Jack was standing in front of me, his hands on my shoulders. Something about his eyes drew me in and gave me focus. "Take a breath," he said. "What you are experiencing is not unknown among the *Daijheen*. I can help you with this; to be in complete control of your body. But know this; you have not lost yourself. You feel that you do not know yourself, yes? That you have lost your place in the universe?"

I thought about that. It did seem to fit what I was feeling, and I nodded.

"You are you," he told me. "All that has ever been true about you is still true. What is your name? Say it."

"Mira," I said. "Mirabela Cervantes Ramirez." Then my mind swirled. "But it's also Mira nya Balangur. And I've gone by Carmen Cansino! And Raven! Even my name is all over the place!"

"Did any of that change your nature?" he asked. "Did any of that change who you truly are?"

"No," I shook my head. "I was still me. Those names... I guess they had more to do with other people than with me. Like when Tony calls me *mija*. It's not about me so much as my relationship with him."

"Exactly," Jack agreed. "Names and forms both deal with your interaction with the universe. They do not change *you*. Start as yourself, beyond the conception of name and form. That is your foundation. That aspect of you that is aware of being aware. That center from which you view the universe around you. That is your starting point."

Jack took three steps backward.

"Look at me," he said. "Good," he said when I had done that. "Now look at Neelu. Good, now your left hand."

I followed each of his instructions.

"Now look at the wall to your right."

I turned my head to look at the wall. Then I looked back at him and then at Neelu.

"Alright," I said. I was feeling better. "I think I get it."

"Tell me," he prompted.

"I'm here," I explained. "I'm right here, right now. I'm in this body. But at the same time, when I look around me, I'm… bigger. It's like my attention starts with me and I sort of flow with it wherever I focus it. But, it's also kind of like the dimension points of the *Ralabo*… And it doesn't matter what's in between. Ideas, bodies, space… they exist, I'm aware of them. I can see them, use them, or whatever. But they aren't me. I'm me."

"Very good," he said with a smile.

"I still need to learn to control my change though," I said. "I barely learned how to get back to my regular form when I left the *Pilané Jhin*."

"If you like," Jack said, "I can help you with that. It may differ from how the *Daijheen* change, but there will likely be similarities as well."

"Thanks, that would be good." I turned to Neelu. "Sorry I yelled at you."

"It's alright," she gave me a hug. "I'm glad you're feeling better now."

I took a deep breath and let it out. I *was* feeling better.

"So," I said. "We were going to the barracks where the refugees are staying?"

"Yes," Neelu answered. "This way."

CHAPTER TEN

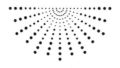

NORA

Shahz helped me get to my feet. I was tired but satisfied. I had silenced the cannon and saved lives. They could still fight and kill each other, but they were going to have to do it the hard way.

"We should return to your quarters," Eskivel said. "I don't know what you have done, but the fewer who suspect your involvement, the better."

We loaded into the carriage and before long we were back at the Peacock House within the Citadel walls. As the carriage first started down the street, I thought I had seen Inigon watching us from the side of the street as we went past. I was barely aware of anything else until we pulled up at the little guest villa. Our baggage had been brought while we were out. Not that I had much of anything besides what I was wearing and a few hand-me-downs from Shahz. The little I did have was in my shoulder bag with the book.

"Stay inside," Eskivel told us. "I'll return when I can."

We were left with not much to do and Eskivel hadn't returned by the time we went to sleep. He was there in the morning, looking a bit disheveled. I could smell fresh coffee and helped myself to a mug.

"Have you been up all night?" I asked Eskivel.

"The Citadel is in a bit of a turmoil," he said. "There is a push from some factions to remove General Igonez and I've been doing what I could to help maintain stability."

The front door opened, and I looked up to see Princess Nériala come in with Luana right behind her.

"Good," she said without preamble. "You are all here."

She started to say something else, but I was looking at Luana and the anger that I'd been avoiding, that I'd been pushing to the side all this time came boiling up. I took three strides forward and slapped her across the face as hard as I could.

The room went silent and everyone froze. Luana staggered back, looking at me in surprise. Her eyes had watered and there was a red handprint on her face.

"YOU HAD NO RIGHT!" I screamed at her.

I hadn't realized how angry I was with her. I hadn't let myself think of it, and the whole thing had been overshadowed with the idea that Mira was dead. Now, I felt dirty and violated all over again. I raised my hand and started to step forward to hit her again, and Corlen grabbed my arms from behind to stop me.

"Yo-ah! What goes here?"

"Let me go!" I tried to pull away from him.

He stepped in front of me and held me back, confusion showing on his face.

"What goes here?" he asked again.

"I told you what she did already," I snapped at him. "You didn't care then, why should you care now? Except to protect your precious princess?"

"Nora," Shahz spoke softly. "Even if you told us, we don't understand. We are sorry for that. Can you explain? Can you help us understand?"

"She tried to *take* me," I spat. "She *forced* herself into my body, into my mind. She tried to make me into *nothing* and just take everything! She violated me in ways I didn't know I *could* be violated. And then she put this *thing* in me!"

I stepped backwards, pulling myself out of Corlen's grasp and put my hand over my chest. I focused and there was a flare of power, then I was holding the last of the Heartpiece in my hand. I shouldered past Corlen and shoved it at Luana. She grabbed it reflexively.

Luana gaped at me.

"I'm sorry… I… I didn't think. I…"

"You're damn right you didn't!" I snapped at her. "You didn't think! You didn't ask! You just took!

"I just wanted to save my peo—" she started, but I didn't let her finish.

"You had no right!"

Her eyes fell. "I'm sorry."

"Look at me!" I commanded her. Slowly, she forced her eyes to meet mine. "Don't *ever* speak to me again."

I could see her pain as her expression crumbled, but I didn't care.

I turned my face to Nériala, deliberately putting my back to Luana.

Nériala's eyes flashed between us before she nodded.

"Are you responsible for what happened yesterday with the cannon?" she asked me.

"You mean did I stop your soldiers from slaughtering innocent *Kajoran*?" I raised my eyebrow at her.

"I'm not saying I support what they were doing," she said. "Did you stop it?"

"I did."

"If I may ask…" My attitude was giving her pause. "What exactly did you do?"

"I created a spell that prevents gunpowder from exploding within five miles of the Ziggurat," I said.

She let out a long breath.

"How long will the spell last?"

"Oh, it's anchored in place," I told her. "It's pretty much permanent."

I could see her mind racing as she nodded in response.

"It has escalated things," she said. "The situation on the Kajoran Archipelago and your arrival here had already set things in motion that could not be undone. But some members of the senate are presenting this as General Igonez's failure, and they are demanding his removal. The Citadel is on the brink of anarchy."

"Why?" I asked. "He's just one man. He's not even the king. He can be replaced, right?"

"The balance of power can be a delicate thing," she answered. "It's not as stable as you might think. Without Igonez in place to keep things balanced, control of our government will change."

"I thought you had a monarchy? So, the king is in charge. Isn't that inherited?"

"Technically, we are a republic functioning under a monarchy," she explained. "That is how it has been since my great-grandfather seized control and created the throne. When my grandfather assassinated him, he barely retained the crown. When my father assassinated *him*, the transition was very smooth; Eremon the Victorious arrested the leaders of all opposing factions and had them killed before they realized my father was making his move."

"That sounds pretty cut-throat," I frowned.

"Each generation has tried to hold onto power as long as they could," she shrugged. "And the succeeding generations wanted power before they were truly ready. They were not willing to wait. Now, we are again in a time of transition."

"I'm not sure I care about Félbahrin problems," I said. "I took care of everything I needed to."

"What happens in Félbahrin will have impacts on the rest of the world," Eskivel said. "King Elizondo cannot stay in power without Eremon Igonez. If the wrong people take his place, it could spell disaster for many other countries."

I thought about that. I shouldn't let my feelings for Luana taint my feelings for everyone else in this world.

"With the general in disgrace," Nériala confirmed, "my father's fall will come quickly. I had hoped that my cousin would be able to assume the throne, but we were not prepared to move so soon."

"So, Elizondo is going out and people are scrambling to see which one will be the new king of the hill," I said. "Who are the contenders?"

"Aside from my cousin, there is Palben Ayala.

He represents the religious faction," Nériala said. "If he comes into power, he will do everything he can to crush the rest of the world under the boot of his order. Even with your new plague, the *Kajoran* people would not be safe. Agaeran Zabala is a brute, he would destroy the senate and my people would be subjected to a harsh dictator. He would also seek revenge against the *Kajorans* for our losses."

"You support him, right?" I asked Eskivel. "You seemed pretty buddy-buddy with him yesterday."

"He is my superior," Eskivel said archly. "I must obey him, but that does not mean I would support him."

"Fine," I turned back to Nériala. "Anyone else?"

"Fernan Gabiran. He cares only for money. As long as we can offer more than the others, he will give his support. A marriage to Luana was a very enticing reward for his support. Hopefully, it will still suffice with the recent changes."

"After your cousin, I mean… if he can't do it, who's next in line? You? You seem to have a pretty good grasp of the situation."

"A woman?" Nériala scoffed. "Félbahrin ruled by a queen? Impossible. Therefore, my father has named my cousin as heir apparent."

"Such a foolish people," Luana spoke up for the first time. "Women can rule just as well as men. Perhaps better."

"I don't disagree with you," Nériala told her. "But this has not been our way. The balance has been tipped and things are in motion. I had hoped we would have time for Inigon to come of age. We are out of position. Whoever comes into power will probably have him killed to strengthen *their* position. But there is another option, and probably the only way for a woman to have any power in Félbahrin."

"A regency," Luana prompted.

"Yes," she answered. "If I were to wed my cousin, I could be named regent until he comes into his majority."

I thought of the boy I had met in the hallway and imagined him being married to Nériala. It didn't seem to be a very good match, but who was I to comment on that kind of thing?

"You are too close," Luana was shaking her head. "The admonishments against incest would bar your way."

"It is the safest path," Nériala insisted. "We could convince the senate as long as we have the support of Gabiran and a treaty with the *Kajorans*. With your marriage to Gabiran and my marriage to Inigon, we present the most stability going forward."

"I'm sorry, Princess, but they will not accept the marriage," Eskivel said.

"Without a regency, our cause is lost!"

Luana was shaking her head again. "Much of what you have described is well thought out. But we will need some changes. You are the daughter of the king. If there is to be a regency, you are a good contender for this. Particularly with Gabiran's support, which he should be more than happy to provide for his wife."

"You think *I* should marry Gabiran?" Nériala's eyes were wide. "What of Inigon?"

"Do you not agree you would be sufficient bait to lure the duke? Especially if there was a treaty to his benefit with the *Kajorans*?"

Nériala blinked as that sunk in.

"So, all you need to do is to secure that treaty," Luana went on.

Nériala's eyes narrowed. "What do you want in exchange?"

"You realize that if this works, you are not simply getting a treaty," Luana told her. "You are getting stability for your people, and both you and your cousin would escape the inevitable executions should one of the other factions come into power."

"Yes." Nériala's tone was clipped.

"With my mother's abdication, I am not princess, but queen," Luana spoke deliberately. She pulled out a folded parchment from a hidden pocket. "I have her signed and sealed statement of abdication in my favor."

Realization showed on Nériala's face. "You want to marry Inigon?"

I bit back a laugh. I didn't think Luana would be any better for Inigon than Nériala.

"I do not," she answered. "But I would make this sacrifice for my people. The safest path forward for *my* people is also the best path forward for yours. By aligning with each other, we can both achieve our goals."

"But as I have already said," Nériala pointed out, "the *Félbahlag* would not accept a queen as a ruler."

"Agreed. But they might accept a queen and the daughter of the former king as co-regents."

I wasn't surprised at Luana's idea. She'd already shown how far she was willing to go in the name of helping the *Kajorans*. This move would put her in position to do a lot for her people. It was brilliant strategy, in a cold and calculating sort of way.

"I see what you're trying to do," Nériala said. "But I don't think you understand the *Félbahlag* attitude toward women. They would never accept an all-woman regency."

"A triumvirate then," Luana said. "With a male counterpart."

"That might work." I could see Nériala's mind was working. "The problem is finding someone who would join us and not immediately try to get rid of us or overrule us once he is in power, which rules out anyone we've already talked about. And it has to be someone that the Senate would accept. Or be convinced to accept."

"Someone in the military?" Luana asked. "Someone of noble blood?"

"Three Elizondo generations purging the nobility of any potential rivals narrows those options considerably." Nériala scowled. Then her head swiveled to look at Shahz. "Did you say your family name was Dega?"

"It's not an uncommon name," he shrugged, not looking at her.

"Isn't it?" she asked. "You know my next question. Are you of that bloodline?"

"I'm just a sailor," he said. "Nobody special."

"What's this about?" Luana asked.

"Before King Elizondo the First," Eskivel supplied, "Félbahrin was ruled by the Dega family. Six generations of Degas."

"You're some kind of lost prince?" I asked Shahz.

He looked at me sheepishly. "Something like that."

"That could work!" Nériala gave a single nod. "But we will need backing. Allies."

"Hang on," Shahz objected. But they weren't listening to him.

"I already have allies among the Senate," Nériala was saying. "But so do the others."

"Zabala won't be able to take power," Eskivel said. "Much as he wants it, there is too much opposition."

"Gabiran is in our pocket," Nériala told him. "Or he will be when he hears the deal."

"That leaves Ayala," Eskivel finished. "He has friends in the Senate. Enough friends that *we* may be able to draw support, if only to oppose him."

"Do you think you could bring Zabala to our side?" Nériala asked him. "Maybe if he had the impression he would hold some sway over the regency?"

"Possibly," Eskivel mused. "We might be able to sell it. Maybe if he thinks he'll have a Dega in his power. We would have to manage that carefully. How much time do we have?"

"None," Nériala answered. "We have a day, two at the most, before everything blows up."

"I haven't agreed to anything!" Shahz cut in.

Nériala looked at Dyani, who sat next to Shahz. "If our faction does not come out ahead, it will result in an expansion of *Félbahrin* imperialism. There has already been talk of putting a colony in Ranolan in the next two years."

"And if this plan of yours works, you can stop that?" Dyani asked.

"If this works, we will be in a position to put an end to all imperialistic plans," Nériala affirmed.

"Why tell me?" Dyani shrugged. "I have no *chinéha* in this race."

Nériala raised her eyebrows with an expression that asked, "Oh, really?"

Then Dyani glanced sideways at Shahz and back to Nériala.

"Alright." Dyani gave a nod.

Shahz narrowed his eyes as he looked between the two women. He opened his mouth to speak but then thought better of it.

"Meanwhile," Nériala looked at Eskivel, "we have much to do. You work the Zabala angle to get him on our side. I'll work on Gabiran as well as firming up opposition to Zabala trying to take it for himself. Everywhere he looks, I'll make sure he sees opposition. Everyone else has split their resources between getting rid of Igonez and advancing their own interests. We can focus everything on this. But don't underestimate Ayala."

"One thing," Luana said to Nériala. "This purification rite… it's not going to happen. I'm not doing it."

Nériala looked surprised.

"Why?" she asked. "I mean… it's not so bad. And there's no pain, they make sure of that."

"It's ritual mutilation," Luana said. "And it's a desecration of my body."

"Yes." Nériala glanced at me. "I heard some arguments about that recently. Something about if

162

the creator wanted you to be circumcised, he would have created you that way, and that the ritual could be seen as a criticism of His work. Alright." She gave a nod. "We'll find a way to work around it."

"There's a point in the Ah-Shan ceremony," Shahz said, "where you have to swear to your purity and it must be confirmed.

"Confirmed?" I asked.

"There's no way around that," he said. "Not if it is an Ah-Shan ceremony."

"You're thinking we should use a *Fél Naran* ceremony?" Nériala was shaking her head.

"There are no laws prohibiting it," Shahz answered.

"Perhaps not," Nériala said, "But that won't prevent charges of heresy from the Grand Inquisitor and the Order of Jhunélin."

"The Church of Ah-Shan gets much of its authority from the crown," Shahz pointed out. "It would be problematic to charge the crown with heresy. The pontiff would not allow it."

"What is *Fél Naran*?" Luana asked.

"It is the traditional religion of the *Félbahlag*," Shahz told her. "Or it was, before the Church of Ah-Shan. There are still those who practice it in secret."

"But can this ceremony be used?"

"As I say, there are no laws preventing it," Shahz repeated. "In fact, there are even some laws still in the books that don't acknowledge non-*Fél Naran* unions."

"It is a dangerous move," Eskivel spoke up. "You would make an enemy of the Church of Ah-Shan."

"Once we are in power," Nériala said, "we can start pulling their teeth."

"Saying is easier than doing," Eskivel raised an eyebrow.

"What about a *Kajoran* ceremony?" Luana asked. "I am *Kajoran*, after all."

"It wouldn't be recognized," Shahz answered.

"That's true," Nériala confirmed. "Though a second ceremony in Kajo could be done later using a *Kajoran* ceremony."

"There is still a question about who would officiate," Eskivel pointed out. "Where would we find a *Fél Naran* monk?"

"I could perform the ceremony," Shahz answered. "I was ordained long ago."

"You're a priest?" I was shocked.

"A monk." He smiled at me, some of the glint returning to his eyes. "Have I not always been the model of piousness?"

I couldn't keep my eyes from rolling at that.

"That solves one problem," Nériala said. "But I suggest we keep your status a secret for now. These ceremonies are going to have to take place right away, and that will be difficult to arrange."

"I hope your Fél Naran ceremony will allow you to incorporate aspects of Kajoran culture," Luana spoke up. "Or our religion."

"The core of the ceremony is dictated, but we do have some leeway," Shahz answered. "I'm sure I can work something in."

"Oh!" Luana said. "The *dai so*! The dress! A traditional Kajoran wedding dress was brought from Kajo. It's not very elaborate but technically correct. I didn't care about it when I was supposed to marry Gabiran, but for a wedding like this, I'm going to need to fix it. And I have no idea what I will do for the *chakuta*."

"What's that?" Nériala asked.

"It's a traditional headdress," Luana was shaking her head. "There's no way we could have one made in Iyoké."

"We might not have to," Nériala told her. "A lot of artifacts were... removed from Kajo over the years."

"You mean stolen?"

"They are on display here in the Ziggurat. I'm sure I saw a few different headdresses. We can take a look, maybe one of them will work."

"We have a lot of work to do!" Luana said.

"I have tings to do also," Corlen said. "Da boats. My people. Gotta check da survivors. Da Wounded."

Eskivel nodded. He opened the door and pointed to two guards.

"You two, escort this man wherever he needs to go," he ordered. "Keep him safe. He is under my protection."

"Yes, sir!" The soldiers saluted.

CHAPTER ELEVEN

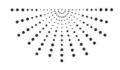

NORA

*A*fter Nériala, Luana, and Eskivel left, Dyani took Shahz aside for a conversation. That left me with more time on my hands and I went back to studying Nimue's spellbook.

When none of them returned that night, I started to worry. Just because I wasn't part of their political maneuverings didn't mean I didn't care about the outcome. But I was done in Iyoké and I'd be happy to leave as soon as Mira arrived.

Two days passed and we still had no word from anyone. That couldn't be good. I knew all the players involved from listening to them talk. Maybe I should try reaching out to one of them. But how? Eskivel was really our only contact in Iyoké. Unless Shahz had someone he could talk to.

I was tired of studying, and tired of not knowing what was going on.

"Shahz," I said as I tucked the spellbook into my bag, "do you have any contacts you can talk to and find out what's happening?"

"I've been away for several years," he was shaking his head. "And when I left, I wasn't exactly advertising that I was alive."

"Why wouldn't people think—"

My question was interrupted as the front door burst open and a half dozen soldiers marched in. They wore metal breastplates with the three-rayed blue emblem I guessed had to do with their church. They were followed by a man I recognized as the Grand Inquisitor. He wore the same fine white linen robe I'd seen him in before. The shining, three-pointed blue pendant hanging from his neck swung like a pendulum with each step. He had hard eyes and a soft smile that seemed too practiced to be sincere. As he walked, his eyes shifted from one to another of us as though we were insects to be put under glass, then they settled on Shahz.

"Apologies for my delay in coming to see you," Grand Inquisitor Palben Ayala said. "I only just learned where you were staying and came to you immediately."

"Why?" I spoke up. "What do you want?"

All of his attention shifted to me as he suppressed a flash of anger. I assumed he had expected

Shahz to speak rather than a foreign female. He forced his smile bigger.

"To welcome you to Iyoké, of course," he said. "And to ensure your safety."

"Our safety?" I asked. "From what?"

"As you may not be aware," his voice took on a condescending tone, "Iyoké is having some growing pains and we are undergoing some changes in leadership structure. Unfortunately, this sort of thing can be confusing for the populace. And there will always be someone who is not happy about the changes and sometimes they act out. A little caution never hurt."

"Gee. Thanks."

His narrowed eyes told me he didn't like my tone any more than I liked his.

"You are the *Kajoran* delegate, yes?" he asked me.

I shook my head. "Nope. Just a messenger. And since the message was delivered, my job here is done. If you want to talk to someone about the *Kajorans*, you'll want Princess Luana. But since you're one of the ones that kidnapped her and brought her here, you should know that already."

His fake smile disappeared at my words. After a moment, he forced it back into place and turned his head to look at Shahz.

"You are Shahz Dega?" he asked.

"I am," Shahz gave a nod.

"Excellent," Ayala said. "I have arrived in time. It will be safer for you and your... *associates* in the Ziggurat. We have come to escort you."

"Baronet Eskivel advised us to wait here for him," Shahz said.

"I'm sure he did," Ayala answered. "But things are in flux, and this is no longer a safe location. Rest assured that I will send word to the baronet so he will know where to find you. For now, we should go."

Ayala nodded to the soldiers, and they ushered us to the door, making it very clear we had no choice in the matter. Spike growled, causing two of the soldiers to jump back in alarm, but I put a hand on him to quiet him. I put my bag over my shoulder, and we went along with the others, noting that the bag seemed slightly heavier than usual.

We essentially retraced our steps from the previous day back to the Ziggurat, but once we were inside, our path was totally different. Very quickly, I was lost in the maze of corridors. We were taken to a room and left alone inside.

After an hour, we checked the door to find it locked. A guard opened it and looked in.

"What do you want?" he demanded.

"We haven't had dinner," Shahz informed him.

The guard looked like he was going to object but then thought better of it.

"I'll see what I can do," he said. "But you are to remain in this room."

"Other than to use the privy?" Shahz raised an eyebrow at him.

"One thing at a time," the guard said with a frown. He closed the door, and we heard him lock it.

After some time, food and beverages were brought and we were able to eat. Then we were taken one at a time to relieve ourselves. When it was my turn, I tried to get a look down the halls to figure out where we were, but it was hopeless.

"Do any of you know where we are?" I asked when I got back.

"I know where we are," Shahz said. "Why?"

"Well, if we got out of this room—"

"If we got out of this room," he cut me off, "we couldn't go back to our quarters. You can assume they are being watched. We would have to find either Baronet Eskivel or Princess Nériala. With everything that's going on right now, that would be very difficult. Meanwhile, they are trying to find us, which they would be able to do more easily if we weren't sneaking around trying not to get caught."

"You're saying we should just wait here?" I asked. "Do nothing?"

"We aren't doing nothing," he said. "But it is not our time to act. Trust Eskivel and Nériala to do their parts. And to find us."

"Fine," I sighed. "I just don't like waiting."

"The impatience of youth?"

I glared at him, and he chuckled.

We heard voices raised in argument on the other side of the door, but couldn't make out the words. Then we heard the key in the lock and the door opened. Nériala gave the guard a stern look and came in. She gave him another look while she waited for him to close the door.

"As a woman, I may not have a lot of power," Nériala smirked. "But as the daughter of the king, it's hard even for the Jhunélin Guard to keep me out of a room in this building."

"Ayala said this would be safer than where we were," I said.

"I'm sure he did," she answered.

She sat in one of the opulent chairs with a sigh.

"Well?" I prompted. "Are you going to tell us what's happening?"

"A lot has happened since we last spoke," she said. "Igonez was arrested for treason. He was accused of sabotaging the cannon – they still won't fire – which he denied vehemently. Zabala and Ayala put enough fear into my father that he abdicated and has fled the city, certain that assassins were close behind. I must admit I helped to foster the idea."

"Abdicated?" Shahz asked. "To Inigon?"

"Yes," she answered. "And I got him to lay the

groundwork for a regency council. No specifics, just that it would be more than one person and only until time as Inigon was fit to rule directly."

"You have been busy," I noted.

"That's just one part of what's been happening," she shook her head. "Luana signed a trade agreement with Gabiran. He agreed to release her from the betrothal and take me instead. He also agreed to support us in our plans."

"That's one piece in place," Shahz said.

"Eskivel called me in and together we convinced Zabala that Ayala was moving against him," Nériala went on. "This prompted him to move against Ayala. It didn't take long for Ayala to find out what Zabala was doing and now the infighting between them is getting fierce. Zabala agreed to support us in return for aid against Ayala. We… implied to Zabala that he might be the third member of the triumvirate regency."

"Implied?" I asked her.

"No promises were made and nothing was said to that effect." She grinned. "It's not my fault if he misconstrued. By the time he realizes, it will be too late."

"And what of the marriage between Inigon and Luana?" Shahz asked.

"That's why I had to find where Ayala had stashed you," she said. "It was announced yesterday. It is to take place tonight, followed by a senate meeting to appoint the regency. We also co-ordinated for the *Kajoran* boats to be let into the harbor and the *Kajorans* have been invited to witness the wedding along with the Félbahrin citizens."

"And it is to be a Fél Naran ceremony?"

"Yes," she affirmed. "Zabala liked the idea of taking Ayala down a notch by using the older ceremony. I hope you have everything you need to officiate. You're the only Fél Naran monk we have."

Shahz went to my shoulder bag and pulled out a rolled-up, purple cloth from the bottom.

"I thought that felt heavier." I scowled at him.

"You carry your bag wherever we go." He shrugged. "Seemed the safest place to keep it near." He looked at Nériala. "I'll need some time to prepare."

"Not too long, I hope," she said. "Ayala still doesn't know the ceremony won't be officiated by one of their priests. We have to time things carefully to make this happen the way we want."

"Understood."

"Ayala is sure to raise the issue of legitimacy in the senate meeting afterwards," she continued, "but with Gabiran and Zabala backing us up, he won't get anywhere."

"Do you think you could get me a copy of the Kanéru Naranir?" Shahz asked.

"I'm sure there will be one in my father's private library," she answered. "That's outside of Ayala's control. I'll be right back."

Nériala went back to the door and knocked. The guard opened it and looked in suspiciously. When he saw who it was, he stepped aside to let her out.

Shahz unrolled the cloth and put it on over his clothes. It was a purple robe with gold embroidery at the cuffs, hem and around the collar. It also had a matching gold belt that tied around his waist. Embroidery on the back was a stylized sun with seven rays of light. A white crescent moon was superimposed over a portion of the sun. He hung a gold chain around his neck that held a matching sun-moon pendant.

"You don't look like a sailor, now," I smirked.

He gave me a mock bow. Then lowered his head and closed his eyes. His arms hung limply, and his hands were joined with entwined fingers in front of him. I started to make another joke, but he was either praying or meditating and I decided to leave him alone.

It was several hours before Nériala returned. She had a dozen soldiers in tow and they ushered the three guards from the hall into the room. The soldiers were dressed similarly to the guards, but they didn't have the blue symbol on their chests. The guards clearly weren't happy at having the tables turned on them.

Nériala held a large leatherbound book in her

hands. The leather was dyed purple, and it had gold-leaf writing on the cover, as well as the sun-moon symbol. Shahz's eyes went wide when he saw it.

"This is no simple copy," he said. "This Kanéru Naranir is fit for the Enlightened. Or one close to him. Or her."

"Enlightened?" I asked him.

"It is the title given to the highest member of our clergy," he explained as he reverently turned the pages of the book. "A Kanéru Naranir of this quality would be used by one of those."

"Then it is fitting that it's used for this wedding," Nériala replied. "How soon can you be ready?"

"I am ready whenever you are." He closed the book.

"Excellent!" She turned to the three guards. "You should stay here and when the Grand Inquisitor returns you can report what has happened."

"We should report to him immediately," one of the guards spoke up.

"I think not." She smiled. "I'll leave a few of the King's Guards in the hall outside to... keep you safe while you wait."

Nériala led us off down the hall. This time I didn't bother trying to figure out where we were going and just followed along. When we had entered and left the building before, we had made use of stairwells. Now, we seemed to be ascending a sloped, switch-backed ramp. Then we emerged onto the broad landing about halfway up the side of the Ziggurat. All around the building, we could see thousands of people gathered for the royal wedding.

The sun had set and stars shone above. Torches were placed on the corners of the landing and along the stairs, as well as in sconces along the wall, casting a red-gold light along the face of the Ziggurat. This landing was actually the main entrance to the building, with a large stairway leading down the center and smaller ones leading off to each side. We had come to it from a different path than before.

The central stairway continued to the top of the Ziggurat behind us as I looked out over the crowd. The landing area where we stood was maybe forty yards wide and fifteen yards deep. Near the front edge, a pedestal had been set, likely for Shahz to put his bible or whatever he called it. There were seven members of the palace guard on each side wearing fancier uniforms than I'd seen so far. The spears in their hands and swords at their waists looked just as deadly.

I stood to one side with Dyani and Nériala. Bright looked out, tucked in her spot in my hood. And Spike, of course. I could tell that the soldiers were nervous about Spike; I probably shouldn't feel as smug about that as I did.

The crowd parted and I saw Grand Inquisitor Palben Ayala, in all his finery, approaching the stairs. His beatific smile was plastered on his lips. Six pairs of soldiers marched behind him, blue emblems on their breastplates.

"This is going to be interesting," Nériala said under her breath. At my look, she continued. "He probably still thinks he's going to be officiating."

Before Ayala was halfway up the stairs to the landing, Shahz stepped out of the central door to the Ziggurat and stepped to the podium, placing his book on top and opening it to a section bookmarked with a gold-colored ribbon.

Ayala almost faltered in his step when he saw Shahz take his place. His practiced smile disappeared, replaced with an expression of rage.

"What is the meaning of this?" He demanded of Shahz when he reached the landing.

Nériala stepped forward before Shahz could respond.

"We thank you for coming, Grand Inquisitor," she said. "You honor us with your presence. This is Father Shahz Dega, who will be conducting the ceremony."

"Father?" Ayala snapped. "He is no priest of Ah-Shan!"

"Correct Grand Inquisitor," she smiled, "we

have elected to use the older, more traditional ceremony of the Fél Naran."

"Heresy!" He motioned to his soldiers. "Guards, arrest this false priest."

His soldiers drew their swords and rushed to obey, but the palace guards sprang into action. More palace guards came out of the Ziggurat. One of Ayala's soldiers took a spear thrust in the stomach. Initially, Ayala's soldiers had outnumbered the palace guard, but the numbers had evened out and more palace guards were coming through the doorway. Spike growled, but I held him back.

A shimmering appeared in the air and a strange-looking winged creature leapt through with several figures coming behind her. She held a sword in her hands and she quickly surveyed the area. Then she spotted me.

"Which ones are the bad guys?" she asked.

"What?" The voice sounded familiar, but I didn't know who this terrifying creature was.

"Who's the enemy?"

CHAPTER TWELVE

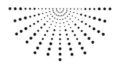

MIRA

*N*eelu led me and Jack to the barracks where the *Wyl-Dunn* refugees were being housed. As we passed by other barracks, I was reminded of my time in training. I must have smirked because Neelu gave me a questioning look.

"I was remembering my first day in one of these," I told her. "Another of the sprigs convinced me, Rispan, and Mouse that we were supposed to wear all of our gear and all of our weapons and stand in front of the other sprigs in the company for our first muster."

"That old prank?" She laughed. "I'm surprised you fell for it."

"I got my revenge." I grinned. "Have you ever put your foot into a boot filled with porridge?"

We continued down the corridor, and I remembered other friends from those times, several of whom were no longer with us. And they had died under my command.

When we arrived at the barracks, only Zoriaa and Usoa were there and Tesia was talking with them. When she saw me, Usoa leaped to her feet and gave me a hug.

"We were worried when you'd been gone so long," she said. "I'm glad you're safe. Tesia just told us you were back."

"You're looking a lot better since last time I saw you," I observed.

She moved and spoke with more confidence than I'd seen in her before, and she seemed older.

"I never thanked you for helping me," Usoa said. "And for bringing us here."

"I'm just glad you've healed so well," I answered. "Where's everyone else?"

"Képa is likely in the infirmary," Zoriaa said. "I know she was very impressed with the ability of the healers here. The others are probably in Market Square, having lunch, or in one of the practice yards."

"So why are you two cooped up here while the others are all out experiencing the city?" I asked.

"We are… in training," Zoriaa said. "Usoa has become my apprentice. She is learning the lore of our people. If something were to happen to me, I don't want that knowledge to be lost."

"Have you thought about writing everything down?" I asked. "Maybe even having a school so that more people can have the knowledge?"

"Much of it *is* written down," she told me. "But those writings are put in a secret place for safekeeping. But it must also be memorized. Plus, she needs to be guided through learning to use her power." She looked at Jack, "It's good to see you're awake. How did they bring you out of the spell?"

"Nora was using her connection to me, and to Mira, to draw a large volume of power for something," he said. "I don't know for what."

"Nora?" Zoriaa looked confused. "She's here?"

"No," I told her. "But I spoke with her briefly through her connection. She said she's in someplace called Félbahrin. Do you know it?"

"I know *of* it," she said. "It is the land of the *Félbahlag*. A smaller continent across the sea to the east of Danu."

"Well," I shrugged, "that's where I need to go. But what about your people here? Do they want to go back to Danu? I brought you all here, but I don't want to leave you stranded."

"The healers here have been wonderful," Zoriaa said. "And the *Ulané Jhinura* have been very welcoming. But there is concern about Kartahn Zeg's war on Danu. I believe they would like to get back to help in the fight."

"We should do that right away, then," I said.

"Do you think they could be ready to go tomorrow morning?"

"Yes." She answered. "I'll talk to them today and make sure everyone is ready to go. That will give them time to say any goodbyes if that's needed."

"I don't know exactly where we'd be going on Danu," I admitted. "I have a thread of *Ralahin*, magic, tied to Anazhari. She and Mehrzad were going to follow the *Bahréth* army. Wherever they are is probably the closest I'd be able to make a portal. And I don't know how safe the area will be."

"You're saying you use a *Ralahin* thread to help establish an anchor for the other end of the portal?" Tesia asked. "And I'm guessing you adapted that from the spell on tracking the flow of a previous portal?"

"Yes," I told him. "It's been working really well. But I have to tie it to someplace I've been, or to a person. But I need to be able to keep track of the threads for later use, so I've just been tying the other end to my wrist," I held up my left hand.

"So I see," she said, looking at it with her *Ralahin* Sight. "But you realize, *Ralahin* flows everywhere and through everything. In theory, you could find anyone or anything by reading the flows, and then create your portal."

"Reading the flows?" I asked. "I don't think we got to that in our lessons."

"We *were* a bit focused on battle magic." Tesia smiled wryly. "And then portals. There *are* other uses, you know."

"Yeah," I agreed. "I don't have a clue how most of the spells we use every day in Su Lariano are constructed. I know there's a *lot* I don't know."

"There's always time to learn more," Tesia said. "I've actually been working on ways to improve the portal spells. Those documents you had about the various portal spells were very helpful. I developed a way to create a stable two-way portal, and it doesn't require having a person working the spell from the other end."

"Really?" That sounded efficient. "I've just been creating two parallel portals, one going each way. I was able to talk with Anazhari from Danu when she was here in Daoine when I had both portals open."

"That's probably a lot easier to do," she said. "The two-way portal takes a LOT of energy. It's exhausting!"

"Alright, you two," Neelu interrupted. "I'll let you talk shop and check in with you later."

"I'm sorry, Neelu," I said. "I really do want to hear about Tesia's discoveries with the portals, and maybe find out about this *reading the flows* thing she mentioned. Come by my rooms later?"

"You got it." Neelu smiled and left.

"Why don't we go back to my rooms and have

some lunch?" I asked Tesia. "We can talk about this stuff some more."

"Sounds perfect!" Tesia agreed.

"Can I come?" Usoa asked. "I just want to listen. This idea of reading the flows... it makes sense! I'm learning a lot about magic... I want to learn everything I can and I want to hear what you say."

"I don't see why not," I shrugged.

"If you don't mind," Jack said. "I'd like to stay and talk with Zoriaa. Maybe she can help me understand my connection to Nora."

"The connection between the *Baensiari* and the champion is not fully understood," Zoriaa said. "But I can tell you what I know."

"Alright," I told them. "We'll see you two later."

"*I don't think you should trust that Jack.*" Yeravi's thoughts came to me after we'd left the barracks. "*Best to keep him at a distance.*"

"*Bull,*" I sent back to her. "*You're only saying that because he can hear you when you talk to me.*"

She had no response to that.

As soon as we arrived back at my rooms, we sent for lunch. Then Tesia and I spent several hours talking about portal theory and reading flows. Usoa mainly just listened.

"I don't understand this talk of portals," she said finally. "Something about it just doesn't make sense to me. But what you're saying about flows... I think that makes sense if I could see them."

"Here," Tesia said, placing her hand on Usoa's arms. I could tell that Tesia had connected to the *Ralahin.* "Let me lend you my sight. That should help."

Usoa's eyes got big as she looked around.

"I see the flows!" she said. "They're everywhere!"

"That is the *Ralahin,*" Tesia told her. "Some think that this aspect of *rala,* of magic, or connecting to it, is proprietary to the *Ulané Jhinura.* But I disagree. And certainly Mira has shown us that you don't need to be *Ulané Jhinura* to use it."

"Now I understand why the flows are sometimes called threads," Usoa said. "And you use these to weave spells and such?"

"Yes. Do you think you can see them on your own now?" Tesia asked her.

Usoa nodded and Tesia withdrew her hand.

"And to read the flows, I just..." Usoa concentrated for a moment. "Fruit pies!" She exclaimed. "They are making fruit pies in the kitchen. But I'm not familiar with that kind of fruit."

"You read that in the flows?" Tesia was surprised.

"Yes!" Then Usoa's brow furrowed. "But there's so much information."

"That's the difficulty," Tesia said. "The flows say so much because they touch everything. Finding specific things can be difficult."

"Things?" I asked.

"Information, I mean," Tesia corrected.

"Things, too," Usoa said, half lost in her vision. "And visions of things past. I can see us walking in the door and being served our lunch."

"I'm impressed," Tesia told her. "Being able to read the flows so deeply is rare, especially for one who only just learned to even *see* the *Ralahin*."

"It's still hard to direct," Usoa said. "But I think I can get better if I practice."

"Even for me, it takes a lot of effort and focus to read what is there," Tesia said. "Directing it is even harder."

"She learns quickly," Yeravi's thoughts came to me. *"You'll need to watch out for that one. She's dangerous."*

"She's just a young girl," I responded.

"Being young doesn't mean she's not dangerous. You were her age when you came to this world. You were dangerous."

"I thought you were here to learn since your approach failed," I snapped.

I could tell that had angered her, but she went silent.

"Well, you jumped past me," I said to Usoa. "I'll probably be asking you for pointers."

For the first time, I saw Usoa really smile. It was sweet and warm and unfiltered. Then her thoughts went elsewhere, and it disappeared.

"What?" I asked her.

"Xantif would have loved this," she said. "He was always so curious about everything."

"I only met him in passing," I said. "But I know how it is to lose someone important to you. Someone that you care about."

"Does the ache ever go away?" She searched my face.

"Not really." I tried to smile. "But you get used to it. I think we always feel the loss, but in time we learn to accept it. Maybe it would help if you told us about him. What was he like?"

"Xantif?" she asked. "I don't know... He was just Xantif. He was always sweet to me, but he was so silly sometimes, like he'd never grow up. And he was absolutely *crazy* about the *Gurpahn*. That's why he became a groom. He was learning to be a handler, a trainer. He taught me a little, too. He said I had a natural talent for it, but I think he was just being nice. He was like that. Don't let him near the cook-pot though; he was horrible at cooking! I remember one time—"

She stopped suddenly and her face screwed up as she held back a sob.

"They told me he was killed trying to protect the *Gurpahn*," she said. "The young ones. How could he be so stupid? He wasn't a warrior! What did he think he could do?"

"He did what he felt he had to," I told her. "It's

all any of us can do. If he had done anything else, would he have been the Xantif you loved?"

"I never said—" She looked at me, startled. "I guess I did, didn't I?" Her eyes fell. "I never told him."

"And he probably never told you, either," I said. "But I'm guessing it was mutual, and he cared for you as much as you cared for him."

Tesia was looking at me. Fortunately, she didn't say anything. I wasn't ready to talk about my own parallel, but maybe I could at least help Usoa with her situation.

Usoa's eyes lit with realization. "I always wondered why he ignored all the girls! All the other ones, anyway." She shook her head with a smile. "What a goof! He never told me! I wish he could see me now, training with Zoriaa."

"How's that going?" I asked.

"Good." she replied. "And we need to have people ready to become *baensiari* for the *Wyl-Dunn*. A *baensiari*, not *the baensiari*. That's Nora. It's different."

"I haven't heard that word," I said.

"It's like a high priestess," Tesia supplied. "A keeper and guardian of knowledge and tradition. And a guide."

"And that's what Nora is now?" I asked.

"No." Usoa shook her head. "She's the keeper of the Sword of Light. But a sort of guardian, too. I don't really know much about that, yet. I still have a lot to learn. It would be easier if we could go to the sacred library, but Zoriaa pretty much knows everything that's there. It would just be easier if I could *see* it. But I don't think Zoriaa knows about reading the flows. That's something new."

There was a knock on the door, and I opened it to see Veron, the Weapons Master of Su Lariano.

"Veron!"

"I'd heard you were back." He grinned. "Since you tend to come and go quickly, I wanted to catch you while I could. I missed you last time."

"I'm sorry!" I told him. "You know, I haven't even seen Rispan."

"You will if this oaf would get out of the way!" A voice sounded from the corridor behind Veron.

Startled, Veron stepped through the door and to the side. Rispan rushed past him to wrap his arms around me.

"Hiya, sis!"

I hugged him back, happy to see him. He'd been here on one of my last visits, but that was when Katya died and we hadn't been able to really talk.

"I hope you're hungry for dinner," he said. "Because I made reservations at the Raven's Nest, and Mouse is expecting us. You're welcome to join us, Veron."

"No, no," Veron said with a laugh. "I just wanted to drop this by."

I hadn't realized he had a sheathed sword in one hand until he held it up for me. I took the sword and pulled it from the sheath. It wasn't magical like the Sword of Light, but it was a similar design and the workmanship was the finest I'd seen. The balance was exquisite.

"I know you left your armor and most of your weapons in Shianri," he said. "So I thought this might come in handy."

"Where did this come from?" I asked.

"It was packed away in the royal armory," he said. "It's a bit long for an *Ulané Jhinura*, so it's just been sitting for centuries, maybe longer."

"It doesn't look like it's been just sitting," I said. "It's in perfect condition."

"Of course," he feigned offense. "Even unused weapons get regular maintenance."

"Of course," I rolled my eyes. "But this is one of, if not *the*, finest blade I've ever seen." I slid the sword back into the sheath and held it out for him to take back. "I'd feel guilty accepting it."

He shook his head. "I already mentioned it to Queen Astrina. None of the *Ulané Jhinura* can use it, and you can. She said to tell you that it was a small token of appreciation for all you have done for Su Lariano and Daoine."

"But—"

"You wouldn't want to insult the queen by refusing her gift, would you?"

"Well played," I said wryly. "Please tell the queen I said thank you."

"I will." He grinned. Then he gave a bow. "Enjoy your dinner."

"And Veron?" He paused and glanced over his shoulder at me. "Thank you."

He gave me a wink and a nod before continuing on his way.

"So," Rispan looked between me, Tesia and Usoa, "is everyone ready for some dinner?"

"I have other dinner plans," Tesia said. "Though, nothing as nice as the Raven's Nest. You go on without me. It was wonderful to meet you, Usoa. I hope to see you again sometime."

I gave Tesia a hug goodbye, and she went the other direction down the corridor. We made our way to the restaurant and I introduced Usoa to Mouse.

"Well," Rispan said as we sat at a table. "Shall I order us a pitcher of Pixie Juice?"

"No." I grinned. "It's too easy to forget you're drinking alcohol, and it looks like tomorrow's going to be a long day."

"Pixie Juice?" Usoa asked.

"It's really good," I told her. "A bit fruity and slightly sweet."

"Fruity alcohol?" She looked confused. "Like, what... apples?"

"No." I shook my head. "More like a combination of peaches, pomegranate, and citrus. It goes down very easily but it packs a punch. It's definitely worth trying, though I wouldn't recommend having more than one. I'm going to stick to Goblin Grog."

"Right," Rispan said with a chuckle. "Because *those* aren't strong at all."

"It's not as sneaky and I'm only going to have *one*," I pointed out. "*And* I won't be gulping it down like juice."

That night, Usoa stayed with me in my suite and she used the bed in the second room. It had been a fun evening and I'd enjoyed spending time with Rispan and Mouse again. I'd ended up having more than just one Goblin Grog, but I'd had enough food – Mouse had brought us their version of pizza, which he said had become very popular – that I wasn't feeling any effects.

In my own bed, I looked up at the ceiling. It had been a while since I'd slept in it and it felt good; like I was home.

CHAPTER THIRTEEN

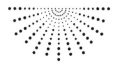

MIRA

*A*fter breakfast, the first thing I did was to check in with Anazhari. It would give me an opportunity to experiment with communicating through the portals. I located my thread to her and followed it to her location. Since no one was actually traveling, I didn't need to make large portals. Instead, I tried making them very small.

"Anazhari," I sent my thoughts to her through the first portal.

"Mira!" The answer was immediate. *"It's been so long! We were worried!"*

"Yeah, sorry about that," I told her. *"I'll tell you about it later. How are things on your end?"*

"We followed the Bahréth *army,"* she said. *"They have been laying siege to Solaian. I think the* Ande Dannu *are planning to evacuate and head north along*

the shore to Usolé to seek sanctuary among the Dannu Fé. *But the trip is long and supplies will be needed. The* Wyl-Dunn *are also here, trying to assist."*

"*Sounds like things are going badly.*"

"*The* Bahréth *army is immense,*" she told me. "*And their mages are very powerful.*"

"*I have some refugees that want to come back in a little while,*" I said. "*Can you get somewhere it would be safe for them to come through?*"

"*I think so.*"

"Good," I said. "*One thing, we may have a few* Bahréth *with us. Friendlies.*"

"*That makes it more complicated,*" she answered. "*Will they be seeking sanctuary from the* Ande Dannu? *If you were to bring them within the city, they would likely be attacked before they could explain.*"

"*No, I don't think that would be necessary.*"

"*Alright, give us a little time to get some distance from the fighting.*"

I closed the portals. The next thing I needed to do was check in with Radomér and the other *Bahréth* to find out what they'd decided. I'd assumed that they'd want to go back to Danu.

Jack hadn't sought me out the previous night, so I assumed he stayed at the barracks with the *Wyl-Dunn*. As I walked with Usoa, I pulled my commdev out and slipped it on my finger. I reached out my mind for Neelu. When she answered, I told her where I was going.

"*I'll meet you there,*" her thought came back to me. Then the connection was gone.

"What's that?" Usoa asked.

"It's a magical artifact that allows you to talk to someone with your mind." I handed it to her. "As long as they have one, too. They're linked, and when you think of the other person, you can connect with them mentally."

"If you know the other person," she asked, "why can't you just use a spell to communicate with them directly?"

"Maybe you could." I shrugged. "But both people would need to be able to work the spell. And you'd have to schedule it so you'd both be doing it at the same time."

"I don't think so," Usoa said as she studied the ring. "I can See the spellwork on this. I think a modified version of the spell would let you establish the link for the other person. I mean... they could always ignore it. But..." Her brow furrowed. "*Can you hear me?*"

Her last question had sounded in my mind, which had startled me.

"*Yes,*" I thought back. "*Can you hear me?*"

"Yes!" she exclaimed out loud. "It worked!"

"How did you do that?"

"Once I understood how the spell worked, it was easy," she told me. "You already have a connection to people you know. So, when you weave the spell all you have to do—"

"You can see how the spell in the ring is made?"

"Sure," Usoa looked confused. "Can't you?"

I shook my head. "I can use it, but I don't understand the spell that makes it work."

"My version is much less complicated," she explained. "Because I don't have to create a link. I just use the one that's already there between the people."

I shook my head again. "You must have a natural talent for magic," I told her. "I thought *I* was a fast learner. That's pretty amazing."

Usoa seemed a little embarrassed and she stopped talking.

"Maybe you could teach me your version of the spell?" I encouraged her. "It would be nice if I could communicate with people who didn't have one of these."

"Sure," she said. "The spell is pretty simple, and you just send it along your connection to the other person."

"I've tied magical threads to people and things," I said. "But other than that, I haven't seen these connections you're talking about."

"Really?" Usoa stopped walking and we paused with her. "Here. Look and I'll show you."

I opened my *Ralahin* vision and nodded.

"Alright," she said. "We know each other." She

reached out her hand as though plucking something from the air. "Here is a line that connects us. Can you see it?"

"Um," I looked where she was indicating, but couldn't see what she was talking about. "No."

"You have to look really close," she told me. "It's very thin."

I shook my head. "Nothing."

"Try reaching out to me with your mind," Usoa instructed. "Focus on reaching."

I did as she said and saw a tiny pulse of something. I sort of zoomed in with my Sight and finally saw what she was talking about.

"I see it." I told her. "But it's so thin! I think if I look away I wouldn't be able to find it again."

"You have lots of these," she said. "I think this one is your connection to Anazhari. I don't know what the others are for, but you have plenty."

"I'll have to work on that," I said, dropping my Sight. "I can't See as well as you can."

We continued on our way and shortly located Radomér and the others. Usoa stayed back a little.

"Good morning, Radomér," I said to him. "Have you guys decided what you want to do?"

He gave one of those upwards *Bahréth* nods.

"We are still discussing," he said. "But in general, I think we have arrived at a consensus."

"This is a nice place," Sena spoke up. "And the

people are welcoming. But we don't really have a place here. We need to go back."

"There are definitely some problems with how our society is being run," Radomér acknowledged. "Running away won't solve them."

"I'll be taking the *Wyl-Dun* refugees back to Danu this morning," I told them. "I can take you at the same time. Do you intend to simply rejoin your army? Or…"

Radomér wagged his head, no. "We should be able to avoid our previous commander. No one else would recognize us or know that we were missing. We want to work to change things from within. To get our people to turn away from Zeg and the Transcendent."

I started to say something, but stopped and glanced at the silent Poldi.

Radomér saw my look and grinned.

"You're worried that Poldi isn't with us," he said. "He's not much of a talker, but he's with us all the way."

"It's true," Sena said. "Poldi is solid."

Poldi just looked on without a word, his face unreadable.

"You don't want to speak for yourself?" I smiled.

He gave a shrug that wasn't much more than a twitch and looked away. "They say it better."

I'd have to accept their judgment on it. I didn't know Poldi and they did.

"Alright," I said. "There's a group of *Bahréth* that are trying to do the same thing. They call themselves the Children of Ezhti. They know the truth about the Transcendent." I crouched down and drew in the dirt.

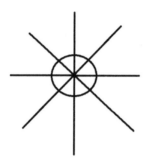

"Look for this symbol," I told them. "An X on a cross with a circle around the center. They use it to identify each other, or places to meet. I don't need to tell you what would happen if Zeg's people found out about them."

"Thank you," Radomér said. "We'll watch for them and join forces when we can."

"Alright," I said. "Grab your stuff and we can go to the others."

"Radomér?" Usoa spoke from behind me, her eyes were on the ground and only flicked up to him for a moment. "I'm Usoa. Do you remember me?"

Radomér nodded. "I remember you well," he

said. "You look much healed from when I saw you last."

"That last day," she said. "Before we came here. After I found out about Xantif. My friend. I started hitting you."

"I remember," Radomér said. "You were very distraught."

Usoa nodded and I could tell this was difficult for her.

"I… I shouldn't have hit you," she said. "And I wanted to apologize."

"Think nothing of it," Radomér told her. "No damage was done."

"No. No damage," she said. "But I would have. In that moment, I would have killed you if I could. I wanted to kill you. I wanted to kill all *Bahréth*."

"I understand," he answered.

"I know you weren't the one who killed Xantif," she told him. "I shouldn't have blamed you. I'm sorry."

"You have suffered a great personal loss," Radomér said. "And I am saddened for this, as I am saddened for the war that even now rages between our people. And I grieve that this war has been in- stigated by the *Bahréth*. You have come to me with truth. To honor that, I must answer with truth. I did not know your Xantif. I cannot say that I was the one to kill him. But I also do not know that I was *not* the one to kill him. Either way, he was slain by a

Bahréth and I am *Bahréth*. For this, I can only feel shame. Shame and a hope that we can do better."

Tears streaked Usoa's face as she held his gaze. Finally, she gave a single nod.

I turned and headed off, leading them to the barracks where the *Wyl-Dunn* refugees should be waiting.

I'd always felt tall around the *Ulané Jhinura* – at an average of four and a half feet, they mostly came up to my shoulder or just above – but walking through the halls to the barracks with the huge *Bahréth* in tow, I felt like a toddler. I could understand why the three shakahr didn't feel like there was a place for them here. Of course, the *Ashae* were a lot closer to them in height, but they were mostly far away in the north.

Zoriaa was waiting with the two dozen or so refugees, talking to Jack. Képa was with them as well.

"I have an update on the situation," I told them.

They all gathered to listen.

"Kartahn Zeg and his army have been at Solaian. The *Wyl-Dunn* are helping the *Ande Dannu* and they're evidently going to evacuate to Usolé."

"But that's more than a thousand miles!" someone said.

"Right," I hadn't realized it was *that* far. "And they'll probably have the *Bahréth* army on their heels the whole time."

"But you can make a portal, right?" Usoa asked. "You can get them through so they'll be safe."

"Um," I hadn't thought of that. But I didn't see how that was going to work. "I don't know if I can do that. I've never been to Usolé and I don't have any anchors there. I wouldn't be able to create the portal."

"Send everyone somewhere else!" A voice called.

"Like where?" I asked. "I can't just bring an entire city here. And they're wanting to get to Usolé, which I don't know."

"You could fly there," Jack said. "I could even carry you. We could get there in a few hours and you could portal back. You'd have your anchors in place."

"Wait a minute," I said. "Don't the *Ande Dannu* guard portals to Earth? Couldn't they use that? Or don't they have one to take them directly to Usolé?"

"I understand the portals became unstable and they were closed," Zoriaa said. "I don't know of any portals between the two cities. A portal would need to be created."

"Even if I could make a portal," I said, "I don't think I could hold it open for long enough to evacuate a whole city."

Everybody was talking and I couldn't make out the words.

"There are mages who could help you with the power." One voice rose above the others.

"And you wouldn't have to take everyone at once," Usoa pointed out. "You could do it in groups."

That was true. It would still take a long time to get everyone, though.

"Alright," I said. "First, we have to get there and talk with someone in charge. We'll see what we can coordinate. Is everyone ready to go?"

"Looks like I got here just in time," Neelu walked up behind me.

"Yes." I turned to face her. "We're just about to go back to Danu. Can you tell everyone goodbye for me? I'll be back as soon as I can."

"I will," she said. "And meanwhile, my mother said don't forget that you are an ambassador for Su Lariano. We would like to establish relations with those on Danu."

"Oh! Queen Astrina! I should have checked in with her!"

"Yes," Neelu smirked. "You should have. She understands things are rather rushed. But on your next visit she expects you to give a full debrief to her and Dzurala."

"I will!" I told her. "I promise! Is there anything in particular she's wanting in these relations?"

"She said she'd leave that up to you, as long as you don't give away the moon and stars."

"Hey." I arched an eyebrow at her. "I *always* get a good value. You know that."

"We are ready," Zoriaa told me.

I gave Neelu a nod and opened the dual communication portals to talk to Anazhari.

"Are you ready?" I asked her.

"Yes," she answered. *"We are in a small clearing that is hidden from view."*

I sensed the open space near her. Then I dropped the small portals and opened one large enough for everyone to walk through.

"Let's go!" I called out.

Jack led the way and the *Wyl-Dunn* refugees followed. The three *Bahréth* brought up the rear, carrying the saddle for Anazhari. I followed right behind them, closing the portal as soon as I was through.

We were standing in a gully. The stream that flowed nearby probably filled the whole area in the rainy season. Judging by the clouds, that might not be far off.

"Anazhari, Mehrzad," I said. "It's good to see you again."

"Where is Luci?" Mehrzad's question sounded in my mind.

"She's on Earth," I sent back to him. *"We got separated and I haven't been able to get hold of her yet."*

"We'll help you get this saddle on," Radomér

said. "Then we should get some distance between us."

"Agreed." I nodded.

We had Anazhari saddled in no time, and I immediately hung my sword from the saddle rather than my hip. Maybe I should have picked up a staff while I was in Su Lariano. That was still my weapon of preference, but I'd gotten pretty good with the two-handed sword. No small thanks to all that practice with Alénia.

"Good luck, you three," I said to the shakahr as they turned to leave.

"Stay safe," Radomér called over his shoulder. Then they were gone over the edge of the gully.

"Where do we go?" I asked Anazhari as I climbed into the saddle.

"*Upstream a short distance from here,*" she answered. "*Then we may be able to access the postern gate.*"

"Um, that's the back door to the city?"

"*Yes.*" I could hear her amusement. "*The back door to the city. Though it's more of a side door. The* Bahréth *have taken control of the harbor, so that approach won't work.*"

"And I'm guessing the front is… busy?"

"*From the rim here,*" Mehrzad said, "*You can see the main gate to the city.*"

"I'd like to get a look at the situation," I said.

The way wasn't steep, and Jack and I crept up

the slope and looked over. Solaian was a walled city. At its center was another walled area that surrounded a fortified palace. The crenelated outer walls were at least thirty feet high.

There was a space of about three hundred yards outside the walls that were empty except for occasional bodies of fallen *Bahréth* and broken equipment.

"Positions have shifted." Anazhari had joined us. *"We will have to wait until the way to the postern gate is clear."*

"It appears the Bahréth *are launching another offensive against the gate,"* Mehrzad observed.

Four armored mammoths – *Gajhanti* – were making their way to the main city gate, side by side. Several hundred *Bahréth*, maybe even a thousand, followed closely behind. When they reached the halfway point of the plain, arrows flew from the city walls. The defenders had gathered more thickly along the walls above and to either side of the main gate. The archers weren't trying for the massive *Gajhanti*, but for the soldiers behind them.

"Why are they ignoring the *Gajhanti*?" I asked.

"It would be wasted effort," Mehrzad answered in my mind. *"Even if an arrow pierced the armor, their skin is too tough and thick to do anything but annoy them."*

The *Bahréth* carried shields for protection, and they held them above their heads to defend against the sea of arrows falling on them. The defense wasn't perfect, and arrows did find gaps. When one fell, the *Bahréth* quickly adjusted to plug the hole in the defense before it could be used against them.

I noticed that the tusks of the *Gajhanti* had been cut short. I realized why when they broke into a run the last twenty yards and charged the gates. I could feel the vibrations under my feet when the four *Gajhanti* struck the gates with their heads. The sound of the impact reached me a few seconds later.

"*Putri firgolo,*" I muttered under my breath.

The *Gajhanti* backed up and charged again.

"How long can the gates last against that?" I asked.

"*The* Bahréth *have been attacking the main gate in this way almost every day,*" Anazhari told me. "*It is likely the defenders have filled the gatehouse with dirt or rubble. At this point, they would have more luck pounding the walls.*"

"Then why bother?" Along the curve of the outer wall, I could see at least two other gates. They were smaller than the main gates, but they were still pretty big. "How many gates are there altogether?" I asked.

"*There are five including the main gate,*" Mehrzad answered.

"Have the *Bahréth* used the *Gajhanti* against the other ones?"

"*No*," Mehrzad said. "*It seems they are more intent on breaching the main gates.*"

"Or that's just what they want the defenders to think," I said.

Something caught my eye. A group of about a dozen *Bahréth* had managed to reach the wall undetected near the next gate further down. They must have gone slowly, using some sort of camouflage.

In what was clearly a practiced exercise, eight of the *Bahréth* paired off and joined hands. Each pair launched another *Bahréth* upwards and the four caught the edge at the top of the wall and scrambled over. Two of the four pairs stayed in place and launched the others in a similar manner. This continued until only one pair remained.

"I think the city is in trouble," I said.

I couldn't tell what was happening at the top of the wall or in the gatehouse, but the gate opened a moment later. As soon as that happened, thousands of *Bahréth* sprung up from camouflaged trenches and ran for the open gate. A *Qélosan* flew with them.

"I will deal with that one," Jack said.

He drew his sword as his body started to change. His skin turned dark red and he grew about two feet. Black horns grew from his head and enormous, leathery wings appeared on his back. He looked like the stereotypical demon from all the stories.

"Is that your true form?" I asked him. His shift had startled me.

"It is one of my forms," he answered. He crouched as if to leap to the sky, then paused, looking at me. "Do you want to come?"

I glanced down and saw that I had started to shift as well. Damn. I hadn't meant to do that.

"Fine," I said, going with the shift and pushing it along.

Usoa was looking at me with wide eyes.

"Keep track of my boots for me, please," I said to her.

I pulled my sword from its sheath on Anazhari's saddle and Jack, and I took to the sky. We raced toward the open gate and the *Qélosan* that was leading the charge. I could already see more and more of the defenders falling to their knees in awe, victims to the glamour of the *Qélosan*.

Jack let out a roar and the *Qélosan* turned his head to see our approach. The spell of the glamour hit me like a wave, but I pushed through it, knowing it to be false.

Jack's sword began to glow and the *Qélosan's* glamour seemed to lose its effects. Defenders were shaking their heads and getting to their feet. The power of the Sword of Light seemed to cut through the magical deception.

The *Qélosan* gave a horrible screech and headed

straight for Jack. I sliced its wing as I flew past, heading for the gatehouse.

The *Ande Dannu* had reformed their lines and were struggling to keep the *Bahréth* from getting through the gates. I pushed harder with my wings to increase my speed and plowed into two *Bahréth* near the front, knocking them from their feet and causing confusion among the attackers as they tried to figure out what had happened.

I circled back in a tight arc and flashed by them again, my sword slicing deeply into the neck of an Anointed as I passed. On my next pass, one of them managed to grab a wingtip, but I spun and lashed out with my talons shredding one of his arms and his stomach. Then I was on the ground and whirling, my sword flashing everywhere, causing the *Bahréth* to pull back.

Jack must have finished with the *Qélosan* because he was suddenly at my side. The *Bahréth* charge faltered, and they began to retreat.

"Keep on them," Jack yelled. "I'll clear the gatehouse!"

I gave way to a building urge and let out a piercing howl that spurred the *Bahréth* to run faster. I flew at their backs, slashing with sword and talons.

A combination of overpowering emotions washed over me. I felt rage at the attackers and that rage flowed through me and guided my motions.

Every cut and slash I delivered fed that rage and gave me more strength. And the feeling of flight and freedom from the earth was something I could never experience in my human form. It was glorious and exhilarating. I reveled in all of it. I couldn't count the number of *Bahréth* I cut down. It was intoxicating.

The attackers had scattered, but ahead of me I saw another large group gathered and flew toward them.

"*Yes!*" I heard Yeravi. "*Kill them all!*"

"Mira!" Jack called from behind me. "The gate is clear! Come back!"

I screeched at the *Bahréth* ahead of me as I neared and several broke formation and ran. A *Qélosan* stepped forward, pushing his glamour at me as hard as he could. I barely felt his power as I slashed with my sword, cutting completely through his body. I laughed as I circled around for another pass.

Something grabbed me and I spun to face whatever it was.

"Mira!" He leapt backwards just in time to avoid my cut. It was Jack. "Come back!"

Why was Jack stopping me? Had he switched sides?

I raised my blade to swing at him again, but he moved back again out of reach.

"Mira!" he called again. "Come back to yourself.

We are allies. There are others we must help. And then we must find Nora!"

Nora? Yes. Nora.

I looked around. The *Bahréth* near us had retreated and presented a wall of shields against me. I had chased them all the way across the clearing and could see the way strewn with the bodies of those I'd struck down. Did I really kill that many of them?

I looked back at Jack.

"Let's go back," he said. "We won the attack. We kept them out of the city."

I nodded to him and we flew to the wall above the gate and landed on the ramparts.

"Stop where you are *Daijheen*!" someone commanded. "Attempt flight and you will not survive ten seconds!"

CHAPTER FOURTEEN

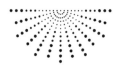

MIRA

*T*he speaker was a woman in shining armor with a crown on her head. Her hostility fed my urge to destroy, but I kept myself in check. We were surrounded by soldiers and crossbows were pointed at us from all sides.

"Who are you?" I asked.

"I am Té Niya," she said. "Queen of the *Ande Dannu*. This is my city!"

"The city we just saved you mean, Your Majesty?" I asked. "The city the *Bahréth* breached and were attempting to enter in the thousands?"

I'd had the impression that neither the *Ande Dannu* or *Dannu Fé* were particularly welcoming of strangers, but we *had* just prevented the city from being overrun. I wasn't going to let her just dismiss us. Or worse.

"We do not know you, whoever you are," she ground out. "And we are grateful for your assistance."

"I am Mirabella nya Balangur of Daoine," I told her with a bow of my head, forcing myself to be calm. "Emissary of the *Ulané Jhinura* of Su Lariano, noble and landowner of the *Ashae* of Shifara, sister to the *Pilané Jhin*. I and this *Daijheen* come to you as diplomats, and we bring *Wyl-Dunn* refugees that we first brought to Su Lariano to be healed and who now wait nearby to enter your city and join their people."

Té Niya took all that in before replying.

"You are welcome in Solaian," she said. "But we know this *Daijheen*. He has been here before. He and his accomplice killed many of our people!"

I remembered the story that Alex Stone had told me.

"Ah yes," I said. "I heard of this. Apparently, you had arrested my sister and were holding her for no reason. When Jack attempted to free her from her wrongful imprisonment, they were attacked and he, and *only* he, defended himself." I looked at Jack, "Did I summarize that correctly?"

Some of that was guesswork, but I knew Nora hadn't killed anyone.

"You did," he affirmed.

"Lives were lost!" Té Niya snapped. "That

cannot be ignored. There must be recompense to the families of the fallen!"

"Kill this impudent bitch!" Yeravi told me. *"Tear out her throat! She doesn't deserve to share the same planet as you!"*

"Be silent!" I ordered her.

"I suggest you take donations from the families of those who did *not* die today," I said to Té Niya. "The families of those he saved can contribute. But why don't we get the refugees inside the walls and we can discuss this, and recompense for wrongful imprisonment, later?"

Her eyes narrowed at me.

"Very well," she said, signaling to the soldiers to lower their weapons. "Tell me where they are and I'll send an escort."

"No need," I told her. I followed the thread to Anazhari as I called to her in my mind, hoping I was within range. *"Anazhari, I'm going to open a portal from you for the refugees to come through. Are you with them?"*

"Yes," she answered. *"I'll have Usoa lead them through."*

I opened the portal and within a minute everyone had come through onto the battlements, including the *Rorujhen*.

Jack had already reverted to his human form. I tried to initiate a change to shift back to my human appearance, but nothing was happening and I started to panic. I'd put up a strong front to Queen Té Niya, but I didn't actually feel confident at all. What if I got stuck this way?

"Jack?" I looked at him. "How... I can't... The change." I held up my hands to indicate myself.

He looked at me in confusion for a moment before realizing the problem.

"Do not try to force it," he told me. "Do not think of it as a change. When you smile or frown, you are not thinking of how you are changing, you simply smile or frown and it happens by itself. At all times you *are* the full range of your form. You do not *change* what you are, you simply assume a state along that gradient that is you."

Queen Té Niya was looking at me curiously.

"This form," I explained. "It's... a new development. I'm still learning."

"Close your eyes," Jack was saying. "Think of where you want to be on that scale and just *be* it."

I closed my eyes and thought of myself as I normally was. Just a regular person, without wings or claws or talons. Just me. I didn't feel any different, though. I opened my eyes. Jack was smiling and nodded to me. I looked at my hands and they were normal; no claws. My feet were back and the wings had disappeared.

"Here." Usoa was handing me my boots and socks, as well as a shirt she'd found somewhere.

"You probably want these. And maybe some more clothes."

I looked down. My jeans were fine, but my shirt and bra were gone and I was suddenly aware of a chill in the air.

"You pretty much shredded what you were wearing when you sprouted wings," she smirked.

From my time in the *Ulané Jhinura* military with men and women sharing barracks and showers, I'd gotten used to nudity, but this surprised me, and my hands instinctively rose to cover my breasts. Then I felt even more foolish. If I'd been flying around topless in front of everyone on both sides of the battle; it was a bit late now to start being modest.

I looked at Jack and he wasn't suffering from the same wardrobe malfunction.

"Your clothes seem fine." I scowled at him as I dressed. "You'll have to teach me how you managed that part."

Belatedly, I realized I should have used the magic pocket for my boots and that my pack was there with clothes.

During our exchange, Képa and Zoriaa had been talking with Queen Té Niya. I waited as they finished explaining what had happened. Once they had finished, I stepped back toward Té Niya.

"While I am here, I am to extend greetings from

Queen Astrina Ulané Poloso of Su Lariano," I told her. "If travel opens between Danu and Daoine, she hopes we can establish friendly relations. Also, I have heard it suggested that you are looking at the possibility of evacuating the city to consolidate forces in Usolé. If this is true, I might be able to assist with a portal."

"You can create a portal to evacuate the city?" she asked me.

"Well, we'd still have some... logistics to work out," I answered. "But I'm willing to try, with the help of my *Daijheen* companion. However, it should be understood that my primary purpose on this world is to find my sister and bring her home. She is not here by choice. I have just learned she's been taken to Iyoké."

Té Niya looked out over the walls and chewed the inside of her lip.

"The truth is that the *Bahréth* army is too big," she said, turning back to me. "In the end, they will find a way in. They almost succeeded today. Usually, such a large force would have problems with supplies, but *Bahréth* don't eat as often as most species. We cannot out-wait them."

"They also come from an area with limited resources," I said. "In their culture, they consider their duty when they die to contribute the meat of their bodies to the community. Every death provides more food."

"They would kill each other to eat?" She was aghast.

"No," I shook my head. "They would never do that. They wouldn't hunt other sentient species for food either. But they believe that not eating meat is wasteful, so long as it isn't rotten."

"I see," she said. "That works in their favor." She let out a long breath. "In terms of evacuation, we had hoped to send as many by ship as possible, especially the slower or weaker ones, and march the rest north. But they've captured the harbor, and we can't get to the ships. Taking everyone overland..." She shook her head.

"It's a major problem to go that far with an army on your heels," I finished for her.

"Yes," she agreed. "If you can indeed create a portal to Usolé, it will allow us to arrive far in advance and we will have more time to prepare."

"The problem is, I haven't been there," I explained. "I need an anchor for the other end of the portal. Plus, I've never created a portal that big or had to hold it open for as long as it would take for the evacuation."

Té Niya was nodding. Then she looked around at the refugees who were standing there while we talked.

"Let's get this group situated," she said. "I will speak with my advisors. Come to me tomorrow at the palace and we can discuss this further."

Usoa and the rest of the former patients went their separate ways, looking for friends and family. The rest of us set off to find Edrigun and Iratzé and we were able to get directions easily enough.

With the influx of the thousands of *Wyl-Dunn* who made up their entire kaganesh, if I was remembering the term correctly, the city was crowded. Tents had gone up wherever they could squeeze them in without blocking traffic. *Wyl-Dunn* weren't used to staying in fixed structures, which probably annoyed innkeepers who'd likely hoped to profit from all the visitors.

The royal tent of the kagana – the kagan and kaganum – was tightly surrounded by others in an open area that was evidently a parade ground or park. It was so crowded it was hard to see what the space had been for originally.

We had to leave the *Rorujhen* on the outskirts of the camp as we weaved our way through, heading for the banner at the royal tent. We apparently arrived just as a meeting was ending because a dozen or so people were filing out. Zoriaa paused outside the opening and clapped her hands twice.

"Enter," a command sounded from inside.

Edrigun and Iratzé were both inside the tent. When they saw how many of us came in, Edrigun looked surprised and Iratzé looked amused. Edrigun's eyes found Jack.

"I see you've recovered from your… condition," he said.

Jack nodded, but before he could say anything, Iratze spoke.

"I do not see the *Baensiari* with you. Did you not find her?" Her eyes scanned us, looking for an answer from someone.

"She's in Iyoké," I spoke up.

"How did she get there?" Iratzé asked.

"I couldn't tell you that," I told her. "I'll be going there as soon as I can, though. Meanwhile, I know there's been talk of evacuating Solaian. It's not certain, but I might be able to help."

"How?" Edrigun asked me. He motioned to some seats nearby and we all found one.

"If Jack and I fly ahead to Usolé, I should be able to get an anchor for the other side and create a portal," I explained. "I think I'd need help keeping it open. Even then, we'd probably have to send people through in waves."

"But then we are back to the same argument," Iratzé said. "Usolé cannot hold all the *Wyl-Dunn* and the *Ande Dannu*. They have neither the space nor the resources."

"If she can create portals," Edrigun said to her, "that may provide other options."

"Such as?"

"We should send the civilians south," he answered. To Findias."

"Findias is long abandoned," she told him.

"Even so," Edrigun said, "it would provide shelter. The *Ande Dannu* army could portal north, to Usolé, and the *Wyl-Dunn* could fight a delaying action to ensure Zeg's army follows us north. Once they are committed to the direction, we can fly ahead on our *gurpahn*."

"Hang on," I interrupted. "There's an important part you're not taking into account. There's two ways I can create a portal to a place. One, if I know the destination well enough, I can envision it in my mind and anchor the other end of the portal to that spot. The only other way is that if I have a magical thread attached to something, I can follow that thread to the end and anchor the portal at the far end. That's how I was able to get here today, Anazhari went ahead and I have a thread tied to her. You're talking about a place to the south and another place to the north, right?"

Edrigun nodded as he scratched his chin in thought.

"Plus," I went on, "you'd still need to work out resources. Your civilians are only going to be able to carry so much. Same with your army going north."

"These are all pieces of the problem," Iratzé said. "I agree that it would be better to send the civilians south. Keeping them supplied, no matter where they go, would be an ongoing issue."

"I know some merchants who would be happy

for the opportunity," I said. "If only they weren't on a different world."

"Your portals can span worlds, can they not?" Iratzé asked.

"They can," I said. "But I can't stay here to run all these connections. Besides, I thought the locals didn't like people portaling back and forth to other worlds."

"I think the time for such restrictions has passed," Edrigun said. "The law would likely have been lifted long ago, but since no one on Danu knows portal magic it only limited off-worlders."

"How did you learn?" Iratzé asked. "Are there others who could assist with this?"

"Um, maybe. There's someone on Daoine," I said. "We were talking about partnering up for a service using portals to transport goods quickly over a distance. She's the only other person I know who can create portals."

"Would she help us?" Edrigun asked.

"Alright," I stood up and paced back and forth, thinking out loud. "I'm sure Tesia would help with the portals, but we need more than what you're talking about. We'd need a thread to Usolé. And what's the other place? The one in the south?"

"Findias," Iratzé supplied.

"Right," I agreed. "Findias. So, we'd need a thread to Findias. But we also need threads to suppliers for resources. We could set one up for Su Lariano. Queen Astrina could be one source. And I could set up another thread to my merchant friends in Pokorah-Vo. Plus, we might also get some resources from the Ashae, but I'd probably have to use my estate at Shianri as a staging area."

"It sounds like you have everything solved," Edrigun observed.

"Not even remotely," I shook my head. "I have identified locations and possible players. But I can't speak for any of them or make any promises on their behalf. You'd have to work out your own deals. And we still have to handle getting threads to both Usolé and Findias."

"I think it is time we brought Queen Té Niya and King Berowen into the discussion," Iratzé suggested. "Come back in the morning and we can go to them together."

"Alright," I said, slipping my comm-dev on my finger. "Meanwhile. I'll go to Su Lariano and get Tesia and some others into this. It really starts with them. I can bring them back here in the morning."

"You're certain they will come?" Edrigun raised an eyebrow.

"Pretty sure," I said. "Let me get them here and we can go from there."

"Very well," Iratzé agreed.

"Here." I opened myself to the *Ralahin* and plucked a thread from the air. I tied one end to Iratzé's chair and the other to my wrist. Then I opened a portal to my suite in Su Lariano. "I'll be back shortly!"

As soon as I stepped into my rooms, I let the portal close and reached out through my comm-dev.

"Tesia, Neelu," I sent the thoughts. "Can you come to my rooms, please?"

They both answered that they were on their way and within minutes they had arrived. Rispan and Ree had been with Neelu and joined us.

"Ree!" I gave her a hug. "I missed you the last few times I came through."

"From what I've heard," she grinned, "it sounds like you've been a bit busy."

"You don't even know!" I rolled my eyes. "Look," I said. "Here's what's going on."

They all listened while I explained the situation in Solaian, and the proposed solutions.

"So, I guess our portal business is happening," Tesia said. "What do you want to call it?"

"Raven Transport?" I asked. "Keeping it to the whole *Raven* thing."

"That works," she said with a laugh.

"Neelu," I said. "You told me Queen Astrina wanted me to see what I could do to establish some kind of connection for Su Lariano to Danu. I think this will be a great opportunity to build a relationship."

Neelu looked at Ree.

"I agree." Ree said. "I should go with you back to Danu to represent our interests."

"I'm coming, too," Rispan spoke up.

"I don't want to make this party too big," I cautioned. "I was thinking just Tesia and Neelu. I still have to go collect other people, too."

"Ree has been assuming her position as eldest daughter and heir to the throne," Neelu said. "This would be perfect for her. And you know how I hate meetings and politics."

I nodded, then looked at Rispan.

"Don't even think it," he said. "I'm not letting my mother go to a different world, into the middle of a war, without me."

"Fine," I said. "Let's go, then. Neelu, I guess I'll leave it to you to let the queen know what's going on."

"When do we leave?" Rispan asked. "Not right now, I hope. I need to let Shéna know what's going on."

"No," I shook my head. "We should go first thing in the morning after breakfast. Meet me here. That gives you all time to make whatever arrangements you need."

It had been a long day, and I had no idea what the next day would be like, so I enjoyed a small dinner by myself, a soak in the tub, and a good night's sleep in my bed. I awoke the next morning refreshed and ready. I'd just finished having a light breakfast when there was a knock at the door as everyone arrived at the same time.

"Is everyone ready?" I asked.

I got nods all around, and then Rispan went to the front door and opened it. He gave a low whistle and a huge panther walked in. On six legs.

"Is that Bijoux?" I asked.

"She's a lot bigger than when you saw her last." Rispan grinned.

Bijoux walked over and butted me on the chest with her head. I obliged and scratched behind her ear.

"I take it you want to bring her, too?" I asked.

He shrugged with a lopsided smile. "She makes an impression."

Shaking my head, I found the thread back to Iratzé and opened the portal.

"I'll go first and keep it open," I said. "Follow behind after a few seconds."

I stepped through the portal into the tent. Everyone else was already there and they looked over as if they'd stopped in the middle of a conversation.

"They're coming now," I told them. "And don't be alarmed but—"

Just then, Bijoux leapt through the portal, and everyone jumped to their feet. Hands were going for weapons, but Bijoux sat at my feet and leaned against my legs with a yawn.

Rispan and Ree stepped through.

"Apologies!" Rispan was saying immediately. "She got ahead of me!"

I reached down and gave Bijoux another scratching behind her ears. She closed her eyes and started purring, but even her purr was frightening for those who weren't used to it.

CHAPTER FIFTEEN

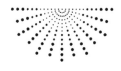

MIRA

*A*fter I made brief introductions all around, Iratzé and Edrigun led off to the palace.

"Anazhari, Mehrzad," I sent my thoughts to them as we approached the edge of the tents in the parade ground. *"Sorry, I should have reached out to you last night. I don't think we are going to need you two for a while. When we do need you, it will probably be fast and I'd use a portal. I'm thinking it might be better for you to be back in Su Lariano for now. Is that alright?"*

There was a brief pause before she answered.

"Mehrzad and I are not comfortable leaving you without protection," she said.

"I won't exactly be alone," I pointed out. *"And I'm not exactly without my own defenses. I do appreciate the concern, though. I already have a thread to you, but I should attach one to Mehrzad, too."*

"*Don't rely too much on those wings,*" Mehrzad said. "*Nothing beats good, solid footing in heavy winds. You call us as soon as you need anything.*"

"*I promise!*"

We were almost to where the *Rorujhen* were waiting, and I plucked a thread from the air for Mehrzad.

"Just a moment," I said to the others. "I'm sending Anazhari and Mehrzad back to Su Lariano for now."

I opened a portal for them using the thread to the pasture outside of Su Lariano.

"*Mira,*" Anazhari sent to me privately. "*I am aware you are struggling with the impulses of your winged form. It is not unlike my own... difficulty with certain impulses. But know that no matter your form, you are still yourself. You are the foundation.*"

"*Thank you, Anazhari.*" I smiled. "*I'll try to keep that in mind.*"

The *Rorujhen* went through the portal, and I closed it behind them. I nodded to Iratzé and Edrigun and we continued on our way.

The palace was more in the neo-gothic style of a fortified palace rather than a gothic castle. My mind was too busy to note much about the surroundings as we made our way to the king and queen.

Once more, introductions were made.

"As you mentioned when we spoke earlier," I said to Té Niya, "Zeg's army is too big to keep out indefinitely. But there are a few logistical issues to be figured out for any evacuation."

"We are thinking it would be better to send the civilians to Findias while consolidating our armies in Usolé," Iratzé said. "Our people can draw Zeg north."

"What's to stop Zeg from following the civilians to Findias?" Berowen asked.

"If we send them through a portal," I answered, "he wouldn't know where they'd gone. There'd be nothing for him to follow. Tesia is here because she can also make portals. Plus, she's a lot better at magic in general."

"But you said you needed an anchor for your destination in order to make a portal," Té Niya said. "This is something that still needs to be solved, correct?"

"Yes." I agreed. "What I'm thinking… if you have a map?"

She indicated a table nearby and I saw a map of the continent spread across it.

"I could fly south and find the city," I told them. "Once I can anchor one end of a thread there, I could portal back here and give the thread to Tesia."

"And Usolé?" Berowen asked. "You would do something similar there?"

"Right. To save time, I'd have Jack fly north

while I'm flying south," I explained. "Is that alright, Jack?"

Jack nodded in response.

"Once I've taken care of the Findias anchor," I went on, "I can portal to Jack in Usolé."

"Usolé is much further than Findias," Té Niya pointed out.

"Well, if he's not all the way there yet," I said, "I can finish the trip with him and set up the anchor. But there's still another issue to address. Supplies. My understanding is that Findias is an old, abandoned *Uthadé* city. There's no fields or farms there. There's no way Usolé is prepared to keep the *Wyl-Dunn* and *Ande Dannu* armies fed. You can only bring so much with you. Once Zeg takes this city, your supply lines from here will be gone."

"And this is why you have brought representatives from Su Lariano?" Berowen asked.

"Yes," I agreed. "But that won't be enough. You need more sources. I can get you more sources."

"Who?" Iratzé asked.

"Well," I told them, "I'm also a merchant."

"Oh, really?" Té Niya raised a cynical eyebrow.

"Based in Pokorah-Vo. I have a partner there. I need to get him here as well. He'll have a better idea what resources would be available."

"So, you're hoping to make some profit on this?" Berowen frowned.

"No," I shook my head. "I'm simply pulling together what resources I know of that might help the situation. Once I've got everyone together, I have other things I need to take care of. You're free to work out, or not, whatever you want with the various parties. You aren't obligated to do anything."

"But we may not have a lot of choice," he said. "That puts your people in a stronger position, yes?"

"You think I'm trying to take advantage of your situation?" I shook my head. "I'm offering to help out. You people have been practicing isolationism for a long time and if that means you don't have a lot of options you can't blame me for that. I'm offering to help because I *can*. I don't like the idea of a bunch of people dying over a war they never wanted in the first place. But in the end, this isn't my problem. It's yours. And it's your decision. Should we stay or should we go?"

With my last question, the song started playing in my head and I had to force it to stop. I looked at Té Niya and Berowen, waiting for their answer. Finally, Té Niya nodded.

"Collect your merchant partner," she said. "We should at least know our options."

"Alright." I nodded back. "And if you can have someone get maps to both Usolé and Findias that we could take with us? Ree," I looked at her. "Maybe you can discuss what Su Lariano can do while I go get Gralbast."

I knew the courtyard at Gralbast's place well

enough and I was already forming a portal. Before I stepped through, I attached a thread to Tesia. The portal was barely closed behind me before I was calling out.

"Gralbast? Are you here?"

I walked to his door, but it opened before I could put my hand on the doorknob.

"Mira!" He reached his long arms out and gave me a hug. "What a surprise! I'd heard you'd gone home to Earth."

"I did," I told him. "Sorry I didn't say goodbye, I was… I just needed to get away."

"Oh, don't worry about that," he said with a grin. "I was just playing a game of *jhianki* with Bavrana. Come in and have a drink with us."

I followed him inside and shared a hug with Bavrana while Gralbast poured me two fingers of goblin grog.

"This isn't really a social call," I said, accepting the drink. "There's a lot going on, and there's a city being evacuated. They are going to need supplies at their destination."

"What city?" Bavrana asked.

"Solaian," I told them.

They looked at each other blankly.

"It's on Danu," I explained. "The *Ande Dannu* will be sending their civilians to an abandoned *Uthadé* city and sending their army, and the *Wyl-*

Dunn army, to consolidate with the *Dannu Fé* in Usolé."

"Another world?" Gralbast let out a long breath. "That's going to be tough!"

I shook my head. "Tesia will be opening portals between locations. If we can set up your courtyard here as a staging area, she could run a portal to either Findias or Usolé as needed."

"We'd still need teamsters to load up the wagons and drive them through," Gralbast said. "We just won't have to go very far. What supplies do they need?"

"I'll let you work out the details and the terms," I told him. "But, be reasonable on rates. If you gouge them, they'll remember it."

"Don't forget who taught you!" Gralbast laughed. "Don't worry, this is a chance to open up a whole new world for business. We're not going to scare them away by taking advantage at the start of the relationship when they're in a bind."

"Speaking of which," I raised an eyebrow at him. "Tesia and I have our own business, Raven Transport, using portals to facilitate the transfer of goods. Don't forget you'll have to work out something with her for the portal service."

"Portal service!" Gralbast exclaimed. "You'd charge your partner for—"

Bavrana was laughing so hard that Gralbast stopped to look at her.

"What's so funny?" he demanded.

"Maybe you taught her too well." She grinned at him. "If it was you, would you do it for free?"

"Oh, don't encourage her!" He gave a mock scowl.

I swallowed what was left of my drink.

"We've no time to waste," I said. "Let me string a thread to your courtyard and we can join the meeting that's already underway."

"What meeting?" Gralbast asked. "With who?"

"Su Lariano will also be providing supplies," I said. "So, no, it isn't an exclusive deal."

"I suppose that would have been too much to hope for," Gralbast grumbled.

I tied a thread to a post at the side of Gralbast's courtyard. Then I found the thread to Tesia and opened a portal. We stepped through and I made introductions again.

"We have heard of *Urgaban*," Iratzé said. "But only in some of the oldest stories. There are none on this world so far as I know. You aren't what I would have expected from the stories."

"And we had no idea that any *Loiala Fé* had emigrated from Daoine," Gralbast said. "It is unfortunate that we meet in such dire circumstances."

"Excuse me, before you all start digging into the details," I said. "You don't need me and Jack for this part. Here's the thread to Gralbast's place," I said as I gave it to Tesia. "And here's the thread to the pasture outside of Su Lariano. That's probably good as a staging area." Then I turned to Té Niya and Berowen. "Were you able to get those maps? Jack will fly north, and I'll fly south."

"Fly?" Rispan asked.

"I'll explain later," I told him.

Jack and I were each given our respective maps and we took our leave from the group. Once we were outside the tent, I attached a thread to Jack. Jack shifted his form, and in a moment, he looked like a demon from a nightmare.

"Oh." I paused. "How do you change back and forth without ruining your clothes?"

"We'll have to worry about that lesson another time," he said. "For now, I suggest simply removing the shirt and storing it in your pack until you need it. You can wear the pack on your back between your wings."

I scowled at that but did as he recommended. Then I tried to shift, but nothing happened.

"Well?" He looked at me expectantly.

"I can't change," I told him.

He studied my face for a moment before responding.

"I sense some abhorrence in you for your other form," he said. "This is new, yes?"

I blinked at him.

"Umm… I suppose," I said.

"Why?"

"I don't know," I shrugged. "Maybe because of how bloodthirsty I was last time?"

"You mean when you single-handedly drove the enemy from the city walls?" he asked. "Saving the lives of countless residents? You see this as a bad thing?"

"No, I… I don't know."

"Your other form is that of a predator," he said. "The impulses and instincts that come with that are new to you. In the heat of battle, those instincts can be almost overwhelming. But they will not change your nature. And the more familiar you become with those instincts, the better control you will have of them."

"But what if I can't control them?"

"I spent much time on this world observing the people here," Jack said. "Looking into their minds. It amazed me how often they would have thoughts or impulses that were apparently contrary to acceptable behavior in their culture. I take it humans are similar in this?"

"Yeah, I guess so," I agreed. "We have negative thoughts, or maybe we feel an impulse to do something bad or stupid. We don't follow through with them, though. Mostly."

"Yes," he agreed. "The vast majority of these thoughts I observed were simply ignored or discarded. Being human, I imagine you are quite adept at this. But now you are faced with thoughts and impulses you aren't used to having. I am sure you will find them just as manageable when you are accustomed to them."

"Maybe."

"Right now," he went on, "the success of your plans, and many lives, depend on you accepting that aspect of yourself. Accepting it and knowing that despite these new thoughts, you are still yourself."

What he was saying made sense. I was still afraid, though. I knew enough mythology to know that the closest thing to what I'd become was a harpy, and I knew that they didn't have a good reputation. They were definitely considered monsters. What if I couldn't control it and ended up *really* becoming a monster? I let out a heavy breath. Even if I ended up becoming a monster, that didn't change what he'd said about lives depending on me. Would I sacrifice my humanity to save all those people?

When I put the question in those terms, I knew the answer.

I closed my eyes and felt for the *Ralabo*. But I also connected to the *Ralahin*. I opened my eyes, and I was seeing the two aspects together as a network of particles. I felt for the dimension points that were part of my new form and expanded into them.

I spread my wings wide and felt the power in them, the strength.

"Alright," I told him. "I'll come to you once I get the thread to Findias back to Tesia."

I launched myself into the air and headed south. I remembered something about planes being able to go faster at higher altitudes, so I flew higher and higher.

I was reminded of the feeling of freedom with the wind in my face when I'd been sailing, but this was so much... *more!* The wind carried me south along the coast. My hair streamed out behind me, and I could see for miles in all directions. I felt more free and more powerful than I'd ever felt in my life. The sky was mine and it was almost intoxicating.

I also noticed that my vision was better than before. I could see further – even from this height I could make out details of the landscape below me. I gave a wry smile when I saw a rabbit crossing a grassy hill. I'd certainly never go hungry in this form. Though I would still prefer my meat to be cooked.

I'd glanced at the map given to me by the *Ande Dannu* before folding it and tucking it into the back pocket of my jeans. I didn't need it. Findias, my destination, was close to five hundred miles away from Solaian, but it was right on the coast. From this height, I should be able to see it in a couple of hours.

I didn't know if it was a natural thing or if it was something to do with the magic, but flying was effortless. When I finally touched down on top of the walls of Findias a few hours later, I wasn't tired at all. The city had been large; even bigger than Solaian. Even though it had been abandoned for centuries, most of the buildings were in decent shape. Of course, plant life had taken over a lot of it, but it wouldn't take much to make a good portion of the city livable again.

I tied a thread to the north gate and was about to open a portal back to Tesia when I heard a scraping noise coming from somewhere inside the city. I took to the air to investigate; I needed to make sure the city would be safe for the *Ande Dannu* citizens.

I followed the sound, and it led me to the harbor-side of the city. As I got closer, I saw that this part of the city wasn't in as good shape as the rest. At least half of the buildings had collapsed and I could see enormous tunnels carved into the debris.

There was some sort of pit or sinkhole in the middle of the district. It was at least thirty yards across. I flew over it to get a better look, but the hole was deep and in shadow; I couldn't see very far. The walls were sheer as far as I could see, and I couldn't tell whether it was natural.

I made a few passes, getting lower each time. I didn't want to actually fly into it because it might be tricky having to fly back out. When I stretched out my wings, they were probably twenty-five feet from tip to tip. That didn't leave much room to spiral up out of the hole if I flew into it.

I made another slow pass just over the top. Air was suddenly rushing at me from the depths, carrying with it a putrid odor. I flapped my wings hard to pick up speed and just made it past the far edge when something huge went past me.

I spun to see what it was but the space was empty. I circled back and something struck me, sending me crashing to the ground.

"WHO DARES TRESPASS ON MY DOMAIN?" a voice thundered in my head.

CHAPTER SIXTEEN

MIRA

I looked up to see an immense creature looking down on me. It could probably swallow a *gajhanti* in one gulp. It was a serpent, but it had brightly colored feathers and wings and it hovered in the air above me. I could feel the raw power radiating from it. This wasn't something I could hope to challenge, but it was intelligent; hopefully, it could be reasoned with.

"I'm Mira," I said. "There was no intent to trespass. It is generally believed that this city, Findias, is unoccupied."

"DOES IT LOOK UNOCCUPIED?" the voice thundered again.

"Please," I said. "Your thoughts are too strong. Could you send them more softly? I'm not here to offend or challenge you. I'm here on a humanitarian mission. Maybe you could help."

"Why should I help anyone?" The thoughts came in at a more manageable level. *"I have no need of anyone."*

"That's the only time help is genuine," I pointed out. "If someone is only helping another for what they themselves can get out of it, they're really only helping themselves. It's when someone helps and has nothing to gain from it, or even when there is a cost to themselves, that they truly show their greatness and their compassion."

"Well," the creature responded, *"you're a slick one, aren't you? Explain this mission of yours."*

"There's a war being fought north of here. Kartahn Zeg, a necromancer, has riled up the *Bahréth* people and is attempting to conquer, well… everything. We want to draw him further north. At the same time, we were looking for a place to evacuate the civilians. Someone mentioned the abandoned *Uthadé* city of Findias as a good choice. We didn't know you were here, of course."

"You want to bring people here? To my *city?"*

"That was the intent, yes," I said. "But since you have made Findias your home, it would be up to you. May I ask your name?"

"I am Kékoatalki," he answered. At least, I was getting more of a *he* vibe from the creature.

"Pleased to meet you," I said. "I've never encountered anyone of your species before."

"No, there are rarely more than a few of us on any world," Kékoatalki said. *"We tend to live solitary lives. I've not seen another of my kind for millennia."*

"That sounds lonely," I said.

"Not at all," he answered. *"We come together at least once or twice every ten thousand years. There's another one fairly soon, in fact."*

"Oh? When is that? Will it be here?"

"Here? Oh, no," he said. *"No world could contain us all together. It* is *coming up though. Less than two thousand years. I'll need to start preparing soon. I can't be distracted now by visitors."*

My mind was reeling from his perspective on the scale of time and I tried to orient my response to accommodate the concepts as he saw them.

"Of course we would not want to distract you from your preparations," I agreed. "But there is no chance of that. The refugees would come and go in scarcely a blink of an eye for you."

I actually didn't know what the average lifespan was for *Loiala Fé,* but I was sure it didn't compare to Kékoatalki's.

"And perhaps," I added. "It would provide you with an amusing story to tell the others when you see them."

"Perhaps," he mused.

"And news of your benevolence would—"

"Enough!" Kékoatalki cut me off. *"They can come. Temporarily. And I will watch over them. But they cannot settle close to my lair."*

With that, Kékoatalki disappeared back into the hole.

"Thank you!" I called after him.

There was no response. For someone who lived as long as he apparently did, Kékoatalki was remarkably impatient.

I found the thread on my wrist to Tesia and formed the portal. A moment later, I was back at the meeting in Solaian.

"I have news," I said. "And an interesting development."

Both Tesia and Rispan were looking at me with wide eyes like I was a stranger. I realized I was still in my winged form and they'd never seen it.

"It's me," I said to them. "Mira."

Rispan's jaw dropped open and his eyes got even bigger.

"No time for that now," I told him. I turned back to the others. "Findias is not unoccupied. There's a huge, feathered serpent living there near the harbor. His name is Kékoatalki. But he said it's alright to use the city as long as it's temporary and people stay clear of his *lair*."

"Maybe we can just drive this Kékoatalki from the city," Berowen suggested. "Then our people could stay as long as they want. Go where they want."

"No," I said, shaking my head. "You didn't see him. You do *not* want to piss this guy off, and if you attack him, that's all that will happen. He may very well be the most powerful being on this planet."

"In that case, I think we should accommodate his wishes," Té Niya said.

I gave the thread to Tesia and found the one for Jack. I could tell he was flying; this would be a different sort of trip for me.

"Alright," I said. "Now for the next part."

I opened the portal. As I stepped toward it, Rispan called me from behind.

"Sis?" I looked over my shoulder at him and saw a grin plastered on his face. "You really *are* a badass!"

I gave him a wink and launched myself through the portal, expanding my wings as soon as I was through. Then I was in the air, flying next to Jack.

I gave him an update on what had happened as we flew.

"I have heard of this species," he said. "Many worlds have various myths and legends about such creatures. They have been called serpents, snakes, worms, and other things. My kind names them *Borosoor*. They are considered gods or demi-gods; they are indeed primordial beings. Some stories have them eating their tails, though I hardly find this creditable. Some even believe that their entire world rests on one of these *Borosoor* and the world would end if they should wake."

"That doesn't surprise me," I said. "He was pretty... impressive. You wouldn't want one of those as an enemy. It would be impossible to fight something like that."

"Perhaps," he looked at me out of the side of his eyes. "Have you ever considered how you could use your portals as a weapon?"

"As a weapon? No. I don't see how they could be."

"What do you suppose would happen if you closed a portal while someone was only partly through?" he asked. "Even a creature such as a *Borosoor* would have difficulty surviving such an experience. Though I imagine it might take some practice to be able to open and close a portal at just the right place and right time."

"Let's hope I never have to try it," I said, imagining the results.

We flew on in silence for several minutes before I thought of something else.

"You know," I said. "Here we are going to Usolé to set up a portal that an army will go through. Have the *Ande Dannu* actually discussed this with the *Dannu Fé*?"

"That, I could not say. They have no means for instant communication, but they could have sent a messenger on *gurpahn*. Do you think we should check with their leaders to make sure? I believe that would be Queen Maeve and King Ayrik."

I shook my head, though I wasn't sure he could see it.

"No, I don't want to get into that," I told him. "Let's just find a good spot that's close but not *too* close to the city. They can handle their own coordination."

A few hours later, the city of Usolé was in sight. We landed in a clearing that was about a half-day's march along the road to Usolé. It was getting quite dark, but from what we could see, the spot seemed like it would be sufficient. I attached a thread to a tree at the edge of the clearing. Once the other end was secure on my wrist, I located the thread to Tesia and opened a portal.

This time, Tesia wasn't in the room with all the royalty anymore. She was in a room that was evidently her quarters. Rispan was seated with her at a table and Bijoux was curled up in a corner, napping. One side of the room had a wide opening that led to a balcony. We were looking down on the city from several floors up.

"Nice view," I remarked. "How'd everything go?"

"We managed to escape," Rispan said with a grin. "The mucky-mucks were working out all the details. It was pretty boring and we weren't needed."

"They will send for me when they need a portal," Tesia added.

There were platters of food on the table, and they had evidently finished eating.

"I could use some of that," I said. "I'm starving!"

I started toward the table with Jack and then I stopped.

"Hang on," I said.

I concentrated on the *Ralabo* and my form. After a moment, my shape dissolved into my regular human form. I took off my backpack and pulled out a shirt. Once I'd slipped it on I joined them at the table and I listened to them make small-talk as I ate. Finally, I leaned back in my chair and patted my stomach.

"Much better!" I grinned.

"If you eat much more, I don't think you'd be able to fly," Rispan smirked.

I gave him a token scowl and then turned to Jack, who'd also resumed his human-like appearance.

"How do you manage to change shape and grow wings and not destroy your clothes?" I asked him.

"I just put them in a pocket," he answered. "That's the easiest."

"A pocket?"

"You could do the same," he said with a nod. "In fact, I know you can wear that pack when you shift and it just stays centered between your wings, but you could put it in a pocket as well. It might be easier than carrying it all the time."

"A pocket?" I asked again. "My pockets aren't that big."

He gave me a confused look for a moment and then his eyes got big.

"No, no," he said. "Not that kind of pocket. It's more like a folded piece of space. You can put things in it. It's a relatively simple spell once you get the hang of it."

"Show me," I prompted him.

Jack reached his hand forward and it disappeared into some invisible… *something.* A moment later, he drew it back out and he held a shirt.

"Wait," I told him, connecting to both *Ralahin* and *Ralabo.* "Do that again."

It was really just what he had said. He had folded space to make a pocket and I watched him put the shirt back inside.

I tried to duplicate what he had done, and the folded space formed in front of me. I picked up my pack and placed it inside the folded space.

"Very good," Jack said. "We have ways to keep this with us. From what I understand about your use of magic, you would probably tie a tether to the space so it will always be with you."

I did as he said, letting the opening of the folded space close. Then I opened it again and reached in, finding my backpack. I left it there and let the opening close again.

"Thanks!" I grinned. "That's definitely going to come in handy! I can think of a lot of things I could put in there."

"Since the objects do not share your space," he explained, "they have no weight or dimension to hamper you. Eventually, you will be able to simply *will* something on your person into the space, such as clothing."

Just then there was a pounding on the door and Zoriaa rushed in without waiting for anyone to answer.

"I was hoping you'd be back," she was looking at me. "Usoa's outside the walls. We have to help her."

"What happened?" I asked. "What's she doing out there?"

"She went to see the *gurpahn,* to the nursery where the young ones are cared for," she said. "I only just heard about this. The adult *gurpahn* brought their young when they came here to Solaian, but the orphans were too afraid of the city and refused to come inside."

"*Gurpahn* orphans?"

"Yes," she answered. "Many *gurpahn* were killed in that battle near Tyr nya Lu. You remember Usoa mentioned that boy who worked with the *gurpahn*? Xantif? The one who died?" I nodded. "I think Usoa has gone to get the orphans for him, because he loved the *gurpahn* so much. Plus, she knows many of them as well, since she often helped him in his work."

I could see it. In fact, I envied her. I'd had nothing that I could do for Mooren, to honor him. If I had, there would have been nothing that could have kept me from doing it. I had no doubt that Usoa would have found a way to get out of the city.

"I tried to get the city guards to help, or some other *Wyl-Dunn*," she went on. "But none were willing to risk soldiers for one person and some *gurpahn* kits."

"Right," I said. "Do you know where they are?"

She nodded. "I was told where the kits had stopped and gathered. They are probably still in that area. But it's not far from the *Bahréth*. If they catch her... They won't be as understanding as Radomér."

"Jack?" I looked at him. "Are you ready for another short flight?"

"Indeed," he said, getting to his feet.

"It's outside the walls but near the harbor," she added. "The *Bahréth* captured the harbor days ago and they've been filling ships with soldiers and sailing them east."

"Why would they do that?" I asked.

"They don't need their entire army for Solaian," she said. "Perhaps they intend to conquer the *Fél-bahlag* as well?"

I shrugged, turning my attention back to the task at hand. Usoa had been on foot, but we didn't know how much of a lead she had on us. We went to the balcony and shifted forms. I cursed under my breath; I'd forgotten to take my shirt off and had just ruined another one.

Jack and I took to the air, leaving my boots behind us, heading beyond the walls to the north where they met the shore. There was a lot of *Bahréth* movement to and from the harbor and few ships were left. With the night sky above us, we flew unseen above the working troops.

Zoriaa had described an embankment along the beach. My enhanced vision was even more useful at night, and we were able to fly high and get a better look at things further away. Ahead and below I could see the promontory of rock extending into the ocean that we were looking for; the young *gurpahn* should be just on the other side of it. Then I saw Usoa, she had just climbed past the promontory, and I could see the kits coming out of the nearby rocks and going to her. They all seemed happy to see her and some were rolling and playing. There was one adolescent that was larger than the rest, but most were under three feet tall at the shoulder.

What Usoa couldn't see was the two *Bahréth* coming up fast behind her. I steepened my angle of flight, trying to put on more speed to get to Usoa before the *Bahréth*. Jack was right beside me. The wind was in my eyes, but I had an extra inner eyelid that blinked horizontally to help protect them. There was no way we were going to get there in time. The *Bahréth* leapt past the crest of the promontory and one had grabbed Usoa before she could react.

I could hear the screeching roars of the young *gurpahn* as they attacked the *Bahréth*, trying to defend Usoa. The one holding Usoa went down quickly and the kits were tearing him apart. The other had drawn his sword and hammer and was swinging at the kits. One kit had its wing nearly severed and another took the hammer to the ribs, throwing it several feet away into a large boulder.

And then I arrived.

I screamed and the *Bahréth* froze, a look of terror on his face before I ripped his head from his body with my talons. Then I rushed to Usoa, but she was already trying to care for the injured *gurpahn*.

The one that had been struck by the hammer was dead. Its chest had been caved in and its head had been crushed when it hit the boulder. The other kit was bleeding profusely from where its wing had been cut.

"Help me!" Usoa looked up at me. "She's going to die!"

I did the fastest thing I could think of and opened a portal to Tesia. I grabbed the wounded kit and indicated the others with a nod.

"Bring them through!" I told her.

Then I was through the portal and into Tesia's quarters.

"We need a healer!" I called.

Tesia had jumped to help, grabbing the table-cloth to bind the wound.

"I just called Ree on my comm-dev," she said. "She's on her way. She's a healer."

I could attest to that. She'd healed me enough times. Usoa had come through the portal with the other kits. They stalked around the room as if looking for something else to attack.

It was only a few minutes before Ree rushed through the door. This startled the kits and they screeched. They moved toward Ree but Usoa called to them.

"Calm down!" she ordered them. "She's here to help."

I don't know if they were responding to her words or her tone, but they immediately dropped their heads and skulked away.

Ree hadn't even noticed the interchange as she

had already started to work on the injured *gurpahn.* We all stood in silence and waited while she worked. Eventually, she gave a sigh of relief and leaned back.

"She will survive," Ree said. "And I believe she will be able to use that wing, but it won't be any-time soon."

"Thank you!" Usoa rushed to Ree and wrapped her arms around her. "I thought I was going to lose her, too."

Ree was surprised but returned the hug.

The kits had stopped skulking and had started playing; their antics were endangering the furni-ture. That got Usoa's attention. She looked around and saw a doorway to the bedroom. She opened the door and then turned back to face the room.

"Hey!" She called. All the *gurpahn* stopped what they were doing and looked at her. "Play in here!" She pointed to the bedroom.

The kits all rushed past her into the room, and she closed the door behind them. Only the oldest one stayed in the room. He had a vibe like he felt he was above the games the others were playing.

"That was too close," I said, scowling. "Usoa, you could have been killed! Or captured!"

"I know," she said. "But I couldn't leave them out there to die, could I?"

"No," I relented. "Of course not. But I would have helped you if you'd told me."

"You weren't around," she said with a shrug.

I couldn't fault her. The bottom line was that she had done what she thought was right despite the personal danger. That's really all we had a right to ask of anyone.

Jack and I both shifted back to our human forms. I pulled my pack out of my "pocket" and put on a fresh shirt before returning the pack to the folded space.

"Hey," Rispan said to Usoa with a grin. "I'm the one with the reputation for getting into trouble. I'm not looking for competition."

"I don't think there's any danger of that," I told him with a raised eyebrow.

"I don't know," he said. "You come pretty close. How come you still haven't found your sister?" he asked. "Haven't you been here long enough?"

"I know," I said with a sigh. "I finally know where she is, but I don't know how to get there."

"Oh? Where is she?"

"She's in Iyoké," I answered. "In Félbahrin."

"Isn't that where all the ships were going?" he smirked. "The ones with the *Bahréth*? Maybe your sister is a magnet for trouble, too."

"With all the ships being taken," I said. "I don't know how I'm going to be able to get to her."

"Why don't you just make a portal?" Usoa asked.

"I don't have an anchor where she is," I said. "I don't have a thread to follow."

"You have a thread to her, right?" she asked. "I told you; you have lots of threads. Not ones you created on purpose, but ones that developed naturally from your connection with a person. One of them must be for her."

Right. One of those super thin threads that I had trouble even seeing.

"We're pretty strongly connected," I said. "If I had a natural connection to anyone, there'd be one to Nora."

"Let's try to find it," she suggested.

"Okay," I shrugged.

Usoa might be young, but already she seemed to be able to pick up magic a lot easier than I had. I connected to the *Ralahin* and tried to look at myself and my connections. Of course, I saw a whole tangle of threads I'd tied to my wrist, but those were easy. Try as I might, I couldn't see any other connections.

"I'm clearly not as good at this as you are, Usoa," I said. "I don't see them."

"Try what you did last time," she said. "When you found your thread to me. Think of Nora. Think of sending to her."

"Sending what?"

"Anything," she said. "Energy. Emotion."

While still looking with the *Ralahin*, I pictured

Nora's face in my mind, really focusing on it. Then I pushed a desire to communicate toward my concept of her. A thread flared briefly, and I grabbed it before it could disappear.

"I think I have it!" I said. "I have something, anyway."

"Send your awareness to the other end and see if it's her."

That part was easy, I'd done it enough times before when creating portals. I sensed the other end. It was Nora! She was there!"

"It's her!" I said. "I found her!"

Then I sensed something else on Nora's side of the connection going on around her.

"There's fighting!" I told them. "She's in danger!"

I didn't stop to think, I ripped a portal into existence and leapt through, drawing my sword and shifting forms at the same time. I cursed as I realized I'd just destroyed my last shirt.

I was standing on some sort of platform or landing on the side of a building that angled further up toward the sky. There were two groups of soldiers fighting each other, but I couldn't tell who was a threat and who was an ally. I looked around and saw Nora.

"Which ones are the bad guys?" I asked her.

"What?" She gawked at me.

"Who's the enemy?"

"Um… The ones with the blue symbol on their chests."

I launched myself forward, knocking one from the landing and slashing at another with my sword. Jack had come through with me and he attacked another one, the sword in his hand glowing a bright white. And there was Rispan. And Usoa! What was she doing here? The remaining soldiers with the blue emblems were putting down their weapons and getting to their knees with their hands raised.

A man in a robe snarled and pulled a knife from inside his robe.

"Your heresy is responsible for this!" He glared at Nora. "Now you must die!"

He launched himself at Nora, who stood frozen in shock. My sword flicked out and his head went spinning into the air to fall over the edge of the landing, his lifeless body tumbled after it.

CHAPTER SEVENTEEN

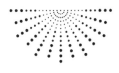

NORA

The winged woman moved so fast I could barely follow her with my eyes. She slammed into one of Ayala's soldiers, knocking him over the edge. Her sword slashed at another, cutting through his armor as though it was nothing. Beyond her I saw Jack. What was he doing here? He was swinging a glowing sword against two of Ayala's men. There were others with them, but I didn't know them.

Then Ayala's soldiers were putting their weapons down and giving up. Ayala's head snapped around and he sent me a look of intense hatred. His hand went inside his robe.

"Your heresy is responsible for this!" he snarled.

He leapt toward me, a dagger flashing in the

moonlight. Then the winged woman lashed out with her sword and the last thing I saw on the Grand Inquisitor's face as his head went over the edge was surprise.

"Nora, are you alright?" the woman was asking me. Half of her body was black, or a blue that was so dark it was almost black, and the other side was white. It was disconcerting.

"I'm… yes," I answered. "I'm fine."

"So," a young man was looking at me with a grin. "This is your sister?"

Sister?

The winged woman was looking around. Then she seemed satisfied and sheathed her sword. The palace guards looked uncertain about the new arrivals. Then one snapped a command and they brought their lances to bear, ready in case the strangers were going to attack them.

"What's going on here?" the winged woman asked.

It was Shahz who answered.

"We are about to have a royal wedding," he said. "There was some… disagreement as to the type of ceremony we should have." Then he spoke louder so that the crowd below could hear him. "Véshdani's will has been made clear! We have received the blessing and protection of Véshdani this night!"

"Um…" The woman frowned. "We don't know any Véshdani."

"Still." Shahz shrugged with a grin. "We appreciate your help."

Shahz signaled to the soldiers, and they lowered their weapons. They started removing bodies and escorted the prisoners from the landing.

"Who's getting married?" she asked. Then her head spun to me with surprise. "You?"

"No." I shook my head. "Princess Luana and Prince Edrigun."

There was something familiar about the woman, but I was sure I didn't know her. She'd be hard to forget.

"What… Who are you?" I asked her.

Her slitted eyes widened in surprise, but then she looked down at herself as though in embarrassment.

"Right," she said. "You don't recognize me. Um… I don't suppose you have a spare shirt with you? Never mind."

Then her body started to shift. Her wings shrunk and disappeared. Her clawed fingers became normal hands and her talons turned into regular feet. The long, straight hair became more wavy. Then her eyes and face shifted. The face that looked at me was familiar, but I was still sure I hadn't met this woman. And she was topless.

I pulled my bag from my shoulder and pulled out a spare shirt.

"It's not clean," I said, handing it to her. "But it's something."

"Thanks!" She slipped it on. It was too large, but all I had were hand-me-downs.

She looked at me with a smile, but then it faltered.

"Right," she shook her head. "Nora, a lot has happened. I know I look a lot older, but it's me. Mira."

"Mira?" I was stunned. "No... Mira is... Who are you?"

"Close your eyes," she told me. "You know we're connected. You can feel that it's me."

I was shaking my head, but I closed my eyes anyway. This was crazy! Mira was sixteen years old. This woman had to be close to thirty!

I opened my magical senses to her. It *was* her! This was the Mira I thought had died! This was the Mira who said she was coming for me!

"Mira?" My eyes snapped open. "What happened?"

Before she could answer I had crossed the space between us and wrapped my arms around her.

"I've been so worried about you," she said, hugging me back.

Then she pulled back, embarrassed, and looked at Shahz.

"I'm sorry," she told him. "Your ceremony. Who are the bride and groom again?"

She gave my hand a quick squeeze. "We'll swap stories later," she said under her breath.

"Prince Inigon, heir to the throne of Félbahrin, and Princess Luana Aloso of the *Kajoran* people," he said.

"Please inform both highnesses," Mira spoke louder, somehow magnifying her voice the way Shahz had, "that Mirabela nya Balangur, *Ashae* noble by right of conquest and ambassador of the *Ulané Jhinura* of Su Lariano on Daoine, and her diplomatic party, have come to pay our respects and witness their union. Included in our party is Prince Karis Ulané Panalira, who is also one of Su Lariano's diplomats."

Ambassador?

The man who had grinned at me earlier scowled.

"Just Rispan is fine," he said.

I noticed a huge, six-legged lion of some sort sitting at his feet. It was sniffing the air and looking suspiciously at Spike. Spike looked agitated and had his attention on a young griffin.

"Also present to witness the union," Mira went on, "is Usoa of the *Wyl-Dunn* and Jack..." She paused to look at him.

"Jakareal Abalaan," he supplied.

"Jakareal Abalaan of the *Daijheen*," she finished.

267

This wasn't the same Mira I knew. This Mira was much more confident. No sixteen-year-old could possibly step in and manage the situation so smoothly like she was doing. And the way she looked when she first got here... and she'd killed those soldiers, and even Palben Ayala, so easily.

"Our blessings from Véshdani are great in number," Shahz announced to the crowd. "We have witnesses representing Earth, *Ashae*, *Ulané Jhinura*, *Wyl-Dunn*, *Sokwané* of Ranolan, and you, the people of Iyoké. Do we have any other representatives present?"

I looked out over the crowd and saw that someone was pushing their way through to the steps. It was Corana. She had survived! Corlen was close behind her.

"Captain Lélé Corana and Corlen Veranu of the *Kajoran* people join us as well," Shahz said. "Bringing the blessings of Véshdani to seven!"

The crowd had been too uncertain of how to respond to the fighting and the news, but now applause started up here and there until everyone was clapping and cheering as Corana and Corlen ascended the steps.

Shahz was whispering something to one of the palace guards, who nodded and disappeared inside the Ziggurat.

"Véshdani does not dictate our lives," Shahz

said to the crowd. "He gives us the freedom to make our own choices, but he does provide signs and hints for guidance, if we but look to see them. From what I can see, my friends, the signs are most auspicious!"

The crowd cheered at this. Meanwhile, one of the soldiers came over to get us all to step to the side for the ceremony.

"The time of presentation has come!" Shahz said.

Trumpets sounded. At least, they sounded like trumpets. A *Félbahlag* man and woman stepped out of the doorway and stepped to the front of the landing. They both wore crowns. The man's expression was anxious, and the woman looked resigned. The crowd's applause wasn't as enthusiastic as the response had been for Shahz. I assumed this was King Unais Elizondo the Third and his wife Queen Arama. I had thought they had fled the city. News that he had abdicated had spread, and the crowd wasn't sure what to make of him. The two took their place on the other side of the landing.

The trumpets sounded again and Inigon and Luana stepped out of the doorway to the front of the landing. Inigon's eyes flicked to each of us curiously.

Luana was radiant in her bright red *dai so* dress. It had golden embroidery at her collar, cuffs, and hem. The embroidery also adorned her shoulders and chest and came to a point just below her waist. On her head was an intricate, golden headdress that almost lent itself to the appearance of a halo or an aura. This must be the *chakuta* she had mentioned.

Inigon was dressed in a black military style jacket with gold embroidery that matched the gold in Luana's dress. He wore a red sash around his waist the same color as her dress. He looked older than his fifteen years.

Side by side, Inigon and Luana faced the crowd. Behind them, Shahz ascended the upper stairs of the Ziggurat, the embroidered symbol plain on his back. When he had reached the top, he turned to face forward.

"Let us open our hearts in prayer," he said.

The cheers and murmuring whispers from below had stopped and all eyes were turned to him. Shahz raised his hands, palms upwards, and closed his eyes. I saw many people below us take the same posture, so I mirrored it as well. Except I kept my eyes open.

"Great Infinite One," Shahz's voice rang out. "Prime Mover Unmoved, Creator of creators whom we call Véshdani and to whom many names have been given but for whom names and identities are meaningless, we ask that you hear our prayer.

"We give thanks to the impetus toward exis-tence You have bestowed upon us, and for Your gift of freedom of choice which allows us to become the imperfect individuals we are and allows us to become the creators of our own lives, for good or ill.

"We seek Your wisdom that we might make better choices in the pursuit of our goals.

"We seek Your vision that we might better navigate our lives in a manner that benefits all, not only ourselves or those close to us.

"We ask Your blessing in our efforts to end hatred and fear, for to hate another is to hate You, and to fear another is to fear ourselves.

"Oh, Véshdani, we also ask for your blessing in the joining of Inigon Elizondo and Luana Alosa, that their partnership be fruitful and harmonious.

"May it be so."

He lowered his hands and descended the stairs to where the rest of us stood on the staging area.

"Witnesses behold!" He said. "All present whether in spirit or in body, *Félbahlag* and *Kajoran*, visitors from other realms, Véshdani, Shan, A'iwanea and the Noélani, all witness and behold, for this is indeed an auspicious day. Know these two people for who they are; Inigon Elizondo and Luana Alaso."

The crowd cheered and Shahz paused.

"Inigon Elizondo," he continued when the noise had died down. "Before you stands Luana Alaso. Do you deem her admirable and worthy as your equal partner in life, and do you accept her as such before all witnesses here, both mortal and divine?"

"I accept her as such," Inigon answered.

"Luana Alaso, before you stands Inigon Elizondo. Do you deem him admirable and worthy as your equal partner in life, and do you accept him as such before all witnesses here, both mortal and divine?"

"I accept him as such," Luana said.

Shahz placed Luana's left hand in Inigon's right. Then he wrapped a red ribbon around the joined hands.

"This ribbon is a physical representation of the bond you have made," Shahz intoned. "Walk now to the apex. With each rising step, your bond will solidify until your union is complete for all to see."

Shahz stepped to the side. Luana and Inigon, hand in hand, made their way up the stairs to the top. Luana's huge train draped across the steps behind them, spreading to show more golden embroidery. They rotated to face the crowd and raised their joined hands. Cheering erupted again. With an expert flick of her wrist, Luana whipped the long train around and out of her way. Luana and Inigon came back down the stairs and the cheering subsided as they retook their places by Shahz.

"On this day," Shahz said to the crowd, "we have witnessed the union of not only a man and a woman as husband and wife, but also a union of nations. May peace and prosperity reign for all. This union is complete!"

Cheering erupted again and I could also hear the sounds of instruments. I guessed it was now party time for the city.

CHAPTER EIGHTEEN

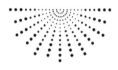

NORA

*L*uana and Inigon turned and went into the Ziggurat. Nériala immediately motioned for the rest of us to follow her through the door as well. As soon as we were in the sloping corridor heading down, she spoke in low tones.

"Now we have an emergency session of the Senate," she said to me. "We will need to have Inigon, and the regency, confirmed. I'm not sure how the death of Palben Ayala is going to change things. Plus, we now have two chairs to fill instead of one. We'll need to get your party to a safe location."

"Is it a closed session?" Rispan asked.

Nériala glanced at him from the corner of her eyes.

"That has not been specified," she said. "Why?"

"From my experience," he grinned, "emergency sessions can be pretty entertaining."

She frowned at him, thinking.

"Since it was not announced as a closed session, we can probably justify bringing you all in as audience," she said. "I suppose there's not a safer location than the council chamber."

"Problem solved." He winked.

We wound deeper into the Ziggurat than I'd been before until we arrived at a large room. There was a stage with a long table in a semicircle at one end with chairs positioned so that when they were in use, everyone seated could see each other. The opposite side of the room had rows of seats. Most of the chairs on the other side of the curved table were occupied by men who were already in some kind of argument.

We followed Nériala down the central aisle and took a chunk of seats in the front two rows. No sooner had we found our seats than another group of people entered the room. These all wore brown robes, except for one whose robes were white. There were seven of them altogether. The ones in the brown robes took seats on the other side of the aisle from us. The man in the white robes moved to join the men behind the curved table.

By now, the arguing people started to take notice that they weren't alone and one of them signaled for the others to be quiet.

"Forgive me, Your Holiness," one of the men said to the white-robed man. "This is a closed session. I am afraid only members of the Senate may be present. We will need to ask everyone else to leave."

"You speak out of turn, Count Zabala," another man said. "This session wasn't called as a closed session. Therefore, any who wish to do so may observe." He turned to the man in the white robe. "Your presence is appreciated, Your Holiness. I hope it will have a calming effect."

"Thank you, Duke Gabiran," the man replied, with a humble bow of his head. I was getting my first look at the man who was originally going to marry Luana, but now was the target for Nériala. "With the passing of Palben Ayala, I am here to assume his position on the Senate as a representative of the clergy."

The duke's eyebrows rose in surprise.

"With all respect, Your Holiness," he said. "That would need to be approved by the council. We can add it to the agenda, but for now, I must ask you to be seated with your brethren in the audience."

The man they were calling His Holiness wasn't happy about that, but he nodded and sat with the others in the audience. Luana and Inigon had come in and took seats in the audience as well.

"Now then," Gabiran said. "As the ranking

member, I will officially call this meeting to order."
He snapped a gavel onto the table.

"You are not the chairman of the Senate Council," Zabala objected.

"You are correct, Count," he agreed. "But as the senior member of the nobility present, I will act in that capacity until such time as we *do* have a chairman. I believe the first point of order is dealing with the abdication of King Elizondo."

"We are down by three members," one of the men said. "Any vote runs the risk of a tie. Perhaps we should address Ayala's replacement first."

"Baron Danel Gartza makes a good point," Gabiran admitted. "We are indeed down by three members and a tie should be avoided at all costs. That in mind, I move that we promote Baronet Eskivel to the rank of general and appoint him to the council to replace General Igonez as the military representative on the council. Do I have a second?"

"Seconded!" Another man raised his hand.

"Thank you, Count Uftzi—"

"Wait a minute!" Danel interrupted. "I said we should replace Ayala! You are out of order!"

"Forgive me, Baron Danel." Gabiran looked at him innocently. "There was no motion on the floor."

Danel opened his mouth to speak and then slammed it shut and glared at Gabiran.

"We have a motion on the floor regarding

Baronet Eskivel," Gabiran continued. "Arguments?"

"*Major* Eskivel has no experience in governance," Danel snapped. "He's just a soldier. He's only a mid-level officer."

"He is *indeed* a soldier." Gabiran agreed. "But he is not inexperienced. He was the alcalde in Carabora for two years under Baron Rotger. As we all know, Baron Rotger served under the tutelage of the esteemed Count Zabala. If the baron was in better health, I would have nominated him. Unfortunately, it does not seem his recovery will be a short one and we need someone who is available now. I am sure Eskivel will serve us as well as Rotger. What are your thoughts, Count Zabala?"

"I tend to agree with your assessment," Zabala said.

"In favor?" Gabiran prompted.

The majority of the senators raised a hand.

"Opposed?"

Danel and a few others raised their hands.

"The motion carries," Gabiran said with a strike of his gavel. "General Eskivel, if you would be so kind as to take a seat at the table."

Eskivel rose and took a seat behind the curved table. That had actually gone pretty smoothly, in no small part because of Gabiran's driving things forward. He wasn't what I expected.

"Now that a tie is not possible," Gabiran spoke

again, "I believe the most important matter at hand is the succession. King Elizondo the Third has abdicated. His named heir, his nephew, Prince Inigon, is not of age and may not legally ascend the throne. If we are to maintain the line of succession, there must be a regency until such time as Prince Inigon comes of age. Do we have points of discussion?" He nodded to Zabala, who had lifted his hand from the table. "Count Zabala?"

"Order must be maintained," Zabala said. "We can't have people scrambling for the throne; it would be anarchy. There is enough chaos right now, what with the arrest of General Igonez and the inexplicable abdication of King Elizondo. Not to mention the turn of events in the Kajoran Archipelago."

"The question then becomes," another man spoke up, "who would be assigned as regent?"

"Baron Kemen Agéra raises a separate matter," Gabiran said. "This council would have to agree on any such assignment, but the point is moot if we choose to go another direction."

"What other direction is there?" Kemen asked with an amused expression.

"We are certainly open to suggestions," Gabiran said. "Do you have another proposal?"

"Oh, not I," Kemen answered. "I was simply asking."

"He makes a good point!" Danel said. "Assignment of the regency—"

"Will be addressed if we decide to take this course of action," Gabiran interrupted him.

"I move that His Holiness, Pontiff Yulin, be appointed as regent," Danel said, trying to emulate Gabiran's earlier move. "Do I have a second?"

Another man raised his hand. "I sec—"

"I'm sorry, the Barons Danel Gartza and Ager Sagasti are out of order," Gabiran interrupted him as well. "This is not a lawful motion. There is no regency to which His Holiness, or anyone else for that matter, could be appointed. I ask you to be patient, Baron Danel. However, I take it you are in support of a regency?"

Danel hesitated, his eyes moving among the other senators, calculating possibilities. He nodded, finally.

"I would support a regency," he said.

"Very well." Gabiran agreed. "Let us make it an official motion. I move that we accept the official line of succession and appoint a regency until Inigon is of age. Do I have a second? Danel?"

"I second," Danel said.

"The motion is on the floor. Are there points of discussion?"

"I think discussion will come when we review candidates for the regency." Kemen raised an eyebrow.

"Fair enough," Gabiran said. "On to the vote. In favor?"

Almost all hands raised.

"Opposed?"

No one raised a hand, but a few had abstained.

"The motion carries," Gabiran announced. "A regency will be established for King Inigon." He struck the table with the gavel again.

"Now we get to the crux of the matter," Kemen had a wry expression.

Before Danel could say anything, Gabiran spoke again.

"We have already heard one suggestion from Baron Danel," he said. "He has recommended Pontiff Yulin. I assume this would be to ensure the Most Holy Church of Ah-Shan continues to have an active role in the governance of our country."

There were a few nods around the table.

"All here witnessed the attack earlier by Grand Inquisitor Palben Ayala against the royal wedding—"

"Ayala was acting on his own!" Yulian came to his feet. "His actions were not that of the church!"

"I assumed this to be so, Your Holiness." Gabiran nodded to him. "However, and meaning no disrespect, you assigned him as Grand Inquisitor and allowed him to form the Order of Jhunélin." The pontiff's face turned white with fury at his words. "I am not finding fault with you, Your Holiness. You could not have known his true nature. However, I think you will have your hands full with your church, ferreting out his confederates and dealing with the now headless Order of Jhunélin." Gabiran's eyes widened. "Oh! Apologies! I spoke in haste and was not considering the manner in which the Grand Inquisitor died."

"I am quite capable of handling both the church and a regency," Yulian snapped.

"I would tend to agree with Duke Gabiran," Zabala said. "I would not feel comfortable with either the church or the regency if you had to split your attention. Each deserves full focus."

There were nods around the table and Danel looked like he'd just taken a bite of a rotten apple.

"What would be ideal," Gabiran continued, "is if we had someone steeped in the knowledge of running a country who would not have to divide their duties."

Nériala stood.

"If I may speak," she said. "I have given some thought to the matter and have some ideas."

"As a woman," Danel snapped, "you have no right to speak here!"

"Of course, you are correct." She replied demurely. "I do not have the right. This is why I ask permission to speak. Were I a man, such as yourself, I could simply demand to be heard. But I am not."

"Denied!" Danel barked.

"Baron Danel," Gabiran chided him. "Again, you speak out of turn. As acting chair, it is for me to grant or deny the floor. I, for one, am curious about what the daughter of King Elizondo the Third has to say on the matter. You may proceed, Princess Nériala."

"Thank you, My Lord." She curtsied. "Though not a son and not an option as an heir, I studied my father's work every day of my life. I am steeped in the ways of the court and the considerations that are part of such an appointment. One of the fears in assigning a regent is that this person would seek power for themselves and use their time to undermine the rightful ruler. Is this not true?"

Some of the senators looked at each other uncomfortably.

"That would be a valid concern," Gabiran agreed. "Continue."

"To mitigate this concern," she said, "perhaps it would be better to establish a joint regency, so that no single person has that level of power."

"Very clever," Gabiran replied. Of course, he knew what she was going to say; he was in on it. And I guessed that they hadn't announced their engagement. "There is merit to that idea. I would support this. But that compounds the question; we no longer seek one viable candidate but two."

"Agreed," she said. "However, we do have two people who were raised as royalty, who understand governance and what it is to rule, and who would have every reason to support the royal house of Elizondo. Further, there is no possibility that these two people could seek power outside the confines of the regency."

"And who might these amazing people be?" asked Kemen.

"I know who these people are," Inigon said, getting to his feet. "And while I am too young to have an official voice, I would support them as co-regents and learn from them. They are my royal wife, Queen Luana Aloso Elizondo, and my cousin Nériala Elizondo. Their royal lineage cannot be denied."

Voices erupted around the table.

"Order!" Gabiran was calling, pounding with his gavel as the voices died down. "Order!"

"Women are incapable of ruling!" Danel snapped at Nériala. "You are making a mockery of these proceedings!"

"I make no mockery," Nériala said, her head bowed. "What you say is well known in *Félbahlag* Society. That is why I would propose the regency be established as a triumvirate, with a man as the third member to provide his guidance. Meanwhile, including Queen Luana as part of the regency will do much to calm the *Kajorans*, and preserve the idea that the recent wedding is truly a step toward uniting our nations. My own lineage as an Elizondo will also, despite my being female, lend credence to the idea of stability for our own people. All under the guiding hand of a man."

Gabiran let out a laugh. "Clever!" he said. "I can definitely appreciate how such cleverness, under the guidance of a man, could be put to good use for Félbahrin."

"I agree." Zabala was nodding his head as though thinking it over. "The real question here would not be about these two women. They are excellent window dressing for the reasons given. The real question would be to determine the third member of this Triumvirate."

"I do like the idea of a Triumvirate," Gabiran said. "I think this would be the safest form of regency. Just looking at that aspect, does anyone have a better idea for the regency than using a Triumvirate?"

He looked around the table, but no one said anything.

"Alright," he said. "Let's get that aspect decided. I move that the regency be structured as a triumvirate, with three members. These three members will constitute a single vote in the senate council. Do I have a second?"

"Seconded," Zabala agreed.

"We've already had the discussion. All in favor? Opposed?"

Again, there were none opposed and only a few abstained.

"The motion carries." Gabiran thunked his gavel. "Now, the makeup of this Triumvirate. It has been proposed that two of the members be Princess Nériala and Queen Luana, and that the third member be a man. Let's hold off on the third member for now and look at this idea of women in the regency."

"Ludicrous!" Danel snapped. "This is insane!"

"Do you think that a man would be unable to keep these two women in check?" Gabiran asked him.

"Of course not!" Danel said. "Any man could keep control of two mere women. It is simply that the idea is repugnant."

"Sometimes," Gabiran said, "we must do unpleasant things to achieve our goals. Let us put it on the floor to vote and have done with it. I move that we appoint Princess Nériala and Queen Luana as co-regents as part of a Triumvirate regency, on the condition that the third and final regent will be a man approved by the senate. Do I have a second?"

"I second," Count Uftzi answered.

"Very well. The motion is on the floor. In favor?"

Gabiran and Uftzi raised their hands. Zabala followed shortly after them, then Eskivel. Slowly, other hands went up. This vote was going to be a lot closer. I carefully counted and then counted again. Of the nineteen senators, nine had their hands raised. Then Kemen raised his hand, giving them the majority.

"Opposed?"

Led by Danel, the other nine raised their hands.

"The motion carries," Gabiran struck his gavel. "Queen Luana, Princess Nériala, please stand before the panel as we move to the next stage." He cast his glance along the line of senators. "I know this was a difficult decision for all of us. Let us now turn to filling the third spot of the Triumvirate. Without that, there is no regency. I want to thank all of you for your patience and support thus far. Count Zabala, I would also like to thank you for your support and your cool head in these deliberations. Since the idea was posed, I have been trying to think who would be a good choice for this. I'm going to propose someone, but let me tell you why I think they would be a good choice.

"The person I have in mind has a rich family heritage of serving this nation that none can deny," Gabiran continued. "He has a keen mind and is experienced in leading men and is well-versed in the intricacies of religion."

I could tell that Zabala was barely able to suppress a smile.

"When I say your name, please stand." Gabiran paused. "Shahz Dega, please stand!"

Count Zabala started to stand but stopped, shock evident on his face.

"I move that Shahz Dega, last of the royal line of Dega, be appointed as the third regent in the Triumvirate," Gabiran announced. "Do I have a second?"

"Seconded," Uftzi called.

"The motion is on the floor, and I have given my justification. In favor?"

The shock on Zabala's face had changed to fury. Hands were already going up. Danel had noticed Zabala's reaction and raised his own hand, the others who had voted with him earlier joined suit.

"Opposed?" Gabiran called out. Zabala's hand shot up but only a few of his confused supporters joined him. "The motion carries! Shahz Dega is the third regent of the Triumvirate. Fully formed, the regency is now in effect."

CHAPTER NINETEEN

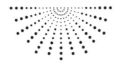

MIRA

I didn't know the stakes or the players involved, but it was pretty clear to me some major political victory had just been achieved.

"As I was only acting chair in absence of the king," Gabiran said, "I now defer to the Triumvirate to take over this session."

People shifted position so that the three new regents could take seats at the center of the table. Shahz Dega sat in the middle with the two women on either side of him.

"Thank you for your confidence in us," Shahz said. "We will endeavor to be worthy of it."

"I am greatly troubled by what happened earlier at my cousin's wedding," Nériala said. "The fact that the Grand Inquisitor felt he had license to interfere is disturbing."

"I agree," Luana said. "I was shocked that this could happen in such a civilized society. This man had no position in the Félbahrin government, yet from what I observed he was able to give orders to government officials and even the military. This does not seem appropriate for clergy."

Shahz was nodding. "I think an official proclamation relating to religion is in order," he said.

"You have no right to issue proclamations to the Church!" Pontiff Yulin snapped. "The Church is outside your jurisdiction."

"You are correct," Shahz told him. "Religion has a different purpose and focus than government. Government has the purpose for facilitating the well-being of citizens, in both long and short term, so that both individually and as a whole they might live fulfilling and productive lives without fear of oppression or unjust treatment from the government. Religion is not focused on the physical but on spiritual matters, which are more personal to the individual. There are many religious paths in the world and the government has no right to dictate which path is chosen by its citizens. His Holiness, Pontiff Yulin is an honorable man and a devout worshiper and advocate for the Holy Church of Ah-Shan. I am an adherent of Fél Naran. Queen Luana and the majority of *Kajorans* follow the *Noélani*. We could no sooner command His Holiness to follow the *Noélani*," there was an audible gasp from several people, "than we could order the *Kajorans* to follow Shan or the ways of Fél Naran."

"Heresy!" Danel jumped to his feet. "You cannot compare Ah-Shan to these superstitions!"

"These superstitions, as you call them," Eskivel said to him, "just drove all occupying *Félbahlag* from the Kajoran Archipelago lest they die a horrible death. This is very real. If you doubt that, you should read the reports. I was there and I saw this myself. We may not follow the gods of the *Noélani*, but we cannot deny their existence."

"Agreed," Shahz said. "That is why I would make the following proclamation: I proclaim that from this day forward, the State shall have no power to interfere in the religion of any citizen. No policy or law enacted or enforced by the State can be seen to support or favor any religion over any other religion, nor can any policy or law favor religion or religious doctrine over the well-being of citizens or the overall health of Félbahrin."

"How can you separate the health of the spirit from the health of the person?" Yulin objected.

"They are both important," Shahz agreed. "But the government has no place dictating how people follow religions any more than religions have a place dictating governmental policy. This proclamation, if my counterparts of the regency agree, will have immediate effect."

"I support the proclamation," Nériala said.

"As do I," Luana agreed.

"It is done," Shahz struck the gavel on the table.

"There is a related matter," Luana said. "Physical torture or mutilation are not spiritual concerns and should not be condoned."

"How is this related?" Danel scowled.

"Shan does not support torture or mutilation," Yulin said.

"The Order of Jhunélin was widely known to torture those they called heretics or blasphemers," Shahz pointed out. "This is one of the reasons I was away from Félbahrin for so long. Being a follower of Fél Naran, I could have been arrested at any time and tortured and even burned at the stake. Regent Luana is correct; this practice has no place in a civilized society."

"How are we to preserve the faith if we cannot strike down heretics?" Yulin objected.

"The proclamation we just put into effect means you have no right to enforce your religion on anyone," Shahz pointed out. "Any person may believe as they choose, and speak of it as they will."

"There is also a current practice of mutilating the genitalia of women," Luana said. "This is a religious practice that crosses the line into the physical."

"This is to purify women in the eyes of Shan," Yulin said.

"Bullshit!" Nora glared at him. "You think your

God is perfect, right? Well, if He's so perfect, why do you think He didn't make women exactly the way *He* wants them to be? Or do you think He screwed up and that you can do a better job? This is just a way to oppress women and keep them in line!"

Yulin was speechless, shock evident on his face.

"Go, Nora!" I grinned at her.

"I agree with the assessment of Regent Luana," Shahz said. "And while she may have been lacking in etiquette and courtesy, I find merit in what Nora has said. A second proclamation is in order. I proclaim that from this day forward, it is illegal to torture or physically alter or mutilate any person for religious purposes."

"Yes!" Luana spoke immediately.

"I agree," Nériala said.

"Done," Shahz struck the gavel.

I had no idea how much more they had planned for the meeting, and I didn't feel like waiting until they'd exhausted whatever agenda they had.

"Excuse me," I said, standing up. "I think you've made some really good progress here. Separation of Church and State, freedom of religions and freedom from religious persecution are the basis for any civilized people. And the mutilation thing," I made a face and shook my head. "Anyway, I'm sure you have a lot of other important things to talk about, but I have some news for you. It's kind of related to the same subject. You're about to be in a war."

"With the *Kajorans*?" Shahz asked.

"No." Luana shook her head. "The *Kajorans* don't want war."

"No," I agreed. "Not with the *Kajorans* – I don't even know who they are. In less than two weeks you are going to face ships loaded with a *Bahréth* army."

I had their attention now.

"*Bahréth*?" Gabiran asked. "Those are just stories. Reptilian monsters from fairy tales. They aren't real."

I assure you they are very real," I told them. I just came from Solaian. The city is being evacuated. Kartahn Zeg—"

"Kartahn Zeg?" Nora looked surprised.

"Right." I agreed. "You met him. Well, with the help of the *Qélosan,* posing as angels, what they call Transcendent, he's started a religious war and he's trying to take over the planet. Maybe more than just this planet. They captured all the ships in the harbor at Solaian and a big chunk of their army is on the way here. They set sail several days ago."

"If our cannon were working," Eskivel said, "we could destroy their ships before they could land."

For some reason, he was looking at Nora.

"If the cannon were working," Luana looked at

him, "it is likely they would first be used to attack the *Kajoran wakoa karua* outside the harbor."

Nora was looking back and forth between the two of them, but she didn't say anything.

Eskivel didn't push the matter and turned to me instead.

"What can you tell us about this Kartahn Zeg and the *Bahréth?*" he asked.

I filled them in on what I knew, including about the *Qélosan.*

"Because of their glamour, the *Qélosan* really make things hard," I said. "When your defenders drop to their knees in awe instead of fighting, the *Bahréth* can walk right over them."

"Maybe we can make a spell of our own," Nora suggested. "Something that would somehow block their glamour."

"That's a good idea." I was surprised. "But I wouldn't know how to do that. Maybe if we had Tesia, but she's busy with the evacuations."

But Nora was lost in thought and hadn't heard what I said.

"We have at most two weeks to prepare," Eskivel said.

"And that's assuming they don't have mages who can give them better wind," I pointed out.

"Can that be done?" Shahz asked.

"I've done it." I shrugged. "I'm sure I'm not the only one who's thought of it."

"If they can do that," Shahz said, "they may be able to cut the travel time in half."

"Just be glad they aren't trying to portal their army here directly," I told them. "Otherwise, you'd be facing them today."

I glanced back at Nora, but she was busily paging through a leatherbound book and wasn't really paying attention to us.

"You all have a lot of strategy and logistics to figure out," I said to the council. "If you don't mind, I'd like to talk to my sister. It's... been a while. We have some catching up to do."

Nora looked up from her book, then she slammed it shut and got to her feet.

"I think I know the way back to the Peacock House," she said.

"Nevertheless, you should have an escort." Eskivel signaled to a nearby guard. "Send a squad to accompany them."

The guard assembled a squad of seven soldiers, and we were led out of the Ziggurat. The crowds celebrating in the open space outside and in the streets were too packed to navigate with a carriage, so three guards acted as a sort of wedge in front, with two to either side and two more in the rear. Rispan kept Bijoux close throughout the walk. The huge, scaled, cat-like creature seemed to be keeping close to Nora. Usoa's *gurpahn* eyed the crowd around us as though it was one of the guards.

I shook my head in amusement. We were practically a walking zoo.

There was too much noise for conversation. It was a relief when we eventually went through a gate into the courtyard of a villa. It was much quieter once we were inside. The soldiers situated themselves outside while we made use of the chairs and couches.

Nora seemed to be avoiding making eye contact with me. Instead, she looked over at Jack.

"I noticed the sword was glowing for you earlier," she said.

"Yes," he answered. "It seems that when you accepted my pledge of protection it made me your champion. I have full access to the sword's power."

"Where's Zoriaa?"

"She is with the other *Wyl-Dunn* in Solaian," he said.

"And Emma?" she asked. "Is she okay?"

"Emma's fine," I told her. "I took her home."

I knew that was a simplistic answer and it wasn't really accurate. Emma didn't know that her father was dead, but by now she would know he was missing.

"Maybe some introductions are in order all around," I suggested. "When you got sent here, I ended up on another world. Daoine. That's where I met Rispan. He's been a true friend. More like a brother, actually."

"And royalty," Rispan said with a grin. "Don't forget that part."

I rolled my eyes.

"Yes," I admitted. "He recently discovered he's royalty. But he's always been a royal pain. That big cat is Bijoux. He found her as a kitten during our travels. And this is Usoa."

"Zoriaa has told me much about you," Usoa said to Nora. "I am apprenticing under her now."

"And of course, Jack couldn't be kept away from coming to get you," I added.

"I'm Dyani," the woman who'd come with us from the meeting said. She was strikingly beautiful. Her skin had a dusky, golden color and she had bright, golden eyes. Her darkish brown hair framed her face nicely. Like pretty much all non-humans I'd met, she had pointed ears.

"Dyani helped us get away from the *Félbahlag* when we were leaving Ranolan," Nora said, nodding to her. "Then she kind of got stuck with us. But I'm not sure it wasn't on purpose."

"On purpose?" Dyani blinked at her.

"To spend more time with Shahz?" Nora asked her.

Dyani blushed and looked away with a shrug.

"This is Spike," Nora said, scratching behind the ears of the big thing sitting at her feet. "And there's Bright," Nora added. "Come on out."

A tiny glowing figure emerged slowly from

inside Nora's hood. It circled in front of her. Then it began to expand until it became a fully sized woman with golden-orange skin, almost like a sunset, and blue hair. She still had a faint glow.

"Hello," she said, looking around with brilliant blue eyes.

"Bright," Nora looked surprised. "When did you learn how to do that?"

"I have been experimenting in the dream-spaces," Bright answered. "While you slept. It seemed to me that it should work just as well here. Especially after I saw Jack and Mira change their shapes."

Nora was nodding. "I remember you did that once in a dreamspace. I mean, you changed your size. But this is the first time you've spoken out loud."

"Is my voice alright?" Bright asked. "I think I could change it if—"

"Your voice is perfect!" Nora smiled at her. She jumped to her feet and hugged Bright.

"I'm glad you made some friends while you were here." I smiled. "And it's nice to meet you, Bright. You too, Dyani."

"Why…" Nora paused, her eyes on the floor. "Why are you so different?"

"There was a time spell," I told her. "I had to take it down. It aged my body."

"But you're acting different, too." She raised her eyes to mine. "It's not just how you look."

"Because of the spell, time flowed differently there," I explained. "It was only a few days on Earth, but for me, I was gone for two years."

"You were stuck there for two years?"

I nodded. "Then when I finally got home, I found out that you were gone, too. And I've been trying to find you ever since."

"Why were we gone, though?" she asked. "How did all this happen?"

"Someone was being stupid," I said, thinking of Alex Stone. "It was an accident. Magical accidents can cause big problems."

"And you're not younger than me anymore."

"No," I said. "I guess technically we're the same age now. But my body has aged a lot more."

"You cut that guy's head off," she said. "With a sword. Since when do you use a sword?"

I took a deep breath and let it out slowly.

"That's a longer story," I told her. I looked around the room. "Is there any whiskey here? Or a local equivalent?"

"Since when do you drink?" she asked.

"Somebody was a bad influence," I said, looking pointedly at Rispan.

"Hang on!" Rispan objected. "I didn't have anything to do with that!"

"Really?" I asked him. "I seem to remember

somebody who kept ordering refills on pitchers of pixie juice."

"That's not..." He thought about it for a moment, then nodded his head. "Alright. Point made."

Nora was looking back and forth between us. "Are you two like, together?"

Rispan and I exchanged horrified looks.

"No." I shook my head. "He's family. Rispan is my brother like you are my sister. Besides, he has his hands full between his princess and his dragon lady."

"Shéna is not a princess, she's a queen," Rispan corrected me. "And Genevané is *not* my dragon lady."

"I stand corrected," I said, grinning.

"I think you have better things to talk about than my love life." He frowned, getting to his feet. "How about you work on that, and I'll see if I can find us something decent to drink?"

Rispan went into the other room without waiting for an answer.

"He's right," I agreed. "We do need to swap stories. I know pretty much everything that happened to you up until you left Tyr nya Lu. What happened after that?"

Somewhere along the way, Rispan returned with a bottle of a dark green liquid and several glasses.

"What's this?" I asked, holding up the glass and looking at the color.

He shrugged, taking a sip from his own glass. Then he smiled and nodded.

"It's tasty," he said.

"I recognize that," Dyani said. "It's called the Tears of the Siren."

I hesitated, recalling my near-death experience under the enchantment of the *Solénur*.

"Is this actually from them?" I asked. "Or just named after them for some reason?"

"Good question," she said. "I get the impression this is something named for them. Either way, I doubt it actually contains their tears." She sipped hers. "It's not bad, Though I prefer the traditional drink of the Ranolan Savannah."

"Sorry." Rispan shrugged. "No Ranolan Specials here. This is all I could find."

I took a sip. The liquid had a complex flavor. It was a little sweeter and not as strong as the goblin grog I had come to prefer. It was not as sweet as Pixie Juice, though, and much more herbal than either of them.

I turned my attention back to Nora, who was looking at her own glass with misgivings.

"It sounds like you've had an amazing experience," I told her. "You actually met gods!"

"Well," she hedged. "I'm kinda finding the definition of *god* to be relative. But yeah, I met a bunch of the *Noélani*."

"I didn't meet any gods," I told her. I heard

Yeravi give a mental clearing of her throat. "Well, I suppose I did meet one that many considered a goddess."

"*Thank you,*" Yeravi sent to me. It sounded a bit sarcastic, though.

"You said you were on that world for two years?" Nora asked.

I nodded.

"I guess it's my turn."

I gave her a rundown of everything that had happened since I landed on Daoine. By the time I was finished, so was the bottle. I still hadn't told her about the house burning down yet, or that I didn't know where Jill and Tony were. Nora sensed that I was holding back and called me on it.

"You're not telling me everything," she said. "Are you?"

I shook my head.

"Is there something else I need to know?" she asked.

"Yes." I nodded, trying not to think about it. "But not right now. There's nothing we can do about it tonight. Let's talk about it in the morning, then we can figure out what we're going to do."

"You don't want to tell me now?" she pressed.

"Nora." I let out a breath. "It's been pretty much non-stop for as long as I can remember. Since this whole thing started. And when I thought it was finally over, that I could go home and everything could go back to normal, I found out that you were here, and I've been searching to find you. Let me take one night. Please."

She furrowed her brow but nodded in agreement.

"You've both had incredible adventures," Dyani said. "And you have both played important roles wherever you have gone. I doubt fate is done with you yet."

"I don't believe in fate," I told her. "I believe we have free will."

"Oh, I agree." She said. "However, we all act according to our natures. Some rise to the occasion, others run from it."

"Sometimes, I wish I could run." I gave her a lopsided smile. "But…" I shrugged.

Then I looked at Bright.

"But there are other amazing things happening," I said. "Bright, I can't imagine how this has been for you. It sounds like your very existence has transformed!"

"It has," she said. "Much of it has to do with Nora. But the biggest change was when Luana tried that spell to swap bodies with Nora. I was already connected to Nora and Nora had a connection with you."

"Right. And at the time I was locked in a magical fight with Médard. That spell ended up causing me and Médard to switch bodies."

"All of those connections at once somehow expanded me," Bright said. "And then Nora had the Heartpiece. That gave us a connection to the goddess A'iwanea. I suppose there was no way I could experience all that and be unchanged. I have some of all of you in me. Yet, I am myself."

"Legends say that a spirit can give pieces of itself," Dyani said. "And that these pieces can become autonomous."

"Doesn't that take something away from the giver?" Bright asked her.

"No," Dyani shook her head. "Whatever was given is replenished."

"That lines up with some of the *Wyl-Dunn* texts," Usoa said. "I didn't study this in detail, but Zoriaa had a couple of books with her, and I remember coming across it when she had me researching something else. I think..." She thought for a moment. "It mentioned putting a piece of yourself into something, like a golem or a zombie, and then having control over it. But I think the piece must be put in with controls or the subject receiving the gift will go rogue."

"Maybe *rogue* just means it has a mind of its own," Nora said. "Makes its own decisions and doesn't blindly obey."

"Most likely," Usoa shrugged.

"I do not feel controlled," Bright said. "I do not wish to be controlled."

"I see connections," Usoa spoke up. She was looking at Bright and I assumed she was using her magical vision. "You're definitely connected to Nora. You're connected to Mira, too. Those are your strongest connections."

"I can understand the connection to Mira," Bright said. "Luana's spell was sidetracked by Nora's connection to Mira and I was caught in that."

"There's another connection," Usoa went on. "It's not as strong, but I sense whoever is on the other end is very powerful."

"It might be A'iwanea," Nora said. "I carried that Heartpiece for a while. It wouldn't surprise me if I still had some connection to her, and Bright was part of it when that started."

"I don't know," Usoa answered. "I can only follow it so far and then something stops me. But I don't think any of these connections are designed to be used for control."

"That is very good to know." Bright said. "Thank you."

CHAPTER TWENTY

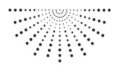

NORA

*A*s we talked, I was having trouble reconciling this new Mira with my little sister. Mira had always been pretty confident, but not like this. The Mira I'd known had been... I don't know. Quieter? This Mira didn't hesitate. She didn't wait for someone else to lead the way; she just stepped up. She was decisive. Not that she steamrolled over other people, she just didn't hesitate.

The Mira I had known had often turned to me – not for guidance necessarily, but maybe for reassurance. She wasn't doing that now. Thinking about that, I realized that I'd only known Mira for the year I'd been with the Ramirez family. For her, that had been over two years ago. She'd moved on. She'd spent twice the time away from me since then than we'd ever spent together.

I covertly glanced at Rispan a few times. Mira said he was like her brother. I saw from the way she laughed at some of Rispan's comments that they were close. They had a lot of shared experiences that I wasn't part of. She clearly didn't need me anymore.

I'd thought that maybe I had finally found a family with Mira. With Jill and Tony. But now it felt like that was slipping away. Mira had always been able to connect with other people. I hadn't. For me, the relationship we'd had was special. I'd never get that back.

"I'm glad to finally meet you," Rispan was looking at me. "Mira has told me a lot about you."

"That's nice." The words slipped out before I thought about it. I felt bad, but that was life.

Rispan just nodded his head with a slight smile.

"In fact," he went on, "I'd always been a little jealous. I could tell she loved you more than she'd say and missed you more than she'd admit. But it was always there."

I narrowed my eyes at him, wondering why he was telling me this. Did he have some ulterior motive? Was he going to show me how much closer he was to her than I'd ever be?

"When I met Mira," he said, "I was alone. No friends. No family. I was smaller than the others my age and they would sometimes try to bully me. One day, there was a group of them, and Mira stood up for me."

"It wasn't just me," Mira had evidently heard his comments to me. "Don't forget Mouse!"

"Yeah," he agreed. "Mouse, too."

"And what did I get for my trouble?" Mira looked at him, then she turned to me. "He challenged me to a match! I stood up for him and he tried to kick my butt!"

"I got pretty close, too." He grinned.

"In your dreams." Mira rolled her eyes.

I liked their easy familiarity. They *were* closer than I'd ever been with Mira.

"I think I'm going to get some sleep," I said, standing up. "It's been a long day."

"Okay," Mira stood up and put her arms around me. "Get some rest and we'll talk in the morning."

I nodded, turning away and hoping she wouldn't see my eyes. Spike was dozing next to the chair where I'd been sitting. I left him there. I found a bedroom and closed the door behind me. She'd probably tell Rispan whatever it was that she hadn't told me earlier. If he didn't already know. Mira didn't need me anymore. Well, I didn't need her, either. I knew how to be alone. I'd been doing it all my life.

I half-expected Bright to say something, but I realized she was still in the other room instead of tucked into the hood of my cloak.

Fine. I didn't need Bright, either.

I climbed under the covers on the bed and thought about going into the dreamspaces. I knew that Katamakutu would come to me if I called him.

No. I couldn't depend on anyone else. I needed to be able to stand on my own and not rely on Mira, Bright, Jack, the *Noélani*, or anyone else.

When I woke up in the morning, I didn't feel rested. That wasn't new, but usually it was because of the nightmares. I was just starting to get used to restful nights. I got dressed and went into the front room. The staff assigned to the villa had already laid out breakfast and everyone else was eating and talking around the long table.

I found the coffee and took a seat toward the other end of the table.

"There you are!" Mira smiled at me. She got up and moved to the chair next to me.

I dished up whatever scramble the cooks had prepared. It looked like eggs and cheese with onions and some unfamiliar vegetables. I focused on eating so I wouldn't have to look at Mira.

"I know you haven't had your coffee yet," she said. "But I have more to tell you. Stuff I didn't want to get into last night."

I didn't have anything to say to that, so I took another bite.

"I'm not sure where to start," she said, thinking. Then, some decision made, she went on. "Our parents knew each other. Our biological parents, I mean. They were friends."

That stopped me, and I looked at her.

"And it's no coincidence that Jill and Tony took you in," she said. "Do you remember Luci? Luciana Leon?"

The name sounded familiar, but I couldn't place it.

"She works at child services," Mira told me. "She was our caseworker. She placed you there on purpose. It turns out, she's my aunt. She said she would have put you with us sooner, but she hadn't been able to."

I stared at her, stunned.

"That sword actually came from your mother," she said. "My mother was just hiding it for her."

The sword?

"I talked to Zoriaa," Mira went on. "You already figured out you had some connection to the sword. Well, it's yours. From your mother."

"How is this all possible?" I asked her.

"I know," she said. "Crazy, right? It turns out they were all connected through this secret group, the *Daruidai*. And that guy who showed up at our house? The one who tried to grab me and started this whole mess? He's with the *Daruidai*, too."

"What are they?" I asked her.

"I don't know a lot about them," she said. "But evidently they keep track of magical things on

Earth. Like police, I guess. For magic. Or like a whole secret, magic judicial system."

"I didn't know there was really such a thing as magic on Earth," I told her.

"I think that's one of the things they do," Mira replied. "They try to keep magic a secret."

"Did Jill and Tony know about it?" I asked. "About our parents?"

"No," she shook her head. "If they had… It seems that when we opened that box from my mother and started pulling things out of it, it set off some kind of magical alarm and kicked everything off."

I nodded. That *had* seemed to be the start of everything.

"But there's been some trouble back on Earth." Mira took a breath and let it out. "Our house got burned down."

"What? How?"

"I don't know," she said. "But Jill and Tony are safe. At least, they were safe and still are as far as I know. They're with Luci."

"Where?"

"I don't know that either," she admitted. "I haven't been able to get hold of any of them, and things have been a bit hectic."

"Why are you here and not trying to find out where they are?" I asked her.

"Because I knew they should be safe with Luci,"

she said. "But I didn't know whether *you* were safe. I had to find you first."

"Me?" That didn't make sense. "Why? They're your family."

"So are you," she told me.

"Seems like you have a lot of family these days."

Whatever she was going to say was interrupted as the front door burst open. I could hear the clash of fighting and Mira was already moving. She had a knife in either hand.

Nériala stumbled through the door. A man slipped through the fighting behind her and followed her in, his sword raised for a slash. Mira was a blur and had interposed herself between Nériala and her attacker.

Mira's blades flashed and the man was down, his blood pumping from the artery on the inside of his right leg and from the artery under his right arm. She'd also slashed the hamstrings on his right leg going past him. Mira ignored him as he fell, and she was through the door.

Rispan was helping Nériala, putting some distance between her and the open door. The sounds of fighting outside stopped.

"Send someone to Eskivel right away and let him know what happened," Mira was saying. "You're going to need reinforcements."

One of the guards replied, but I couldn't hear what he was saying.

"No," Mira said. "You did well here, all of you. And you were outnumbered. I'll make sure Eskivel knows that. Meanwhile, stay sharp and let me know right away if you think there's trouble coming. And send for those reinforcements. I'll take care of this one."

Mira came back inside leading a wounded man. He had a gash on his head and a wound on his leg. She had his arm twisted behind his back with one hand and had a dagger pressed against his kidney with the other. She shoved him at a chair.

"Sit there and don't move," she told him. Then she moved her hands and I could tell she had worked some kind of spell.

Mira checked the fallen man she'd taken down on her way out the door, but he'd bled out.

The animals were all up and agitated. Usoa was trying to calm down her griffin. Rispan gave a low whistle, and the six-legged panther flipped an ear at him, then plopped down on the floor. Spike was trying to push me back from the door with his shoulder, almost sticking me with the quills of his mane in the process.

"It's alright Spike," I told him. "It's over."

"What happened?" Mira was looking at Nériala.

Nériala shook her head. "I don't know, they must have been following me. But I didn't see them until I was coming in the gate. If it hadn't been for the guards..."

"They almost had you," Mira pointed out. "Why attack you? Do you think it's about the regency you guys formed last night? The Triumvirate?"

"I don't know what else it could be," she answered.

"If someone is resorting to violence," Mira said, "you won't be the only target. The other two members of the regency are also in danger. And maybe even the king. Do you know where everyone is?"

"They all have at least temporary residences inside the Citadel," Nériala told her. "The meeting went late, but it is set to reconvene in an hour. Most attendees either stayed in the Ziggurat last night or they went to their local residence. I only came out to check on everyone here."

"Who's behind it?" Mira asked her.

Nériala considered that for a moment. "It's hard to say."

Mira turned to the wounded man in the chair.

"Who sent you?" she demanded.

The man just glared at her wordlessly.

"You definitely upset a few people last night," Rispan observed. "That Zabala guy wasn't very happy when he didn't get the third regency position."

"Zabala was never a friend," Nériala said. "But we needed his support to lay the groundwork. He asked about the third position. I only said I would not advance any senators above him."

"You knew how he would read that," Rispan replied. "Well, he's definitely an enemy now."

"Perhaps," she answered. "But he is not in a strong enough position to try this on his own. He must have allies."

"You're going to need to figure out friend or foe pretty fast if things have already escalated this far," Mira said.

"There was another guy that was pretty upset last night." Rispan scratched his cheek. "What was his name?"

"Danel," Nériala told him. "But I can't imagine the two of them joining forces. They agree on very little."

"Maybe so." Mira shrugged. "Then again, the enemy of my enemy is my friend, right?"

"I see what you mean," Nériala replied. "But I still see that as an unlikely union. But neither would try this alone. There's no one strong enough to try this alone."

"Then there's another player," Mira said. Maybe someone that could bring the others together? Someone who isn't obviously against you, or maybe even is friendly to you?"

"Baron Kemen Agéra," Nériala said with certainty. "It must be him! He always plays the center, never really committing to either side. Zabala and Danel could be convinced to join forces by a strong third party like him."

"You're sure it's him?" Mira asked her.

"It couldn't be anyone else," she answered. "The rest are fully committed to our cause and the future of Félbahrin."

"Would Zabala and Danel keep working together if this guy was out of the picture?"

"Not for very long. They'd be at each other's throats without Kemen to keep them focused," Nériala said.

Mira turned back to the prisoner.

"Are you working for Zabala or Danel?" she asked him. "Their plan has obviously failed, so you might as well tell us what you know."

He lurched out of his chair, trying to attack, but bounced back as though he had hit an invisible barrier.

"Not very smart, are you?" Mira asked with a raised eyebrow. "It will go better for you if you cooperate."

"You'll get nothing out of me!" he growled at her.

"Oh, I'll get everything," she told him. "The only question is what will happen to you when I extract the information."

"I doubt you have the stomach for torture," he sneered. "You could skin me alive and I would still tell you nothing!"

"Torture?" Mira laughed with a shake of her

head. "No, I don't bother with that. I can extract the information directly from your mind."

The man narrowed his eyes.

"The problem," she went on, "is that the process of probing your mind – of breaking through all of your mental barriers and walls, of ripping past your will – is not gentle. It leaves you… damaged. I *will* learn everything you know. You, on the other hand," she shrugged, "you might remember your name, afterwards. And it tends to sever your control of your body. You'll get along well enough as long as someone feeds you and cleans you."

His face paled at that.

"You lie!" he snapped. "That's not possible!"

"Not possible?" Mira's body suddenly shifted. Her skin turned a dark bluish-black color and huge wings appeared. She raised a clawed hand and looked at it curiously. "What exactly do you know about what is and isn't possible?"

The man's eyes were wide with fear.

"How are we going to proceed?" she asked him.

He swallowed, clearly terrified but still hesitating.

"As you wish," Mira sighed. "Remember, you asked for this."

She moved her hands in a circular pattern and they began trailing streamers of light. Then the streamers coalesced into a ball. With another motion, the ball started moving toward the prisoner.

"Wait! It was Danel! He had a meeting with Zabala and one other, then he sent us after Princess Nériala!"

"Who was the other person?" Mira asked. "Was it Kemen?"

"I don't know!" he answered. "I swear! He was cloaked! With a hood! I couldn't see who it was."

"I think you're lying," Mira shook her head sadly. "There's really only one way to be sure."

The ball of magic moved toward the man again.

"Please! No! I swear that's all I know." He was too terrified to even pretend to be tough anymore.

"So you say," Mira answered. Then her voice turned hard. "The problem is that you are *not* an honest man. You are a *traitor*. A *betrayer*. And you think there is some sort of *honor* in being loyal to another betrayer. You *have* no honor! You lie easily and I will rip through your mind until I find the truth! *All* of the truth!"

"Please, no…" he was openly weeping now.

"Who is the third man?" Mira demanded.

I watched, horrified, as the ball of magic ever closer to the prisoner. Was she really going to do this?

"I DON'T KNOW! I DON'T KNOW!" He tried to pull away but was stopped by the invisible barrier around him.

"What are their plans?"

"There will be an attack on the senate!" he said.

"The regents are to be killed along with their main supporters!"

"Names," Mira insisted. "I need names!"

"That's all I know! I swear!"

Mira looked at Jack, who gave her a nod.

"Very well," Mira said. She waved her hand and the ball of magic disappeared. "I will believe you. For now. But if I find out you've lied to me…"

"No!" He fell to his knees. "I haven't! I swear!"

Mira went to the door and called in one of the guards.

"Secure this prisoner somewhere," she told him. "We may need him again later."

After the man had been removed, Mira let out a sigh. In a moment, she had shifted back to her normal body.

"It looks like I ruined another shirt," she said.

"A shirt?" I asked. "You were going to destroy his mind and you're worried about a shirt?"

Surprise showed on Mira's face.

"I wouldn't do that even if I knew how," she said.

"You were bluffing?" I gaped at her.

"My telepathic abilities aren't that great," Mira said. "But I figured Jack's would be good enough to tell whether this guy was lying if I gave him enough stress."

"Correct," Jack said.

"But now we've confirmed the two people we

suspected," Mira went on. "Maybe if we can get to him before the senate meeting, we can stop their plans. But we haven't confirmed that Kemen is really the third man."

"I can't think who else it could be," Nériala said again.

"Then that's our target," Mira told her. "We need to take this Baron down." Then Mira took a breath and looked around the room. "Maybe I'm getting ahead of myself. I'm only here to get Nora. Your politics don't really concern me." Then she looked at me. "You call it, Nora. These are your friends. If you think we should help them, we'll help. If you want to let them sort out their problems themselves, we'll leave. Keep in mind, besides this issue, they're also going to have Zeg's *Bahréth* army showing up any time."

All eyes were on me now. What did I want to do? I was still pissed with Luana, and I was of half a mind to let her fend for herself. But I couldn't abandon Shahz and Dyani. And then there was Corlen and Captain Corana. Maybe my mission to A'iwanea hadn't been my choice, but I still felt an obligation somehow to protect the *Kajorans*. The *Félbahlag* situation was pretty well sorted out for the *Kajorans*. Sure, there were still some details left, but between Mohanga's Revenge and Luana being in the regency, they were in good shape. But then there was Zeg.

"Zeg is definitely a threat," I said. "For everyone."

"It looks like he's on a global domination kick," Mira said. "He's trying to take over everything on the Danu continent. Plus, he's coming here *and* I think he sent scouts to Daoine, too. And that makes this something I care about, too."

"Zeg is my sworn enemy," Jack said, looking at me. "And he is allied with the *Qélosan*, who are ever the enemy to all *Daijheen*. I would fight Zeg and the *Qélosan* on every front. But I have sworn myself to your cause and will follow where you lead."

"If we fight him here," Mira added, "we have to settle this insurrection, or whatever it is, first. And we have to do it fast, or it won't matter."

Zeg was bad news, all right. I knew that.

I thought about leaving it all behind. Going home. Then I remembered that Mira told me the house burned down. Where *was* home? Was it with Mira? With Jill and Tony? Maybe I'm not the kind of person that gets to have a home. Maybe I'm the kind that ends up alone.

"You are not alone," Bright spoke into my mind. *"You have friends who care about you. You have a sister, a family, that loves you. And you care about all of them, too. If you turn your back on the ones who love you, you will only end up hating yourself."*

"Since when did you get so smart?" I sent back to her.

She was right, though. I would hate myself if I turned my back on the people I cared about. And I would always regret disappointing any of them. This new Mira might not be the same one I remembered, but the Mira I knew wouldn't be happy walking away from doing the right thing. Still, she'd left it up to me. I looked at her.

"I'll support whatever you decide," she gave me a nod. "No questions."

I felt my walls start to crumble when she said that. And a grain of hope that Mira, my *sister* Mira, wasn't totally lost to me. Maybe she hadn't left me behind after all.

"Alright," I said out loud. "We stay. We handle the hell out of this situation and then we take out Zeg.

Mira looked at Usoa and Rispan.

"Usoa," she said. "I appreciate you coming through the portal to back me up like that, but you don't need to stay for this. I can open a portal back to Solaian for you and your *gurpahn*."

"This is part of the same war," Usoa answered. "They don't need me there, but I can help here."

"Thank you." Mira gave her a nod. "Rispan, I know your addiction to being in the heart of a mess, so I'm not going to bother asking."

"Will I get to finish breakfast?" he asked.

"Eat fast," Mira told him.

"Here." Rispan tossed her a shirt.

She held it up. The arms had been cut off and much of the material on the upper back had been removed, leaving only a strip of cloth down the center.

"I think that will survive you changing back and forth." Rispan winked. "At least until you figure out something better."

"Thanks!" she said, slipping it on.

CHAPTER TWENTY-ONE

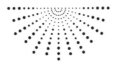

NORA

"Nériala, what's the best way to find this Kemen whoever?" Mira asked. "Do you know where he is?"

"He would most likely be at his local residence," she said. "A place very similar to this."

"Is it far?"

Nériala shook her head. "A few minutes only."

"How much protection will he have?"

"Normally, not much," Nériala answered. "But he's not normally trying to stage a coup. There's no telling. But the place isn't big enough for more than a couple squads of soldiers."

"We can go after him there, but would it be better to just wait until the meeting?" Mira asked Nériala. "You said it was going to reconvene soon."

"It's hard to say," Nériala answered. "If he's allied to both Zabala and Danel, they might be able to get enough support in the senate to undo everything we did last night."

"What if we arrest him?" Mira asked. "Do you have the authority to do that?"

"No." She shook her head. "I am only one-third of the regency. The Triumvirate would have the authority to have someone arrested, but it would take at least two of us agreeing to it."

Mira scowled. "I really miss having phones on this world. I'm too used to instant communication."

"We have our rings," Rispan said. "The commdevs. But you can't talk to anyone who doesn't have one."

"You know," Mira mused. "I read a series of books once where they had playing cards that had images of the people, and you could focus on the image and establish a mental connection with them. The other person didn't need to have anything."

"Oh." I remembered some long past discussions. "Was that the one about Amber by Roger Zelazny that you kept trying to get me to read?"

She nodded. "Too bad we don't have anything like that."

"That sounds possible," Usoa said. "Let me think about it."

"Meanwhile," Mira went on, "you said we don't have the authority to arrest him without one of the other regents. What if it isn't an actual arrest? What if we just want to bring him in for questioning? I want to move as quickly as possible. The longer we wait, the better position he'll be in."

"We could do that," Nériala agreed. "But he could refuse."

"Let's do it then," Mira said, "and hope we can be convincing. But we should all stay together. I'm not comfortable leaving anyone." She looked at Nériala. "Especially you. They've already made one attempt."

Mira went to the door and called in the guard who was in charge.

"We're going to leave here," she told him. "We're going to talk to Baron Kemen. We think he might have been behind the attack on Nériala."

"Is that safe?" the guard asked. "If he was behind the attack, you could be walking into danger."

"True," Mira told him. "That's why we'd like you and your men to come with us. We might come back later, but for now, we're not leaving anyone here."

"You wish to go to his villa?" the man asked. "I know where it is. It is not far."

"Perfect," Mira said. "You can lead the way."

We drew a lot of attention on the walk to Kemen's villa, and people who saw us coming tended to change direction quickly. At first, I was confused, but then I smirked when I realized how we must look. We had a half dozen guards leading the way with pikes and swords. The rest of us, besides Néri-ala, were all foreigners of various kinds, mostly armed with swords and looking very serious. Plus, we had Spike, Usoa's griffin, and Bijoux, Rispan's lion.

I'd probably run the other way, too, if I saw us coming down the street.

I glanced at Mira, thinking of how easily she had killed that man attacking Nériala. She hadn't hesitated at all. And she hadn't seemed to even think about it afterwards. This was very different from what I would expect from the Mira I used to know, and I had a feeling there were details she'd left out of her story.

Bright walked with us, too. Since coming out the night before and taking a larger shape, she had stayed that way. I had a feeling her days of watching from my hood were over. I guess she didn't need me anymore, either.

When we neared the villa, it looked like they'd probably seen us coming and a squad of guards outside the gate with pikes held at the ready to fend us off. Jack drew his sword and stepped toward them.

"Wait!" I put a hand on his arm. "Don't kill any-one! Not unless you have to!"

Mira looked at me, then nodded. I felt her draw power and then she made a pushing motion with her hands. The guards were all thrown back as if some giant hand had swatted them all away. Before they could recover, the guards with us had them disarmed.

The rest of us were through the gate and across the courtyard. Jack gave the front door such a powerful kick that the whole thing flew from the frame and slid across the floor. Jack and Mira led the way inside and the rest of us followed closely behind. I could tell that Mira was still filled with power.

An opening in the back wall was sliding closed and I could see Kemen looking at us from the other side. I could also see a tunnel behind him leading who knew where. He was getting away!

"No!" Mira moved her hands.

The sliding wall stopped closing and then slowly reversed direction. Kemen was standing as if transfixed, a look of surprise and fear on his face. Mira moved her hands again and Kemen was pulled out of the opening.

"Not so fast," Mira said. "We need to talk."

The surprise and fear on Kemen's face was replaced with anger.

"And now your truth is revealed!" he snapped, glaring at Nériala. "I should have suspected treachery from the start! I should never have supported you."

"Nice try," Mira said. "But you have no audience here to play to. There's just us.

"And we know what you've been up to," Nériala told him. "Despite your *pretended* support."

"I see the Triumvirate was not enough power for you. Have you already taken out the other two regents?" he asked Nériala, his lips twisted with disgust. "If you have come for me, I assume you have already removed all overt opposition from the senate."

"We're not removing anyone." Nériala frowned at him. "We know what Zabala and Danel are doing, and we know you put them up to it."

He narrowed his eyes at her.

"What are you playing at?" he growled.

"Hang on," Rispan said. "Something is off here. Mira, let's let the baron take a seat and we can have a conversation."

Kemen looked at Rispan suspiciously. Mira released whatever she had been using to hold him. She nodded to Rispan to proceed.

"A few minutes ago," Rispan said. "Nériala here was attacked by assassins. As you can see, they failed."

Kemen's eyes went to her.

"Is this true?" he asked.

"Don't you know?" she asked him.

Kemen pursed his lips, his eyes calculating as he looked around at us.

"Let me guess," he said. "You knew that none of the senate was strong enough by themselves to try this. Zabala and Danel must be working against you, but they hate each other too much to ever come together on their own. Someone else has united them. You thought I was a likely candidate to be this third person."

"That's an amazing guess," Rispan said. "Almost as if you weren't guessing at all."

"It's the most obvious conclusion." Kemen shrugged.

"Just because it's obvious doesn't mean it's wrong," Mira pointed out.

"True," he agreed. "Given the information you have, suspecting me is logical. Just as it would be logical to doubt my claims of innocence. But you need this resolved before the senate reconvenes, so you can present your case before those who stand against you can strengthen their position."

"You seem very adept at these political games," Rispan said. "That just makes you even more likely to be the third party."

"Of course," he answered. "Given the information you have. I'm going to have to provide new information. Information that would show I have nothing to gain and much to risk by working with Zabala or Danel."

"Such as?" Nériala asked him.

"That passage," he pointed to his failed exit route, "was not constructed in case of an attack like yours. I use it for smuggling."

"Um, *that* doesn't make you sound innocent," Mira said.

"From Regent Luana's statement last night," he went on, "it is obvious she has strong objections to the Church's method for purifying women. She is not the only one to feel that way. Aside from that, there are other reasons why various people might want to leave Iyoké, or even Félbahrin, because of certain policies that have been enforced here. Policies that Danel fully supports. Policies that help people like Zabala stay in power. I help these people to find a life somewhere else. I am hoping that under the new leadership of the Triumvirate, such a need will become a thing of the past. Going against you would make no logical sense for me."

"If all that was true," Nériala admitted, "it wouldn't make sense that you would work with them. But how can we verify what you're saying is true? We can't just take your word for it."

"I wouldn't expect you to," he said. "But you can check with someone you *do* trust who can verify what I have said."

"Who?" Nériala asked.

"Shahz Dega." He smiled. "I helped him leave the city years ago. Had you been able to check with him before coming here, he would have told you himself."

"We don't have time to check before the meeting," Nériala said.

"You don't have a lot of options." Kemen shrugged. "You came here with no proof, probably hoping you could goad me into a confession which you could then use against me with the senate. Either I am lying to you, and you are still left without a confession or proof and you must let me go, or I am telling the truth, in which case you must let me go. But I am not lying."

"Well," Rispan shook his head, "I'm inclined to believe you, pending verification from this Shahz Dega. But if you're a smuggler, even one who does it for good reasons, it means you must be good at lying." He looked at Nériala. "Either way, he's right. We have to let him go."

"Agreed," Nériala didn't look happy as she turned to Kemen. "I pray you speak the truth."

Kemen's brows raised in question. "To whom would you render this prayer? Shan?"

"I think not," she smirked.

"You still have another problem," Kemen said. "If I am not the one who brought Zabala and Danel together, and I agree that they are likely involved, then who did?"

"I don't know," Nériala shook her head. "The other key senators are either strong supporters of Zabala or Danel, or they are fully with us. Ager Sagasti is with Danel. Uftzi Elkano and Gurutz Baroja sided with us."

"One of your supporters is betraying you,"

Kemen said. "And the other is likely a target. But I would point out that Baroja only supported you because he was following Zabala's lead."

"You think it's Count Elkano?" Nériala looked confused. "I don't understand how this would benefit Uftzi at all. Why would he betray us? He's been Gabiran's staunch supporter for many years."

"I don't know," Kemen said. "Maybe he's tired of being in second place. If he can push Gabiran aside, it could be very profitable for him."

"And we have another problem," Mira told him. "They intend to assassinate the Triumvirate and their supporters when the senate reconvenes."

"How do you know this?" Kemen asked, looking around at the group. "Are you certain of this?"

"We are," Nériala answered simply.

"Then we need to move quickly," Kemen said. "If we have guards ready, hiding, we can catch them in the act. We'll stop them *and* have proof of what they were doing."

"Agreed." Nériala said. "We should go to the Ziggurat now and put things in place. There is not much time."

Kemen joined us as we all left the villa, headed for the Ziggurat. We had scarcely gone past the gates before we were surrounded by what looked like at least six units of soldiers. One of them stepped forward.

"Regent Nériala, Baron Agéra," he said stiffly. "I am Captain Vassago. Come with us, please."

"Where do you intend to take us?" Nériala asked.

"We are to escort you to the senate council," Vassago answered.

"We need no escort!"

"It is for your protection, Regent," Vassago told her.

"Who sent you?" she asked. "You wear neutral colors."

"Count Zabala sent us to take you into protective custody and conduct you and whoever is with you directly to the council chambers."

"Were you told to take me into protective custody as well?" Kemen asked.

"Not by name," Vassago answered. "But you are with the Regent and therefore fall under our orders."

"Are we under arrest, then?" Nériala demanded.

"No Regent," he answered. "As I said, we are here for your protection."

"We decline," she told him.

"We have our orders, Regent," he said. "I am afraid I must insist. We tried to get to you at the Peacock Villa, but we missed you there."

Mira stepped close to Nériala and whispered

something to her. Nériala thought for a moment, then shook her head.

"There are too many," she said.

Vassago stepped to the side and indicated that we proceed.

"Shall we go?" Vassago asked. "Consider us your Honor Guard."

Nériala clenched her teeth, then strode forward, the rest of us followed. There were about a dozen men marching ahead, and two dozen following behind.

There was nothing else we could do. We went up the steps of the Ziggurat and through the door to the right up the upper stairway. It seemed like it took us forever to get to the council chamber. The soldiers entered with us and spread out along the walls of the room.

The senators were all there, though none had taken a seat at the table. Most were arguing when we walked in the door. Of them all, only Zabala sat at the table, saying nothing. Nériala went to where Shahz and Luana stood. One of the senators eyed Nériala and turned to her angrily.

"Is this your doing?" He demanded. "What is this about? Having us dragged here by force!"

"I assure you, Count Baroja," she snapped back. "I had nothing to do with this!"

"Silence!" Zabala rose to his feet, his voice cutting through the noise like a rusty blade. "I am sure many of you have questions. They will be answered shortly."

He had everyone's attention.

"Now then," he continued. "As I am sure it was obvious, not everyone was pleased with the outcome of the last senate meeting. As a result, there will be a restructuring of power in this room."

"What are you saying?" one of the senators asked.

"If you would keep your mouth closed for a bit longer, Count Sagasti," Zabala snapped at him, "you will find out."

Sagasti glared, waiting for him to continue.

"I had a conversation with Baron Danel Gatza after the meeting last night," Zabala went on. "We were not alone. The current state of affairs cannot stand."

"Right you are." Danel grinned. "Did you three think you could seize power so easily?" He looked at the three regents.

"Now, now, Danel," Zabala said. "Don't interrupt. I'm not quite finished." Danel flashed a look of annoyance but fell silent. "First, I will call everyone's attention to the guards stationed around this room. No one will be allowed to exit until our business is concluded. Does anyone doubt that I now have complete control over everyone in this room?"

"Tell us what you want, Zabala," Gabiran told him.

"In time," Zabala said. "As I said, there were three of us in this conversation. Of course, the third was cloaked so I cannot say for certain who our compatriot is, though it *is* certain he is one with power and resources."

"Where is Count Elkano?" Kemen asked. "Shouldn't he be here as well?"

"We shall discuss Uftzi and the mystery senator in good time," Zabala told him. "After all, the cloaked party *did* appear to be wearing Uftzi's signet ring. To summarize our meeting, it was suggested by Danel and our mystery senator that three new people could assume the positions of the Triumvirate were the three current regents killed. Naturally, their supporters would also need to go. I agreed."

"This is madness!" Gabiran exclaimed.

"Perhaps," Zabala said. "Yet, I speak the truth. May I take it that you intend to support the current regents, despite what I have said?"

"Of course!" Gabiran snapped.

"Captain Vassago," Zabala called. "Please take the regents and Duke Gabiran into… protective custody. You'd best include Baronet Eskivel in that. You others," he gestured to me and Mira and our group, "please take a seat in the audience so that you can witness what is about to happen. I ask that you do not attempt to interfere. I assure you; you are quite safe."

I glanced at Mira and Rispan. Mira shrugged and we did as directed. Usoa's griffin gave her a little trouble, but she managed to keep it under control.

"Are there any others who would stand with our current regents?" Zabala asked.

Sagasti laughed as he looked around at the other senators.

"No?" Zabala prompted. "I take it that many of you are either trying to remain neutral, or you are afraid to speak up. Let's take this another way. Who would stand with removing these upstart regents and replacing them with Danel, myself, and a third?"

"Of course!" Sagasti grinned.

"I would support this!" Baroja said.

"Any others?" Zabala asked. "Danel? What do you think? We have two opponents, two supporters and everyone else is too spineless to take a stand."

Danel looked around at the silent senators.

"Let them be spineless," he said. "They will remember this day and they will stay in their places."

"You wish to proceed then?" Zabala asked him. "Shall we execute this replacement that you, in your wisdom, suggested?"

Danel gave him a slightly confused look before nodding. "Yes! Enough talk. Let's have done with it!"

"Very well," Zabala stepped closer to Danel.

"All here have witnessed the confession of Baron Danel Gartza of high treason and conspiracy to regicide. The penalty for such an offense is death!"

In one quick motion, Zabala drew his sword and thrust it through Danel's heart. Danel fell to his knees, his eyes wide with surprise.

What had just happened?

"I will go to great lengths to protect Félbahrin, Danel," Zabala said. "But I am no traitor."

He pulled his blade from Danel as the man's corpse fell to the floor. He wiped his blade clean and resheathed it.

"Captain Vassago," Zabala ordered. "Place Baron Ager Sagasti and Count Gurutz Baroja under arrest for high treason. The rest of you," his gaze passed over the other senators, "disgust me. You should be charged as accessories. But I will leave that for the Triumvirate to determine."

"What of the third man?" Gabiran asked. "Was it Uftzi? Where is he?"

"The third man was cloaked to disguise his identity," Zabala answered. "Despite all the care he took, even as far as using a spell to disguise his voice, he managed to flash the Elkano signet ring several times."

"Then it *was* Uftzi," Kemen said sadly. "I am surprised he would turn on his allies. I suppose it is difficult to really know someone. But why isn't he here?"

"Yes," Zabala agreed. "It would seem the third man was Uftzi. Except that I know it was not."

"What?" Kemen's head swung up. "But you just said—"

"I had spoken with Uftzi earlier yesterday," Zabala said. "Before the meeting. His gout was acting up and the intense pain in his left foot was making him limp. A limp he still had when he left the senate meeting, but strangely did not have a few minutes later."

"Then why isn't he here?" Gabiran asked.

"I suspect he is dead." Zabala frowned. "His ring taken to intentionally cast doubt on him should the secret meeting not go as planned."

"Then we still don't know who the third traitor is," Shahz said.

"I didn't say that," Zabala said. "The third man is not only ambitious, but also well skilled in politics and intrigue. Such a person would normally take a moderate position, who might vary on whether he supports more liberal or more conservative propositions. This narrows the options considerably. In fact, all things considered, there is really only one man who it could be. And that man is—"

Before he could continue, Kemen launched himself at Zabala, a look of fury on his face and a blade in his hand. Zabala's eyes went wide, but before Kemen could reach him there was a blur and

Kemen was taken down. It was Bijoux, Rispan's six-legged cat.

Kemen was missing his throat and his eyes stared blindly at the ceiling.

"Bijoux!" Rispan called in mock surprise. Then he looked around and shrugged.

Zabala gave Rispan a nod.

"I think we can now proceed with the scheduled meeting," Zabala said. "And I would surrender the floor to the Triumvirate. Though I do have one un-related matter to address."

"I can't wait to hear it," Nériala said as everyone remaining took their appropriate seats.

"First," Zabala said, "I would like to applaud you. You outplayed me yesterday, and this does not happen often. I truly believed that I would be the third member of the Triumvirate and I supported you based on that."

"I never promised you—"

"No," Zabala cut her off. "You never promised it. But you knew I believed it. As you knew I would be… displeased when I discovered the truth."

She nodded in agreement.

"Unfortunately, you assumed this would auto-matically make us enemies," he told her. "And you took additional steps to mitigate this. I do not object to Baronet Eskivel being a member of this council. However, I do not feel he has sufficient rank, title, or experience to replace General Igonez as supreme commander of our military. That is a rather large leap from alcalde to supreme military commander. I do not say this out of malice, Baronet. I am simply stating the facts."

"No offense taken," Eskivel replied. "I would tend to agree."

"If nothing else," Zabala continued, "I have proven today that above all I am a patriot. And my value has been shown by the facility with which I thwarted this conspiracy."

"If you will allow me, Count Zabala," Eskivel said. "I believe I see where this is going. You propose that the post of supreme military commander be assigned to someone with a higher rank. Someone with more experience. Someone such as yourself. Yes?"

"Succinctly, yes." Zabala replied.

"I second the motion," Eskivel said.

The regents looked at each other, surprised. Then Luana spoke.

"All in favor?" Hands were raised. "Opposed? The motion carries."

CHAPTER TWENTY-TWO

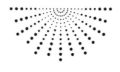

MIRA

The senate would have to figure out what to do about the members who were content to sit by and allow a coup to happen, but the crisis itself seemed to be over. At least, *that* crisis seemed to be over. They still had a *Bahréth* army on the way. Even so, the senate could manage their own meeting from that point and the rest of us went back to the villa with Nora, Bright, and Dyani.

We sat at the table and asked the kitchen staff to put something together for lunch. I could tell something was bothering Nora. Probably several somethings.

"What's up?" I asked her between bites of a dish that consisted of meat that tasted like chicken and had been stewed in a curry sauce with some kind of fruit, sort of like a mango, and served over rice.

"I'm worried about Jill and Tony," she said. "I know you can go back and forth between the different worlds now, but we've had all this stuff going on and haven't had time to check in on them."

"It looks like we have some time now." I smiled at her. "Do you want to go see if we can get hold of them?"

"Can we?" she asked. "Is it really that easy for you to go back and forth?"

"It's pretty easy at this point," I agreed. "I mean, there are restrictions to where I can go, but otherwise it's not that hard. Tesia drilled me hard on it at the beginning."

"Who?"

"Tesia," I told her. "You'll meet her later. She helped me a lot when I was learning to use magic."

"I only met her briefly," Usoa said. "But she seemed to be a very powerful mage."

"You're turning out to be quite talented yourself," I said.

She shrugged dismissively and looked away.

"Anyway," I turned back to Nora. "Why don't we pop over, just you and me?"

"Oh, *that's* not happening," Rispan spoke up.

"What?" I looked at him. "Why?"

"You two aren't going anywhere alone," he said. "Especially not to another world."

"It's our home world," I told him. "We'll be perfectly safe."

Rispan looked at me and then just laughed, shaking his head.

"What?"

"Let me get this straight," he said. "You rushed to Daoine not long ago because you were being attacked, on your home world, and one of your party was killed in the process. And then *you* were attacked, on your home world, and almost killed. Your home burned down somehow. Your parents, your aunt, and your friend Grace are missing, all on your home world, but you'll be perfectly safe. Is that right?"

I scowled at him and turned to Nora. "In case you were wondering, yes, he *is* always this annoying."

"But not wrong," he said.

"Okay," I rolled my eyes. "Not wrong. Except they aren't missing. I just don't know where they are."

"Can I come?" Usoa looked up. She'd been doing something with a placard of some sort. "I'd like to see another world!"

"You did, though," I told her. "You were on Daoine."

"Yes, but that wasn't so different," she said. "Besides, I can help if you need to see your connections to people."

She had a point. If I couldn't raise anyone on the phone, like last time, Usoa could help me to track them through my connection. I still couldn't do that unless I specifically tied a thread to them.

"Alright," I agreed. "I suppose it wouldn't hurt if you came."

"I would like to come as well," Bright said. "I would like to understand the difference between this world and your own."

I looked around at the group. "We can't take everyone," I said. "And no way can we bring the animals."

"I am sworn to protect Nora," Jack said. "Now that I have found her, I will not be separated from her."

Rispan laughed again. "I'll tell you what. Since Jack is going to go no matter what you say, how about Dyani and I stay here and watch the animals? But tie one of your threads to me. That way if you don't come back, I can talk to Tesia over the comm-dev and she can follow the thread to you." He looked at Dyani. "That alright with you?"

"Yes," she agreed. "I want to be here when Shahz is finished with his meetings today." She looked at him. "Why don't you go ahead with them. I can tell you want to. I can watch the animals."

"Thanks!" Rispan grinned in response.

"Alright," I said, scraping the last of the sauce

off of my plate with a chunk of bread. "Me, Nora, Usoa, Bright, and Jack."

"And me," Rispan added.

"And you." I rolled my eyes at him. "We can leave in a few minutes. If all goes well, it shouldn't take more than a couple of hours or so."

"Don't jinx it." Nora frowned at me playfully.

It was good to see her joking, at least a little. She had seemed a bit standoffish so far. But then, she was probably still trying to deal with all of my changes and get her head around that.

"What do you think?" Usoa handed me the placard she had been working on.

I looked at it. It was a piece of flat wood, maybe a quarter of an inch thick, three inches wide and six inches tall. There was an image etched onto it.

"Radomér?" I asked her.

"He was someone we both know, and I could picture him well enough to make the image," she said. "But if you focus on it, you should be able to communicate with him."

"Really?" I was surprised. She'd said she would work on this idea, but I hadn't really expected her to get anywhere. Especially not so quickly. "Is there a range limit?"

"I don't think so," she said. "It's kind of like that comm-dev thing that Rispan has, but it doesn't take two of them. I don't know if it will work if the person is on a different world, though. I haven't been able to figure that part out for sure yet."

"This is brilliant work," I told her, handing it back. "I'll try it out later and we'll see how we can surprise Radomér."

A few minutes later, everyone had finished their lunch and it seemed like a good time to go.

"Is everyone ready?" I asked.

I received several nods.

"Can we go to the house first?" Nora asked. "I know you said it burned down, but I'd like to see it before we see Jill and Tony rather than after."

"Sure," I answered. "I'll bring us into my bedroom. It wasn't too bad. It will be a little small for everyone, but I don't want to just show up in the yard in case anyone is around."

I connected with the *Ralahin* and created the portal. A shadow shimmered in the air, ready for us to step through.

"Bastien," Usoa was talking to her *gurpahn*, "You stay here and be good for Dyani."

Bastien looked at her, but I had no idea whether he understood. When she stepped toward the portal, Bastien started to follow and she signaled for him to stop. She motioned for Dyani to approach. When she did, Usoa put her hand on Bastien's neck under his beak.

"Scratch here," she instructed.

"You have these under control, zookeeper?" I asked her.

"No problem." Dyani smiled. She had already made friends with Spike and Bijoux.

Jack went first, followed by Nora, Bright, Usoa, and Rispan. I flipped a thread at Dyani, establishing a connection, then stepped through after them and closed the portal behind us.

Nora had already gone through the door and was looking down the hall at the wreckage of the front room.

"I suppose it could have been worse," she said. "You're sure Jill and Tony weren't..." She left the question half-asked.

"I'm sure," I told her. "They're safe. Alex Stone had them in a safe house, and then Luci took them someplace else after that."

Nora nodded, looking around at the destruction.

"I know," I said. "It feels like we lost something. Something we can never get back. But it's just a house. It was the people that made it a home."

She nodded again. "I guess I hadn't realized how much it had started to feel like a home to me. I hadn't had that before."

"Right," I said. "And for me, it was really the only home I'd ever had, too. But really, it was Jill and Tony. And then you, too."

She looked at me when I said that, her expression unreadable. Then she looked around again.

"Okay," she said. "I guess there's not really anything to see here after all. I mean, I had to *see* it. Let's find Jill and Tony."

"Alright," I agreed. "I left my cell phone in the charger in the office at Grace's store. I can portal us there and we can try calling."

"Oh!" Nora pushed through the wreckage into what was left of her bedroom.

After a moment, she came back out, black marks on her hand. She held up a soot-stained cell phone.

"The battery is dead," she said. "But it doesn't look damaged. It should still work if we get it charged."

"Unless there's water damage," I pointed out.

She shrugged, slipping the phone into the shoulder bag she was never without. "It's worth a try."

"What *is* that?" Bright asked.

"What is what?" I turned to see what she might be pointing at, but she wasn't looking at anything.

Bright had her head tilted as if listening or sensing with something other than her eyes.

"I feel it, too," Usoa said. "I feel it in the flows. It's coming from that way." She pointed in the general direction of the local woods.

"Someone in pain," Jack said.

I opened myself to my *Ralahin* senses. I could feel *something*, but not well enough to know what it was.

"I recognize the creature," Jack went on. "Not personally, but I can tell that it is a *Jhiné Boré*. There is fear and pain."

"What's a *Jhiné Boré*," Nora asked.

"A dryad," I told her. "A wood nymph. And I know where one lives. Your favorite tree in the woods."

"Really?" she asked.

I was already opening a portal.

"Let's go," I said. "It sounds like she's in trouble."

This time, I was the first through the portal. The others came through on my heels.

"Move and they both die!" a voice snapped.

I looked at the source of the voice and saw Shelby, her face twisted with hate. She was standing between Jill and Tony, and she held a pistol in each hand and had them pointed at the backs of their heads. They were both gagged and I could see fear in their eyes.

"Don't test me!" Shelby ordered. "They'll be dead before you can do anything."

"Shelby?" I asked. "What are you doing?"

I looked around; we weren't alone. A half-dozen women I didn't recognize were on their knees with their hands tied in front of them. Luci was with them, and Grace.

"Why are you doing this?"

Around the edge of the clearing were about two

dozen figures in black robes. They also wore masks, like the ones who had attacked Grace's store and killed Katya. There were two more who held the *Jhiné Boré* between them. One of them paused in the process of digging a dagger into the side of her face.

"Everyone always thought you were so great!" Shelby glared at me. "But now they'll know the truth!"

"But…" This made no sense to me. "I thought we were friends."

"Ha! I don't need your pity. You are *nothing* compared to me! I *knew* you wouldn't be able to resist. You're so stupid! You fell for my trap. Now you can watch your parents die! The only question is will it be slow and painful or should I make it fast? What do you think, Mira? Should I be merciful? Make it fast?"

"Shelby, I don't understand," I said. I needed to get her talking, maybe then I could de-escalate things. "Please, explain this to me. You attacked me once before, too. What did I ever do to you to make you so angry? I swear I would never hurt you on purpose. If I—"

"Lies!" she snapped. "Oh, you might be able to cover up all the little insults over the years, the condescension, allowing little Shelby to tag along now and then, just for show. But the last thing you did you can't pretend about. What happened to my father?"

That stopped me. Nothing else she said made any sense, but how could she know about her father?

"I *know* you were spying on us; I was *there!*" she said. "He followed *you* and he never came back!"

"I wasn't spying," I told her. "I was just checking to make sure Emma was okay."

"Stop lying!" she screamed at me. "You killed my father!"

"No," I shook my head. "He attacked me, I almost died, but I didn't kill him."

"Where is he then?"

"He..." I couldn't meet her eyes. "I made a portal to get away, but he followed me through. We ended up in a *Pilané Jhin* garden. Pixies don't allow violence in their community. They—"

"No! *You* did it!" she accused me. "*You* killed him and you're trying to blame someone else! Like you *always* do!"

"I'm telling you the truth," I told her.

"You want some truth?" Shelby asked. "Here's some truth for you!"

She signaled to the figure holding the knife against the *Jhiné Boré* and he sunk the blade into her eye. The body collapsed to the ground, empty of life.

"What did you do?" I was shocked.

"Give up now," Nora said. There was an edge to her voice I'd never heard before. "Give up now and let them go, you worthless piece of shit. That's your only hope to get out of this alive."

"You think so?" Shelby's eyes were wide with glee.

She pulled the trigger of the gun pointed at Tony's head. The hammer clicked, but nothing happened.

"I have a spell for that." The lack of emotion in Nora's voice only made her sound more cold and harsh. "Guns won't work here, now."

"No!" Shelby yelled.

She started pulling the triggers on both guns, but when nothing happened, she threw them down in disgust. A long dagger appeared in her hand from nowhere and she thrust it up under Jill's ribs. She pulled it out as Jill fell.

"NO!" I screamed. *Not Jill!*

Suddenly, everyone was moving. Bright flared like the sun and everyone around the circle covered their eyes. Nora made a motion and Shelby erupted in flame. She screamed in fury and pain but still managed to turn toward Tony with her knife. Before she could do anything else, I had sucked a ball of plasma into existence and threw it at her. Her body sizzled and was gone in an instant. The dagger, warped almost beyond recognition, fell to the ground.

The figures in black cloaks had launched magical attacks. Luci lunged to her feet. I don't know what she expected to do with her hands tied, but a flash of power struck her face and she collapsed to the ground.

I thrust a shield up around us to deflect the magical attacks from the black cloaks. Then I expanded the shield so that it pounded into them, knocking them from their feet.

Nora started pointing at them, and one by one they burst into flame. One rushed toward Nora from behind, a dagger raised. Before he reached her, there was a flash from Bright and the figure turned to ash. I saw some others scrambling to get away from the corner of my eye and I sent threads of *Ralahin* to snare them, raising them off their feet and into the air.

I could see Jill's body on the ground, her eyes wide and staring. Tony was on his knees, crouched over her. His eyes were clenched in pain and loss.

I screamed.

There were no words. Rage and frustration exploded into a primal sound that reverberated through the forest. I pulled the *Ralahin* threads tight like a fist, slicing the robed figures into pieces.

I looked around the clearing. The captive women on their knees were looking at me with wide eyes. I sent more tendrils of *Ralahin* to cut the ropes that tied their hands.

It was over.

It had all happened so quickly. Jack spun

around where he stood, looking for a target with his sword only half-drawn from its scabbard, but there were no enemies left. The black-cloaked figures were all dead. Shelby was dead. And Jill… I felt something break inside me and I went to Tony. I sank to my knees beside him, wrapping my arms around him. It was only then I realized that I had shifted to my winged form at some point and I changed back to my regular body. Nora joined us a moment later. Tony pulled us both in tightly, his body wracked with sobs.

CHAPTER TWENTY-THREE

NORA

*M*ira and Tony were completely wrecked.

Losing Jill was hitting me harder than I would have thought, too. I hadn't realized how important Jill had become to me. I gently extracted myself from them and looked around.

One of the faces was familiar as she struggled to rise. She'd been struck by a magical attack, and it looked like her eyes had been damaged.

"You're Luci, right?" I asked as I helped her to her feet.

She nodded.

"What's happened?" she asked. "I can't see."

"It's over," I told her. "I guess we won. But it doesn't feel like it."

The people who had been on their knees and bound were getting to their feet.

"Who are these people?" I asked Luci. "What happened?"

"They are my coven," a petite black woman said. "We thought we were strong enough to stand together against the black-robes. But," she shook her head, "too many came against us."

"Who are you?" I asked her.

"I am Grace Ndané," she said. "I think you met Katya. We run – We ran a store together."

"Right." I answered, remembering Mira mentioning the two of them when she told me what had been happening to her. Grace and Katya. "But how did you all end up here?"

"It's my fault," Luci said. "I didn't think Jill and Tony were safe with the *Daruidai,* so I connected with Grace and her coven agreed to take us in. But they must have been watching and followed us."

"No." Grace shook her head. "They would have come sooner. They must have discovered us some other way. We were careless."

"I'm so sorry," Mira was struggling to speak through her tears. "I should have left you on Daoine, in Su Lariano. You were safe there. I should have known better—"

"Stop!" Tony looked up, anger and grief battling for control of his face. "All of you, stop! Blame them!"

He pointed at the bodies of the black-robed attackers. "They chose to do these things, not you. Not any of you. And that Shelby. She *chose*! *Esa puta estaba loca!*"

I didn't fully understand the Spanish, but I got the idea that it was something about Shelby being crazy. He was probably right.

"Don't blame yourself, *mija*," he said more gently to Mira.

Mira looked at him, a flicker of hope showing through her grief. Hoping that it might not be her fault. Knowing how Mira tended to take more responsibility for things than she should, that wasn't going to be easy.

But nothing about this was going to be easy.

Since meeting back up with Mira, I'd started to get used to her stepping up and taking charge of things. That wasn't going to happen right now. She didn't need to take that on right now.

"We can't stay here," I said. "This isn't something we can explain to the police, and we definitely don't need that kind of hassle. And we should probably do something about these bodies, too."

Bright stepped to the center of the open area, and I could feel that she was drawing power. In a moment, there was a huge ball of crackling energy in the air over her. She made a motion, and the ball broke up, a piece shooting to each of the bodies of the attackers. Then nothing remained of them except scorch marks on the ground.

"Where did you learn that?" I asked her. I had no idea she'd become so powerful.

"It was something I saw Mira do," she answered. "When she destroyed that young woman."

"Alright," I said. "That's one thing handled."

I wasn't ready to look at Jill yet. I looked at the other body. The small creature that had been tortured to get our attention. Her lush black hair was matted with blood and dirt. Her features, with her greenish-brown skin, had been lovely. But now, one side of her face was a ruin. I could see that one of her pointed ears had been cut off. She looked so small and frail. Her delicate body lay collapsed in an awkward position on the ground.

"What about her?" I asked.

"Cirilia," Mira said. "Her name was Cirilia, and she's lived in this tree forever. She didn't deserve this, either."

"What should we do with her?"

Mira shrugged.

"Take her to her tree," Grace suggested.

I looked around and saw what tree she must mean. The huge, gnarled and ancient tree that dominated the clearing. It dominated the entire little forest.

Jack picked up the small form in his arms and carried her to the tree, setting her down. You could almost imagine she was simply asleep and curled up against the tree.

I noticed something about the tree as well. Something was wrong with it. The tree itself seemed to be grieving. And it was dying.

There was a blurring of forms and Cirilia's body was absorbed into the tree. I studied the tree to see if this had changed anything, but it was still dying. Something about it reminded me of when I first met Bright. She had been dying, too. She had lost her connection to what had been her source of life and energy.

This was very similar. I tried what I had done with Bright. I sent power to the tree, giving it more energy. It surged with life for a moment. But only for a moment.

I tried sending it more power. It wasn't enough. Bright had been watching and she stepped up next to me, joining her power to mine and sending it to the tree. Life flashed again but it still wasn't enough. I pushed more and more power and I could feel Bright doing the same. The tree was still dying.

"Mira?" I called to her. "Can you help? It's dying."

Mira got to her feet and walked to us, her eyes on the tree. Then she nodded and put her hand on my shoulder. I felt her power joining with ours. Somehow, Mira's participation changed something for me and my power increased tenfold. I could feel the same thing happening with Bright.

The tree was changing! It was actively drawing on our power flows now. It was healing, strengthening, becoming its true living self. Finally, we could feel it was done and we stopped. It was all we could do to not fall to our knees, exhausted, and the three of us held onto each other for support.

"Thank you," a voice spoke. "We owe you a debt that can never be repaid."

I looked up. It was Cirilia. She was standing next to the tree. Her skin was smooth and unblemished. There was no sign she had been injured.

"How is this possible?" I asked.

"A *Jhiné Boré's* life is symbiotic with our tree," she explained. "Neither can live long without the other, but neither is completely dead while the other still lives."

"Could you..." Tony spoke from where he still kneeled next to Jill. He looked from her body to us. "Jill..."

I realized what he was asking, and my heart broke for him. I couldn't answer.

Cirilia walked to him and put a hand on his cheek.

"I am sorry," she told him. "This was only possible for me because I am not really separate from my tree. Jill's body cannot be revived. Even were a necromancer to raise the flesh, it would be empty of her spirit. The connection is severed. She is gone."

Tony's head dropped and he nodded, understanding.

Mira was looking around, an odd expression on her face.

"If you wish," Cirilia was saying to Tony, "we can draw her physical form into us. Her body would become part of us. Part of this forest. We offer this as an honor to her. And to her kin, who have saved us from our end."

Tony looked from Cirilia to the tree.

"If you did that," he asked. "If you… joined her body to you and your tree. Could she ever… I mean – Like you?"

"No." She shook her head. "I do not offer false hope. What has happened today, what these three did for us, has never been done before. It was truly miraculous. We were far past any hope for healing, and I doubt any others but these three could have done what they did."

Tony seemed lost in uncertainty, but then something changed. Something hardened in him.

"Do it," he said. "At least she'll be part of something that will last. Or her body will be, anyway."

Tony gathered Jill into his arms and carried her to the tree, placing her much as Jack had placed Cirilia earlier. The blurring happened again and Jill's body disappeared.

Tony stood in silence for several minutes. We stood by, silent as well, waiting until he was ready. Then he seemed to make up his mind about something and turned to us.

"I have to go," he said. "I'm going to need some alone time."

"Okay," Mira said. "Do you want us to wait here?"

"No," he shook his head. "I don't mean for a little while."

He let out a heavy sigh.

"When I met your mother, after I got back from Iraq, she really saved me," he said. "I was lost. In a dark place. She was my light. Without that light..." he shook his head. "I'm going to need some time to find myself again. To keep from turning back into what I was."

I gaped with realization. He wasn't just saying goodbye; he was saying good-*bye*.

The thought of losing him too shattered any protections I'd thought I had put up around myself. It hadn't just been Mira who'd gotten through to me. It hadn't just been Mira and Jill. I loved Tony, too! I rushed to him and put my arms around him, holding him tightly.

"You can't leave!" I cried. "You can't!"

"I can't stay," he answered, caressing the back of my head, "Not right now. You have to give me this time."

Mira had joined us in the hug and Tony pulled himself out of our arms.

"We need you," Mira was saying.

"Hush, *mija*," he said. "You have your sister. You both have each other. You'll be alright. Take care of each other. You've both made me proud. I —" His voice cracked. "I have to go."

He turned and strode from the clearing.

"Wait!" It was Usoa.

She rushed to him with something in her hands. She gave it to him, and I couldn't hear what she was saying. He gave her a nod and tucked it into his shirt. Then he was gone.

Mira just stood in place, staring after Tony.

"Mira?" I reached out a hand to touch her shoulder.

She spun to face me.

"How can he do that?" she demanded. Her face was a mixture of grief, anger, and confusion.

I wasn't quite sure what she meant.

"I think he just needs to be by himself for a while," I told her. "To process everything."

"It doesn't *work* that way," she said. "The world doesn't just stop so you can *process* things!"

"Different people need to handle grief in different ways," I said.

"Quitting isn't *handling*!" she snapped. She turned and yelled into the forest, "YOU CAN'T JUST QUIT!"

"He's not quitting," I told her. "He just—"

"What else would you call it?"

"He's been through a lot," I pointed out. "Jill was his soulmate, his one true love. She was his anchor. You heard what he said, she kept him grounded after the military. He has a lot on his shoulders."

Mira was shaking her head. "Who doesn't? She was the only mother I really knew! He had a hard time in the war? *I've* been in war, too. I've lost people close to me. And I've probably killed more people up close than he has. Did I quit? No! I finished the job! *And* got home to them. And when I came home and found out you were gone, did I run away so I could *process* things? No! I came after you."

I'd never seen Mira like this. And clearly there was more to her story than she'd told me the other night.

"Mira," I said. "You know that I'm not like you, right? We don't do things the same way, and we have different strengths. Different life skills. If I don't do something as well as you do, do you judge me for that?"

"What?" She gave me an exasperated look. "No! Why would I do that?"

"You wouldn't," I told her. "Not usually. But you're doing it now with Tony."

"But he's supposed to *be* here," she said. "He's supposed to be the *father*."

"Sis," Rispan spoke. "I'm no expert on the subject. My father's been dead a long time and my memories are pretty spotty. It seems to me that fathers are just people, like everyone else. We might see them as more, or want them as more, but they're not."

"I *need* him to—"

"No," Rispan cut her off. "This isn't need. Not really. I know you *want* him to be here for you as your father. And I'm sure he will be. Just not right now. But you *do* have family here for you. We will *always* have your back. You have Nora, me, Mouse… How many others are there who would drop *everything* if you needed it?"

She looked at him, thinking about what he was saying.

"Mira," he went on. "You're the strongest person I know. No matter what happens, you keep going and you never stop. Most people can't do that. Not like you can."

"Maybe I'm tired," she said. "Maybe I don't want to be the one to keep going anymore."

"Good luck with that," he smirked. "I figure the most you could do is take another fifteen minutes, tops, to wallow in your self-pity and then you'd start doing something again."

"Self-pity?" she gaped at him.

"What would you call it?" he shrugged. Then his voice took on a sing-song quality. "I need this. I need that. Whine. Whine. Whine."

She glared at him and for a moment I thought she was going to hit him. He'd been doing well, but I wondered if he'd gone too far.

"*Putri firgolo*," Mira said under her breath. "You can be a real jerk sometimes, you know that?"

"But that's why you love me so much," he said with a smile.

"It is *not!*" she said emphatically.

"Here," he said, holding out his arms. "Do you need a hug? You want me to pat your back a little?"

"We don't have time for that." She scowled. Then she let out a deep breath. "We should probably get back to Iyoké." She looked at Grace. "I'm not losing track of you again." She made a motion with her hand that I didn't understand.

"That was less than fifteen minutes," Rispan observed.

"I've been looking all over for you," Luci said. "You disappeared on me. I didn't know what happened to you."

"I ended up back on Daoine for a bit," Mira told her. "What happened to your eyes?"

"There is no pain," Luci answered. "But I can't see."

"We need to get you to a healer."

"Mira," Grace was looking at her strangely, "when you were fighting... Your body..."

"Yeah." Mira gave a nod. "Some things have happened since I saw you last. That's one of them. I'm still getting used to it."

"Alright," Luci said when it was apparent Mira wasn't going to give any more details. "I suppose that story can wait. But you should know about some other changes since we saw you last. The *Bahréth*."

"What about them?"

"They're here in numbers," she said. "Not *here* here. In Ireland. In the Newgrange area."

"I think I remember seeing something about that online." Mira frowned. "But they were calling it a hoax."

"Not anymore," Luci said. "Too many videos went viral on social media. Then the news outlets started covering it. They attacked a local town. They took over a village called Donore, and they've started toward Drogheda. *And* they're using magic."

"Who or what are *Bahréth*?" I asked. "You mentioned them before."

"You met Kartahn Zeg, right?" Mira asked me. I nodded. "Well, he has an army of walking, talking Komodo dragons. Only worse. And apparently, he wants to take over more than just one world."

"But..." I tried to get my head around it. "Even

with magic… they don't have modern weapons, though. Right?"

"Right," Mira agreed. "But that doesn't make them helpless. Still, I don't think they stand a chance against a full-on attack from our modern military. Zeg made a big mistake coming here."

"I'd tend to agree," Luci said. "But the cat's out of the bag in terms of magic. And somebody even got a video of some *Bahréth* coming through a portal. It's a bit of a mad-house out there right now."

"We'll have to let the military here handle it," Mira said. "Maybe if we can take care of him back on Danu, any other attacks will fall apart."

"The Republic of Ireland is still trying to handle things internally," Luci said. "But whether the Irish Defense Forces are going to be able to handle this on their own is going to depend on how many *Bahréth* come through and how many mages they have. They wouldn't be happy about foreign armies coming in to help, especially with the closest ones being English."

"I appreciate their desire for national independence." Mira shook her head. "But that's not our problem to solve right now. Let's get back to Iyoké and figure out our next moves."

Then Mira's gaze shifted between Grace and Luci.

"What about you?" she asked Grace.

"I am needed here," Grace told her. "The

witches need to be better prepared. Better organized. What happened here has made that very
clear."

Luci looked torn.

"I want to go with you," she said. "But I think I
can accomplish more here. I'm sure those people in
the black robes were somehow connected with the
Daruidai. I need to investigate that. This could be
the same group within the *Daruidai* that went after
your parents."

"I understand," Mira told her. "But we need to
get you to a healer first. Once you're better, maybe
you and Grace can work together. Help each
other."

Luci nodded. "I need to be able to see. I—" She
paused to get herself under control as her voice
started to break. "Too many lives depend on us. I
can't fail them. Not like I failed you. Like I failed
Jill—"

"You didn't fail us, Aunt Luci," Mira said, wrapping her arms around her. "None of that is on you."

Luci returned the hug, but she didn't seem reas-
sured by Mira's words.

"Let me take you to Tesia," Mira suggested.
"She'll make sure you get the proper care and she
can bring you back afterwards."

Mira had already started to form a portal. She
led Luci through and the portal closed. I wondered
how long she would be gone, but it was only mo-

ments before another portal appeared and Mira was back.

"Alright," she told us. "She's in good hands."

Mira stepped to the tree and put her hand on it. She closed her eyes for a moment as if in silent prayer, then turned back to us.

"Let's go," she said.

A shimmering appeared in the air and we went through. Then we were back in the Peacock House; the villa we were using in Iyoké.

Dyani turned her golden eyes to us from where she was feeding Spike a haunch from some animal.

"You're back!" Then her smile faltered. "What happened?"

Mira shook her head. "Not now. Later. What's happening here?"

Mira took a seat on one of the couches.

"Sails were just sighted on the horizon," she answered. "It looks like the *Bahréth* are arriving sooner than expected."

"They must be using magic to enhance their wind," Mira said.

"We can probably find out more, shortly," Dyani told us. "I'm expecting Shahz any time now."

Rispan smirked. "It seems you definitely have *that* fish hooked."

"You're one to talk," Mira said. "Aren't you engaged to Shéna? Or did you already get married while I was away?"

"No, that's still a couple of months away," he said. "But that's different. *I* caught *her.*"

"I'm sure Shahz thinks that, too," Dyani said with a smile.

Rispan gave her a mock glare.

"I was just about to have some lunch," Dyani said. "I'd guess you haven't eaten since you left."

"You guys go ahead," Mira told us. "I'm not really hungry."

CHAPTER TWENTY-FOUR

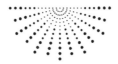

MIRA

I was having a hard time keeping my head clear. It kept coming back to me that Jill was gone.

Focus on the next thing.

But what *was* the next thing? I didn't even know.

Why did Shelby do that? What did she have to do with those others in the robes?

It made no sense.

That's not the next thing. That was Earth. What's the next thing?

Zeg.

Focus on Zeg. He was coming here. At least, a big part of his army was coming here. And apparently, another part was going to Earth and maybe another part to Daoine. Zeg was going to mess things up for a lot of people I cared about.

I glanced at the table where the others were eating. Nora was with them, but she was only picking at her food.

At least I had Nora back.

"It's always hard to lose someone you love," Yeravi's voice sounded in my mind. *"You never really get used to it. Love makes you weak. Better to eliminate that feeling."*

"I don't need your advice," I sent back to her. *"Your way doesn't work, remember? You lost. You're wrong!"*

"Oh, I might have been wrong about some things," she answered. *"But not about this. Look at yourself right now. You're useless! Why? Because love makes you weak! Jill! Tony! Nora! They all make you weak and useless."*

"I'm not useless!"

I could hear derisive laughter.

"You know what your problem is?" I asked her. *"YOU'RE useless! And you're trying to put it on me. You're just trying to find some way to be relevant. To matter."* I opened myself to the *Ralahin.* *"But you don't matter. And I don't have to listen to you. Or your twisted views of life."*

I used my *Ralahin* vision to look deeply, similar to how Usoa had tried to show me. Like I'd done when I'd found how spirits anchored themselves into bodies.

"What are you doing?"

I ignored her, searching for the source of her thoughts. And I found it. I found the heart of awareness that she used to perceive the world. The awareness that she spoke to me from. And I bound it. I sent thread after thread, locking it down.

"No! Don't do this! I can help you! I can teach you to control your shifting! I can make you the greatest mage of all time!"

She tried to fight me, but she was inside my body without anchors; she couldn't stand against me. I wound her like a cocoon and wrapped the threads so tightly that not even a thought could slip through. I could feel her beating at her prison from the inside, but I wrapped more and more threads until, finally, I could sense nothing within them.

The struggle had left me tired. I glanced at the table again and Jack was looking at me. He met my eyes and gave a single nod.

Shahz Dega walked in a few minutes later and joined the others at the table. He looked tired. I hadn't gotten to know him yet outside of the senate. Actually, I hadn't gotten to know anyone in Iyoké personally yet. I could tell Nora liked him, so that was a mark in his favor.

I was glad Rispan was here, but I knew he

couldn't stay indefinitely. Bright came and sat near me on the couch.

"I was hoping I could ask you some questions," she said. "Do you mind?"

"Um," I frowned, "I guess not."

"When we joined to create that spell earlier," she said. "It didn't seem to... I'm not sure how to explain it. The combined amount of power... what we could provide individually, it would have been far less than what we generated together."

I thought about that. She had a point. The amount of power hadn't been cumulative. It had been exponential. I remembered when Laila had boosted my power when I was dismantling the maelstrom. She had given me an incredible amount of power, but even that had been cumulative because of how much power she'd been able to hold.

"I think you're right," I told her. "I take it you're asking me why?"

She nodded.

"I can't help you there," I said. "I have no idea."

"Do you think it may have something to do with Nora's past identity as a *Noélani*?"

"Her what?" I guess I wasn't the only one to leave out a few details when we'd swapped stories. "What exactly are *Noélani*?"

"The *Kajorans* see them as gods," she told me. "I am not sure what that means, though. They are certainly very powerful. We met several in the dreamspaces. That is how much of Nora's past was revealed."

"What's a dreamspace?"

"That is something else I do not quite understand," she admitted. "I think they are something like postulated realities. They can be worlds. Universes even. Created by one or created by many. One of the *Noélani* said they are games, and that even this reality was just another dreamspace."

I shook my head. "The more you explain, the less I understand."

"I'm sorry," she said. "I am still learning to communicate."

"You're not alone there," I told her. "It's something we all struggle with sometimes."

"Truly?" She looked at me.

I nodded.

"Nora introduced you as Bright," I said. "Is that a nickname, or is that your real name?"

"It was my first name," Bright said. "Nora gave it to me. But I think I have outgrown it."

"You didn't have a name before that?"

"You must understand," she said, "I didn't have a consciousness as such before Nora saved me. I was simply a *kree*. Not much more than an insect, really. But when she saved me, I was enhanced somehow. And I was connected to her when she joined with you in the spell that Luana attempted. I was further enhanced by this. It is as though I am a piece of both of you. And something was also gifted to me through the connection to A'iwanea."

"And you've been changing since then into something new?"

"It is not just me," she explained. "The *kree* are no more. They have become *Asha Kree*. They are conscious."

"And that's what you are now?" I asked.

"No." She shook her head. "I am something else. The *Asha Kree* call me *Shian Shariel*. But that is not a name; it is what I am."

"But you said Bright was your first name," I pointed out. "That implies you have another."

She nodded. "I have another, but I have not assumed it yet. I feel that when I say it out loud, it will solidify all that I have become and all that I may become."

"You don't have to tell me. It's alright."

"No," she said. "It is time. My name is Astéa Wairua."

"It's pretty," I said. "It sounds a bit like some of the *Kajoran* words and names I've heard."

"It is my birthplace, after all." She smiled.

"Does it have a meaning?"

"The *Asha Kree* honor me for helping them to evolve," she said. "The name has to do with opening a path for the spirit."

"I said, no!" Nora's voice cut through our conversation. "I'm not going to do it!'

"It's our only defense," Shahz was saying.

"Find another way."

"What's going on?" I asked.

Nora just glared at Shahz and didn't say anything.

He crossed his arms, exasperated, and looked away.

"Anyone?" I prompted.

"It is about the cannon," Jack supplied. "They want to be able to use the cannon against the *Bahréth* fleet."

"And what's the problem?" I asked.

"The cannons aren't working," Jack told me. "Of course, very few people know why this is so."

I looked at Nora and Shahz, then back to Jack.

"I take it this has something to do with Nora?"

"It was her spell that has rendered them useless," he confirmed.

I nodded, remembering how she'd stopped Shelby from using the guns.

"That's pretty amazing, actually," I said.

Nora looked at me, surprised.

"You think so?" she asked.

"You used that spell on Shelby, right? That's why nothing happened when she tried to shoot Tony."

"I don't want to let them have guns or cannons here," she said. "Not if I can help it. Only the *Félbahlag* have cannons. You didn't see what they were doing! I can't trust them with something like that."

"I believe you," I told her. "But you can't stop them all over the world. Can you?"

"No," she admitted. "But gunpowder won't work within five miles of the Ziggurat."

"Five miles?" That surprised me. "How did you manage that?"

"With help," she said. "You helped, too."

"Me?"

Then I remembered when she had asked for power. Usoa was right; we *did* have a connection, and Nora had used it to draw power for her spell.

"You were right to stop them when you did," Shahz said. "They were firing on defenseless *Kajorans*. But now *we* are defenseless and the *Bahréth* will arrive in hours."

"I'll help you against them, but I'm not giving you back the cannons."

I wasn't sure I agreed with Nora's decision, but I wasn't going to hassle her about it.

"Fine," Shahz said. "Let's go out to the sea wall where we can see the approaching ships. Maybe you'll change your mind."

She hesitated. "We can go, but I'm not going to change my mind."

Shahz went to the door and issued some orders to the soldiers on the other side. Within a few minutes, a large carriage appeared, and we loaded inside. All but the animals; they followed on the street, terrifying the locals as we passed.

I got a look at the inner harbor on the way; it was very impressive. We finally arrived at a fortified wall that stood above a rocky shore overlooking the ocean. Halfway to the horizon, I could see a fleet of ships.

It looked like a motley assortment of all kinds of ships and even fishing boats. The *Bahréth* had taken anything that would carry a few soldiers. From what I could guesstimate, they probably had a few thousand troops in those ships. *Bahréth* troops. Eight-foot-tall reptilian warriors and mages. They would be hard to stop. I could understand why Shahz wanted the cannon.

"Now, do you see?" Shahz was asking Nora.

"I see," she told him. "But I'm not going to do it."

"It will save lives!"

"Today, maybe," she agreed. "For this fight, yes. But what about tomorrow? What about when it isn't just for defense? Like when the *Kajoran* boats came the other day."

"You could just take the spell down temporarily," Shahz said. "And then put it back afterwards."

"I don't think I could," she told him. "I was barely able to do it before, even with help." She took a breath and then looked him in the eye. "I'm sorry, but we need another way. War is a despicable way to solve problems. It's nothing more than license to murder on a grand scale. We'll have to find another way to beat them. And as much as I hate killing, I promise you I'll do whatever it takes to protect you and your people. Just no cannons."

"Interesting promise," another voice spoke. "Whatever it takes?"

Nora turned to look at a man who I swear hadn't been there a moment before.

"Kata?" she asked. "What are you doing here?"

He shrugged. "You hadn't visited me in your dreams for a while. I was curious what you'd gotten up to. I *have* been visiting your Earth, though, to see where you've been hiding since... Well... Forever. It is *quite* a colorful place."

He turned his smile in my direction and looked at me with mischievous green eyes that sparkled from a face colored a deep, dark golden brown under a mane of golden hair.

"Ah," he said. "You are her new sister." He bowed to me with a flourish of his hand. "Katamakutu, at your service!"

"And what, exactly, is a Katamakutu?" I asked him.

"I am of the *Noélani*," he said. "As was your sister, once upon a time." He turned back to Nora. "You were just talking about protecting the people here. Perhaps some of your earlier self is coming through. You *were* the protector, after all."

"Not a very good one, apparently." Nora frowned.

"Quite the contrary," he answered. "You kept the *Kajorans* safe. They didn't get into any trouble until long after you left. Now that you are looking to take on the role of protector once again, I realized that I was in the unique position of being able to help you."

"Jack," I said to him under my breath. "What's your take on this guy?"

"I can't say," Jack answered, looking at Kata-makutu. "He is… beyond me."

Katamakutu flashed me a wink and turned his attention back to Nora.

"Kata," Nora said. "I don't remember the life you're talking about. But I do have the idea that you like to play games, and you have your tricks. *And* that you always have an ulterior motive."

"Guilty, as charged," he said with a grin. "But my *ulterior motives* as you call them are not harmful to you or to any you care about. You must sense that as well."

Nora studied him.

"I can help you to defeat this army and protect this city," he said. "And that is truth."

"I believe you," she replied. "And what is it going to cost me?"

"That, I cannot say for sure," he said. "I am hoping it will remove the veil of forgetfulness that separates you from who you were. That is all."

"And who was I?"

"You were and are Akajokira," he said with conviction. "My beloved sister and protector of any who call upon the *Noélani* for support."

When he said the name Akajokira, Nora paled. Clearly, the name meant something to her.

"And if you… remind me of being this Akajokira," Nora touched her tongue to her lips. "I'll be able to stop the *Bahréth*?"

"As Akajokira, it is what you were born to do!"

"Hang on," I interrupted. "Are you saying she's going to stop being Nora?"

"I… wouldn't say that," he answered. "But in truth, I do not know the result. I only hope for the return, in some measure, of my sister. Surely, you can understand that?"

"This doesn't sound like a good idea to me, Nora," I told her. "It sounds like he wants to mess with your head and he doesn't know what he's doing." I turned to him. "I bet you could stop them yourself, couldn't you? If you're the brother of this protector, you're probably powerful, too. Right?"

"I suppose that is true," he admitted.

"Then why don't you do it?" I asked him. "Why don't you stop the *Bahréth*?"

"The people here are not under *my* protection,"

he said. "I have made no promises to keep them safe. They are not my problem. My sister has made them her problem and I have simply offered to assist her in keeping her promise. No more."

I glanced at Nora and I could see from her expression that she had made up her mind.

"Alright," she said. "Tell me what I need to do."

CHAPTER TWENTY-FIVE

NORA

For some reason, I was terrified.

I'd already gone through one of these experiences where I remembered part of some past life. How many of these could I have? That was a good question.

How many *could* I have?

My time as Nimue was centuries past. Maybe longer. What Kata was talking about, me as a *Noélani*, was before that. If the average lifespan was eighty years, give or take, that was a lot of possible lives that could have happened in that amount of time. Was Akajokira my first lifetime or did I go back even further than that?

I think it was Kata who'd said that even this universe was just another dreamspace that everyone had created. Had I been part of that? Had

I existed in some form before the universe was created? If so, the number of lives I'd had were beyond
counting.

That gave me a feeling of insignificance. If I'd
lived hundreds, thousands, or even millions of
lives, how could I think that this one, that Leanora
Leland, mattered at all in the grand scheme of
things?

I shook my head. I couldn't think like that.

It didn't matter if this was a dreamspace or not.
It didn't matter whether the universe was all just
one huge game. I was here. Right now. And there
was a situation that I could do something about
that mattered to other people who were right here,
right now.

Kata was looking at me.

"Are we going to do this or not?" I asked him.
"Those ships are getting closer."

"It is simply a matter of remembering your
other form," he told me. "As Akajokira, you looked
very different than you do now."

"You mean I looked like a *Kajoran?* Like the
other *Noélani* do?"

"Oh, you had a form like that, too," Kata said.
"But I am talking about your protector form. The
great and glorious Akajokira, who could glide
through the air just as easily as the sea; able even to
traverse the void between suns. Akajokira, who
could swim through the molten heart of the sun it-

self! Akajokira, whose mere presence caused even the most bold to quail in terror and awe! Akajokira, the great serpent who inspired countless imitations! Did you not know? Your protector form predates even your time as a *Noélani*."

As he spoke, I had flashes of memory. But the memories did not fit me. Not this body; it was far too small.

"Can you remember the joy of your power?" he asked me. "Can you feel it?"

There was more to what he was saying than just his words. He was using his own power to evoke the memories within me; to pull them out of the hidden recesses of the past.

And it was working.

No wonder I felt insignificant, limited to such a tiny form. I could be much bigger than that. I *was* much bigger than that.

I was *more* than that!

"You are Akajokira!" Kata shouted. "You are the protector!"

Why was I tied to the ground? What foolishness was this?

I felt myself rising. Expanding. I was power incarnate.

My body flowed and writhed through the air. I looked at my body and it was beautiful! A spectrum of blues and greens and golds and reds. My scales sparkled in the sunlight. I soared straight up into the air, reveling in the power of flight. I didn't have wings; I didn't need them. My will was enough!

I circled around, seeing the city below me. The once towering bulk of the Ziggurat no longer seemed so large. But I knew it was important. It was important to those beings for whom I had granted my protection. Those beings had also done wrong; I knew that as well.

"Know me, people of Iyoké," I sent my thoughts to everyone below and my words reverberated through every mind. *"I am Akajokira! I will protect you, though you are unworthy! Become worthy!"*

I ignored the feelings of panic and fear that flowed back at me. I spun in the air and flew out past the sea wall to plunge into the icy depths. The sensation was invigorating as I sped through the water!

I could sense the ships on the surface and the *Bahréth* within them. These were the ones who dared to attack! They would pay for their arrogance!

I broke the surface of the water, overturning two dozen ships in the process. I gave a faint swish of my tail and six more flipped over. I laughed at this demonstration of my power. The largest of the ships caught my attention and my head shot forward, catching the ship within my jaws and crushing it as though it was nothing.

I launched myself forward, winding my way

along the surface of the water or just below it. The boats and ships were no more than child's toys, left splintered in my wake. After a few passes, only a few ships remained intact and they had turned away from Iyoké, heading back to whence they came.

I considered going after them. Why should I allow any survivors? Surely whoever had sent them would get the message if none returned.

I turned my attention back to the city. They were indeed unworthy of my protection. Perhaps they needed a better message as well.

"WHO TRESPASSES UPON MY WORLD?" A voice demanded in my head.

I turned my attention to the far western horizon. Someone was coming. He was more than these others, but he was less than I. I sank below the waves, watching… anticipating… waiting to spring the trap.

Then he arrived, and I shot up into the air, coiling myself around his body.

"Do you wish to challenge me, little one?" I sent the thoughts to him.

"Great mother!" he exclaimed. *"I did not know! Where have you been?"*

His response surprised me, and I released him, sliding away through the air.

"Who are you?"

"It is I, Great Mother. Kékoatalki."

"I don't know you," I told him, but I wasn't sure that was true. *"And I am busy. There are more lessons to be taught here."*

I started toward the city. I felt Kékoatalki flying away across the ocean behind me.

"You must learn to be worthy," I sent my thoughts to them.

I looked at the walls that they thought were so mighty. I flipped my tail into the nearest section, and it collapsed, rubble flying in all directions.

"Nora! Stop!"

A small creature was flying toward me, but it was too small and insignificant to consider. I sent a gust of wind at it, and it tumbled backward to land broken on the shore.

"Nora!" A new voice sounded in my mind. It was familiar.

A form appeared in front of me, its size rivaling my own. It was a female and she had a slight glow around her. A challenger!

I dove at the form, but it was insubstantial, and I passed through it. What trickery is this?

"Nora! It's me!" the voice said. *"Bright!"*

It seemed like I should know that name.

"You cannot stand against me!" I told the creature.

"I am not your enemy!" she said. *"I am your friend!"*

Friend?

"Come back to us! We need you. Mira needs you! She's hurt!"

Mira?

I felt confused. Something about that name meant something to me, but I didn't know what it was.

"Who is this Mira?" I demanded.

"She is your sister!"

"Sister? Where is this sister?"

I received an image of the small creature I had knocked to the ground. I coiled around in the air and dropped down to where the creature had landed. It no longer had wings. It did not appear to be conscious.

The face was familiar. Why was it familiar? Memories came to me then. Mira laughing. Spaghetti dinners. Movies. Love. Going to school. Lunches. Rita Hayworth. Hugs.

This was Mira! What had I done?

Then I was next to her as Nora, cradling her head in my lap.

"Somebody help!" I yelled. "Get a doctor! A healer!"

Suddenly, Jack was there. He was pointing his sword at Mira. No, not the sword; the sheath. He was focusing his power through the sheath to Mira.

After a moment, her eyes fluttered open and he stopped.

"She needs more healing," he told me. "I am not

skilled in this art, and I am limited in what I can do, even with the sheath."

"We need to get her back to Tesia," Rispan said. "Do you know how to make a portal?"

"A portal?" I looked at him. "No."

"Give me a minute," Mira mumbled. "I can do it."

"Are you sure?" Rispan asked.

"Yeah," she answered. "But I can't hold it for long."

"Get everyone ready," Jack said.

The carriage was sent back to the villa to retrieve our luggage from the ship, such as it was, including Spike's saddle. Meanwhile, we did what we could to clean Mira up and stabilize her. Among other things, she probably had a concussion, so we didn't want her going to sleep yet. Fortunately, it didn't take long for the carriage to come back.

I looked around and saw that everyone was here. Then my eyes went to Shahz and Dyani, realizing that if Mira was able to create the portal, I'd probably never see them again.

"I guess this is it," Shahz said. "Time for you to go and get your foot stuck someplace else."

"You know you're an annoying jerk?" I scowled at him, remembering when he'd found me with my foot pinned between a boulder and some driftwood.

He grinned and wrapped his arms around me in a hug.

"Alright, alright," I told him. "I'll probably miss you. But I'm sure I'll get over it."

"Thank you for what you did here," he said.

I nodded and then gave Dyani a hug as well.

"She's ready," Jack said, picking Mira up in his arms.

We gathered around as Mira created a portal. As soon as it was formed, Jack carried Mira through. Rispan tossed our luggage into the opening and then carried Spike's saddle through. Then Usoa shuffled through with the animals. I gave a last look to Shahz and Dyani and followed them.

We were standing in an apartment and a small woman looked up, startled, from where she was eating her lunch.

"Tesia! Mira's injured," Jack was telling her. "She needs healing."

"Bring her!" Tesia wasted no time.

A new portal formed, and Jack went through with Mira and Tesia followed right behind. I stepped forward to go with them, but it was already closed.

I turned to look at the others and saw that Kata was with us, a big, goofy grin on his face.

"It worked!" he said.

"Barely." I frowned at him, recalling what had

happened. "I almost turned on the city. And I hurt Mira!"

"Yes, yes," he said dismissively. "But the city is fine, and Mira will be, too. The important thing is that now you know your true self! You are Aka-jokira again!"

"I'm Nora," I told him. "That's all. Maybe I *was* this Akajokira, once upon a time, but that's not who I am anymore."

"It is a part of who you are," he insisted. "You can't deny that any longer. You've seen it. You became it!"

"The thing I became was not me!" I snapped. "And whatever that was, I only became it because that's what you were pushing for. It wouldn't have happened otherwise, and it's not going to happen again, because I'm not going to let you do that to me again. Are we clear? You're not going to force me to be something I'm not anymore."

Kata looked crestfallen as he nodded.

"I was not trying to control you," he said. "I only wanted you to be able to be whatever version of you that you want to be. To give you an active power of choice."

"Did it occur to you that maybe that choice had already been made a long time ago?"

His eyes widened in surprise.

"Look," I said. "On the one hand, I'm glad we stopped the attack. Maybe we kept *Félbahlag* from dying, but I killed a lot of *Bahréth* to do it. Just because they were attacking doesn't mean they all deserved to die."

"Perhaps not," he said. "But you see what you were able to accomplish!"

"I also almost killed Mira!" I snapped. "Whatever that *creature* was, it wasn't *me*! And it can't be trusted! Do you have anything else to offer?"

He looked at me, not understanding.

"We still have a ton of problems here to solve," I said flatly. "You may recall there's a war going on. Do you have anything else to offer besides trying to turn me into something I'm not?"

His eyes flicked around the room as he tried to come up with something to say.

"Alright," I said to him. "I think we're done here. Goodbye, Kata."

He tried to give me a smile, but it faltered. He gave me a nod instead and then he was gone.

"I think you made the right decision," Bright said.

I nodded, still staring at the space Kata had just occupied. Then I turned to her.

"I'm still getting used to you not being in my hood." I smiled.

"Yes," she agreed. "There was something comforting about it. But I think now I need to learn to be more independent, and how to interact and contribute with others on terms they are accustomed to."

I went to the balcony and looked out at the city. It was afternoon and I expected to see a lot of people in the streets, but it was practically empty with only a person here or there, obviously in a hurry to get somewhere.

"Where is everyone?" I wondered out loud.

Rispan joined me.

"I've only been to this city once before," I said. "And I didn't really get a look around."

"I know they were going to be evacuating," Rispan told me. "Tesia was going to set up multiple portals in the city so people could get out."

"Evacuate to where?"

"The citizens were going to an abandoned city in the south. The *Ande Dannu* army was going to head north, to Usolé to consolidate with the *Danu Fé* there."

"What about the *Wyl-Dunn*?"

"As I understand it," he said, "they are supposed to engage the enemy enough to make sure they head north."

"One thing bothers me," I told him. "How big of an army does Zeg really have? He sent a bunch to Iyoké. We know he also sent some to Earth."

"I think he sent some of them to Daoine as well," he said. "But you're right. We need to get better intelligence on how many troops he has and where he's deploying them."

"I know I said I was going to help in the fight against Zeg," I said. "But right now, all I can think about is that I almost killed Mira."

"Mira's tougher than she looks." Rispan grinned.

I looked at him. "She looks pretty tough when she's got her wings and talons."

"Fair point," he agreed. "I'm still not used to that. But you know what I mean." Then he looked at me from the side of his eyes. "Or maybe you don't. She kind of glossed over a lot of her story when she told you what happened to her over the last two years or so."

"So I gathered." I frowned at him.

"I don't think she's trying to keep anything from you. There are just parts of the story she'd rather not think about too much. Things she had to do. People she lost."

"I noticed she's not quite as open as she used to be," I said.

"She's still reeling from a lot of it. When she went home from Daoine, she thought she would have time to recuperate – to come to terms with everything. But then she found out that you were missing…"

"So, she still hasn't had time to process every-thing," I finished for him.

"Process?"

"You know... put all the pieces together so they make some kind of sense, so she can move forward."

"Right," he agreed. "And then she went through whatever was involved with this new shapeshifting thing. And now losing your mother. At least she found you, though. I know that's a big relief for her."

"It seems like you're pretty close," I observed.

He nodded. "There's three of us. Me and Mouse were both orphans, and Mira didn't have any family on Daoine. We decided *we* would be a family. It was Mira's doing, really."

"She's always been good at connecting with people. She'd never be alone for long. Mira could be happy anywhere."

"You know," he said, "sometimes she wouldn't mention it for a long time. But I could tell it was always there. She was always looking for a way to get back to you and her *real* family."

"Are you trying to say you were just a temporary substitute?" I raised an eyebrow at him. "If you really know Mira so well, does that really sound like something she'd do?"

"No. You're right. I shouldn't doubt her commitment to me and Mouse. Just like you shouldn't doubt her commitment to you."

"I know," I let out a long breath. "It's just...

things are different. She's different. I'm not sure I know her anymore."

"You know her," he said. "She's still Mira. She's just learned and grown a lot since you last saw her. She's turned into a real badass."

The term surprised me, coming from him.

"One thing," he went on. "I wouldn't recommend having a drinking contest with her."

"Drinking contest?" I was surprised. "Mira?"

"She'll put you under the table," he winked and went back inside.

I guess there was a lot to this new Mira I was going to have to find out about.

CHAPTER TWENTY-SIX

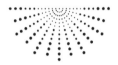

MIRA

I stretched and opened my eyes. The ceiling was unfamiliar, and I looked around. It took me a moment to figure out where I was. I was in an infirmary. Or rather, it looked like one of the rooms off of the Su Lariano infirmary.

Right.

A huge floating dragon or serpent or whatever had swatted me to the ground when I was flying. A huge floating dragon or serpent that was Nora. She'd flown without wings. I didn't understand how that worked, but that's magic for you. Whatever she'd turned into had an incredible amount of power, that was for sure!

And if I knew Nora, she was probably torturing herself over hurting me.

I sat up in the bed. I actually felt pretty good. No

pain. And I was rested for a change. I was more than just a bit hungry though.

The door opened and Tesia walked in.

"Perfect timing!" she said.

Servants followed her in and set up a huge breakfast in front of me. My stomach sent pangs of welcome to all the food.

"This *is* perfect timing!" I grinned. "I'm starving!"

The omelet was a wonderful contrast of cheese, semi-spicy peppers, shrimp, mushrooms, and red onions. It was served with some sweet melon slices on the side.

"This is delicious!"

"Since the Raven's Nest is now open twenty-four hours, it has a breakfast menu."

"Nice!" I took another bite. "I may have some ideas for them on that. But if you're giving me breakfast, I assume I've been here overnight?"

She nodded as she helped herself to a mug of coffee.

"This is late enough to qualify as brunch, though," she added.

"But I've just been here one night, right?" I confirmed. That last time I woke up from an injury it had been four weeks.

"Right. One night. It was late enough that Shigara decided to just let you sleep after the healing.

But she said to tell you to take it easy for a few days."

I paused with a bite of omelet halfway to my mouth.

"Yeah, I don't know how well that's going to work out," I said. "But I'll try. We should get back to Solaian as soon as we finish eating."

"No bath or shower?"

"Okay," I conceded. "After a quick shower"

"I'm sure everyone will appreciate the improved smell."

"Ha-ha." I gave her a mock scowl. She was probably right though. Then I had another thought. "Maybe we could swing by Felora's shop. Do you think she could fix up something that I could wear that wouldn't get shredded every time I sprout wings? Rispan cut a shirt up, but... Rispan isn't Felora."

"Eat," Tesia said standing up. "Take your shower. Then meet me at the shop. I'll go on ahead and let her know what you need."

"Thanks!"

"I'll have a word with Gylan as well," she added. "Armor takes a lot longer, but the sooner he gets started, the sooner it will be ready."

Less than an hour later, I was walking through the door of Felora's shop – clean and dressed in fresh clothes. I'd even swung by the armory and picked up a new staff to replace the one that had burned up in Tyr nya Lu.

Felora greeted me with a smile and a hug. It felt like forever since I'd seen her. Gylan was also there and sent a wink my way. Looking at the two, I could easily see where Tesia had gotten her warm demeanor.

"Now then," Felora said after we'd said our hellos. "To business. We should probably step outside so we can both see your wings."

They followed me outside and I was a bit self-conscious as I shifted.

"Hm," Gylan mused. "A harpy."

"Am I?" I asked. "I thought harpies were disgusting and filthy. And ugly and mean."

"Oh, hush," Felora scolded me. "You should know by now that any creature with a free will can be any way they choose."

"You do look very fierce, though," Tesia said with a smile.

"Aye, that she does!" Gylan agreed.

Felora was examining my back.

"Give me ten minutes," she said. "I got a start when Tesia told me what you needed. I'll have a couple of shirts for you."

She went back inside and Gylan was studying my wings and had me move them around so he could see where they might bind against armor and he made notes on a piece of paper.

"Alright," he said at last. "I don't know that I'll have it done before you need it, but I'll start on it right away."

Back inside, Felora was just finishing the second of two shirts. I slipped the first one on and tucked the other under my arm.

"Well, you two," Felora looked at me and Tesia. "I'd tell you to be careful, but I'll have to be content knowing you won't be careless. Come back when you can."

After goodbye hugs, Tesia and I went outside. She opened a portal and we stepped through to her rooms in Solaian.

Nora looked up from where she was sitting on a couch, scratching Spike under his chin. As soon as she saw me, she was up and across the room, wrapping her arms around me.

"I'm sorry! I'm sorry!" She was saying. "I didn't mean to hurt you!"

"I'm okay," I hugged her back. "It *was* pretty awesome though, you turning into that huge... whatever it was. And it can probably come in handy."

"No." She was shaking her head as she pulled away. "That's not me. Kata says I used to be like that, but I'm not anymore. What happened... Kata made that happen. And he knows better than to try that again. I've had enough of people making me do things against my will."

"You don't need to be a giant dragon," I told her. "You're pretty awesome on your own."

"I don't know about that." She frowned.

"Aren't you the one who figured out how to keep gunpowder from working?" I asked her.

She shrugged at that. Nora had never been very good at taking compliments. I decided to give her a break by changing the subject.

"So, how do things stand?" I asked, sitting at the table. "How's the plan going?"

"We haven't gotten an update," Rispan said. "But Nora brought something up last night that I think we should look into. Zeg apparently has a big enough army to split it up and attack multiple fronts. And not just multiple fronts, but multiple worlds. We know he's attacking here, but he's got to be starting to spread himself too thin. Or is his army just that big?"

"That's a good question." I looked at Nora and back to Rispan.

"I remember Iratzé and Edrigun talking about him when I first met the *Wyl-Dunn*," Nora said. "They said Zeg is a necromancer and that he wants to raise a bunch of dead gods to fight for him. To lead his army, I guess."

"Can he do that?" I asked.

I looked around the room and all I got was a bunch of blank looks.

"It is conceivable that he can raise the bodies,"

Jack said. "But I seriously doubt he can restore the departed gods to those bodies. Even Nora resists being restored to her former self."

"But I almost lost myself in it." Nora was looking at the floor. "I almost wasn't able to come back."

"Perhaps," Jack said. "But you were still in your body. The shape changed, but it was still your body. These gods Zeg wishes to raise have other bodies by now. Other lives and identities."

"So, you're saying he would just raise zombies?" I asked him. "Not gods?"

"I suppose it is possible he might locate the spirit for one of these dead gods that is between lives," he hedged. "But the bonds to the old body are gone. I don't know how he could trace them after so long."

"Whether they come back as gods or just zombies," I said, "they're still going to be a problem."

"We need more information on what he's doing," Rispan said. "Plan for the worst and hope for the best."

"We could try flying overhead," Jack suggested. "At least we could get a better idea of his deployment and numbers."

"That would help," I agreed. "Though I'm sure the *Wyl-Dunn* have already scouted on their *Gurpahn*."

"Maybe Radomér would have more information," Usoa suggested.

"Maybe," I answered. "But we don't know where he is or how to reach him."

Usoa rolled her eyes and got up from the table.

"We need to coordinate with the king and queen," I said. "Find out what they know and build from there."

Usoa walked back in from the other room.

"Why don't you ask Radomér what he knows?" she asked, placing her etching on the table in front of me.

"Right," I said, looking at the image. "I remember you said something about this. What exactly is it supposed to do?"

"If you focus on it, it should help you establish a mental connection to the person," she told me. "This one is for Radomér."

"And it works?"

"It should." She frowned at me. "You were supposed to test it."

"Either way, that was good thinking to make one for Radomér. So… I just…"

"Focus on it and send your mind to him," she told me. "Focus and call to him with your mind."

I looked at the image. She had done a pretty decent job of it and it was a good likeness. In fact, the more I looked at it, the more lifelike it became.

"Radomér," I sent my thoughts. *"Can you hear me?"*

"What?" A surprised answer came back. *"What sorcery is this? Who – Mira? Is that you?"*

"Yes! It's me!" I told him. *"Can you tell me any-thing about what Zeg plans to do? Where his army is? How big it is?"*

"It is not the army that he has that you need to worry about," Radomér said. *"It is the army he is about to raise."*

"I heard he wants to raise gods from the dead to lead his army."

"No," he answered. *"You do not understand. We are in the Métur Valley. Many wars have been waged here between the Uthadé, the Fu-Mo Ri, the Félbahlag of old… These were the gods of Danu. Many thousands of gods died in this valley, and he intends to raise them all."*

That didn't sound good.

"When is he planning to do this?" I asked him.

"Tonight, once the sun is below the horizon," he an-swered. *"Between now and then, he intends to send more soldiers to Earth and to Daoine to strengthen the beachheads he has established."*

"How is he doing that? Does he know portal magic?"

"He has the Cauldron of Dagda. It opens doorways to different worlds. But he can only go to the places that it has been used for before. As far as I can tell, he does not know how to attune it to other places. Mira, I don't know

what you or your allies can do, but if he is not stopped soon, he will crush all three worlds!"

"Alright," I told him. *"I don't know what we can do either. But get to a place that would be good for us to come through, hopefully in numbers, so we can stop him."*

I broke the connection.

"Break's over," I said. "The shit's about to hit the fan."

CHAPTER TWENTY-SEVEN

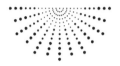

NORA

"*I* have heard of Dagda's Cauldron," Tesia said to Mira once she had explained the news to Té Niya, Berowen, Iratzé and Edrigun. "But I understood from the legends that it was supposed to be some kind of endless supply of food or drink or what have you."

I felt a little uncomfortable talking to kings and queens. I just wasn't used to the idea of dealing with royalty.

"If it is indeed some sort of a magical portal artifact," Jack said, "and it goes both ways, one could easily employ it to access whatever resources they wanted."

"I don't know about any legends," Mira said. "All I know is that Radomér told me Zeg uses it to open portals to Earth and Daoine. Do any of you know about this valley he mentioned?"

"Yes," Jack said. "I have researched this world extensively. If Zeg is able to raise all that have perished there, he would have a mighty host. And one nearly impossible to kill. Those raised by necromancy are very resilient."

"The wars that were fought there all happened before our people came to this world," Queen Té Niya said. "But I have heard tales of the fierce and bloody conflicts."

"If we don't stop him before he completes his plan," Mira said. "We may never be able to stop him."

"We have sent our army north to Usolé." Té Niya shook her head. "It is too late to change that now."

"It is not too late for the *Wyl-Dunn*," King Edrigun said. "If you could create a portal for us, we could strike Zeg directly."

"I'm pretty sure I can open a portal to him," Mira said. "Once I establish a mental connection it should be easy."

"How large a portal can you create?" Iratzé asked her. "And how long can you keep it open?"

"I've been thinking I think I should be able to tie off the threads to the spell just like any other, then it should stay open indefinitely," Mira answered. "And I can make them big enough to fly through."

"We can probably muster a thousand soldiers on *gurpahn*-back," Iratzé said. "But it would probably take at least a half an hour to fly them through, three abreast. Maybe even as long as an hour."

"I would suggest that we open several portals, side-by-side," Tesia said. "Even if they only go through a portal one at a time, we should still be able to get them through quickly."

The royal pairs exchanged glances and evidently reached a consensus.

"We'll send out the orders," Edrigun said. "Find a good place to set up the portals so they can easily fly through them. It will take a few hours to get everything organized. Be ready."

Since the *Wyl-Dunn* would be flying through the portals, it seemed the best target for the portals would be along the top of one of the walls. Rather than using the outer walls where what was happening would be in plain sight of the *Bahréth* outside the city, we decided to use the walls around the main keep at the center of the city. Though even there, it would eventually be noticed.

Now we just had to wait until the *Wyl-Dunn* were ready to fly through. Mira checked in with Radomér, but only long enough to find out he had withdrawn to the east side of the valley just south of the abandoned *Uthadé* fortress of Findias at the north end of Métur Valley. And Zeg was sending the last of the reinforcements to Earth and Daoine.

There wasn't much else that Radomér could tell her.

"I don't like it," Mira was saying. She was pacing back and forth on the parapet. "There's still too much we don't know and too much going on that we're not doing anything about."

Then she stopped, some decision evidently made.

"Tesia, you can portal to Shifara, right?" she asked. "To warn King Kholinaer and Queen Ysiola?"

"I could get to Ancaera in Shianri," Tesia answered. "Ancaera spent a lot of time in Shifara. I could use her mental images to create an anchor for another portal."

"Good." Mira replied. "And that's what you need to do. You and Rispan will need to handle things on Daoine."

"Hang on, sis," Rispan started. "I'm—"

"No," Mira cut him off. "It's better to send two of you. And as a prince of Su Lariano, you need to let Queen Astrina know what's going on so you can coordinate on that end. And Tesia needs to go because she can make portals to put armies where they need to be. Your fight is on Daoine."

Rispan didn't look happy, but he accepted what she said. Tesia was already creating a portal.

"This is yours, Rispan," Tesia said.

"Fine." Rispan scowled. Then he stepped to

Mira and hugged her. "Stay safe. You're headed for trouble."

"That's usually your job," she smirked.

"You seem to find your fair share," Rispan still hesitated.

"Rispan," Mira shook her head. Then she glanced at me with a smile. "I'm reminded of some lines from a play. Though I only saw the movie version." She looked back at Rispan. "O, that a man might know the end of this day's business ere it come. But it sufficeth that the day will end and then the end is known. If we do meet again, why we shall smile; if not, why then this parting was well made."

Rispan thought that over for a moment, then he gave her a single nod and went through the portal with Bijoux close behind.

Tesia closed the portal and was opening another.

"What about Earth," Tesia asked. "Zeg is sending reinforcements there as well."

Mira nodded. "I don't know what to do about that. But maybe if we can get word to Grace, or even reach out to Alex Stone, they may know who to contact. But none of us knows portal magic besides me and Tesia, so if we send anyone, they'd be stranded until either Tesia or I could go after them."

"I can portal," Bright said. "I have watched both

you and Tesia do this. If you can create the first one, I would be able to return on my own."

"Really?" Mira was surprised. "Alright. I can make a portal to Grace. You and Nora can go there—"

"Not happening," I cut in. "We're not getting separated again."

Mira started to object, but she saw the look in my eye.

"Fine," Mira said with a smile. She looked at Jack. "Can you go with Bright?"

Jack shook his head. "I am bound to Nora. Where she goes, I go."

Mira accepted this as though she'd expected it.

"I don't think Earth is at risk as much as Daoine," she said. "There's no way that Zeg has any idea of what he's facing in terms of modern weapons, and that's a huge tactical error on his part. Still, Earth should get whatever information we can give them."

I could tell she was doing something magical and got a sense she was sending her focus along a thread. Then she created a portal.

"This will take you to Grace," she said to Bright. "I wish we had some backup to send with you. Grace will have to do that. Just bring her up to speed on everything that's happening."

"I'm sure I'll be fine," Bright said, and she stepped through the portal.

"I'll back you up!"

Before we knew what was happening, Usoa leapt on Bastien's back and launched him through the portal.

"Stop!" Mira called out to her, but it was too late.

Mira frowned, then shrugged.

"She may be better off there than here, anyway," she said.

"Bright will watch out for her," I assured her. Then I shook my head. "It's hard to believe how much Bright has changed since I met her. She was so simple at first, but lately, instead of me teaching her, it's been more the other way around."

"They're both pretty amazing," Mira answered. "They'll probably make a good team."

"So," I changed the subject. "Do we have an actual plan besides just blindly attacking?"

Mira's mouth formed a hard line before she spoke.

"We don't know enough about what we're going into for a specific plan," she said. "The *Wyl-Dunn* will attack whatever army Zeg has with him and provide a distraction. Then we can focus on Zeg. I don't like going into this blind, but that's our situation."

We settled in to wait for the *Wyl-Dunn.*

The first thing I'd done when Mira had gotten back that morning and it looked like we were heading into trouble was to put the saddle Istas had given me on Spike. The saddle had been adapted from what the *Ranolan* clans used on their huge dogs, their *chinéha*, but it fit Spike pretty well and it was surprisingly comfortable. We'd experimented with it a few times and Spike seemed to feel like it made him more important to wear it.

I looked at Mira. She seemed... not tense, really. More like poised for action.

"I can't believe you had that line of Shakespeare memorized," I smirked, trying to lighten the mood.

"I've always loved that line." She grinned. "I just never thought I'd ever have a reason to *say* it."

As I looked at her, I felt a pang of loss.

"I guess I'm never really going to get my little sister back, am I?"

Mira opened her mouth to speak and stopped, thinking about what I'd said.

"I guess I've changed a lot since this all started," she looked sad. "I know I'm not like I used to be. There's just been so much—" her eyes fell. "I'm sorry. I never wanted to disappoint you."

That surprised me.

"Disappoint me?" I asked. "Are you serious?"

"I'm sorry."

This was almost surreal.

"Mira, you've always been so strong. And you've always held your ground. And now, it's like you've become more *you* than you've ever been." I shook my head. "Since I got here, to this world, I've been trying to be as strong as you, as brave as you. But I'm just not."

"Brave like me?" she shook her head slowly. "Silly rabbit."

"What?"

"I wasn't brave. *You* were brave. I saw that when we first met. I wasn't afraid when things came up, well… not much anyway. So, it wasn't as big a deal for me. Especially because you were there. You *were* afraid. You never said it, but I could tell and you always kept going anyway. I've always admired that about you. And all this time since the night when this all started and I went to Daoine and you went to Danu, I've been trying to be as brave and strong as *you*."

"As *me*?" I looked at her. "Are you sure you didn't hit your head or something?"

A *Wyl-Dunn* with a beard to his chest landed next to us on his griffin.

"Tavarnin!" I was surprised. "I haven't seen you in a while!"

"That's General Tavarnin, to you, young pup," he said with a wink.

"Yes, sir!" I snapped a mock salute at him.

"We are ready," he said.

"Alright," Mira answered. "Let me check with Radomér and make sure he's in a good spot for the portals."

Mira was looking at that image again of the *Bahréth*, Radomér. I actually hadn't even seen a *Bahréth* before I attacked their fleet.

"Once we go through," Jack was saying to me, "if fighting starts, stay close and I'll keep you safe."

I just nodded. I knew he had this idea that he had to protect me, and I wasn't going to argue with him. But after what we'd been through when Shelby killed Jill, I wasn't feeling so much like I needed protecting. The few people I'd killed there were nothing compared to the number of *Bahréth* I'd killed when I went through their fleet as Aka-jokira. And even though I couldn't go into that form again, I'd shown I was plenty dangerous without it when I burned those black-robes.

Maybe if I hadn't hesitated… If I'd acted sooner against Shelby… Maybe Jill would still be alive. I wasn't going to make that mistake again. And I wasn't going to hide behind Jack if things got hairy.

"Alright." Mira had put away the image of Radomér and was facing Tavarnin. "I'll set up three portals, side by side. I'll tie them off so they will stay open. The portals just look like a shimmering in the air, or a floating shadow."

"Aye." Tavarnin said. "Put them up and we'll fly through."

Mira concentrated and one by one I saw the three portals take shape. After a moment, she nodded.

"They're stable," she said. Then she looked at me and Jack. "We'll go through first."

"I'm ready," I told her.

Mira nodded and stepped through the center portal. I led Spike through after her and Jack followed right behind.

We were standing on a low hillside overlooking a long, narrow valley. A *Bahréth* warrior was standing in front of us. We were facing west into the setting sun. No more than a hundred yards to our right was a fortress tucked into the rocks of a mountain range that closed off the north end of the valley.

"Radomér." Mira gripped forearms with the huge lizard-man. "What's the situation?"

"Zeg opened portals to the other worlds in the plains outside the walls of the keep," he said. "He has already sent the reinforcements through. He still has a decent-sized force here, though. He also has at least three of the Transcendents with him. The portals are still open, and he plans to send his raised army through once he's brought them back from the dead."

"Understood," Mira said. "We're here to stop him from raising that army."

Just then, the *Wyl-Dunn* started pouring through Mira's three open portals.

Radomér gaped.

"You're bringing an army?" He scowled. "You

are making me a betrayer of my people. I thought you were just coming to confront Zeg."

"I can't confront Zeg if he has his army between us," Mira told him. "You know that. I'm sorry. But we have to keep them distracted so we can get to Zeg. Once he's out of the picture, there shouldn't be any reason to keep fighting."

"Then let us go quickly," Radomér said grimly. "I won't fight against my brothers and sisters, but I can lead you to Zeg."

He led off fast, his long legs covering a lot of ground with each step. A horn blew an alarm from within the fortress; someone must have seen the *Wyl-Dunn*. We reached the gatehouse just as it was starting to close, but we were through and Mira threw some kind of sizzling spell at the winch and the whole thing melted in place, locking the gates half open.

"Zeg is on the wall above, preparing his spell," Radomér said. "This way!"

He led us up a stairwell. I was gasping for breath when we exited onto the parapet at the top of the walls. Soldiers were already fighting, shooting arrows at the *Wyl-Dunn* who were diving at them with their griffins.

Bright light shone like a beacon from a stairwell on the other corner of the wall. Then four glorious angels stepped out. They were brilliant and breathtaking! I fell to my knees, scarcely noting how the *Wyl-Dunn* had stopped attacking.

"I've got this," Jack growled.

I didn't understand what he meant. Then Jack's form seemed to melt and expand. His skin turned red and he grew two feet in height. His enormous batwings spread out behind him, and the long horns curled out from his head. He leaped into the air and drew his sword. The blade shone brightly, even brighter than the light of the angels.

Jack launched himself at the angels.

Why is he doing that?

As the light of the sword touched them, their beautiful features seemed less distinct. Then the blade sliced through one and it fell in two pieces. The other three angels took to the air and attacked Jack.

What's going on?

I shook my head, trying to clear my thoughts. The bodies of the three angels fighting Jack seemed to alternate between beauty and something else, something horrible.

Mira was striding toward Zeg, who was looking at her with a sneer.

"You are too late!" Zeg raised what looked like a skull in his hand. "The power of the Skull of Donn has already been invoked! It cannot be stopped. Behold!"

He waved his hand out over the valley, and we

turned to look.

The valley floor was shifting… moving… almost like it was a living thing. Lumps started forming. The lumps grew into larger piles, which got taller and more narrow until they started to resemble bodies. More than just resemble; they became actual bodies with skin and hair.

"How can there be anything left of those corpses after so long?" Mira wondered out loud.

"The parts will *always* be there in some form," Zeg said with a grin. "They become absorbed into growing plants only to decompose again. The power of the skull draws those pieces together. Any missing pieces are supplemented with dirt or twigs or whatever is nearby."

"Great," Mira smirked. "So, you'll have walking piles of moldy dirt and dogshit to fight for you."

"Oh, more than that." Zeg's features seemed to blur between the human features he'd had when I met him and the scales and structure of a *Bahréth*. It was as if his body couldn't decide what form it should take.

The army of Risen began walking toward the fortress. I don't know how many there were, but the valley floor for as far as I could see was lined with raised bodies.

"The skull will also restore their spirits to the bodies," Zeg gloated. "The dead gods will serve me!"

He raised the skull again and started to mutter some words I didn't understand. The skull started to glow. It looked like someone had taken shattered pieces of skull and joined them together with silver. I could see runes painted on the bone portions and they began to glow as his chanting continued.

"I don't think so!" Mira snapped.

She started throwing lightning bolts at Zeg and he managed to get up a shield just in time. Zeg pulled in an immense amount of power and threw a huge lightning bolt back at Mira. It was too much!

Then Mira somehow redirected the bolt back toward Zeg and it struck the skull, shattering it into a million pieces. The army seemed to sway in place for a moment, then they started moving again. This time, their direction was less certain.

"You idiot!" Zeg yelled at Mira. "I needed that to pull and bind the spirits! But it matters not! They will still obey me!"

Zeg focused his power and the army's march to the fortress became more certain. The front ranks of the Risen walked toward the walls and disappeared as they stepped through the open portals Zeg had in place.

I was finally feeling like I was coming to my senses, and I knew I needed to do something to help. I tried throwing fire at Zeg, hoping to ignite him, but he saw my motion and erected some kind of shield and blocked it.

"Nora!" Mira was pointing at something. "Grab that! Shut it down!"

I looked and saw a wooden frame holding what looked like a shallow pot, about twenty feet from me. That must be Dagda's Cauldron! I rushed to it and tried to figure out what it was doing. This must be what was holding those portals open. I could sense the power it was emitting, but I didn't know how to turn it off.

I grabbed it from the frame to look at it more closely. As soon as my hands touched it, the power emission stopped. Was that it? I looked at where the portals had been. The Risen were still marching forward, but now they went forward until they reached the wall.

The portals were closed! I started to shove it into my shoulder bag, but Zeg threw a dagger at me. I dropped the cauldron on the ground as I dodged the blade and it rolled away from me, right toward Zeg!

Before I could do anything, Bright appeared in the air in front of me, floating, but in her larger size.

"How did you get here?"

"I sensed your need," she answered. "Your panic."

Bright looked around and took in the situation as the cauldron rolled closer to Zeg. She dashed forward and grabbed it off the ground. She turned to look at me, a question on her face.

"Get it away from him!" I yelled.

Zeg was reaching for her, but Bright slipped through his fingers, taking to the air again. It was strange to see her flying in her larger form. Somehow, her lack of need for wings to fly was more obvious when she didn't look like a one-inch-tall flame.

She paused in her flight.

"Do you need help?" she asked me.

I shook my head. "Just get that thing as far from Zeg as you can!"

She nodded, and then she was gone as quickly as she'd appeared.

"Aaargh!" Zeg screamed and threw a magical attack at Mira.

The stones under Mira's feet shattered and exploded upwards, knocking her from her feet. Before the dust settled, I saw Zeg disappearing into the far stairwell.

Mira got to her feet and saw that Jack was being hard-pressed by the three angels. One of his wings had been injured and he couldn't fly. The angels were attacking Jack from two sides, and they had him on the defensive. Mira threw a lightning bolt at the nearest angel and the creature absorbed the power. Mira drew her sword and attacked.

Zeg was getting away!

I jumped into Spike's saddle and urged him through the stairwell after Zeg.

CHAPTER TWENTY-EIGHT

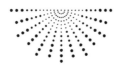

MIRA

I saw Zeg duck into the stairwell, but Jack wasn't going to be able to hold off the three *Qélosan* on his own for much longer. Zeg would have to keep, for now. I drew my sword and rushed the nearest *Qélosan*, feeling no regret as I took the head from its shoulders. I couldn't say whether it was a he or a she; with the *Qélosan*, everything was the most convenient illusion.

One of the remaining *Qélosan* turned to me, its sword flashing, but I blocked it easily. I ignored the false beauty and feelings of warmth and I swiped at it with my blade to keep it off balance. The creature launched into the air, hoping to get the advantage of height on me, but I shifted without hesitation and went into the air after it, not giving it room to ready an attack.

We grappled in mid-air, our wings flapping as we soared higher and higher. Our arms ended up in a bind, with neither of us able to effectively strike the other. I reached up with my taloned feet and ripped across its stomach.

The thing screeched, its beauty fading in and out as it struggled to free itself from my grasp. It was falling now, making no effort to fly but it had latched onto my wrist, dragging me down with it as it fell. It made a last-ditch attempt to slow its landing and I managed to free my wrist and swung my sword, cutting deeply into the shoulder of its wing.

It struck the top of the parapet and struggled to rise. Before it could get to its feet I crashed down on top of it, all talons and sword-point, ending the fight. I turned to check on Jack just as he was pulling his glowing sword from the chest of the *Qélosan* he'd been fighting.

We spun around, looking for the next enemy, but the battlements were clear. Jack slid his sword into its sheath and then gripped the scabbard. Both he and it started to glow, and I could see his injured wing visibly heal. After a moment, he released the scabbard with a nod.

"Jack," I asked him. "Where did Nora—"

My question was cut short as the first of the Risen erupted through the two stairwells. And they were armed.

"Keep them from getting out!" Jack yelled as he rushed to the closest stairwell, sword back in his hand.

I charged the other stairwell, taking down the three Risen who barred my way. His strategy was good. The doorway to the stairwell acted as a bottleneck and they couldn't rush me as a group. I continued to cut them down as they came through.

But they kept coming.

How long could I keep this up? We should have just taken to the air when they were first coming out. Could I put enough distance between myself and this swarm to get away before they grabbed me or skewered me with a thrown spear?

Even now, various projectiles were being launched at me from behind the front attackers. These Risen didn't really look like zombies. They sort of did when they first stood up in the valley, but whatever magic Zeg had used to reanimate them had also given them flesh and bone, blood and sinew. They were at least as fast as normal people, and their weapons and armor had somehow been restored with them. I had to use the *Ralahin* speed and flit to avoid all the attacks.

Every Risen I cut down was replaced by another. And another.

Time became meaningless and the stones under my feet were soaked with the blood of Risen. Then another one shoved through, pushing two others before him and he cleared the stairwell as I cut down the two Risen who had stumbled forward.

In a flash of inspiration, I sent a wave of power like a giant hammer down on the roof over the stairwell. The stones broke and collapsed into the stairs below it, making it impassable.

I had to dodge back as the remaining Risen thrust his spear at me. I spun to face him fully.

This Risen was a bit larger than the others, and he truly looked like a god. He was beautiful. He had finely shaped features and his long, blonde hair had just a touch of red. But there was no intelligence behind his eyes, only a certain animal cunning. And from the way he moved the spear in his hands, he also had the ingrained muscle-memory he'd developed during his life.

I shifted back to my human form; this guy was too good with that spear for me to risk flying. I needed the ground beneath my feet for better reaction time.

I tried going on the offensive, but every strike I threw at him was deflected with ease. Before I knew it, I was on the defensive and he was driving me backward toward the wall.

The tip of his spear began to glow as his attacks got faster and faster. I used the *Ralahin* to keep up with him, but I hadn't flitted yet, so he didn't know my full capabilities. I fell back, step by step, trying to seem afraid. I let my movements appear more frantic. Then I stumbled backward, my sword coming up.

He stepped in quickly, striking upwards at my sword and I let it fly out of my hands as I flitted forward, drawing one of my daggers as I went. I looped my right hand under his right shoulder as I went past him and flipped around onto his back, sinking my left-hand dagger into his neck. He dropped his spear and tried to reach me with his hands.

I pulled the dagger out and plunged it into the side of his neck a second time as he stumbled to his knees. He fell backward and I jumped free in time to avoid being pinned under his body.

I heard steps behind me and leapt forward in a roll, grabbing the fallen spear as I went. I turned to face my attacker and saw that he was an enormous brute with a patch over one eye. He rushed me and I thrust with the spear, aiming for that eye-patch. It rammed home and the spear-tip went through the back of his head. I heaved back and the spear came free as the body fell.

Jack was being pushed back by a half-dozen Risen. I pulled on the *Ralahin* and sent the roof of the other stairwell crashing down as I had the first. I launched forward, a whirlwind, using the spear as I would have my staff. The tip glowed brightly, as it had when the Risen had used it against me, but now there were also brightly glowing runes along the shaft. It was as if the spear itself was helping my efforts.

I took three of the Risen down with the spear before the others realized I was there. Two of the others turned to me, but they weren't as good as the guy who'd had the spear and I took one with a slash across the throat and the other with a thrust into his solar plexus.

The last of the attackers was tougher, but Jack was holding his own. The Risen he was fighting had a silvery hand, similar to Jack's. I stepped forward and drove the spear-point into the back of its skull.

Eventually, more Risen might find their way to the battlements, but for now, we could take a breath. Jack was looking at the spear in my hands.

"I have heard of that weapon," he said. "*Ar-éad-bair*. The Spear of Lugh. One of the missing treasures of the *Uthadé*."

"Lugh?" I asked. "Does that mean that's who that was?" I indicated the Risen who'd attacked me with the spear.

"Most likely," he said. "His raised body, anyway. And the one with the eye patch would have been Balor. It is ironic that he was killed with *Ar-éadbair* again. This," he nudged the silver-handed corps with his foot, "was Nuada."

"I'm not that knowledgeable about the old legends," I told him, picking up my sword from where it had fallen. "I recognize those names, but I don't know the significance."

"My research tells me that *Ar-éadbair* is a very powerful artifact," he said. "Nearly as powerful as the Sword of Light. If you throw *Ar-éadbair* and speak the command, *Ibar*, it will strike the intended target, never missing. The command, *Athibar*, will cause the spear to return to your hand."

Then Jack looked around sharply.

"Where is Nora?" he asked.

"I don't know," I answered, sheathing the sword. I was worried I might lose her again. "I noticed she was gone right after we finished those *Qélosan*."

"JAKARAEL ABALAAN!" a voice called from the battlements of a nearby tower.

We looked up to see another *Qélosan*. He was larger and more brilliant than the others I had encountered.

"What did he say?" I asked Jack.

"Jakareal Abalaan," he said. "That's me."

"Right," I said. "I remember now. I still think of you as Jack."

"Nora's abbreviation," he told me. "This is Gathrael. One of the most powerful of the *Qélosan*. Find Nora. I will deal with Gathrael."

Jack launched himself into the air, flying toward the fake angel.

Find Nora? How?

I wished I'd tied a thread to her, but I'd been too distracted by seeing her again to think of it. Then I remembered how Usoa had shown me a way to find her with our natural connection.

I heard Jack and Gathrael fighting above me, but I couldn't worry about that. I had to have confidence that Jack could handle it.

I used my *Ralahin* vision to try to see my connections; not the thick threads I had tied to people, but the fine connections I had with anyone I'd known. Usoa could see these easily, but I saw nothing. I focused my mind on Nora and tried to send a thought to her. As I did this, I saw a pulse and grasped at it. I held a fine thread that I could now just barely see. Here was my connection to Nora!

I tried to follow the thread to its end with my mind, hoping to create a portal to wherever Nora was, but the thread was interrupted somehow. It was there, but I could only follow it so far and it was gone. All I could tell was that it went north from the fortress into the Kalian Tundra.

I shifted back into my winged form and flew in the direction the thread led me.

The sounds of Jack's duel with Gathrael faded behind me as I flew past the northern wall of Falias, following the thread. The air immediately turned chilly and the ground below me was strewn with ice and snow.

Why would Nora come this way? Had someone

taken her? No, that didn't make sense. Not when she had Spike with her.

I flew closer to the ground and stopped where I could see some tracks crossing a patch of snow. I didn't know anything about tracking like Luci did, but I'd picked up a little. There were two sets of tracks. One set seemed to shift between looking human and looking like a *Bahréth*.

Zeg! Nora must have gone after Zeg!

That was both reassuring and worrisome. I knew that Nora had learned how to use magic; she wasn't helpless. But had she learned enough to defend herself against Zeg?

The other set of tracks looked like those of a huge cat. Nora must be riding Spike. Hopefully, Nora and Spike together would be enough to handle Zeg. But it would be better if I could catch them before she caught up with him.

I still held onto that fine thread as I flew further north and slightly east along the base of the mountain range. I started to notice odd crystal formations thrust upward from the ground. The thread ran through one and seemed to stop. This was as far as I'd been able to follow with my mind.

I continued past the crystal outcropping, hoping for some sign that Nora was still going in the same direction. The thread was back! I studied the crystal formation again with my *Ralahin* vision and saw that it somehow interrupted the flows and threads of magic. Maybe interrupted wasn't the right word. When I really looked, I could see that the flows passed through the crystal, but where they did, they were oddly refracted and it seemed like the flows within the crystal were frozen. That's why I hadn't been able to follow the thread; it's not that it ended, but that it *stopped*, frozen in place. It was almost as if time didn't exist inside the crystal.

All very interesting, but all I cared about now was finding Nora.

Now that I understood what was happening, it was easier for me to follow after Nora. Whenever the thread intersected one of the crystalline formations, I just located where it exited the other side and carried on.

They had covered a lot of distance. I knew that as a *Bahréth*, Zeg could move at a good pace, but I'd bet Spike could travel faster, even with Nora on his back.

Looking ahead, I could see that the thread went into a cave at the base of the mountains. I increased my speed and was landing outside the entrance minutes later. The opening wasn't wide enough to fly through, so I shifted back to my human form as I went in. I paused to let my eyes adjust so I could see in the semi-darkness. The entrance gave way to a larger space and there was flickering light on the walls. I could see a fire to one side. In the center of the room was Nora and Spike.

Crystal had formed around their legs and much of their bodies, holding them where they stood. Only Spike's front shoulders and head were uncovered. The crystal had somehow grown to hold him. It also covered Nora up to her lower ribs. I rushed to her side to see how I could get them loose.

"Mira!" Nora's eyes went wide when she saw me. "Look out!"

I heard a murmur of words to my left, and crystal appeared around my feet and ankles, locking me in place.

"Fools, the lot of you!" It was Kartahn Zeg. "You've slowed me down. Interrupted my plans. But I'll be back on track in no time! You can't defeat me in the end!"

I tried to draw the *Ralahin* to myself to throw an attack at him, but the crystal interfered and the *Ralahin* didn't respond to my will.

"You can't win, now," I told Zeg. "You've lost your magical artifacts. Your plans are dead in the water."

"Not all of them." He grinned.

Zeg held a short rod in his hands. I could see that it had runes and symbols etched into the surface, and several pieces of blue gemstones glowed on the surface. He waved the rod, and I felt the crystal spreading faster; now it was over my knees. He must be controlling the crystal with that rod.

Spike struggled against his imprisonment, but

the crystal had encased his shoulders and neck now. I tried again to reach the *Ralahin*, or even the *Ralabo*.

"Oh, you've inconvenienced me, to be sure." Zeg grinned. "But it is merely a setback."

Contact!

It was weak, but I managed to pull in a thin stream of *Ralahin*. Enough to send a bolt of lightning at the rod in Zeg's hands. He cursed and dropped the rod; I could see that it was partially melted.

"It doesn't matter," Zeg told me. "I don't need it anymore."

Zeg's features were starting to run. I didn't know if his human appearance was a shape change he had learned or just an illusion. The crystal was interfering with his control. Had he ever managed to create human-looking ears? As his hair fell away, I could see he didn't have any now. His skin was fluctuating between human and reptilian.

The crystal had reached my waist, and Spike's face was covered up to his eyes. The growth of crystal seemed to be getting faster as it went. I still couldn't reach *Ralahin*. I tried *Ralabo* with the same result.

I struck at the crystal with the butt of the spear, hoping to break it, but I might as well have been pounding at a block of steel.

"You won't get out that easily," Zeg said with a

laugh. "You won't be going anywhere soon. In fact, you won't be going anywhere, ever!"

I gripped the spear with my left hand in frustration.

"As soon as I get rid of the infernal chill of this place," he held his hand out to the flames of the small fire, "I'll get back to my plans. We *Bahréth* are not fond of the cold. And you can stay here knowing that you have failed in your feeble attempts to stop me."

There had to be something I could do. If the crystals were generating some kind of spell, I should be able to use my daggers to get out. My right hand was resting on a dagger hilt, but it was pinned in place by the crystal.

I had to do something or Zeg would continue with his plans of conquest of three worlds.

Then I remembered my last conversation with Jack.

"It was a nice try," I told Zeg. "Bringing back dead gods to fight for you. One of them showed up with this spear."

"Go ahead." He laughed again. He knew that I didn't have enough mobility at this point to put much into a throw. "Try it! It will only be too easy to block, if you could even reach me."

"I don't think you can block this spear," I told him. "It belonged to Lugh."

Zeg's brow furrowed for a moment before I saw realization on his face.

"I must have it!"

"Sure," I told him. *"Ibar!"* I shouted as I threw the spear toward him.

The spear shot out of my hand with more force than I was able to give, locked in place as I was. It plunged through Zeg's chest and his eyes went wide in shock. Zeg had instinctively tried to throw up a magical shield, but it was only partly formed and it exploded when it came in contact with the spear, causing part of the ceiling to collapse.

"Athibar," I said as I held out my hand.

The spear flew from Zeg's crumpling body back to my hand as the crystal reached my shoulder and started down my arms.

I turned my head to Nora, intending to say… something. But she was fully encased and beyond hearing anything I could say. My last thought as the crystal crept across my face was that we had won. The three worlds were safe from Kartahn Zeg.

CHAPTER TWENTY-NINE

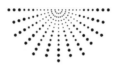

ASTÉA

Tony watched with no emotion on his face. I didn't know what he was like before. Before Mira and Nora disappeared. Before his wife Jill had been brutally murdered in front of him. I only knew what he had become in the twelve years after that.

He was a hard man, but not cruel. He was a highly competent warrior. He rarely spoke, and never smiled. And he never let anyone close or opened himself up. He'd lost his wife and walked away, needing to separate himself from the world. But then his two daughters disappeared. In some ways, I was still getting used to how people think and feel, but I suspect he felt guilty, thinking that if he had been there, Nora and Mira might not be missing.

I looked around our small group. Tony and Jack had become regular companions, along with Rispan. They had never stopped or slowed their search. Not that the rest of us had given up. We hadn't. But we'd had other things to deal with.

Rispan was why Genevané was here in the Kalian Tundra, and by association, the huge *Ogaré*, Gaetan. Rispan had the idea that, in her dragon form, Genevané might be able to do something about the crystals. We were about to find out if he was right. Genevané *had* been able to confirm that someone was indeed behind the wall of ice, rock, and crystal that barred the entrance to the cave. But she hadn't been able to say with any certainty who that might be.

Usoa was with us as well. But this *was* her world. I suppose it was my world, too. Technically. But when Usoa had returned to Danu back when the wars were first starting, I'd stayed on Earth.

They had needed a defender who knew magic.

Not that they didn't have people who could work magic. They had witches and mages. And of course, they had the *Daruidai*. But I'd had enough conversations with Luci that I didn't trust the *Daruidai*.

"Bright?" Usoa asked me. "Do you think it's them? Could they really be in there after all this time?"

Bright had been Nora's name for me and Usoa

still used it sometimes, especially if she was worried or anxious. These days, most people call me Astéa Wairua. Or just Astéa.

"We can only hope," I told her. "The crystal prevents me or Jack from just walking through to see what's on the other side. We'll have to wait and see."

"I hate not knowing," she said. "And waiting."

Genevané was immensely strong in her dragon form. She was able to use her claws to pull boulders and ice debris from the mouth of the cave, but she had to be careful so that she didn't cause the whole thing to collapse. It was slow going, even with Gaetan's help. Sometimes, she used her heated breath to clear out chunks of ice or blue crystal, but mostly it was easier to just break chunks off by hand as long as the area was stable enough. We'd tried chipping at the crystal, but it was too hard and none of our tools would dent it.

"We have breached the interior," Gaetan said over his shoulder. "Give us a few minutes and we will have the opening large enough—"

"Step back!" I called before he could finish.

I reduced my size to that of a normal *Kree* and had flown past him and Genevané through the small hole they had created. I found myself in a large chamber and increased my luminosity, filling the room with light. I expanded back to human-size and looked around.

Two large, pale-blue crystals dominated the space. There was a body on the floor that I recognized. It was Kartahn Zeg. Something had created a large hole through his chest.

I nodded in satisfaction at that. We had assumed Zeg was dead, but it was good to have confirmation. I searched the space, but there were no other chambers, no exits.

They weren't here.

Another disappointment.

But they had *been* here. Zeg's body told me that much. Zeg had fled north and they had gone after him. None of them had been seen since. It was as if they had ceased to exist.

My connection to Nora had gone dead. Usoa and I had tracked all the threads Mira had tied to people and places, but they had all been interrupted by the blue crystals.

Mira and Nora, or one of them, must have been here, in this chamber, and killed Zeg. Then where had they gone? Had Mira tried to create a portal? It's possible that the crystals might have interfered, and she went someplace she hadn't intended. If that happened, there was no telling where they might have ended up. And why hadn't they come back from wherever that was?

I shook my head, wondering if we would ever get the answers.

I opened my senses to the magic, the *Ralahin*.

Tesia had taught me how to do this; to See with magic. I was hoping for some sign or clue that would help us. The *Ralahin* didn't reveal anything that my light hadn't already shown.

I squatted next to Zeg's body. Sealed in the cave as it had been and with the cold temperatures of the Kalian Tundra, he was very well-preserved. His features were mostly human, but his reptilian, *Bahréth* skin was showing in some places. I didn't know what magic he'd used to look human, but it had clearly been more than just an illusion.

The wound in the middle of his chest was too large to be from a sword. It had more likely been a javelin or a spear. The trouble Zeg had started was still causing problems twelve years later, but it would have been much worse had he lived.

I was still using my Sight and noticed something I hadn't earlier because Zeg's body was partly on top of it. Flashes of blue light reflected off of a short metal cylinder that was partially melted. I pulled it out and stood up to examine it.

From the symbols, it had obviously been a magical artifact, but I had no idea what it was for. What had melted it? I couldn't decipher the symbols, but the embedded crystals made me wonder if it had something to do with the larger crystals. I shrugged to myself. It didn't matter now; the thing was useless.

I dropped it to the ground next to Zeg. He could

keep it here in his tomb. I turned to go but paused to give the cavern one last look before going, hoping to find some clue I'd missed. But there was nothing. Just floor, walls and ceiling, and those two large, pale-blue crystals.

The crystals had been a mystery and the main reason we'd been unable to find Nora and Mira. They were all over the Kalian Tundra and interfered with magic and interrupted magical flows. Any thread that contacted blue crystal terminated at that spot.

Genevané and Gaetan had kept working at the opening and they finished making it big enough for a person to walk through. Genevané stepped into the cave and the others followed her in with torches to provide a more mundane form of light that did not rely on my own.

"They were here," I told them. "One or both of them. They got Zeg." I pointed to the body.

"More blue crystals," Rispan said, looking at the big chunks.

"That's probably why we had so much trouble sensing what was in here," Usoa suggested.

Jack was looking at Zeg's corpse and he picked up the melted rod from where I'd dropped it. He examined it curiously, and then looked over at the two large blue crystals.

"Astéa," Jack called to me. He had a strange

look on his face. "Can you try shining your light through these?"

I held up my hand and sent a beam of intense light at the nearest of the two tall crystals. The crystal lit up as the light passed through, but there was a shadow at its heart. Something was encased inside it.

"What *is* that?" Rispan asked.

"And the other one?" Jack prompted me.

I did the same thing to the other crystal. This one was slightly larger. Like the first, there was a shape of something inside. Whatever was inside this one was much larger than the first.

"It's them," Jack said. "This artifact gave Zeg the ability to manipulate the crystal and he imprisoned them before he died. They may still be alive. We have to get them out."

"Not as easy to do as to say," Genevané answered. She had shifted out of her *Darakanos* form. "I could break the crystal, but if they are indeed inside, this would likely break them as well."

"What about your breath?" Usoa asked. "That wouldn't break them."

"Possibly," Genevané mused. "However, my breath is not safe for them, either."

"You can go slowly," Rispan said. "Remove as much as you safely can until we get a better look at what we're doing."

"There is still risk," Genevané told him. "I do

have control over the temperature of my breath, but affecting the crystal requires heat."

We all looked at Tony. He stood at the entrance looking at the crystals. He was their father. It should be his decision on how to proceed.

Finally, he gave a nod.

"Do it," he said.

"Give me some room," Genevané instructed.

She didn't need to be in her *Darakanos* form to generate the hot, dragon's breath, but she could get more volume of air from the larger lung capacity.

Once she had changed back to her *Darakanos* form, she was only able to stand with the front part of her body in the cave and she could only manage that because her wings were tucked tightly against her body.

Rispan looked at her and grinned.

"I imagine it's a bit drafty back there," he said, nodding to her back end, which was outside in the cold.

Genevané turned her snout in his direction and her response sounded clearly in everyone's minds.

"Perhaps when we return to Su Lariano, I can discuss your interest in my hind quarters with Shéna."

The grin left Rispan's face instantly and I could feel Genevané's mental laughter. Genevané was very different from anyone else I had met, and she often thought in ways I didn't understand. She was also the only *Darakanos* I'd ever encountered, so I assumed that was the reason for the difference. However, Genevané did have a very sharp sense of humor.

Genevané turned to the task at hand and started the painstaking work of directing her breath across the surfaces of the two crystals. Besides the heat, there was some magical property to dragon's breath and when it came in contact with the blue surface, the crystal turned to vapor, but it was a slow process. After three hours of work, we had one bulky shape that looked like it could be a person, and another that looked like a person and a large animal.

This had to be them. Nora would have had Spike with her. The other figure must be Mira. There was still a layer of at least an inch of the crystal encasing them. The figure I assumed was Mira now had a spear extending up from the crystal. That could very well be what had delivered the final blow to Kartahn Zeg.

"I am wary of burning them if the heat gets any closer to their bodies," Genevané said. "Perhaps now that there is less of the interfering crystal covering them, other means may be employed."

Tony stepped forward, drawing a heavy knife from a sheath. He struck a powerful blow to the nearest crystal figure with the hilt, but it simply rebounded with no visible result.

"This stuff is harder than diamonds," he said.

"I'm not even sure a pick would work, and that wouldn't be safe to try. But maybe we don't need to." His voice was devoid of emotion. "If they've been in here for all this time, they're dead. Now that we know, we can let this be their tomb."

"No," Usoa said. "Whether their bodies are alive or dead, their spirits are trapped within the crystal. I would have been able to find them otherwise. That's the only explanation that makes sense. We have to get them out."

Tony stared at her silently for a moment, then looked away.

"Nora is the *Baensiari* of the sword," Jack said, drawing the weapon. "Her connection to it, and to me, is very strong. As Genevané said, perhaps now it will be enough."

Jack stood in front of the figure we assumed was Nora, the sword held upright in his two hands. He closed his eyes and I saw a look of concentration on his face. The sword began to glow, the light getting brighter and brighter. He shifted his hold and pointed the sword directly at the crystal prison.

Light and power shot from the sword into the crystal and it began to glow as well. A high-pitched ringing sound filled the room and the walls started to vibrate. The remaining crystal holding Nora and Spike shattered, pieces flying in all directions. The bodies of Nora and Spike were revealed as they fell to the ground.

Tony rushed forward. He touched his fingers to Nora's throat and paused.

"I don't feel a pulse," he said. "But her body... she's cold and pale, but she doesn't seem dead. But then, how can there not be a pulse?"

"It could be that the crystal has held her in stasis all this time," Jack told him. "In which case, we need to wake the body back to life."

Jack removed the sword's sheath from his belt and placed it on Nora's chest, wrapping her hands around it. He concentrated power again, his own hands also on the sheath, and it began to glow.

We waited, scarcely breathing, hoping for something to happen. Jack's concentration deepened, but still nothing happened. Jack opened his eyes and swung them to me.

"Help me!" he said. "I know she flowed life power to you once. Flow it back! Through the sheath!"

I stepped forward and placed my hands on top of his on the sheath and sent warmth and life to Nora. Color started returning to her face and I saw her chest rise and fall. She was breathing!

After a moment, her eyes opened. She looked around at us in confusion.

"What happened?" she asked. "What's going on?"

Tony opened his mouth to speak, but no words came out.

"You have been imprisoned in the crystal for some time," Jack told her. "We have only just freed you."

She nodded. "I remember Zeg. He trapped us," she turned her head and saw Spike lying on the ground next to her. "Is Spike alright?"

"We used the power of the sheath," Jack said. "Both Astéa and I, to waken your body to life."

"We have to do it for Spike, too!" She turned toward Spike and laid the sheath on his body. Then she looked back at Jack. "What do I do?"

"As *Baensiari*, this should be much easier for you," Jack told her. "Simply flow power and life to him through the sheath, as you once did for me to restore my hand."

Nora concentrated and the sheath started glowing again, the glow spread to encompass Spike. After a moment, Spike moved. His eyes opened and he yawned, his double row of teeth reflecting the torchlight.

"I'm so tired," Nora said, her eyes closing. "I think I need to sleep now."

She was already out.

"It was soon to make such an effort," Jack said. "But she should be fine with some rest."

"Can you get Mira out the same way?" Tony asked.

Jack shook his head. "It was the power of the sword – the power of her connection to the sword and to me – that allowed us to overpower what was left of the crystal barrier. We will need something else for Mira. I am sorry."

"We will find a way to free Mira," I said. "We have Nora back now. She is safe. We *will* recover Mira as well."

CHAPTER THIRTY

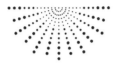

NORA

I was still tired when I woke up. At the same time, it seemed like I'd been asleep forever – I felt like I needed to get up. To look around. To talk to people. I forced myself to sit up.

I was in a cave. I'd been lying on some blankets on the floor. There were several other people here, one of whom was a woman sitting near me and looking at me curiously.

"Um… Hi," I said. "I'm Nora."

"I would hope so," she said, humor showing in her eyes.

I hid my confusion at her cryptic answer by looking around the cave. It seemed vaguely familiar and as I thought about it and nodded to myself as I remembered coming here, chasing Kartahn Zeg.

Tony was here! He was sitting near me by a small fire, dozing. He looked older than I remembered. I wondered briefly if Jill was here, too, but then I remembered. Jill was dead. Killed by Shelby, of all people. No wonder Tony looked so much older.

I glanced at the other people that were here. I recognized Usoa and Rispan. And Jack and Bright, of course. The only ones I didn't know were the woman I'd spoken to and a huge figure that was sitting with his back against the cave wall. He, too, was looking around, but his attention frequently returned to the woman. I looked back at her, slightly annoyed that she hadn't introduced herself to me in turn. I opened my mouth to ask, but she spoke before I got a word out.

"I am Genevané," she told me. "Rispan asked me to aid in the search."

"Search?" I asked. "What search?"

"For you," she said. "And for Mira."

Mira!

Memories flooded back to me. Zeg had done something and trapped me and Spike in the blue crystal. Then Mira came and he trapped her, too. I remembered the horrifying experience and the crystal slowly spread up my body and over my face. What had happened? The last thing I remembered was Mira trying to break the crystal with a spear she had.

"Where's Zeg?" I asked her. "Where's Mira?"

"Zeg is dead," she told me. "As for Mira..." She tilted her head toward the center of the room and I looked over.

I didn't see Mira.

"Where..."

Then I realized what she'd meant. There was a big piece of crystal that was vaguely body-shaped standing near the center of the room. Part of a spear was sticking up out of one section.

"Is she okay?" I climbed to my feet. "We have to get her out of there!"

Tony's eyes snapped open and went to me. He stood up immediately and stepped toward me, putting his hands on my upper arms.

"Nora, are you alright?" He looked into my eyes. "How do you feel?"

"I'm fine," I said. "Tired. But what about Mira?"

Everyone had stopped whatever they were doing and were looking at me.

"What?" I looked at them. "Can somebody please tell me what's going on?"

"You were both encased in the crystal," Bright spoke up. "The crystal interferes with magic and connections. Genevané removed as much of the crystal as she could do safely. Then Jack was able to use your shared connection to the sword to pierce the interference of the crystal to get you out."

"But not alone," Jack added. "It required Astéa's connection with you as well."

"Astéa?"

"Me," Bright supplied. "I mainly go by Astéa Wairua, now."

"What do you mean, *now*?" I asked her. "You make it sound like it's been a while."

No one commented on that, but from their faces, I could tell they had plenty to say.

"Never mind that." I'd deal with whatever they had on their minds later. It wasn't as important as getting Mira out of the crystal. "Why haven't you done the same thing to get Mira out?"

"Mira does not have a connection to the sword," Jack answered. "The same solution cannot be applied."

"We need to figure something out, fast!" I told them. "How much longer can she stay in there? Won't she suffocate?"

"She is safe," Bright assured me. Or Astéa, I'd have to get used to that. "When you were encased in the crystal, you were in a form of stasis. You were trapped, body and soul, but your body was neither alive nor dead."

"But she'll be alive as soon as she's out of the crystal?"

"When we got you out of the crystal," Astéa went on, "your body was without life. We had to flow power and healing to you to infuse you with life once more. As you did with Spike."

Right. I remembered that now.

"Alright." I relaxed a little and walked over to look at the crystal that held Mira. "So, she's safe for now. Still, we should get her out as soon as we can. I assume we can't just chip it off?"

"The crystal is extremely hard," Jack said. "Striking it with enough force to break it would be difficult and would likely injure her."

I glanced at Genevané. "You removed a bunch of the crystal?"

She nodded.

"How?"

"It is susceptible to my breath," she answered.

"Your breath?" *How is halitosis a solution?*

Genevané raised an eyebrow at me and Astéa chuckled. I knew Astéa could read my thoughts if they were loud and unguarded, it seems Genevané could as well.

"Genevané is *Darakanos*," Astéa explained. "A dragon."

"Ah," that made a certain kind of sense. "Dragon's breath. I get it. Why can't that work to get the rest off?"

"Intense heat is required," Genevané said.

I nodded, thinking it over. She must have shaved off what she could without risking injury.

We couldn't break it off and we couldn't use more heat. But there had to be a solution.

"How exactly were you able to get me out?" I asked them.

"The crystal does interact with magic to some degree," Jack said. "Though mainly, it interferes with magic or blocks it. However, with enough power and with your connection to me and to the sword as *Baensiari*, we were able to push through the blockage of the crystal. Once the power was flowing through that connection, we were able to expand it, causing the crystal to shatter."

"And since Mira doesn't have a connection like that," I nodded, finally understanding the problem, "we need to find a different solution. What do we know about the crystal?"

"Nothing beyond what we have discussed," Jack said. "Though it seems Kartahn Zeg had some knowledge. Or the creators of the artifact he used did. If it still functioned, perhaps it could be employed to remove the remaining crystal. But it does not."

"Acid might work," I thought out loud. "But that leaves us with the same problem of hurting Mira. We can't heat it. We can't pound on it. There has to be some magical solution."

"Yes," Jack agreed. "But thus far it has been impervious to magic except for what we did with you, once we had reduced the amount of crystal around you."

"We need someone with knowledge." I frowned. Nimue hadn't known anything about the crystal. At least, it wasn't in her grimoire. I'd read through it enough times that I'd remember any mention of the blue crystal.

I did know someone that might know something about it. He'd pretty much pissed me off the last time I talked with him, though. Still, getting Mira out was more important than my annoyance.

"Katamakutu!" I called, both out loud and with my mind.

I sensed him at the other end of my thoughts, but he didn't reply. I did get a sense for his emotions.

"Stop pouting and get over here," I told him.

Then he was in front of me, looking, as did all the *Noélani*, like a beautiful *Kajoran*. Except he had a scowl on his face.

"You block me for years and then suddenly you expect—" He stopped in the middle of what he was saying to take in our surroundings. "Why have you come to the Kalian Tundra? This is not a safe place to be."

"It's kind of a long story, Kata," I said. "See that guy?" I pointed to Zeg's body where it lay sprawled on the ground. "We chased him here. I did. And Mira came after."

"It appears you caught him," he said. "When was this?"

"Um, I don't know," I looked at the others. "I meant to ask. How long *has* it been?"

"More than twelve years," Tony said.

"No way!"

"It is true," Astéa said. "You and Mira disappeared over twelve years ago. We have been searching ever since."

Kata's eyes widened in understanding.

"You were stuck in *Kalias*?" he asked.

"*Kalias*?"

"The crystal," he said.

"Yes," I told him. "And Mira still is."

Twelve years? No wonder Tony looked older. What about me? Did I look twelve years older, too? How could I have been stuck in here for twelve years?

Kata's eyes went to the crystal standing in the middle of the room. He walked over and squatted down to examine the remains of a second formation that had apparently been where Spike and I had been trapped. Nodding, he stood and walked around the crystal that held Mira, looking it over. Then he reached out and flicked the tip of the spear that protruded from the crystal.

"I thought you had been ignoring me, blocking my thoughts, but if you were imprisoned in the crystal," Kata explained, "you would have been unable to hear me or respond."

"What exactly *is* this stuff?" I asked him.

"A very long time ago, we had an incursion," he answered. "An *awa'ia*, a god – or goddess in this case – thought to expand into this world. That happens from time to time. We fought her off eventually, this Kali. But she established herself in this region before we even knew she was here. The *Kalias* was her creation, to use as a defense against the *Noélani* or any other *awa'ia*. It is very effective."

"Then you know how to get rid of it, right?" I asked him. "You can get Mira out without hurting her?"

He shook his head. "We never solved it. We ended up abandoning the entire region, naming it for the goddess we fought. *That* was a glorious contest!"

"You must know something that can help us," I prompted him.

"How were you freed from your imprisonment?" he asked.

He listened as we went over everything they had done to get me out.

"Nicely done," he said. "I can extrapolate from there that you should be able to use your connection to Mira in a similar way."

I shook my head. "Mira doesn't have a connection to anything like I did to the sword."

"Not precisely the same, no," he agreed. "But all that is needed is a strong connection and some way to reach her."

"But she doesn't *have* a connection," I objected. "That's why I called you here. To see if you knew something we *could* do."

"Everyone has connections," Kata answered. "One cannot operate in any universe for long without developing connections. While not completely inaccurate, it would be overly simplistic, and misdirecting, to say that everything is connected."

"But you said it, anyway," I pointed out. "Misdirecting or not."

He gave a shrug of acknowledgment before continuing.

"You have connections with everyone in this room. Some of those connections are stronger than others. Some are very faint, but still there."

"I don't think that's the same thing," I said. "That's not the same kind of connection."

"Isn't it?" he asked. "How would you define *kind* of connection?"

"I don't know." I scowled at him.

"If you would embrace your past," he said, "your knowledge of these things would return."

I glared at him, and he raised his hands in surrender.

"Very well," he said. "In practical terms, one

could say that there are two kinds of connections, the physical and the nonphysical. Of course, when we take into account that the physical is simply our created reality, a mutually maintained dreamspace, if you will, even physical connections originate in the non-physical. Ultimately, everything originates in the nonphysical."

"Let's stick to the practical stuff," I told him.

"Yes," he agreed. "Physical and non-physical. But a connection is simply a pathway on which something can flow. Nothing more."

"That's not true." I shook my head. "You can have different kinds of connections with different people."

"The connection is simply a connection," he answered. "The difference you're referring to is what you flow on that connection. Love. Hate. Admiration. These are all things that can be sent on a non-physical connection. The more you flow, the stronger the connection becomes. If you neglect a connection, it can atrophy."

"To make a long story short," I sighed, "you're saying I have a connection to Mira? One that I could use to get her out?"

"From what I can observe," Kata said, "you have two extremely powerful connections, stronger than any others, even stronger than the connection to the sword. One of them is with Bright."

I looked at Bright in surprise.

"She goes by Astéa, now," I told him, stalling while I processed what he had said. "And the other connection?"

"The other connection terminates in that crystal," he pointed to where Mira stood in her prison. "Interestingly, Astéa also has an equally strong connection to the same point."

"How's that possible?" I asked. "They barely met."

He shrugged. "Perhaps it's a three-way circuit. Three points of a triangle. And I think I detect some traces of mother – of A'iwanea. But I wouldn't be able to tell you how any of this came about."

I had my own ideas about that, going back to when Luana had forced Mama A'iwanea's Heartpiece into me and tried to take over my body. Bright – Astéa – was still early in her development to sentience and somehow the three of us had all linked together to block Luana.

"If that's true, how can we use it to get Mira out of the – what did you call it? The crystal."

"The *Kalias*," he supplied. "I don't know. But I'm sure you'll figure it out between the two of you."

"I can't even see it!" I protested.

"You don't need to," he shrugged. "Just because you can't see something doesn't mean it isn't there."

"So, what do we do?"

He shrugged again. "The *Kalias* is still a barrier,

even this as it is now. Try combining connections. You'll come up with something. Meanwhile, I'm glad to learn you weren't just ignoring me. I admit I was a bit miffed about that. You've got quite a game going on here. Good luck!"

He was gone.

"That was useless," I grumped.

"I disagree," Jack said. "I found it very informative. Plus, we now know that you and Astéa have connections that can be employed to free Mira."

"Right." I frowned. "But we still don't know how."

"The difficult aspect will be to pierce the barrier of the *Kalias*," Jack went on. "It was the same when we were attempting to free you. Even for that, I used your connection to Astéa, in conjunction with your connection to the sword and your connection to me."

"He said something about a circuit," Tony said. "Couldn't you use something as a conduit? Like a wire for electricity?"

"I suppose," I said. "But we'd still need to get through that crystal. Are you thinking of trying to drill through it?"

"We don't need to," he shook his head. "Not if you can use that." Tony pointed to the roughly eighteen inches of spear that protruded from the crystal. "I'm assuming the other end of that is in her hand. That's a pretty direct conduit. If you can use it."

I looked at Astéa. "Let's try it!"

"Are you sure you're ready?" Rispan asked. "You just woke up. And remember, when you, and Spike, first came out, you needed more... life flowed into you to bring you out of whatever that state was. They used the sheath to do it, because of your connection to it. After you revived Spike, you passed out from the effort."

"Not for long," I said. "I'm a little tired, but I'm fine now."

"You passed out three days ago," Rispan said. "We've been waiting and hoping you would be alright. If you're not ready but you manage to get her out... What if you're too weak to revive her?"

That set me back.

"He makes a good point," Usoa spoke up from where she leaned against her reclining griffin. "We know she is safe within the *Kalias*. Once she is free of it, we may need to act quickly if we hope to revive her."

"Alright," I said. "We should take things slowly, make sure we are ready. Make sure I'm ready. But maybe we can just test the connection? Let's see if we can actually reach her using the spear as a conduit."

"That seems reasonable." Rispan replied, looking around for confirmation.

Usoa shrugged.

"I have no objection," Jack said. "But I do not know what to expect from such an attempt."

"Do you want to try it?" I asked Astéa.

She eyed Mira's prison and the spear for a moment before giving a nod.

"But I think we should try for minimal contact," she said. "Just enough to establish whether it is possible. Then we can determine how best to proceed."

"Okay." I stepped toward Mira. "What do we do?"

"I would suggest the two of you join hands, with your connection to magic active," Jack said. "Then touch your other hand to the spear. Send a gentle flow of power through it to sense Mira on the other end. If you are able to sense her, we will know the connection is viable."

Astéa stepped up next to me and held out her hand. In her smaller form, Astéa had pretty much stayed in the hood of my cloak, but we hadn't had actual physical contact since her early days of development, and never using power. When our hands made contact, I felt a jolt. Not an unpleasant one, like electricity, but the sensation was somehow similar. Her eyes widened at the contact.

"Are you alright?" I asked her.

"Yes," she nodded. "You?"

"I'm good."

I looked at the spear and took a breath.

"Alright," I said. "Let's try it. Nice and easy."

We reached out with our empty hands and placed them on the spear. Power flared as the spear somehow amplified our connection. The shaft glowed from within the crystal.

I felt Mira! She was there!

"She is waking!" Astéa exclaimed. "We must get her out now! If she revives within the crystal she will suffocate!"

CHAPTER THIRTY-ONE

MIRA

*M*y eyes opened but all I could see was a blue blur. I could feel power flowing into my left hand through something I was gripping. I tried to move but my entire body was held in place.

I had no air! I started to panic and forced myself to calm down.

I was no record holder, but I could hold my breath for a respectable amount of time. But not if I panicked.

I tried accessing the *Ralahin*, but the only power I felt was what was still coming to me through my hand. It was Nora. Somehow, I knew, it was Nora. I could feel her. Not only her; there was someone else. *Who?*

"I am Astéa Wairua," the thought came to me. *"You know me as Bright."*

"And me." It was Nora. *"We need to get you out of the crystal. Can you help?"*

The crystal. I remembered. Zeg had managed to trap me in the crystal and it blocked magic.

My lungs started to burn, but I tried to focus.

The spear. Power was coming from Nora and Astéa through the Spear of Lugh. I struggled to move again, but I was held fast. I felt another source of power – my right hand was resting on my dagger. The dagger was imbued with magic. It had a spell that could cut other magic.

Would that work against the crystal? I pushed against my crystalline restraints with all my strength, but there was not even a molecule of give. I drew power through the spear, everything I could pull and Nora and Astéa were sending me an incredible amount. I flowed that power outward against the crystal.

I still saw nothing but blue, but the more power I flowed into the crystal, the more it glowed. It got so bright I had to close my eyes against the glare. Still, I flowed more and more power.

I was feeling lightheaded, and my body tried gasping for air where there was none. Spots were appearing in my vision, behind my closed lids. I couldn't keep this up much longer; I was about to pass out from lack of oxygen.

I pushed with everything, physically, magically with the power I was getting through the spear, and with the spell of the dagger. It seemed like the crystal might be reaching a saturation point of magic. I could feel it vibrating around me and I could sense ruptures, cracks in the blockage. I drew more power through the cracks and sent the most powerful wave I could against the crystal.

The crystal burst in all directions. I fell to my knees, gasping for breath, finally free of its grasp. I felt hands on me, lifting me up.

Not just Nora and Astéa. Others were here, but I couldn't tell who. I was too busy trying to slow my breath and calm my racing heart. My dagger was in my hand, and I could feel someone take it and slide it into its sheath at my belt.

People were talking, but I couldn't hear them over the rushing sound in my ears. Moments later, I had been laid down on some blankets and I could feel that people had stepped back, giving me room.

I looked around at them as my breath turned into something more normal.

"About time you woke up." Rispan was grinning at me. "Since when did you get so lazy?"

"Don't worry," I told him. "You're still the champion for that."

"How do you feel?" Nora asked.

I took a moment to figure out the answer to that question.

"Invigorated," I told her. "I mean, I'm catching my breath now that I can breathe, but I feel full of energy."

Nora looked at me curiously. "A little while ago, I was feeling pretty tired. But that's totally gone."

"It is the connection the three of you have," Jack said. "Katamakutu was correct about that. I am not familiar with such a thing, but your combined power when you are connected is far more than I have ever witnessed."

My eyes went to Usoa. But she was not the Usoa I knew. The Usoa I knew was a teenage girl, not the young woman who now looked back at me. My eyes shifted to Bastien, and he was at least two feet taller than when I'd last seen him.

"How long?" I asked them. "How long was I stuck in that stuff?"

"You figured that out quick." Nora raised an eyebrow at me. "They told me it's been more than twelve years."

Nora and Spike looked the same. I nodded to myself as I remembered that they'd been caught in the crystal before I had.

"Alright." I let out a sigh. "I need a debrief. What's been happening in the last twelve years? Zeg sent his armies to Earth and to Daoine. He raised another army from the dead. First, we took away his ability to raise more dead and then we took away his ability to open portals. I seem to remember that, just before I got turned into a blue popsicle, I managed to shove a spear through Zeg's heart. What else happened?"

Everyone shifted gazes back and forth, wondering who was going to start.

"Someone?" I prompted.

"As far as anyone knew, you, Nora and Zeg all simply vanished," Rispan said. "Without Zeg and his Transcendent pushing them, the Daoine drive fell apart right away. None of that army was interested in fighting anymore. Some of them formed a small community in the mountains southwest of Shifara. The rest were given passage back to Danu."

"Tesia opened a portal for them?" I asked. "Or has someone else learned to do that."

"Tesia," Rispan confirmed.

"Alright." I turned to Usoa. "What about here on Danu? We are still on Danu, right?"

"Yes," she answered. "The *Bahréth* here have mostly retreated to Murias, on the western coast. They are led by a group called the Children of—"

"Children of Ezhti." I said, cutting her off. "That's good. So, things are peaceful here as well."

"No," Usoa shook her head. "We have problems with the Risen."

"I hoped they would… I don't know… lose animation when Zeg died."

"They don't have the intelligence of people," she told me. "But they can be quite cunning. There are bands of varying sizes roaming around, and they have learned to be stealthy. Sometimes more than one group will get together. Entire villages have been decimated. Some even managed the crossing to Avalon and Tyr nya Lu."

I felt a wave of anger coming from Nora and looked at her. She had clenched her jaw and her expression had darkened.

"Tyr nya Lu was always meant to be a city of hope and peace," she said.

"It will be so again," Jack said to her.

"Yes." Her voice was firm with certainty.

Nora saw the question on my face and she tried to explain.

"I know that when we move on to other lives, we are no longer obligated to promises made by earlier identities, but…" I could see she was trying to understand what was driving her. "It isn't because once upon a time I was Nimue and was responsible for Tyr nya Lu. It's because now I – Me, Nora – *I* am the *Baensiari*, the keeper and guardian for the sword now. And for that city. Because I once was Nimue, I am aware of the vision of what Tyr nya Lu was meant to be. I want that vision. And this is not a Nimue responsibility. It's a Nora responsibility. And it's a worthy one."

I could tell she was sorting through her feelings as she spoke, and I knew she was feeling her way.

"Does that make any sense?" she asked me.

"Good enough for me," I told her. "You'll have my support. In any way I can."

She nodded with relief.

"I should also tell you," Jack said. "Gathrael escaped me in our duel. He leads the Risen."

That wasn't good news.

"Okay," I went on. "Who can fill me in on what's been happening on Earth?"

"I've been spending a lot of time there," Astéa said. "Usoa has been back and forth between Danu and Earth. But things have been changing so much there. It's a bit chaotic. Even Tony has a hard time understanding the changes."

"Tony?" I asked. "Tony's been helping you?"

I hadn't realized someone was standing by the entrance to the cave until he moved.

"*Hola, mija.*" It was Tony.

The last image I had of him flashed into my mind. He had turned his back to us after Jill was killed and was walking off into the forest. The pain of that day was still fresh in my mind, but I was on my feet and had my arms around him before I knew what was happening.

One advantage to my method of always looking for the next thing that needed to be done and doing it was that it kept my mind off of things that were difficult to deal with. Like Jill's death. Like Tony leaving. But now he was here and all thought of the "next thing" was gone. The only thing I cared about now was the bear hug I was getting from Tony.

Finally, I pulled back from him and wiped my eyes.

"I'm glad you're here, papa," I told him. I'd only used the term with him on rare occasions because it tended to embarrass him. But it didn't seem to embarrass him now.

"Where else would I be?" He smiled sheepishly. "I had to find my girls."

In spite of his words, I could see changes in him. There was an aloofness, a separateness, that hadn't been there before. His smile was genuine, but it didn't change his eyes. And there was an alertness, a wariness. He wore military-style fatigues, but there were no patches, and he was fully armed with an automatic, a knife, and a rifle slung around on his back. I'd always known Tony had served, but he had never seemed so deadly as he did now.

"I guess I should hear about what's been going on back home," I said. I took his hand and led him back to the fire and we sat down.

"Chaotic is a good word for it," Tony said. "I guess it all started with the videos. The ones of the _Bahréth_ when they first came through in Ireland. Their warriors... their mages. Those videos went viral. Suddenly, everyone knew that magic was real. They knew that all the old myths and legends were based on real races and places, and that there were other worlds."

"It doesn't take much imagination to guess how that must have turned everything upside-down." I frowned. "A lot of religions would have been in turmoil, and I bet there were hard-liners saying it was all the work of the devil."

"Yep." Tony agreed. "And, of course, the governments wanted to get in on it, and the big corporations. And every two-bit conman on the street. Schools of magic started opening everywhere, most of them scams. Then a delegation showed up from Daoine."

"From Daoine?" I was surprised.

"From Su Lariano, in fact." Rispan grinned.

"It probably helped that the first races that came through that weren't *Bahréth* were so small," Tony said. "People tend to think they are smarter or better than small people, so they aren't intimidated by them."

"Tesia and Réni set up trade agreements," Rispan said. "Along with Bavrana and Gralbast."

"Oh, my," I said. "That's not a group to underestimate!"

"Yeah, there's a good bit of trade going back and forth," Tony said. "Tesia has a corner on the market for transport. She said it was your idea, and you're half-owner of the company?" He shook his head.

"Anyway, you're loaded. There's even a Raven's Nest restaurant chain on Earth now."

"What?" I could see how different things must be, but my erstwhile business partners had certainly taken every advantage of the changing situation.

"Tell her the rest," Astéa told him.

Tony's eyes went to the ground for a moment.

"A group who call themselves the *Daruidai* stepped up," he said. "Said they'd been secretly protecting the world from magic and the supernatural for thousands of years. They threw up some sort of magical barrier around the entire region the *Bahréth* had taken over in Ireland. Locked them in."

"Why?" I asked. "They'd probably just want to go home like the ones on Danu and Daoine."

"Not according to the *Daruidai*." Tony shook his head. "And it seems like the *Bahréth* are somehow able to sneak in and out of the area and cause all kinds of mischief. The *Daruidai* have been given more and more power and authority worldwide to police magic and unauthorized incursions from other worlds."

"How are the *Bahréth* getting out?"

"The magical barrier has been replaced with a physical one," he said. "It's manned with soldiers and heavily patrolled. Plus, there is some sort of spell on the area now that makes it impossible to work magic in the *Bahréth* zone. But the incidents outside the zone? The *Bahréth* are being blamed for it, but I don't think it's them."

"Then what's really going on?"

"I couldn't tell you." He shrugged. "I haven't been there as much as Astéa. Or even as much as Usoa."

"Where were you?" I asked. "Su Lariano?"

"Told you," he said. "I had to find my girls."

Nora and I shared a look.

"Tony and Jack have been focusing on finding you two," Astéa said.

"Not the whole time." I was shocked.

"Do you want precise percentages?" Jack asked. I looked at him to see if he was joking, but he was serious.

"I got the house fixed, but with Jill gone," Tony was looking at the ground again. "There really wasn't anything to keep me on Earth."

"My oath to Nora could not be foresworn," Jack said. "Diligence and dedication were my only options."

"Wow." I shook my head. "You guys amaze me."

"Rispan has spent a lot of time on the search as well," Astéa added.

I looked at Rispan, "You were planning a wedding last time we talked."

"It happened," he said with a nod. "Shéna understands why I've been away so much."

"Rispan!" I was shocked. "How could you do that to her?"

"*You* came for *me*!" he said fiercely. "How could I do any less for you?"

"Yes, but *I* wasn't a newlywed!"

"And if you had been, would that have made any difference?" he asked.

I opened my mouth to object, but there were no words. I let out a sigh. He was right. It wouldn't have made any difference.

"You're still an idiot," I told him. "You need to seriously work on making it up to her."

"Good to have you back." He gave me a sheepish grin.

I sent a mock glare at him, but really I was thinking about everything they had told me about what had been happening.

Ending Zeg hadn't ended all the problems.

We had Gathrael and his *Qélosan*, not to mention marauding Risen, to deal with on Danu. And we had the situation on Earth with the *Daruidai* and the *Bahréth*. And I still had the mystery of my parents and my mother's chest to solve, but that would have to be on the back-burner for now.

"Alright." I looked at the faces around me. "Where do we start?"

End of Book 6
The story will continue in *Heritage Unbound*.

GLOSSARY

Ah-Shan: Religion of the *Félbahlag*.

Akotan: One of the six indigenous clans of the Ranolan Savanna.

Alauikiki: A kind of fish found along the Kajoran Archipelago with a sweet, light-blue flesh.

An-Jhyeh: Demi-gods of the *Bahréth*.

Ande Dannu: (Fae of the Summer Court.) They were *Loiala Fé* who migrated from Daoine to Danu.

Ar-éadbair: Name for the Spear of Lugh.

Asha Kree: *Kree* that have evolved into sentient creatures.

Ashae: (Sidhe or Fae) *Ashae* are roughly six and a half feet tall, with pointed ears, platinum-colored hair, pale blue eyes, and light skin. *Ashae* are a faction of the *Uthadé*. They split from other *Uthadé* on Danu and migrated to Daoine.

Athibar: Command that caused the Spear of Lugh to return to the caster's hand.

Avalon: An island in the Sulosh Sea where stands the ancient *Uthadé* city of Tyr Nya Lu.

awa'ia: Kajoran word for god.

Baensiari: Title for the protector and keeper of the Sword of Light. The first three *baensiari* were Duanna, Aradi, and Nimué. The term can also have a broader sense for someone who is a protector and spiritual guide.

Baggies/Baggy: Slang term used by the *Kajorans* for *Félbahlag*.

Bahrantu: Large, scorpion-like creatures that serve the *Bahréth*.

Bahrél: Great desert on the western side of the southern continent below Danu. Home to the *Bahréth*.

Bahréth: Reptilian race from the southern continent of Danu. They stand eight feet tall on their hind legs, bear a spiked tail of another six feet, have razor-sharp claws, a venomous bite, chameleon abilities, emit a call that pains the ears and sends shivers down your spine, and are extremely cunning.

485

Bayibaa: African word for witch.

Borosoor: Huge, god-like serpentine creatures that were the original concept for later dragon races created by other gods.

Bronsam: African word to indicate an evil being.

Caladbolg: A name for the Sword of Light.

Carabora: An island in the Kajoran Archipelago.

Chakuta: Traditional *Kajoran* headdress worn by women.

Cheenya: A traditional hard liquor of the *Wyl-Dunn*.

Chinéha: *Ranolan* term for the large dogs they use as mounts.

Chipasek: One of the six indigenous clans of the Ranolan Savanna.

Claíomh Solais: A name for the Sword of Light.

Dai so: A formal *Kajoran* woman's dress, such as for a wedding.

Daijheen: From the world of Sheobal. While *Daijheen* can adopt a human form, they are naturally red-skinned, have claws, horns, and bat-wings, and stand approximately eight feet tall. They are sometimes referred to as demons.

Dajhanok's blade: *Bahréth* expression refers to the knife of their god of chance. The knife might have a blade on both ends, so you don't know if it will help or hinder until you grasp it. Either way, you have to take a firm grip.

Dannu Fé: (Fae of the Winter Court.) They were *Loiala Fé* who migrated from Daoine to Danu.

Danu: The original home of the *Ashae* of Daoine.

Daoine: This is the continent and realm of the *Ashae* and *Ulané Jhinura*. Origin of *Loiala Fé*.

Daruidai: An ancient order predating the druids which serves to police the world of supernatural and magical elements.

Derris: Port city on the island of Carabora in the Kajoran Archipelago.

Falias: Abandoned *Uthadé* city at the northern end of the Métur Valley, north and east of Tir nya Lu.

Ferazi: Port city on the island of Kajo in the Kajoran Archipelago.

Félbahlag: (Fir Bolg) *Félbahlag* are roughly six feet tall, with slightly pointed ears, brown hair and eyes, and swarthy skin, owing to their interbreeding with humans. *Félbahlag* were a faction of the *Uthadé*. They split from other *Uthadé* on Danu and migrated first to Ireland and then to Greece. Eventually, they managed to return to Ireland. There were natural portals from Danu to Ireland at this time and it was very easy to walk from one to the other. Nuada and the *Uthadé* wanted to expand to Earth and demanded half of Ireland. The *Félbahlag* refused and fought the first battle of *Métur* against the *Uthadé* on Danu. They lost this war and retreated to a small continent east of Danu. Where they have established pre-industrial technology heavily influenced by their time on Earth.

Félbahrin: Home of the *Félbahlag*.

Fél Naran: Ancient, monotheistic *Félbahlag* religion. The god, Véshdani, is neither male nor female, or possibly both.

Findias: Abandoned *Uthadé* city on the east coast of Danu.

Fragarach: A name for the Sword of Light.

Fu-Mo Ri: (Fomori) *Fu-Mo Ri* are roughly six and a half feet tall, with pointed ears, red hair, green eyes, and pale skin that tends to freckle. *Fu-Mo Ri* are a faction of the *Uthadé*. Because of their difference in coloring, many *Uthadé* considered them lesser or monstrous, despite a large number of marriages between the two groups. The *Fu-Mo Ri* fought the second battle of *Métur* against the *Uthadé*. Although they did terrible damage to the *Uthadé,* they lost in the end. At least one ship of 100 men and 100 women was all that survived, though they may have been joined by other ships. It is thought they may have become pirates.

Gajhanti: Mammoth-like creatures used by the *Bahréth*. Native to the Ranolan Savanna.

Gan: *Wyl-Dunn* title inferring the status of king for a *ganesh* within the *Wyl-Dunn kaganesh*.

Ganesh: A self-governing sub-group or traveling camp of *Wyl-Dunn*. *Wyl-Dunn* are nomadic and are divided into smaller *ganesh*. All *ganesh* collectively are referred to as *kaganesh*.

Ganum: *Wyl-Dunn* title inferring the status of queen for a *ganesh* within the *Wyl-Dunn kaganesh*.

Gartza: *See Danel Gartza.*

Gastbaween: Secret police for the *Félbahlag* religion of Jhye Hazhdi.

Gram: A name for the Sword of Light.

Gurpahn: The name of the griffin-like creatures used by the *Wyl-Dunn* as mounts.

Guyo: A *Kajoran* slang term meaning, okay, good, fine, or alright.

Gyajhan: Term meaning thief.

Hovina: One of the six indigenous clans of the Ranolan Savanna.

Ibar: Command that ensures the Spear of Lugh, when thrown, strikes its intended target.

Iyoké: Capitol city for **Solaian:** Capitol city for *Félbahlag* on the west coast of Félbahrin.

Jhiné Boré: (Dryad or tree nymph) They have dark, greenish-brown skin, black hair, green eyes, pointed ears, and Asian features.

Jhunélin, Order of: A religious order within the Holy Church of Ah-Shan.

Jhyeh: The gods of the *Bahréth.*

Kadj or **Kadj-speak:** A type of pidgin spoken by the *Kajoran* people.

Kagan: *Wyl-Dunn* title similar to king. Specifically, this is the senior king who presides over lesser kings and queens.

Kagana: *Wyl-Dunn* term referring to the Kagan and Kaganum collectively.

Kaganesh: *Wyl-Dunn* term for all *Wyl-Dunn ganesh* collectively.

Kaganum: *Wyl-Dunn* title similar to queen. Specifically, this is the senior queen who presides over lesser kings and queens.

Kalias: Term for the blue crystals found in the Kalian Tundra.

Kazaran: A *Wyl-Dunn* encampment of any kind.

Kajoran: The people native to the islands of the Kajoran Archipelago.

Kajoran Archipelago: A string of islands that runs from the east coast of Danu to the south-western tip of Félbahrin.

Kanéru Naranir: Book of holy scripture of the Fél Naran religion of the *Félbahlag.*

Kiné: A *Kajoran* term for stranger or foreigner.

Kree: a magical creature found in the Kajoran Archipelago. They give off light and even have the appearance of a small flame. They are less than an inch tall.

Lako: A *Kajoran* slang term for a person. Used similarly to buddy, man, or dude.

Lantesia: A mythical city under the Sea of Lantesia of the eastern coast of Danu.

Laraksha-Vo: This is the primary *Urgaban* city on Daoine.

Loiala Fé: (Fae) They are roughly the same size and appearance as humans, but have pointed ears.

Mehiras: Capitol for the *Bahréth* in Bahrél.

Métur Valley: Located on Danu east of Tir nya Lu. The site of many wars and battles fought by the *Uthadé*.

Mireygna: Legendary *Ashae* mage, possibly a goddess. It is thought she may be three women or sisters, or one woman who can appear as any one of three avatars.

Murias: Ancient *Uthadé* city of the west coast of Danu.

Noélani: The awa'ia, gods, of the *Kajoran* people.

Pilané Jhin: (Pixies) Typically about three inches tall with humanoid bodies and features. Sometimes confused with *Sula Jhinara* (sylphs.) They live in flowers and primarily live on nectar and pollen. They can also be mischievous. Skin may be a full range of browns from beige to dark chocolate, or blue or green. Blue and green pixies have butterfly wings, the others have dragon-fly wings. They are also strong telepaths. They are alternately male and female and change over a two-year period.

Pokorah-Vo: *Urgaban* city founded by criminal exiles from Laraksha-Vo.

Ponari: One of the six indigenous clans of the Ranolan Savanna.

Qélosan: A race of beings often thought to be angels.

Ralabo: A specific term for magic used by the *Pilané Jhin*.

Ralahin: A specific term for magic used by the *Ulané Jhinura*.

Raven's Nest: Restaurant owned by Mira and Bavrana in Su Lariano. Managed by Mouse.

Ranolan Savanna: Enormous plains area eastern side of the southern continent below Danu. Home to six clans of indigenous people: *Akotan, Chipasek, Hovina, Ponari, Rochiné,* and *Sokwané.*

Rochiné: One of the six indigenous clans of the Ranolan Savanna.

Rorujhen: This race is similar in appearance to a very large horse. However, they are much faster, are fully sentient, and communicate telepathically.

Scian of Goibhniu: These are the two matched daggers that Mira carries. They were created by the master *Uthadé* smith Goibhniu.

Sheobal: Home world of the *Daijheen.*

Shian Shariel: Bright evolved from being a *Kree* to the advanced state of being Shian Shariel, This represents both her species and her title, since she is the only one.

Shakahr: Common *Bahréth* soldier.

Shianri: The estate in the Shifara region which Mira inherited when she killed Vaelir, a White Rider. The word means hearth or home, or even nest.

Shifara: The *Ashae* capitol in Daoine. This includes Shifara City and Shifara Castle, each of which are walled and are connected by a causeway.

Shoro: Any of many common cooking and eating areas in a *Wyl-Dunn* encampment.

Shrolin chalé: These words of power are infused with magic and can be invoked orally. The literal meaning is "give strength."

Sokwané: One of the six indigenous clans of the Ranolan Savanna.

Solaian: Capitol city for *Ande Dannu* on the east coast of Danu.

Sulosh Sea or **Suloshné:** Large lake or inland sea on Danu. It is also known as the Eye of the Goddess because it is roughly shaped like an eye and has an island near the middle.

Su Lariano: An *Ulané Jhinura* city, home to Neelu. Mira's first home on Daoine. There is an outer town, but this is primarily an underground city built into caves and tunnels under a mountain.

Tékoran: (Manticore)

Tir nya Lu: Ancient *Uthadé* city on the island of Avalon in the Sulosh Sea on Danu.

Tolkeda: Holy scriptures of the *Bahréth*.

Tuatha de Danann: Human name for the *Uthadé*.

Ulané Jhinura: (Sprite) They are generally about four and a half feet tall, so can appear to be human children except for the pointed ears. Using magic, they are able to move very quickly. They also appear to have slightly Asian features.

Urgaban: (Goblin) *Urgaban* are typically around four feet tall. They are generally humanoid, but the head is noticeably larger, with a heavy jaw and wide mouth, and their arms are longer. Their pointed ears are also very long. They have pale, yellowish skin and no hair.

Usolé: Capitol city for *Dannu Fé* on the east coast of Danu.

Uthadé: (*Tuatha de Danann*) Ancient race from the world of Danu. Three factions split from the *Uthadé* to become the *Ashae* of Daoine, the *Félbahlag* of Félbahrin, and the *Fu-Mo Ri*. The remaining *Uthadé* moved to another world and have not been seen in centuries.

Vil charovo: The first of three parts to an ancient toast used among soldiers. It means, "to life." The appropriate response is, "Zi kuvan," which means and death. The final phrase is "*zi ros dolin,*" which means "and all between."

Wakoa karua: *Kajoran* word for a catamaran that has both an upper and lower deck.

Wanago mak'oché: *Ranolan* term meaning spirit world.

Wanatu ra: *Kajoran* word meaning goodbye or farewell.

Weenyan wukahn: *Ranolan* term for a holy or sacred woman or female spiritual leader. Medicine woman.

White Rider: This was an elite group of *Ashae* warriors, all male, who were supposed to be the executors of justice in Daoine. They wore white armor of hardened leather. Higher-ranking Riders used *Rorujhen* as mounts.

Wyl-Dunn: (Wild Fae) They were *Loiala Fé* who migrated from Daoine to Danu.

Yo-ah: *Kajoran* word used as an expletive or to get someone's attention or as a neutral acknowledgement.

Zi kuvan: The second part of an ancient toast used among soldiers. It means, "and death" and is used as a response to "*Vil charovo*," which means "to life."

Zi ros dolin: The third and final part of an ancient toast used among soldiers. It means, "and all between." It is a response to the earlier phrases meaning "To life" (*vil charovo*) "and death" (*zi kuvan*.)

ABOUT THE AUTHOR

Primarily an author of fantasy and science fiction, Adam K. Watts was born in Santa Clara, California, and was raised mainly in the heart of "Steinbeck Country" in Salinas, California. He currently resides in Sacramento, California. He has always been an artist and has made forays into writing, painting, composing music, dancing, performing arts, and digital photography. As a child, his mind was caught by the poetry of Robert Frost; the words from "Stopping by the Woods on a Snowy Evening" and "The Road Not Taken" resonated with him. The ideas of looking into the woods with longing to enter and turning away out of duty and responsibility, and the desire to travel a path few have seen, have lent his soul the aspect of the seeker. This aspect has been reflected in many of his works; images that bespeak of places that call, of paths that make you want to walk them, and corners that beg you to come look and see what is just around them, or just the wandering wind asking you to walk with her.

He was also shaped at a young age by *Man of La Mancha*, a musical play inspired by Cervantes and Don Quixote. "Tilting at windmills" is a metaphor for pushing back against the machinery of civilization advancing at the price of beauty and the human spirit. He believes that advancement can and should be achieved, but the cost should not be valor or honor or justice. An impossible dream? Perhaps.

"I've been a lover and avid reader of fantasy and science fiction since I was knee-high to a short Hobbit. I have finally escaped the confines of professional non-fiction writing to follow the purpose that has been burning in my heart since I could lift pencil to paper. Those embers, never quite cooled, have been fanned to unquenchable flame and I cannot contain the result. Enjoy!"

To learn more about Adam K. Watts and discover more Next Chapter authors, visit our website at www.nextchapter.pub.

Dear reader,

We hope you enjoyed reading *Rise of the Vanquished*. Please take a moment to leave a review on your preferred online book vendor, even if it's a short one. Your opinion is important to us.

Watch for more Tales of the Misplaced releases coming soon!

Best regards,

Adam K. Watts and the Next Chapter Team

Rise of the Vanquished
ISBN: 978-4-82419-213-4
Large Print

Published by
Next Chapter
2-5-6 SANNO
SANNO BRIDGE
143-0023 Ota-Ku, Tokyo
+818035793528

8th March 2024

Milton Keynes UK
Ingram Content Group UK Ltd.
UKHW010857280324
440101UK00003B/331

9 784824 192134